Dear Sweet
Filthy World

Dear Sweet Filthy World

CAITLÍN R. KIERNAN

Subterranean Press • 2017

First Edition

ISBN
978-1-59606-819-3

Subterranean Press
PO Box 190106
Burton, MI 48519

subterraneanpress.com
www.caitlinkiernan.com
greygirlbeast.livejournal.com
Twitter: @auntbeast

For Angela Carter and Shirley Jackson,
my Jachin and Boaz.

What I dread is this: that you'll be understood
Only by someone whose smile is helpless,
By someone who's lost.
What anguish – to search for the right word,
To lift sick eyelids,
And with lime-corroded blood
Gather night grasses for an alien tribe.

Osip Mandelstam,
"1 January 1924,"
from *The Eyesight of Wasps*

Table of Contents

Werewolf Smile

I don't know whether it's true that Eva slept with Perrault. Probably it is.
I know she slept with plenty enough men – men and other women –
those nights when she'd slip away from me, wrapped in a caul of cigarette
smoke, perfume, and halfhearted deceit. She'd laugh whenever anyone
dared to call her polyamorous. Unless, of course, she was in one of her
black moods, and then she might do something worse than laugh. I never
called her polyamorous, because I knew that she never *loved* any of them,
any more than she loved me. There was no amour in those trysts. "I fuck
around," she would say, or something like that. "It doesn't need a fancy
fucking Greek word for it, or a fucking flag in a pride parade. I'm a wanton. I sleep around." Then, she might ask, "What's got me wondering,
Winter, is why you *don't?*" She almost never used my actual name, and
I never asked why she'd started calling me Winter. We met in July, after
all. On a very hot day in July. But, sure, she might have slept with Albert
Perrault. She liked to call herself his disciple. I heard her call herself that
on more than one occasion. She fancied herself somehow favored by him.
Favored beyond the bedclothes, I mean to say. It pleased her, imagining herself as more to him than a mere student, as though he were some
unholy prophet, Eva's very own *bête noire* come to lead her down to places
she'd spent her life only half imagining and never daring to dream she
might one day glimpse. She assumed – from his paintings, from *what* he
painted – *he* had glimpsed them. She assumed he had something to show
anyone *besides* the paintings. Eva assumed a lot of things. But don't ask
me what he truly thought of her. I hardly ever spoke with him, and then
only briefly, and it was never anything but the most superficial sorts of
conversation. Our exchanges were cursory, perfunctory, slipshod, though
never exactly awkward. I don't know what he thought of her as an artist,
or as a lover, or if he derived some satisfaction from my suspicion about

the two of them. Sometimes, I wanted to warn him (I'd often wanted to warn others about Eva), but I never had the nerve, or I never had the heart, and, besides, that probably would have been like warning Herod about Salomé. And, likely, I'd have only succeeded in appearing jealous, the disgruntled green-eyed third in a disconnected *ménage a trois* trying to jam up the works. I can see how my feelings for Eva might be misinterpreted. But I do *not* hate her. I love her, as I have loved her since the hot July day we met, almost five years ago, and I know that's why I'm damned. Because I cannot push away. I am unable to push away. Even after all her lovers, after Perrault, and the Dahlia, and all the things she's done and said, the hideous things I've seen because of her, all that shit that's going to be in my head forever and ever, I still love her. I seem to have no choice whatsoever in the matter, because I have certainly *tried* to hate Eva. But I have found that trying not to love her is like someone trying to wish herself well; thinking, for example, I could simply will a gangrenous wound back to healthy pink flesh again. You cut away necrosis, or you die, and I plainly lack whatever cardinal resolve is necessary to cut Eva out of *me*. And I wonder, now, if she ever had these same thoughts, about me, or about Albert Perrault? I cast her as I have, and as she claims herself to be, a willing plague vector, but perhaps Eva was also merely one of the infected. She may well not have been a Typhoid Mary of the mind and soul. I can't know for sure, one way or the other, and I'm weary of speculation. So, better I restrict these meanderings to what I at least *believe* I know than to speculate, yes? And when I sat down to write about her and about Perrault, I had in mind the Dahlia, in particular, not all these useless (and generally abstract) questions of love and fidelity and intent. How can I pretend to have known Eva's intentions? She called herself a liar as frequently as she called herself a wanton and a slut. She was the physical embodiment of the pseudomenon, a conscious, animate incarnation of the Liar's Paradox.

"Oh, Winter, everything I've ever told you or ever will tell you is a lie, but *this,* this *one* thing is true."

Now, work with that. And I'm not speaking in metaphors, or paraphrasing. And I do not, here, have to rely upon an inevitably unreliable memory, because when she said those very words, I was so taken aback, so galled at the audacity, that, less than an hour later, I scribbled it down in the black Moleskine notebook Eva presented me on the occasion of my thirty-fifth birthday. That *is* what she said. And I sat very still, and

I listened, because how could I refuse to hear the one truth uttered by a woman who will never be permitted to speak one truth? I sat on the floor of my apartment (I never thought of it as *our* apartment), and I listened. "It scared the living shit out of me," she said, "and I have never seen anything so beautiful." This, I suppose, was her one true thing, which, perforce, must also be false. But she continued for quite some time thereafter, and I sat beneath the window, not *not* listening. There was a Smiths CD in the stereo, set on repeat, and I think the disc played twice through before she was done describing to me plans for Perrault's new installation. "The parallel is obvious, of course, and he acknowledges that up front. *Le Petit Chaperon Rouge*, Little Red Riding Hood, *Rotkäppchen*, and so forth. The genius is not in having made the association, but in the execution. The cumulative effect of the assembled elements, both his paintings and the reproductions of various artifacts relating to the murder of Elizabeth Short." Eva laughed at me when I told her it all sounded pretentious and unspeakably morbid. She laughed loudly, and reminded me of games that we had played, of scenes beyond counting. "I know, Winter, you like to pretend your heart's not as rotten as mine, but do try not to be such a goddamn hypocrite about it." And there's our lovely paradox once more, because she was absolutely right, of course. I don't recall interrupting her again that night. I can't even recall *which* Smiths CD was playing. Not so much as one single song. "You know," she said, "before the 'Black Dahlia' moniker stuck, the newspapers in Los Angeles were calling it the 'werewolf murder.'" She was silent a moment, then, just staring at me, and I realized I'd missed a cue, that I'd almost forgotten my line. "Why?" I asked belatedly. "Why did they call it that?" She lit a cigarette and blew smoke towards the high white ceiling. She shrugged. "Albert tried to find out, but no one seems to know. Back then, LA journalists were always coming up with these lurid names for murders. Lots of times, they had to do with flowers. The White Gardenia Murder, the Red Hibiscus Murder, and so on. He thinks the werewolf thing maybe had something to do with the smile the killer carved into her face, pretty much ear to ear. That it sort of made Short *look* like a wolf. But that still doesn't make much sense to me. I assumed that the newspaper men were referring to the murderer as the werewolf, not to the victim." That's the only time I ever heard Eva disagree with Perrault. She shrugged again and took another drag off her cigarette. "Either way, it's a great angle, and he means to make the most of it. He hasn't told me exactly how, not exactly, not yet. But I know he's been talking to a taxidermist. Some guy he worked with once before." And she went on like this, and I sat and listened. "It's very exciting," Eva continued, "seeing him branch out, explore other media. He did that thing with the stones last year in New York, the stones inside their cages. That's what really set him moving in this direction. That's what he says. Oh, and I haven't told you. He got a call from someone in Hollywood last week. He won't say who, but it's someone big." I promise, for what that might be worth, I am not trying to make Eva sound any more or less insipid or sycophantic than she actually did that night. She knew I didn't care for Perrault's work, that it gave me the willies, which is probably why she spent so much time talking about it. Come to think, that's probably why she started fucking him to begin with (assuming that I am not mistaken on that count, assuming she actually *did* fuck him).

But wait.

I've said too much about that night. I didn't intend to drone on about that night, but merely present it as prologue to what came afterwards. It was winter, late winter in Boston, and an especially snowy winter at that. I'd just started the bookshop job, and sometimes I picked up a spare shift at a coffee house on Newbury Street. I don't think Eva was working at the time, except she'd taken to calling herself Perrault's personal assistant, and he'd taken to letting her get away with it. But I'm not sure any genuine work was involved; I'm certain no money was. Eva was only a slut. She never had the requisite motivation to be anything so useful or lucrative as a whore. But, playing his PA, she was involved in all the nasty shit he was getting up to that winter, planning the show in LA, the Dahlia. Perrault decided early on to call the installation "The Voyeur of Utter Destruction," after some David Bowie song or another. I heard through Eva that Perrault had landed a book deal from a Manhattan publisher, a glossy, full-color folio affair, though it wasn't paying much. I heard from Eva he didn't care about the small advance, because he'd gotten color. Frankly, I heard most of what I heard about Albert Perrault through Eva, not via my own afore-mentioned perfunctory conversations with the man. Anyhow, the same day Eva told me about the book, she also told me that she was going to be his model for several of the sculptural pieces in the installation. Lifecasts had to be made, which meant she had to fly out to LA, because he had a makeup-artist friend at some special-effects studio or another who'd agreed to do that part free of charge. I understand Perrault was quite good at getting people to do things for him for free. Eva, for example. So, she was gone most of a week in February, during the worst of the snow, and I had the apartment and the bed all to myself. When I wasn't working or slogging *to* or home *from* work through the black-grey slush drowning the streets, or riding the T, I slept and watched old movies and halfheartedly read from a collection by Nabokov, *A Russian Beauty and Other Stories.* The book was a first edition, signed by the author, and actually belonged to Perrault. He'd loaned it to Eva, advising her to read it, cover to cover, but Eva rarely read anything except astrology and self-help crap. Oh, she had subscriptions to the *New Yorker* and *Wired* and *Interview,* because she thought they looked good lying on the coffee table. Or rather, because she thought they made her look good. But she never read the magazines, and she'd not read a page of the Nabokov collection, either. I read most of it while she was gone to California, but can only recall one story, about a midget named Fred Dobson. Fred Dobson got someone pregnant and died at the end, and that's about all I remember. Eva came home on a Friday night, and she was uncharacteristically taciturn. Mostly, she sat alone in the kitchenette, smoking and drinking steaming cups of herbal tea. On Saturday night, we fucked, the first time since she'd started seeing Perrault. She had me use the double-ended silicone dildo, which was fine by me. I came twice. I'm not sure how many times Eva came, because she was always so quiet during sex, always so quiet and still. Afterwards, we lay together, and it was almost like the beginning, right after we met, before I understood about necrosis. We watched the big bay window above the bed, flakes of snow spiraling lazily down from a Dreamsicle sky. She said, "In Japan, they call them *harigata,*" and it took me a moment to realize she was talking about the double-ended dildo. "At least that's what Albert says," she added, and the illusion that we might be back at the start, that I did not yet know the truth of her, immediately dissolved. I lay still, Eva in my arms, watching the snow sticking to the windowpane. Some of it melted, and some of it didn't. I asked her if she was okay, if maybe something had happened while she was away in Los Angeles. She told me no, nothing had happened, but it was intense, all the same, working that closely with Perrault. "It's like being in his head sometimes, like I'm just another canvas or a few handfuls of clay." She fell asleep not long afterwards, and I got up and pissed, checked my email, and then watched TV almost until dawn, even though I had to work the next day. I didn't want to be in the same bed with whatever she was dreaming that night.

I didn't see her again for two or three days. She took the train down to Providence, some errand for Perrault. She didn't go into the details, and I didn't bother to ask. When she came home, though, Eva was mostly her old self again. We ordered Chinese takeout, moo goo whatever, kung pao pigeon, and she talked about the life castings she'd done. Her body nude and slicked with Vaseline, and then they'd covered her with a thick coating of blue alginate, and when that had set, they'd covered the alginate with plaster bandages, making the molds for Perrault's sculptures from her living corpse. I asked if they put straws up her nose so she could breathe, and she laughed and frowned. "They don't do that," she replied. "They're just careful not to cover your nostrils. It was claustrophobic, but in a good way." She told me that each mold would be used only once and then destroyed, and that they did five separate lifecastings of her in five days. "When it hardens, you can't move?" I asked, and she frowned again and said, "Of course you can't move. That would ruin everything, if you were to move." I didn't ask exactly what Perrault intended to do with the casts, and Eva didn't say. It was the next evening, though, that she produced a photograph of one of his paintings and asked me to look at it, please. Eva never, ever fucking said please, so that was sort of a red flag, when she did. She was sweating, though it was chilly in the apartment, because the radiator was acting up again. She was sweating, and she looked sick. I asked if she had a fever, and Eva shook her head. I asked if she was sure, because maybe she'd picked up something on the plane, or while she was in LA, and she made a snarling sound and shoved the photograph into my hands. It was in color, an 8x10 printed on matte paper. There was a sticker on the back with the paintings title typed neatly, black Courier font on white. It read *Fecunda ratis,* and there was a date (which I can't recollect). Written directly on the back of the photo, with what I took to have been a ballpoint pen, were the words *"De puella a lupellis seruata,"* about a girl saved from wolf cubs, circa 1022-1024; Egbert of Liège. "So who is this Egbert of Liège," I asked. She glared at me, and for a second or three I thought she was going to hit me. It wouldn't have been the first time. "How the hell am I suppose to know?" she snapped, trading in my question for a question of her own. "Will you fucking look at the *front?* Winter, look at the front of the picture, not the goddamn back of it, for Christ's sake." I nodded and turned the photograph over. I recognized it immediately as one of Perrault's, even though I'd never seen that particular painting before. There's something about the easy violence, the deliberate carelessness of his brushstrokes. Almost like Edvard Munch trying to forge a Van Gogh, almost. At first, any simple representational image, any indication of the painting's composition, refused to emerge from the sooty blur of oils, the innumerable shades of gray broken only by the faintest rumors of green and alabaster. There was a single crimson smudge floating near the center of the photograph, a chromatic counterpoint to all the murk. I thought it looked like a wound. I didn't say that to Eva, but that's the impression I got. As if maybe someone, Perrault or someone else, had taken a knife or a pair of scissors to the canvas. Heaven knows, I've wanted to do it myself, on more than one occasion. I would even argue that, at times, his art seems intended to provoke precisely that reaction. Art designed, premeditated, to elicit the primal fight-or-flight response, to reach in and give the hindbrain a good squeeze, dividing the predators from the prey. "What do you see?" Eva asked me. And I said, "Another one of Perrault's shitty paintings." "Don't be an ass," she replied. "Tell me what you *see*." I told her I'd thought she wanted my honest opinion, and she gave me the finger; I had it coming, I suppose. I looked at her, and she was still sweating, and was also chewing at her lower lip. Peering into her eyes was almost as bad as trying to make sense of *Fecunda ratis,* so I turned back to the somber chaos of the photograph. "Is this one going to be in the show?" I asked. "No," she said, and then, "I don't know. Maybe, but I don't think so. It's old, but he says it's relevant. Albert doesn't have it anymore, sold it to a collector after a show in Atlanta. I don't know if he still has access to it." I listened, but didn't reply. Her voice was shaking, like the words were not quite connecting one against the other, and I tried harder to concentrate on making sense of *Fecunda ratis.* I wished I had a drink, and I almost asked Eva for one of the American Spirit cigarettes she'd begun smoking after meeting Perrault, though I'd stopped smoking years before. My mouth was so dry. I felt as though my cheeks had been stuffed with cotton balls, my mouth had gone so dry. "What do you see?" she asked again, sounding desperate, almost whispering, but I ignored her. Because, suddenly, the blur was beginning to resolve into definite shapes, shadows and the solid objects that cast shadows. Figures and landscape and sky. The crimson smudge was the key. "Little Red Riding Hood," I said, and Eva laughed, but very softly, as if she were only laughing to herself. "Little Red Riding Hood," she echoed, and I nodded my head again. The red smudge formed a still point, a nexus or fulcrum in the swirl, and I saw it was meant to be a cap or a hat, a crimson wool cap perched on the head of a nude girl who was down on her hands and knees. Her head was bowed, so that her face was hidden from view. There was only a wild snarl of hair, and that cruel, incongruent red cap. Yes, that *cruel* red cap, for I could not then and cannot now interpret any element of that painting as anything but malevolent. Even the kneeling girl, made a blood sacrifice, struck me as a conspirator. She was surrounded by pitchy, hulking forms, and I briefly believed them to be tall standing stones, dolmens, some crude megalithic ring with the girl at its center. But then I realized, no, they were *meant* to be beasts of some sort. Huge shaggy things squatting on their haunches, watching the girl. The painting had captured the final, lingering moment before a kill. But I didn't think *kill.* I thought *murder,* though the forms surrounding the girl appeared to be animals, as I've already said. Animals do not do murder, men do. Men and women, and even children, but *not* animals. "I dream it almost every night," Eva said, near to tears, and I wanted to tear the photograph apart, rip it into tiny, senseless shreds. I'm not lying when I say that I loved and still love Eva, and *Fecunda ratis* struck me as some sick game Perrault was playing with her mind, giving her this awful picture and telling her it was *relevant* to the installation. Expecting her to study it. To fixate and obsess over it. I've always felt a certain variety of manipulation is required of artists (painters, sculptors, writers, filmmakers, etc.), but only a few become (or start off as) sadists. I have no doubt whatsoever that Perrault is a sadist, whether or not there was a sexual component present. You can see it in almost everything he's ever done, and, that night, I could see it in her eyes. "Eva, it's only Little Red Riding Hood," I told her, laying the photograph face down on the coffee table. "It's only a painting, and you really shouldn't let him get inside your head like this." She told me that I didn't understand, that full immersion was necessary if she were going to be any help to him whatsoever, and then she took the photograph back and sat staring at it. I didn't say anything more, because I knew nothing more to say to her. There was no way I would come between her and her *bête noir,* nor even between her and the black beasts he'd created for *Fecunda ratis.* I stood up and went to the kitchenette to make dinner, even though I wasn't hungry and, by then, Eva was hardly eating anything. I found a can of Campbell's chicken and stars soup in the cupboard and asked if she'd eat a bowl if I warmed it up. She didn't reply. She didn't say a word, just sat there on the sofa, her blue eyes trained on the photograph, not sparing a glance for anyone or anything else. And that was maybe three weeks before she flew out to Los Angeles for the last time. She never came back to Boston. She never came back to me. I never saw her again. But I suppose I'm getting ahead of myself, even if only slightly so. There would be the one distraught phone call near the end of April, while Perrault would still have been busy working on the pieces for his installation, which was scheduled to open on June 1st at a gallery called Subliminal Thinkspace Collective. It's easy enough, in retrospect, to say that

I should have taken that phone call more seriously. But I was working two jobs and recovering from the flu. I was barely managing to keep the rent paid. It's not like I could have dropped everything and gone after her. I make a lousy Prince Charming, no fit sort of knight errant. Anyway, I'm still not sure she wanted me to try. To save her, I mean. It's even more absurd to imagine Eva as a damsel in distress than to imagine myself as her rescuer. Which only goes to show the fatal traps we may build for ourselves when we fashion personae. Expectation becomes self-fulfilling. Then, later on, we cry and bitch, and pity ourselves, and marvel stupidly at our inability to take action. The therapist I saw for a while said this was "survivor's guilt." I asked him, that day, if the trick to a lucrative career in psychology was to tell people whatever might make them feel better, by absolving them of responsibility. I look around me, and I see so many people intent upon absolving themselves of responsibility. On passing the buck, shifting the blame. But I'm the one who did not act, just as Perrault is the one who messed with her head, just as Eva is the one who needed that invasion so badly she was willing to pay for the privilege with her life. All I was paying the therapist was money, and that's not even quite the truth, as I was piling it all on a MasterCard I never expected to be in a position to pay off. Regardless, during our very next session, Dr. Not To Be Named Herein suggested that some of us are less amenable to therapy than are others, that possibly I did not *wish* to "get better," and I stopped seeing him. I can be a guilty survivor on my own, without incurring any additional debt.

Eva called near the end of April. She was crying.

I had never heard Eva cry, and it was as disconcerting a sound as it was unexpected.

We talked for maybe ten or fifteen minutes, at the most. It might have been a much longer conversation, if my cell phone had been getting better reception that afternoon, and if I'd been able to call back when we were finally disconnected (I tried, but the number was blocked). Eva was not explicit about what had upset her so badly. She said that she missed me. She said it several times, in fact, and I said that I missed her, too. She repeatedly mentioned insomnia and bad dreams, and how very much she hated Los Angeles and wanted to be back in Boston. I said that maybe she ought to come home, if this were the case, but she balked at the idea. "He needs me *here*," she said. "This would be the *worst* time for me to leave. The absolute worst time. I couldn't do that, Winter. Not after everything Albert's done for me." She said that, or something approximating those words. Her voice was so terribly thin, so faint and brittle in the static, stretched out across however many thousands of miles it had traveled before reaching me. I felt as though I were speaking to a ghost of Eva. That's not the clarity of hindsight. I actually *did* feel that way, *while* we were speaking, which is one reason I wouldn't permit my therapist (my ex-therapist, now that we're estranged) to convince me to lay the blame elsewhere. I clearly heard it that day, the panic in her voice. Hers was such a slow suicide, a woman dying by degrees, and it would be reprehensible of me to pretend that I'm not cognizant of this fact, or that I did not yet have my suspicions that day in April. She said, "After dark, we drive up and down the Coast Highway, back and fucking forth, from Rendondo Beach all the way to Santa Barbara or Isla Vista. He drives and talks about Gévaudan. Winter, I'm so sick of that goddamn stretch of road." I didn't ask her about Gévaudan, though I googled it when I got home. When we were cut off, Eva was still sobbing, and talking about her nightmares. Had it been a scene in a Hollywood melodrama, I would surely have dropped everything and gone after her. But my life is about as far from Hollywood as it gets. And *she* was there already.

A few days later, the mail brought an invitation to the opening of "The Voyeur of Utter Destruction." One side was a facsimile of a postcard that the man purporting to have murdered Elizabeth Short, the Black Dahlia, sent to journalists and the police in 1947. The original message had been assembled with pasted letters snipped from newspapers, and read "Here is the photo of the werewolf killer's/I saw him kill her/a friend." There was an indistinct photo in the lower left-hand corner of the card, which I later learned was of a boy named Armand Robles. He was seventeen years old in 1947, and was never considered a suspect in the Dahlia killing. More mind games. The other side of the postcard had the date and time of the opening, please RSVP, an address for Subliminal Thinkspace Collective, etcetera. And it also had two words printed in red ink, handwritten in Eva's unmistakable, sloppy cursive: "Please come." She knew I couldn't. More than that, she knew I *wouldn't,* even if I could have afforded the trip.

Like I said, I googled "Gévaudan." It's the name of a former province in the Margeride Mountains of central France. I read it's history, going back to Gallic tribes and even Neolithic people, a Roman conquest, its role in Medieval politics, and the arrival of the Protestants in the mid-16th Century. Dull stuff. But I'm a quick study, and it didn't take me long to realize that none of these would have been the subject of Perrault's obsession with the region. No, nothing so mundane as rebellions against the Bishop of Mende or the effects of WWII on the region. However, between the years 1764 and 1767, a "beast" attacked as many as two hundred and ten people. Over a hundred of them died. It might have been nothing more than an exceptionally large wolf, but has never been conclusively identified. Many victims were partially eaten. And I will note, the first attack occurred on June 1, 1764. From the start, I saw the significance of this date. After Eva's call, I could hardly dismiss it as a coincidence. Perrault had knowingly chosen the anniversary of the beginning of the depredations of the infamous *La bête du Gévaudan* as the opening night of his installation. I spent a couple of hours reading websites and internet forums devoted to the attacks. There's a lot of talk of witchcraft and shape shifting, both in documents written during and shortly after the incident, and in contemporary books as well. Turns out, Gévaudan is one of those obscure subjects the crackpots at the fringe keep alive with their lavish conspiracy theories and pseudoscientific, wishful blather. Much the same way, I might add, that the true-crime buffs have kept the unsolved Dahlia case in the public eye for more than half a century. And here, Albert Perrault seemed intent upon forging a marriage of the two, along with his unrelenting fairy-tale preoccupations. I thought about the lifecasts and wondered if he'd chosen Eva as his midwife.

I stuck the postcard on the fridge with a magnet, and for a few days I thought too much about Gévaudan, and was surprised by how much I worried about Eva and how frequently I found myself wishing that she would call again. I sent a couple of emails, but they went unanswered. I even tried to find a contact for Perrault, to no avail. I spoke with a woman at Subliminal Thinkspace Collective, a brusque voice slathered with a heavy Russian accent, and I gave her a message for Eva, to please have her get in touch with me as soon as possible. And then, as April became May, the humdrum, day-to-day gravity of my life reasserted itself. I fretted less about Eva with every passing day and began to believe that this time she was gone for good. Accepting that a relationship has exceeded its expiration date is much easier when you always knew the expiration date was there, waiting somewhere down the road, always just barely out of sight. I missed her. I won't pretend that I *didn't*. But it wasn't the blow I'd spent so much of our four years together dreading. It was a sure thing that had finally come to fruition. Mostly, I wondered what I should do with all the junk she'd left behind. Clothing and books, CDs and a vase from Italy. All the material ephemera she'd left me to watch over in her absence, the curator of the Museum of Her. I decided that I would wait until summer, and if I'd not heard from Eva by then, I would box it all up. I never thought far enough ahead to figure out what I'd do with the boxes afterwards, once they were packed and taped shut. Maybe that was a species of denial. I don't know. I don't care.

June 1ˢᵗ came and went without incident, and I heard nothing more from her. I don't think of myself as a summer person, but, for once, I was glad to have the winter behind me. I welcomed the greening of Boston Commons, the flowers and the ducks and the picnicking couples. I even welcomed the heat, though my apartment has no AC. I welcomed the long days and the short nights. I'd begun to settle into a new routine, and it seemed I might be discovering an equilibrium, even peace, when I got the letter from Eva's sister in Connecticut. I sat on the bed, and I read the single page several times over, waiting for the words to seem like more than ink on paper. She apologized for not having written sooner, but my address had only turned up the week after Eva's funeral. She'd OD'd on a nortriptyline prescription, though it was unclear whether or not the overdose had been intentional. The coroner, whom I suspect was either kindly or mistaken, had ruled the death accidental. I would have argued otherwise, only there was no one for me to have the argument with. "I know you were close," her sister wrote. "I know that the two of you were very good friends." I put the letter in a drawer somewhere, and I took the postcard off the refrigerator and threw it away. Before I sat down to write this out, I promised myself I'd not dwell on this part of the story. On her death, or on my reaction to it. That's a promise I mean to keep. I will only say that my mourning in no way diminished the anger and bitterness that Eva's inconstancies had planted and then nourished. I didn't write back to her sister. It seemed neither necessary nor appropriate.

And now it is a cold day in late January, and soon it will have been a year since the last time I made love to Eva. The snow's returned, and the radiator is in no better shape than it was this time last year. All things considered, I think I was doing a pretty good job of moving on, until a shipment of Perrault's book arrived at the shop where I (still) work. It came in on one of my day's off and was already shelved and fronted, the first time I set eyes on it. The dust jacket was a garish shade of red. Later, I would realize it was almost the same shade of crimson as the girl's cap in *Fecunda ratis*. I didn't open it in the store, but bought a copy with my employee discount (which made the purchase only slightly less extravagant). I didn't open it until I was home and had checked twice to be sure the door was locked. And then I poured myself a glass of scotch, sat down on the floor between the coffee table and the sofa, and scrounged up the courage to look inside. The book is titled simply *Werewolf Smile*, and it opens with several pages of introduction by a Berkeley professor of modern art (there was also an afterword by a professor of Jungian and Imaginal Psychology at Pacifica Graduate Institute). I saw almost immediately that Perrault had dedicated the book to "Eva, my lost little red cap." Reading that, I felt a cold, hard knot forming deep in my belly, the knot that would soon become nausea as I turned the pages, one after one, staring at those slick full-color photographs, this permanent record of the depravity that Albert Perrault was peddling as inspiration and genius. I will not shy away from calling it pornography, but a pornography not necessarily, or exclusively, of sex, but one effusively devoted to the violation of anatomy, both human and animal. And the freeze-frame violence depicted there was not content with the canvas offered by only three dimensions, no, but also warped time, bending the ambiguities of history to Perrault's purposes. History and legend, myth and the grand guignol of *les contes de fée*.

I am becoming lost in these sentences, in my attempt to convey in mere words what Perrault wrought in paint and plaster, with wire and fur and bone. The weight and impotence of my own narrative becomes painfully acute. Somehow, I've already said too much, and yet know that I will never be able to accurately, or even adequately, convey my reaction to the images enshrined and celebrated in Perrault's filthy book.

I am a fool to even try.

I am a fool.

I am.

He festooned the gallery's walls with black-and-white photos of Elizabeth Short's corpse, those taken where she was found in the weedy, vacant lot at 39th and Norton in Leimert Park and a few more from the morgue. These photographs were so enlarged that a great deal of their resolution was lost. Many details of the corpse's mutilation vanished in the grain. There was also a movie poster from George Marshall's 1946 film noir, *The Blue Dahlia,* written by Raymond Chandler, which may (or may not) have served as the inspiration for Short's sobriquet. Hung at irregular intervals throughout the gallery, from invisible wires affixed to the ceiling, were blow-ups that Perrault had made of newspaper accounts of the murder, and there were the various postcards and letters taunting the LAPD, like the one that had been used for my invitation to the installation's opening.

I have decided not to surrender
Too much fun fooling the police
Had my fun at police
Don't Try to find me.
– catch us if you can

Scattered amongst these gruesome artifacts of the Black Dahlia murder were an assortment of illustrations that have accompanied variants of the "Little Red Riding Hood" tale over the centuries. Some were in color, others rendered only in shades of gray. Gustave Doré, Fleury François Richard, Walter Crane, and others, many others, but I don't recall the names and don't feel like searching through the book for them. They would have only seemed incongruous to someone who was blessedly unaware of Perrault's agenda. And, displayed in among the postcard facsimile's and the red-capped girl children were 18th-Century images of the creature believed to have been responsible for all those attacks in the Margeride Mountains. From my description, it may seem that the installation was busy. Yet somehow, even with so many objects competing for attention, through some acumen on the part of the artist, just the opposite was true. The overall effect was one of emptiness, a bleak space sparsely dotted with the detritus of slaughter and lies and childhood fancy.

But this odd assemblage, all these sundry relics – *every bit of it* – was only a frame built to mark off Perrault's own handiwork, the five sculptures he'd fabricated from Eva's lifecasts and, presumably, with the aid of the taxidermist acquaintance she'd mentioned to me. The centerpiece of "The Voyeur of Utter Destruction" and, later on, *Werewolf Smile*. The desecration made of the body of Elizabeth Short, as it had been discovered in that desolate lot in Leimert Park at about 10:30 a.m. on the morning of January 15, 1947. Here it was, not once, but repeated five times over, arranged in a sort of pentagram or pinwheel formation. The "corpses" were each aligned with their feet towards the wheel's center. Their toes almost, but not quite, touching. There are twenty or so photographs of this piece in the book, taken from various angles, the sculpture that Perrault labeled simply *Phases 1-5*. I will not describe it in any exacting detail. I don't think that I could bear to do that, if only because it would mean opening up Perrault's book again to be certain I was getting each stage in the transformation exactly right. "It's not the little things," Eva once said to me. "It's what they add up to." That would have served well as an epigraph to *Werewolf Smile*. It could have been tucked directly beneath the author's dedication (as it happens, the actual epigraph is by Man Ray: "I paint what cannot be photographed, that which comes from the imagination or from dreams, or from an unconscious drive.") What I will say is that *Phase 1* is an attempt at a straightforward reproduction of the state in which Elizabeth Short's naked body was discovered. There's no arguing with the technical brilliance of the work, just as there's no denying the profanity of the mind who made it. But this is not Elizabeth Short's body. It is, of course, a mold of Eva's, subjected to all the ravages visited upon the Black Dahlia's. The torso has been bisected at the waist with surgical precision, and great care has been taken to depict exposed organs and bone. The arms are raised above the head, arranged in a manner that seems anything but haphazard. The legs are splayed to reveal the injuries done to the genitalia. Every wound visible in the crime-scene photos and described in written accounts has been faithfully reproduced in *Phase 1*. The corners of the mouth have been slashed, almost ear-to-ear, and there's Perrault's "werewolf smile." Move along now, widdershins about the pinwheel, until we arrive at *Phase 5*. And here we find the taxidermied carcass of a large coyote that has been subjected to precisely the *same* mutilations as the body of Elizabeth Short, and the lifecasts of Eva. It's forelimbs have been arranged above the head, just as the Dahlia's were, though they never could have been posed that way in life. The beast lies supine, positioned in no way that seems especially natural for a coyote. It was not necessary to slash the corners of the mouth. And as for phases 2 through 4, one need only imagine any lycanthropic metamorphosis, the stepwise shifting from mangled woman to mangled canine, accomplished as any halfway decent horror-movie transmutation.

The face is only recognizable as Eva's in phases 1 and 2. I suppose I should consider this a mercy.

And at the end (which this will not be, but as another act of mercy, I will *pretend* it is) one question lingers foremost in my mind. Is this what Eva was seeking all along? Not enlightenment in the tutelage of her *bête noir,* but this grisly immortality, to be so reduced (or so elevated, depending on one's opinion of Perrault). To become a surrogate for that kneeling, rep-capped girl in *Fecunda ratis,* and for a woman tortured and murdered decades before Eva was even conceived. To stumble, and descend, and finally lie there on her back, gazing upwards at the pale, jealous moon as the assembled beasts fall on her, and simply do what beasts have always done, and what they ever more will do.

Vicaria Draconis

Scádda stands in the restless three-dimensional shadow cast by the vast and rotating tesseract. She is nineteen today, and almost every morning, afternoon, and evening of her life has been spent learning the worm's dance, so that when *this* day arrived, she could perfectly align herself with the shadow's frequency. There is only one woman born, into each five generations, who may stand within the penumbra of the seven cells, bounded by those eight shifting cubes. Only one who can endure this orthogonality, and only one who may grow up to perceive, simultaneously, each of the polychora. Scádda was born with the marks to show that, while still within her mother's womb, she had been touched by the barbs of the dragon. The rotating tesseract isn't the least fraction of the dragon's mind, but may be numbered among its merest considerations. Still, it is the most that will ever be revealed to any mortal mind.

Like the seven priestesses, Scádda is blind, for no one may look into the mind of the dragon and survive. However, her blindness is congenital, not an injury delivered by ceremonial daggers carved from milky green soapstone. Each priestess anointed her in turn, and recited the Litany of Realignment, before they led Scádda down from the highest pinnacle of the golden ziggurat into the bowels of the mountain. Through narrow corridors carved ten thousand years ago, four of the seven walked ahead of Scádda and three followed behind. Eight figures moving through perfect blackness, clothed only in their skin and sweat and the various unguents of this Sacrament. Where the corridor ends, they came upon the worm's well and the circle chiseled into the floor round about its yawning circumference. From the well's lip projects a precarious span, terminating in a small dais. The span vanishes into the tesseract's shadow, and the dais is suspended above the very center of that presumably bottomless gulf.

Only Scádda is permitted to step across the periphery of the circle, but she needed no guidance nor helping hand to gain the dais. Every deliberate, precise step was long ago committed to memory. She knows the way, as surely as she knows the rhythm of her own heart or the voices of all those who have kept her safe and prepared her against this moment. She stands alone within coruscating waves of light that are almost crimson and not quite violet. The light roars like a mighty tempest, like the rush of a cataract smashing itself against stones. It roars, and it wails, and it resonates with paeans to the fabric of the world.

"I have come," Scádda says, her words lost to all but the dragon and whatever elder godthings whose hearing may pierce the tesseract's cacophonous veil. "Before I first drew breath, was I claimed by you, and yet, by my *own* choice have I chosen and walked this road to stand before you upon this day."

And far above the subterranean chamber, the moon passes between the earth and sun, and another sort of shadow falls across the golden ziggurat, and across the city rising from the jungle, and across the jungle and everything that crawls and creeps and skulks and flits beneath its hot green canopy. A terrible hush takes hold as this strange, premature twilight spreads across the land. The men and women of the city know that only by the dragon's will may the sun ever be returned to them. They know the old stories, how the sun so loved the world, but the jealousy of the moon swelled until the one could not even set eyes upon the other. "She will freeze in darkness," said the moon, every word wrapped in spite. "She will never again know your warmth, nor your adoration, and I shall hold her *always* unto me."

And so the jungle was clothed in evening, and only those beasts who rule the night flourished: the jaguar rejoiced in its great good fortune, while the parrots and macaws fell to dreams, and of all the many tribes of monkeys, none but the night-dwelling douroucouli could be heard moving through the trees. Without the sun, the corn and potatoes and all other crops withered and rotted. But one woman defied the jealousy of the moon, and she prayed for the sun to send a warrior to drive back the moon and free them from the unending cold and gloom. And so passionate were her words, they slipped past the arrogant, unmindful moon and reached the sun.

Her name was Scádda, the same name that would be worn by all the sun callers to come. When He Who Loves the Earth heard Scádda's pleas, he spat forth the dragon from the roiling furnace of his gut, and the dragon fought and won a battle against the moon, so that it was forced, at last, to retreat and move once again across the sky, in that groove set aside for it when all the universe was young.

But in its struggle with the moon, the dragon was gravely injured, and the moon swore vengeance. And this is why the sun instructed Scádda that her people must always be ready, once in every five generations of women, to send a bride unto the ailing dragon, from whom it might draw the strength it would need to revisit its victory against the envious, hating moon.

"You will know her," the sun said to Scádda, "for the dragon will make plain his choice." And always, in those appointed seasons presaging the celestial battle, have the people in the city deep within the jungle looked for the marks of the dragon's desire. There are none between the mountains and the sea, none who travel the wide river, who do not know and heed this story.

On the dais at the center of the tesseract, this latest Scádda raises her arms, accepting and welcoming her sun-born husband. The very earth shakes, then, and the retinue of priestesses standing around the circle are thrown violently to their knees. The walls of the chamber strain and groan as dirt and stones sift down from above, peppering the blind women. But not Scádda, for nothing and no one but the sun callers may ever enter the facets of the tesseract; its geometry is strict and unforgiving. And, also, Scádda does not feel the tremors as the earth shudders, as the dragon responds to the sun caller's invocation. She is held safe within the cubes, and it would be incorrect to insist that she continues to exist in the same reality as her seven companions, or any other woman. For five years, the dragon must rest in this cosmic anteroom, this interval between time and space if it is to heal from the wounds incurred during each battle with the moon. But it has heard Scádda's call and has responded.

"You will open yourself to me?" it asks, words spoken without tongue nor palate nor teeth nor larynx. For, indeed, its voice is as silent as its waking was uproarious. It is a voice that Scádda has heard often in her dreams, and briefly she wonders if she is only dreaming now. "You would wed me, and give of yourself completely, that I might do battle with the moon and free the world of this shade?"

"I would," she replies. "I would, and I will, if you will *have* me for your wife. All my life has led me here."

"Always was there a *choice*," the dragon purrs, and that purr resonates in each and every cell of Scádda's body. "And the agents of the moon are everywhere, waiting, watching, eager. The land teems with their number. You might have followed *them,* and served in the present darkness as a queen."

"I am only *your* queen, for there is no fit world without balance. I offer my life that balance will be restored. I offer it freely. I ask that I be deemed worthy."

Something not unlike laughter ripples through her, and Scádda stumbles, but doesn't fall. The dragon answers, "You would not *stand* here, bride, had I not deemed you worthy while you were still a senseless nub of flesh floating in the ocean of your mother. But you *know* this. *Always* have you known this."

And she says yes, she *has* known this her whole life. The dragon laughs again and, gently, he chides her false deference and self deprecation.

"There is very little time," he says, then, and the sun caller lowers her arms to her sides. "The moon gloats in the purple sky, and your people, and all the peoples of all the world, cower in fear that *this* time the sun shall not return."

"No sun caller has ever failed in her duty," Scádda says. "Down all the generations have we stepped into the unseen light and stood in this place and accepted our province."

"Yes," the dragon agrees. "You have. Are you afraid?"

"I will not lie," Scádda replies. "There is a terrible fear in me, though it shames me to say so, to admit this weakness."

"All who came before you were afraid," the dragon assures her. "There is no need for shame. As for fear, there are dangers, and there will be pain, and you will never again be who or what you were. These are things any sane woman would fear, are they not?"

"They are. Of course, they are."

"Then you'd do well to banish any ignominy for your fear. It is merely a testament to your wisdom." And then, again, the dragon says, "There is very little time."

"I am ready," Scádda says, whether it is entirely true or not. "I will receive you, my groom."

"There have been no men who have loved you?" the dragon asks her.

"None," she says. "Only the blind sisters have readied me for your bed. I have known no male lover."

"Then the time has arrived, and we shall be one. And *if* we know victory this day, then we *will* be one until the end of your life. Once filled, the vessel can never empty itself."

"I am here, and I am ready," she says, and then there are no more words, no more questions or reassurances or warnings. She knows that outside the tesseract, in the world above, ground is being lost. The jaguars and many of the serpent tribes will have already gathered to enter the city, when they are certain of the moon's victory, that *this* time they will not be driven back into the leafy shadows. That they will not once more feel the spears of men or know the humiliation of defeat.

And the dragon, birthed of the sun's unquenchable desire, enters Scádda. She is no virgin, for, as she said, the blind priestesses have prepared her for the dragon's ministrations. But no act performed upon her in their secret halls within the holy ziggurat, no matter how savage or merciless, could ever have steeled her for the dragon's caress, for that tangible intangibility that rises from nowhere at all and thrusts itself roughly between her legs.

Neither might they have prepared her for the almost suffocating flood of visions that instantly fills her mind. For the first time in her nineteen years, Scádda *sees,* and she sees with the eyes of the dragon, which are almost the eyes of the sun. She sees, and she knows all the ages past, all those sun callers before her, and all the battles won. She knows the fury of the moon's gray and cratered face, and she knows, too, the love of the earth for blue skies and the single, distant white eye of the sun. She wraps both hands tightly about that part of the dragon leading into her sex, opening herself wider still, and marvels at the beauty and the horror, sensation and the simple fact of color.

And, high above the dais, in that existence continuing beyond the tesseract, the moon squints down into its own umbrage. And the advancing jaguars and vipers pause and hold their breath. The prayers of men and women falter and trail off as the unnatural dusk about them seems to brighten by almost imperceptible degrees. For a moment, even the sea, not so very far away, grows calm, and the river, for that same moment, ceases its ceaseless journey to the sea.

There is no language equal to Scádda's climax, nor to the dragon's, and no vocabulary that might ever hope to convey the act of transmutation that followed. Where there were two, there now is only one. It is neither Scádda nor the dragon, and it is every bit of both of them. It is mother and father and their daughter-son, bound together in a single form. Around it, the tesseract collapses, sucked back into the worm's well with such force that the seven priestesses are pulled down as well, to fall forever in that endless, awful night.

The moon howls its old rage, and once again waves crash against beachheads and the river gurgles between its muddy banks. And the thing that stands upon the dais, its breast armored in scales harder than the hardest stones, its eyes blazing with the seething fission of its father star, gazes upwards. It stares towards the ceiling of the chamber, towards the supplicants kneeling on the steps of the ziggurat, towards the warriors driving back a horde of jungle beasts. Then it looks past all these distractions, directly into the moon's dusty face. That which was Scádda and the dragon spreads wings of flame and opens jaws that steam and drip vitriol and glowing magma. The moon hears it and shivers despite the millennia of bitterness and determination that gird its hollow soul.

Within the ziggurat, immemorial machineries of basalt and iron and bronze awaken, mechanisms crafted of the earth, and corridors shift. Floors and walls slide away in hissing curtains of steam, preparing a path for the sun-caller's gift.

A flint-headed lance pierces the hide of a great spectacled cat, and the head of a venomous snake is crushed beneath the heel of a warrior's sandal. And then all eyes turn away. *All* eyes. For not one among the living or the dead dares look upon the molten champion of the sun and the earth as it rises now to shine and do battle with the moon.

Paleozoic Annunciation

She drifts like any stray bit of flotsam, somewhere in the warm subequatorial seas south of barren Laurentian shores. On this Mid-Cambrian day she is a traveler, some five hundred and ten million years before the evening of her birth. No more conscious or oblivious than any hibernation, she rides currents that have carried her from the point of temporal insertion south and east, away from the submerged edges of the continental shelf and into the wide Iapetus. She's crossed the narrow abyss of an oceanic trench, coming finally to the reefs and lagoons fringing this back-arc scatter of volcanic islands and microcontinents. Raising her sleeping head above the surface, she draws several long breaths, hyperventilating before the dive, though, of course, this dream body needs no oxygen for its continued survival. But old habits persist, and she trails silvery bubbles as she slips below and descends towards the reef. No latter-day reef of corals, this, but a reef whose composition is almost as alien to her eyes as if it had been found on some other world than Earth, some other world orbiting some other star.

Great swaths of the rocky seafloor rising up to meet her is obscured beneath a carpet of calcified cyanobacteria and the branching lobes and solitary cups of archaeocyath sponges. There are knotted clusters formed by problematic chancellorids, an enigma to taxonomists, who must place all organisms in *this* box or *that* box; the chancellorids may be only sponges, or they might be slug-like halkieriids, protected inside their skins of star-shaped, calcareous sclerites. She is the only human yet ever to have seen chancellorids alive, even if she may not say they are being looked upon with waking eyes. Here and there, she recognizes corallimorphs, which seem to represent some transitional stage between anemones and the most primitive of corals. There are true anemones, as well, their stinging cnidarian tentacles waving lazily, sifting the brine for food. A submarine forest of sessile animals and algae and colonial microorganisms in an era when forests have not yet appeared *above* the water. Nestled in the understory are the shells of brachiopods and snails, monoplacophoran and hyolith mollusks and stalked eocrinoids, a menagerie of suspension feeders clustered in the gloom.

And yes, this is a most gloomy forest, for as she draws nearer to the reef – now almost thirty meters down – the sea absorbs all visible wavelengths of light excepting blue. There are no greens or yellows, no reds, only this dim palette comprised of shades of cyan and gray and black beyond counting. Regardless, her eyes adapt, and she can observe the comings and goings of those creatures that must (or have the freedom to) move about, crawling, creeping, slithering, swimming through the living and dead mineralized canopy of the reef. There are jellyfish, or things very *like* jellyfish, and dense swarms of trilobites of many shapes and sizes. There are animals almost too bizarre to describe, which she has only ever seen as fossils. A five-eyed *Opabinia* passes her, propelled by undulations of its segmented body and flabelliform tail. It probes among the sponges with its long proboscis and the sharp jaws set at the distal end of that appendage. But for all its grotesqueries, *Opabinia* is a very small nightmare, next to an enormous *Anomalocaris* lurking not far away, like some ravenous, two-meter-long fusion of fish and insect. The *Opabinia* swims too near and is snared by the twin "arms" protruding from the head of the *Anomalocaris* and drawn quickly towards its devouring mouth. But she must push all these beautiful, arresting distractions aside. She has not dreamed her way across so many eons merely to marvel at the wonders of a vanished ecosystem. Though she *is* a paleontologist, she has not been summoned *as* a paleontologist, but only as a human woman, an ambassador for another age, another species, another civilization. She dreams shutting her eyes, blocking out this ancient spectacle of life and death.

The agency handler is helping her into the tank, and the clear gelatinous substance filling it closes, not unpleasantly, around her calves. The conductive jelly has been precisely calibrated to match her body temperature. And still she shivers, and her handler asks if she's okay.

"I'm fine," she says, and the man nods, reassured.

Or here, long before she'd ever heard of the Burgess Project, she kneels in a quarry of brick-red slate, splitting slabs of stone to reveal the fossils of tiny, eyeless agnostid trilobites. Here are fourteen or more laid out on a single bedding plane. Their fossil carapaces are black and stand out against the ruddy matrix. She wipes sweat from her face with a paisley handkerchief and stares up at the summer sun shining high above the Rocky Mountains.

"You won't be alone," her handler says, and now she's sitting in the transfer tank, and she thinks he smiles exactly the way her father used to smile. "But you *must* focus," he says. "Once you're asleep, the subliminal prompts can only do so much to help you stay on track."

Her hammer and chisel split another slab beneath the white sun and the wide Wyoming sky, and there are more trilobites. But there's something else, too, and she thinks it bears more than a passing resemblance to a fossilized microchip, crushed and distorted and permineralized, mashed almost flat by the weight of sediment and time and the violent orogenies that raised these peaks. Six months from this moment, a team of seven MIT and Harvard scientists will confirm this first impression.

Her hammer strikes the stone, and a spark flies.

A single rivulet of sweat runs into her eye, and she winces and blinks at the pain.

The ocean within me, bleeding out. We all carry the ocean within us. We all, each of us, carry the scars of evolution's path.

The handler makes sure that all the electrodes are in place and checks the cable feeding from the mainframe into the implant at the base of her skull. She begins breathing through the rubber mouthpiece and lies down in the transfer tank.

Half a billion years pass in the space between one heartbeat and the next, and she opens her eyes, naked and dreaming and hovering a few meters above the floor of a reef composed of extinct sponges and cyanobacteria. There is no fear. There is no discomfort. There is only wonder, the sensation of being almost weightless, and the knowledge that she is the first pilgrim on this road. "The First *Time* Traveler" the news feeds proclaimed, even though her *body* was moved backwards not even by a single nanosecond. Better to call this temporal projection than time travel, and look to the spiritualist ramblings and nonsense of a Madame Blavatsky or an Edgar Cayce than the reasoned science fiction of an H. G. Wells, if one is to begin to grasp the psychophysics and mechanical leaps made possible through the paradigm shift triggered by the integrated circuit she discovered preserved in those brick-red shales.

She is not more, nor less, insubstantial than an electromagnetic wave effortlessly riding along unimagined frequencies. She peers down into the murk, and the *Anomalocaris* has gone, swum away to seek out new prey somewhere else in this broken, inconstant chain of Taconic islands that stretches more than 5,600 kilometers west to east. The vestiges of the broken Pannotian supercontinent lie to the south, out beyond the arc and other oceanic basins. Feet down, arms held at right angles to her slender body, and the nimbus of her red hair to frame her face, by choice has she become the uncrucified, though reconfigured, martyr to mankind's curiosity, and the one chosen to answer the call of the beings who have built their cities in the deeper places between the reefs. Like a demon, they have conjured her from unrealized time.

They rise to meet her, half a dozen indistinct forms in the twilight. She continues to sink towards the bottom as they draw nearer. All is as planned, everything proceeding according to Hoyle, and in only a few minutes more, she will have achieved First Contact, and the project will have entered its third stage.

In a future that is both certain and which also may never arrive, her unconscious *corpus* sleeps in its gelatin bed while her handler watches anxiously on and the mainframe struggles to keep her alive in the absence of that portion of herself which has been pulled free and sent spiraling towards an afternoon four hundred million years before the coming of the earliest proto-dinosaurs. She is entirely unaware of any umbilicus linking *then* and *now* (if these terms even retain any objective meaning for chrononauts). And watching the approach of her hosts, the memories of her life prior to the alignment and transfer have begun to assume a spectral, intangible nature. She is forgetting herself, and never mind the warnings of the men and women who trained her for this mission. They could not have known. They could not even have imagined.

Her hosts come, gradually coalescing from this perpetual twilight, becoming defined one from the other, and they have voices.

They are singing to me, she thinks. *They are reeling me in.*

Something small and faintly bioluminescent swims quickly past her face, a jawless agnathan progenitor of the first fishes, perhaps. She watches it go, momentarily distracted from the advancing forms.

If you lose focus, we may not be able to bring you home, her handler said before she went under. *Locking your coordinates is largely dependent on the beta readings, and signal clarity degrades when you're not concentrating.*

They are singing to me, she thinks again. *No one ever said that they could sing.*

And then they are upon her, the agreed-upon six that comprise the encounter team, one enormous female and five males hardly a third the female's size. They are no more trilobites than the members of *Homo sapiens* are lemurs or tarsiers, but to her unprepared mind, with no alternate frame of reference, they appear very much *like* trilobites. But she also thinks they might be angels, freed of the strictures of mythology and expectation. In the end, though, these beings are nothing she *needs* them to be, but only what they are. She wishes that she might glimpse herself through their bulging compound holochroal eyes and gape at her own preposterous physiology. The female looms over her, a fantastic array of spines trailing away from the pleural lobes of its thorax and pygidium. She has been told not to look them directly in the "face," as this may constitute a threat. But she finds it impossible *not* to look, not to admire the intricacies of the interdigitating sutures of the female's cephalic doublure, the hypostome jutting, almost like a beak, from beneath the protective shield of its rostral plate. The hypostome opens, revealing its mouth, and even now she feels no fear, whether from the benzodiazepines being pumped into her brain by the mainframe or by some instinctual knowledge that these creatures mean her no harm. They have not brought her here only to do murder. The female's antennae twitch in the currents, and its feathery gills vibrate, and the many pairs of jointed, hairy legs beneath its carapace move to and fro, as though signing an unspoken language of gestures that this soft human woman will never learn.

They have found me, she thinks, and the thought heralds a swell of euphoria. *I am dreaming, and yet this is no dream. They have found me, and I am here.*

One of the males, hardly larger than herself, breaks formation and moves nearer. Whether this is part of some prearranged protocol, or instinct, or a response to the giant female's instructions, she cannot say. There was never any clear idea what she would encounter at the apogee of her journey.

A moment later, and the male is on her, clinging, probing, forcing her head back so that she stares upwards at the faraway underside of ocean's surface. She offers no resistance; this much, at least, *was* expected.

Consider this sex as diplomacy, the lead xenosociologist said to her, during one of the interminable briefings in the project's Huston compound. And, as her vagina would hardly be compatible with the copulatory organs of her hosts, she was offered two options: urogenital surgery based on their best guesses or a mentally constructed virtual prosthesis that might suffice. When told how much more likely the surgery was to prove successful than the prosthetic construct, she'd agreed to undergo the procedure, though it would be irreversible and render her incapable of normal sex with members of her own species. She'd signed another round of release forms and moved another step nearer consummating the patently impossible.

The male enters her, and she closes her eyes. There might be discomfort, if she could feel. There might be pleasure, but she'll never know. In the half-light behind her eyelids, she recalls the face of her handler, and the transfer tank, and there is a faint sense of disappointment and anxiety as she realizes that it's almost over. Soon, the stream will reverse itself, and she'll be drawn backwards, which, of course, is forwards, if the mind accepts a simple, linear view of time.

Five hundred and fifty million years away, her crack hammer strikes a terra-cotta stone, and the friction of steel against shale throws a spark. Sweat runs from her hairline into her left eye, and she winces and blinks at the stinging salt.

The salt is all about her.

The ocean within me, bleeding out. We all carry the ocean within us. We all, each of us, carry the scars of evolution's path.

When she opens her eyes again, the male has withdrawn. She has just begun to contemplate whether they will each have a turn at her, when the female abruptly and unceremoniously takes her leave. The others follow, and soon they have abandoned her to this Cambrian tableau. And she drifts there, watching the cloud of blood and thick, dark mucus leaking from between her legs. Her hand moves towards what the surgeons fashioned from her clitoris and labia, and then she feels the hypothalamic tug and knows that retrieval has commenced.

There is another faint pang of disappointment, and then she spills back across the eons, or they spill through and over her. It hardly matters which.

And, after what seems no more than the briefest, shining instant, she opens her eyes in the transfer tank, and there are three pairs of hands raising her up into a sitting position. The gelatinous medium drips from her in what seems like slow motion. When the breathing apparatus has been removed from her mouth and nostrils, they tell her not to speak, that it can wait, that she can tell them everything soon enough. As if she is eager to report. She finds the presumption strangely offensive, but doesn't say so.

Almost a month passes before the pregnancy is detected, and she isn't offered the option of aborting the hybrid growing just beyond her remodeled cervix. But, in truth, in point of fact, the thought never crosses her mind.

Charcloth, Firesteel, and Flint

She doesn't know how or where or why it began. She cannot even say when. These memories are as lost to her as is her own name. Sometimes, in the empty hours between burning, she has concocted scenarios, both elaborate and unadorned, mildly implausible and entirely outlandish, to explain how a woman might become the midwife of infernos. These fictitious consolations have numbered in the many tens of thousands, and most are soon forgotten. They rise from her like blackened bits of paper, glowing brightly about the edges and buoyed higher and higher by the updrafts of her singular desires. They are wafted away, to settle on unsuspecting rooftops and in patches of dry brittle grass, to lie smoldering in mountainous chaparral scrublands. In this way, they bear a great resemblance to the longings of all lonely persons.

"I am the daughter of Hephaestus and a mortal woman," she whispers to the darkness. Or, "I was born in the Valley of Hinnom and am a child of Gehenna. The corpse of my pregnant mother was left there amid the rubbish and the dead, but I survived, however scarred." Or she assures herself that she was only raped by a Catalan dragon, or that she is a salamander who was freed by a careless Arabian alchemist and thereafter assumed human form, so that she would not ever be found out.

"In the bright crucible of Earth's molten birth," she says, "I was conceived, a stray and conscious spark thrown from that accreting, protoplanetary disc. I swam seas of magma, and sank, and later slept long eons beneath the cooling lithosphere, waiting to be born from some stratovolcanic convulsion."

Of course, she *believes* none of her tales, not even for an instant. They are fancies and nothing more. But without them, she would be lost. And were she lost, who would bear witness to the fires?

On a deserted stretch of Midwestern highway, half an hour past midnight on a hot summer night, a young man sees her in the glare of his headlights.

She is not hitchhiking. She's not even walking, but merely standing alone in the breakdown lane, gazing up at the broad, star-freckled sky. When he pulls over, she lowers her gaze, meeting his through the windshield, and she smiles. It's a friendly, disarming smile, and he asks if she needs a ride and tells her that he's going as far up I-29 as Sioux City, if she's headed that way.

"You're very kind," she says, the words delivered in an accent he has never heard before and thinks might be from someplace in Europe. She opens the passenger-side door and slides in next to him. He thinks that he's never seen hair even half so black, though her skin is as pale as milk. She laughs and shakes his hand, and, by the dashboard's glare, her eyes seem golden brown, shot through with amber threads. Later, in a motel room on the outskirts of Onawa, he will see that her eyes are only hazel green.

When he asks her name, she decides on Aiden, as it's a name she hasn't used in a while (though Mackenzie, Tandy, and Blaise also came immediately to mind). She doesn't volunteer a patronymic, and the young man, whose name is only Billy, doesn't ask her for one. He notices that her unpolished nails are chewed down almost to the quick, and as she shuts the door, and he shifts the car out of neutral, he catches the faintest whiff of wood smoke. He doesn't ask where she's come from, or where she's bound, as it's no business of his; he keeps his eyes on the road, the broken white line rushing past on his left, while *she* talks.

"My father is a fireman," she lies, though it's an old lie, worn smooth about its periphery. "Well, not exactly a fireman, no. He's a certified fire investigator. He's the guy who decides whether or not it was arson, the fires, and if so, how the arsonists started them."

She talks, and Billy listens, and the indistinct smoky smell that seems to have entered the car with her comes and goes. Sometimes, it's wood smoke, and sometimes the odor is almost sulfurous, as if someone has just struck a match. Sometimes, it makes him think of the rusted-out old barrel his own father used for burning trash, the way the barrel smelled after a hard rain. He keeps waiting for her to light a cigarette, but she never does.

"Did you know," she asks, "that before gasoline was ever used to fuel internal combustion engines, it was sold in pretty little bottles to kill head lice? People sprayed it on their hair." And no, he says, I didn't know that, and she smiles again and stares up at the stars, the wind through the open window whipping at her ebony hair. "It wasn't called gasoline back then," she says, "Just petrol."

"Wasn't that dangerous?" he asks her.

"Calling it petrol, instead of gasoline?"

"No," he replies, only pretending to sound exasperated. "Folks putting gasoline in their hair."

She laughs, and *when* she laughs, he thinks that the burnt smell grows slightly more pungent. "Why do you think no one does it anymore?" she asks, but Billy doesn't answer. He drives on, shrouded by the west Iowa night, and she lets the wind blow through her hair and talks to keep him awake. He never mentions that he's sleepy, or that he's been on the road since just after dawn, but she sees it plainly enough on his face and hears it in his voice. He offers to turn on the radio, but says there's nothing out here except preaching and a few honky-tonk stations, and she tells him no, the night is fine without the radio, without music or disembodied voices threatening brimstone and damnation. It never once occurs to her that he might find it odd, how the topic of her conversation (which is really more a monologue, as he says very little) never strays far from matters of conflagration. She has too little understanding of thoughts other than her own to suspect, or even care, what anyone else might find peculiar. And, in truth, he's so grateful for the company of this strange girl that her single-mindedness is an easy enough thing to overlook.

She recounts Algonquin, Creek, and Ojibwa myths, and in all three a rabbit or hare steals fire and gives it to humanity. She talks about Prometheus and the Book of Enoch and the relative temperatures of different regions and layers of the sun. He has to interrupt and ask her to explain Kelvins, and when she converts the numbers to Celsius, he has to ask what that means in Fahrenheit.

"5,800 Kelvins," she says, referring to the surface of the sun, and speaking without a hint of condescension or impatience in her voice, "is roughly equal to 5,526 degrees Celsius, which comes to a little more than 9,980 degrees Fahrenheit. But you go deeper in, all the way down to the *core* of the sun, and it's very close to 13,600,000 degrees Kelvin, or almost 25,000,000 degrees Fahrenheit." And then she informs him that, by comparison, the highest temperature ever recorded on the surface of the earth was a mere 136 degrees Fahrenheit, in the deserts of El Azizia, Libya, on September 13th, 1922.

"That was sixty years before I was born," he says, and tacks on, "Libya. Now, that's in Africa, right?"

"Yes," she replies. "Now, and in 1922, as well." He laughs, even though she'd not meant it as a joke.

"So, what's the hottest place in America?"

"North America?" she asks. "Or do you mean the United States."

"I mean the United States."

She only considers the question for a few seconds, then tells him that, sixty-nine years before he was born, a temperature of 134 degrees Fahrenheit was recorded in Death Valley, California, on July 10th, 1913. "In fact, the hottest place in the US, or anywhere else in the Western Hemisphere, is Death Valley, which averages 98 degrees in the summer."

"Ninety-eight," he says. "That's not so hot."

"No," she agrees. "It really isn't."

"You learn all this stuff from your dad?" Billy asks her. "A certified fire investigator, does he need to know all about Indian legends and how hot it gets on the sun?"

"My father is a fireworks manufacturer," she says, as though unaware, or merely indifferent, that this lie contradicts the earlier one. "He specializes in multi-break shells and time rain. He has factories in Taiwan and China." And then, before Billy can object, she's already explaining how different chemical compounds produce different-colored flames. "Copper halides give you blue," she says. "Sodium nitrate, that makes a nice yellow. Cesium burns indigo."

Billy flunked eleventh-grade chemistry, and none of this means much of anything to him. But he asks her how they get red, anyway.

"Depends," she sighs and leans back in her seat, pushing windblown strands of black hair from her face.

"On what?"

"What sort of red you're after. Lithium carbonate gives off a very nice moderate shade of red. But if you want something more intense, strontium carbonate's always your best bet."

"And green?"

"Copper compounds, barium chloride."

"And gold? What do you have to burn to get golden fireworks? The gold ones have always been my favorite. Especially the big starburst ones." And he takes a hand off the wheel long enough to pantomime an exploding mortar and the gilded stream of sparks that follows.

She turns her head and watches him a moment, then says, "Daddy uses lampblack for gold, usually."

On his right, a reflective sign promises an exit, with motels, restaurants, and a truck stop, only five miles farther along. He checks the gas gauge and sees that the red needle is hovering just above empty. "I don't want to seem ignorant, but I have no idea what lampblack is," he says to the woman calling herself Aiden.

"Lots of people don't," she replies and shuts her eyes. "It's just an old word for soot, really. You know what soot is?"

"Yes," Billy says. "I *know* what soot is."

"Well, lampblack is a very fine sort of soot, sometimes just called blacking, gathered from partially burned carbonaceous materials. It's been used as a pigment since prehistoric times and is considered one of the least-reflective substances known to man."

"I'm just gonna to take your word for that," he says, and she smiles her easy, disarming smile again and opens her eyes that only seem to be golden brown with glittering amber streaks. "I'm also going to take the next exit, cause we need gas and I could use some coffee."

"I have to pee," she says, and briefly wishes she had a roadmap, because the positions of the stars and planets above the plains and cornfields can only tell her so much.

"You drink coffee?" Billy asks, and she nods her head.

"I drink coffee."

"I'm guessing you drink it with milk, but no sugar."

"I drink coffee," she says again, as if perhaps she failed to make herself understood the first time. "I drink it, though I've never much cared for the taste. It's bitter. I don't like bitter things."

Billy only nods, because he doesn't much like the taste of coffee, either. And then they've reached the off ramp, and he cuts the wheel right, exiting the interstate into the gaudy glimmer of convenience stores and gas stations. The exit for Onawa distinguishes itself in no way from most remote highway exits, just another oasis of electric light, parked automobiles, and towering billboards touting everything from beer to a local strip club. The woman who's name is no more Aiden than it is MacKenzie spots a McDonald's, a Dairy Queen, and a Subway, and here and there, a few stunted, unexpected trees. Mostly, this is farmland, and she suspects the fast-food places are more welcome than are the trees. Billy steers into the parking lot of a BP, not far from a motel; both lots are crowded with semis and pickup trucks.

"We could maybe get a room," he says, as matter-of-factly as it's possible, considering he only met her a few hours before. "We could get a room, grab a little sleep before driving into Sioux City."

"We could get a room," she replies, the words passing indifferently across her lips, hardly more than an echo. "I need to pee," she tells him again, changing the subject as though it's settled, and he stops the car beside the pumps, beneath the halogen shine of the station's aluminum canopy. When he's cut the ignition, she gets out and goes inside. The restrooms are in one corner, near an upright cooler filled with sodas and energy drinks. The women's room reeks of urine and cleaning products and sickly sweet cakes of toilet deodorizer. But she's smelled much, much worse, times beyond counting.

When she's done, she goes back out to find him shutting the trunk. Though she doesn't ask, Billy hurriedly explains, "Something was shifting around back there. Making a racket. Turns out, the lug wrench had come loose." It's as good a story as any, and she doesn't dispute it.

"You heard it, yeah?" he asks.

"No," she answers, and then gets back into the car.

He pulls his car from the BP's lot into the parking lot of a neighboring Motel 6, and she waits alone while he goes into the lobby to register. Billy offers to pay for the room, since, after all, it was his idea, and she doesn't object. While she waits, she stares up at the night sky past the windshield, trying to pick out the stars through the orange-white haze of light pollution. But they've been blotted out, almost every one of them. Only the brightest and most determined are visible, even to her, and she knows the night sky better (as they say) than the back of her own hand. It occurs to her, in passing, that neither of them got coffee at the BP station.

When Billy returns, he has a small paper envelope with the motel's logo printed on it and a plastic card, the sort with a magnetic strip on one side.

"I miss real keys," she says. "The old brass-colored keys, attached to big diamond-shaped chunks of plastic with the room numbers stamped on them. You could steal them, those keys, and have a souvenir. But that," and she pauses to point at the envelope, "that doesn't make for a very interesting souvenir."

"Where are you from?" he asks, squeezing the car into an empty space nearer their room. "I don't recognize your accent."

"Would it really matter?" she asks. All he has for an answer is a shrug, and neither of them says much of anything after that. It may be they've passed the point where talk is necessary. That's what she would say, if the question were put to her. The night has gathered sufficient momentum it no longer needs to be propelled by small talk.

Inside, she goes to the sink and splashes her face and the back of her neck with ice-cold water. Billy switches on the television, to some channel that shows old movies, 24/7, and he turns the volume down low. She doesn't recognize the film that's playing, but it's in black and white, which suits her fine. It helps to counter the garish, mismatched wallpaper and comforter, the ugly carpet and the uglier painting hung above the queen-sized bed.

"I was only fourteen, my first time–" he begins, but she places a wet finger to his lips, shushing him.

"It doesn't matter," she says. "Not to me, not to anyone." And then he sits down at the end of the bed and watches her undress. She's thin, but not as thin as he'd expected. Her breasts are small, her belly flat. Her pubic hair is as black as the hair on her head, a sable V there between her pale thighs. She folds her dingy, road-weary clothes neatly and sets them aside, which surprises him more than the crimson triangle tattooed between her shoulder blades. He asks her what it means, and she tells him that it's the alchemical symbol for fire, though it may mean many other things, as well. He asks where she got it, and when, and she tells him, truthfully, that she doesn't remember.

"But it was a very long time ago," she says, and then begins undressing him. She pulls the T-shirt off over his head, undoes his belt buckle, and then Billy takes it from there. The bed is soft and cool, and the white sheets are heavily perfumed with a floral-scented fabric softener. When he kisses her, she tastes like cinders, but he doesn't say anything. She climbs on top, and he enters her effortlessly. He comes almost immediately, but she doesn't seem to mind, and whispers soothing words in his left ear, while she grinds her hips roughly against his. The thought occurs to him, then, that he might only be dreaming, because it all seems somehow so unlikely, because he hasn't gotten off with anything but his own hands and tubes of KY in years. And because the words she's whispering are coalescing into such vivid pictures in his mind, images so clear he can't be entirely sure that he's not *seeing* them through his eyelids. She fucks him, and her teeth and tongue and spittle and palate taste of cinders, and the visions spill freely from her lips – dazzling, exquisite apparitions of holocaust – and he comes again. He opens his eyes and gasps loudly, and she smiles and kisses him again.

"Close your eyes," she says, and there's a tone in her voice that's almost enmity. "*Keep* them closed. Close them as tightly as you can."

Billy does as he's told, and he understands now that the bright visions are not so much what she *wants* him to see, but what he *needs* to see.

"That's a good boy," she whispers and places a hand on either side of his head. The rhythm of their lovemaking has assumed a cadence, a force, that he will later describe, in the spiral-bound notebook he uses for a diary, as violent. *I almost thought that she was raping me,* he will write. *But it wasn't rape. It wasn't rape at all.* He will also write about how quiet she was, the unnerving, heavy silence of her orgasms, but mostly, he'll write about the fires.

He will write, *I think maybe she was Hawaiian. She was a Hawaiian woman, and her great, great grandmother made love to the goddess Pele.*

She fucks him, and the fire licks at his mind, at the inside of his eyelids, and at the chintzy wallpaper of the motel room.

"This is my gift," she whispers. "This is the only gift I have to offer."

For half an instant, it is another summer night, July 18th, one thousand and forty-five years before the night he finds her standing at the side of an Iowa interstate highway. And *he* stands on a Roman street, outside a cluster of shops near the Circus Maximus. It's two nights past the full moon, and the fire has already begun. It will burn for six days and seven nights, and Nero will accuse Christian arsonists of starting the blaze.

Billy can feel her hands on him, those short nails digging into his scalp and maybe even drawing blood. But he doesn't open his eyes, and he doesn't tell her to stop.

That half instant passes, taking Rome away, taking century after century, until he finds himself on the banks of the Sumida River, looking out across the Japanese caste town of Edo. It is the second day of March, 1657, and hurricane-force winds are sweeping down from the northeast, fanning the flames devouring the city of wood and paper houses, bamboo still tinder-dry from a drought the year before. But Billy hardly even feels the wind. It barely touches him. The sky overhead has been blotted out by smoke, underlit by the fire so that the gray-black billows glow as hellishly as anything Dante or Milton will ever imagine. Over the next three days, more than a hundred thousand people will die.

And then he's sitting on a crowded wooden bleacher, beneath the big top of the Ringling Brothers and Barnum & Bailey Circus. It's a humid summer day in July of 1944, and far overhead, the Flying Wallendas have just begun their trapeze act. In only a few seconds, the tent will begin to burn. The canvas has been waterproofed with a mixture of paraffin and white gasoline. In less than eight minutes, the tent will be consumed, and the melting paraffin wax will drip down like a rain of napalm upon the heads of the sixty-eight hundred people trying to escape the fire. Near the end, Billy thinks he's hearing wild animals screaming, but no, she says, no, those are human voices. Not a single one of the cats or elephants or camels was killed that day.

"Enough," he whispers and tumbles from that day to another. But he doesn't tumble very far this time. Not so very far at all. Hardly more than a year, and it's August 6, 1945, Hiroshima, and somehow Billy is not vaporized when the atomic bomb codenamed "Little Boy" detonates 1,900 feet overhead. The subsequent fireball reduces sand and glass to bubbling, viscous pools, and everything burns. Some of the 140,000 who die are so completely obliterated that they leave behind only shadows on bridges and the sides of buildings. Some leave even less than that.

And it does not matter how many times or how desperately he asks that she make it stop. He cries out, and he screams, and he sobs, and the immolations unfolding behind his eyelids, inside his skull, continue unabated.

"I was there," she says. "For every one, I was there. I carry the memories, and this is my gift to you."

April 18th, 1906, and, in San Francisco, more than three thousand perish in the earthquake and firestorm that proceeds it.

Dresden, Germany, a few minutes past midnight on the morning of February 14th, 1945, the holy day of Ash Wednesday, and hundreds of British bombers drop hundreds of tons of high explosives and incendiary devices on the seventh largest city of the Fatherland. Billy huddles in the largest of the public air-raid shelters, below the central train station, him and sixty thousand others. Almost all of them will be dead soon. By sunrise, much of the city will be at the mercy of a fire whose temperatures will peak at more than 2,700 degrees Fahrenheit. He watches, unable to turn away, and is aware that the woman who calls herself Aiden is somewhere nearby. Near enough that he can hear her as she reads words a survivor will someday put to paper.

"We saw terrible things," she reads, "cremated adults shrunk to the size of small children, pieces of arms and legs, dead people, whole families burnt to death, burning people ran to and fro, burnt coaches filled with civilian refugees, dead rescuers and soldiers, many were calling and looking for their children and families, and fire everywhere, everywhere fire, and all the time the hot wind of the firestorm threw people back into the burning houses they were trying to escape from."

"I do not know why you are showing me this," he says, shouting to be heard above the cacophony of explosions and screams.

"Yes you do," she whispers, and he hears her perfectly well. "You know precisely why."

And there is more, conflagrations beyond reckoning, though, later, he *will* try to write them all down. The burning of Atlanta, as ordered by Union General William Tecumseh Sherman. October 8, 1871, and on the same day as the Great Chicago fire, the town of Peshtigo, Wisconsin burns, along with the Michigan towns of Holland, Manistee, and Port Huron. Hundreds die in Chicago, and in Peshtigo, men and women who try to seek refuge from the heat in the river that divides the town in two are boiled alive. The firestorm generates a tornado, flinging houses and box cars into the air like incandescent toys.

"Open your eyes," she says, and he does. And now there's only the dingy motel room, the murmur of the television, and the naked girl straddling him. He's sobbing, and she watches him as one might watch some outlandish phenomenon that can never truly be understood. She climbs off him, and Billy sits weeping at the edge of the bed. Almost fifteen minutes pass before he says anything.

"I won't do it again," he says. "I promise. I won't ever fucking do it, not ever again."

And she laughs, and it sounds like steam escaping a punctured pipe. A laugh like a thunder crack, that laugh, like lightning finding its mark.

"I didn't come to *stop* you, Billy. I came to be sure you'd *never* stop."

His mouth tastes like cinders, and when he blinks and wipes his eyes, the air dances with the afterimages of a trillion embers sparkling against the backdrop of innumerable smoky skies.

"I didn't think I'd have to explain that part," she says, remembering all the ones who have kneeled at her feet and groveled and, after she was done with them, begged for still *more* revelations.

"I was only fourteen the first time," he says again.

"I know. You've done well, I think. You'll do great deeds, before you're finished."

And then she dresses, except for her shoes, which she carries, and leaves him alone in the room. No longer calling herself Aiden, the woman who doesn't know how or where or why it began, or even when, walks across the parking lot. She passes his car, and the homemade pipe bomb hidden in the trunk, packed snugly beneath the spare tire, in its locked aluminum carrying case. She'll be in Sioux City when it goes off, of course. But right now, she needs to walk. The eastern horizon is going shades of pink and violet as the world rolls towards a new day, and by the time she reaches the northbound lane of the interstate, she's begun telling herself a new story, about the phoenix that might have been her mother, and how she helped the great bird build a nest of frankincense and myrrh twigs. How she set the nest ablaze...

Shipwrecks Above

This one, she rides the tides. She has been hardly more than a shade drifting between undulating stalks of kelp, and she has worn flickering diadems of jellyfish, anemones, and brittle stars. The mackerel and tautog swap their careless yarns of her. For instance, that she was once a dryad, but then fell from Artemis' favor. Weighted about the ankles, so was she drowned and whored out to the sea, cast down from all sylvan terrestrial spheres, from all pastures and forests that have *not* been drowned. But this is no more than the bitter fancies that fish whisper to one another, tales told *in* school, and such stories have even less substance than what has been left of her. She was never a dryad. She was only a woman, very long ago, though not so far back as the tautog and mackerel might have you suppose. The imagination of fish knows no bounds.

She was once only a woman, as I've said, and a woman who had the great misfortune to attract the attentions of something that was *not* only a man. He loved her, or at least he *named* it love, knowing no other word for his desires and insatiable appetites. He loved her, and so must she not, by right, be his? After all, she was the daughter of *his* sister, and had he not *loved* his sister and shown to her all the ruthless dedication of that love, before she ungratefully fled from him? Hence, might not this fatherless Székely child – christened Eórsebet Soffia by some mangy Calvinist priest – be reasonably considered flesh of his own flesh? Yet, when the noble boyar claimed her, his impertinent sister dared protest the allegation. So he had her killed, and István Vadas, hero of the Thirteen Years' War and cherished ally to the Wallachian Prince Michael the Brave, did take the girl away from her village in the year 1624.

On that day, Eórsebet was sixteen and seven months and had never yet looked upon the sea.

Her father and lover, her self-appointed Lord in *all* matters of this world and in any to come hereafter, ferried her high into the Carpathian wilderness, up to some crumbling ancestral fortress, its towers and curtain walls falling steadily into decrepitude. It was no less a wreck than the whalers and doggers, the schooners and trawlers that she has since sung to their graves on jagged reefs of stone and coral. And it was there, in the rat-haunted corridors of István's moldering castle, that she did refuse this dæmonic paramour. All his titles, battlefield conquests, and wealth were proved unequal to the will of a frightened girl. When he had raped her and beaten her did he have her bound and, for a while, cast into a deep pit where she believed that Archangel Michael, bringer of merciful Death, might find her and bear her away from this perdition unto the gilded clouds of Heaven.

"You have chosen to spurn the Light of my devotion," István told Eörsebet Soffia, his dry lips pressed to the hagioscopic squint of her cell door, murmuring through that "leper's window" rather than allow her to glimpse even the flickering of torchlight. "Therefore, it seems more than just that I should *aid* thee in seeking out the lightless realms." István went away, leaving her with no further explanation of intent, but at the dawn of the next day, upon the crowing of the cock, his jailer blinded the girl with an iron poker heated in glowing coals. The wounds were bound with the finest Chinese silk, taken from ravaged Ottoman caravans. Her screams were nothing new to the rats, or to the mortar, the spiders, or the limestone blocks of the keep, for her Lord knew well the worth of torture, just as he knew the worth of a good warhorse or a Karabelá sabre.

In a greater darkness than she had ever imagined, and in greater pain than she'd had cause even to suppose could exist, Eörsebet wept and prayed her delirious, fevered prayers to St. Michael. She knelt in filthy straw and dirt and offal, beseeching *any* angel or saint to intervene on her behalf. But, as before, all her supplications went unanswered.

And when another Transylvanian night had crept across the mountainside, the sun abandoning the steep Bârgäu forests to the wolves, István Vadas came to her again. Her father told her, solemnly, that she might serve him still, for what need had he of a bride who could see? "You are not diminished," he assured her, his voice as smooth as honey and cold as a serpent's blood. "You may yet attend and obey me in matrimony, and know my mercy. Merely assent, and you will be set free, and never again know pain or the humiliation of imprisonment."

But, straightaway, she named him a liar, and worse things, too, and István made a grand show of having been stung through and through by her words.

"You murdered my mother, your own sister," Eórsebet whispered, her voice raw from tears and the wasted prayers. "I shall *follow* her, rather than submit and willingly permit thy seed to enter me. I shall make for thee a *happy* corpse, before I call thee husband or bear fresh imps to assume the strangling yoke of thy name.

"Only show me to the well," she said, "for gladly will I go down into that gullet and be drowned. It would be a kinder fate than what you offer."

"If this is as my belov'd wishes," he replied, pretending to crushing disappointment. "If this is her last word on the matter, so be it. I will demonstrate to thee my complete adulation, in due course, and hold you here no more. I will break the shackles and throw open the door to this cell, and none shall risk my judgment by blocking thy retreat from me."

Even in her agony and bewilderment, Eórsebet was a girl wise beyond her ten and six years, and she saw through the boyar's promises. Or, more precisely, she saw how it was that he said one thing and meant quite another, how it could be he would hold true to every syllable of these oaths he'd spoken and *still* insure her doom. It was only sport to him, a grim diversion which he would win even if he lost.

An old lobster once came near to guessing the truth of her, so she devoured him, leaving nothing but an empty shell to settle amongst the sausage weed and sea lettuce.

While Eórsebet sat in her cell, awaiting whatever form her undoing would assume, the boyar called upon the dark gods to whom he'd always paid tribute. The true deities to which the *Sárkány Lovagrend,* King Sigismund's *Societas Draconistrarum,* had long ago pledged itself, all the while hiding behind a proper papal mask. And by these agencies was the warlord and sorcerer István Vadas granted the power to rain down upon his daughter a terrible curse. He spoke it in her nightmares, as she managed to doze fitfully in that decrepit oubliette. He whispered in some unhallowed grove, and the winds brought his words into her dreams.

"Daughter," he said, and "Dear heart," and "Beloved." Immediately, her dreaming mind did recognize that voice, but Eórsebet found herself poisoned by some sedative potion and unable to awaken.

"Thou wouldst have darkness, which I have already gifted to thee, rather than look upon my face. Thou wouldst be drowned, against our marriage, and this request will I also honor. You shall be drowned, my sweet Eórsebet, and so set free. But, in good conscience, I cannot commit thy soul to this garrison's well, no. I will see thee to far more majestic waters."

This is the secret that doomed the old lobster, and if it is known to any others within Poseidon's mansions, they have wisely kept it to themselves.

"Now, my *second* gift to thee, Eőrsebet," the boyer spoke within the confines of her dream. "For all eternity wilt thou wander the deep places of the world, carried to and fro by the whims of the tides. Thou wilt be of the water, and the water will be thine womb. But thou shalt hunger, as do those *strigoi* who must feed from off the living. And yet, only once in every year may thee leave the sustaining waters to slake thine thirst on the blood you will ever more crave. And, even then, you may not wander far from the shore. This is my gift, daughter, in lieu of matrimony, though I fancy it makes of thee another sort of wife."

So Eőrsebet's prison was opened, and a coach made ready to receive her. But, before her departure, the jailer branded the girl's back with such unnamable symbols as the dark gods had insisted to István she should here-after wear, if the curse were to be lasting and irrevocable. She was dressed in a fine gown of golden threads and driven away from the boyer's keep, down from the mountains and into Wallachia. The coach saw her through the gates of Bucharest and to a bridge spanning the Dâmbovița River. Shackled in irons, she was cast upon the waters. She has long since forgotten the drowning, the short fall from the bridge and the shock of hitting the icy torrent below. She cannot now recall the fire as her lungs filled, or the brief panic before her dissolution and rebirth. The Dâmbovița carried her to the Argeș at Oltenița, which bore her forth to the Danube, her wide, rolling road towards the Black Sea, just south of the ancient city of Constanța.

This small inland sea was her first tomb, and for many decades it seemed to her a boundless vault of wonders, as tombs go. She found a voice she'd not had in life, and with it she trilled raging storms and canted days when the waters grew so becalmed all sails hung limp upon their masts. She sang to sailors and to fishermen from Sevastopol to Varna, from the coasts of Georgia to the port of Odessa. She appeared, sometimes, to sui-cides, inviting them, and with her melodies she did draw to their deaths men and women and children, and even cattle and wild beasts, when the mood found her.

Sometimes, she would feel István's eyes upon her again, for his evil doings and services had earned him strange powers and another sort of undeath. From broken minarets, where he now had only rats and beetles and quick green lizards for company, he watched her with eyes turned black as coal. And finding that gaze intolerable, his siren would seek out some convenient undertow and sink down and down, passing into silty, anoxic nights so dense that not even his eyes could penetrate them.

Once a year, and only once a year, she stepped from the waves and walked waterfronts and streets and alleyways, as any woman would. She chose her victims carefully and stole away the salty crimson oceans locked up inside each and every one.

And this was the round and rut of her existence, until the thing that death and István's spite and sorcery had fashioned of Eörsebet found her way to the narrow straits of the Bosphorus. By this route, she came, slowly, to the Turkish Sea of Marmara and, finally, past Gallipoli and through the Dardanelles into the Aegean. But this was all so very long ago, as I have said, in the days and nights *before* she became a shade drifting through the perpetual Atlantic twilight, an oceanic phantom of kelp and driftwood.

She followed dolphins and mercurial shoals of fish to the stony shores of Crete, then into the Ionian Sea, where it is said the body of the son of Dyrrhachus was tossed, after his accidental murder at the hands of Heracles. She came to know the affection of whales, who also sang, though to other ends than her own. She followed pods of spermaceti from one end of the Mediterranean to the other, skirting the northern capes of African deserts, and was delivered, finally, to Gibraltar.

Perhaps it was only a matter of time (and she has no end of time, surely, excepting that one day the world might conclude, and so she with it) before storm waves and abyssal currents carried her north to the mouth of the Thames, and then west to London. In the year 1891, during the gloaming of Victoria's England and more than three full centuries after the boyar's men had shoved her from a bridge in Bucharest, Eörsebet Soffia raised her head above the stinking, tainted waters of that river befouled by industry and sewage and gazed sightlessly upon its fetid, teeming banks.

One day, a poet will write, "The river sweats/oil and tar." But this day, it also sweats *her,* the boyer's daughter, the sea's prostitute. She wends her all-but silent way between the close-packed clipper hulls, and no one notices when she slips from the water and onto the noisome squalor of St. Katharine's Docks. Amid the bustle, there in the shadows of the ships and warehouses, who's to take exception at the spectacle of one more bedraggled doxy? Who will look closely enough to note the scars where her eyes were, or a few barnacles dappling her gaunt cheeks and the backs of her hands? The docks are a riot of "...solid carters and porters; the dapper clerks, carrying pen and book; the Customs' men moving slowly; the slouching sailors in gaudy holiday clothes; the skipper in shiny black that fits him uneasily, convoying parties of wondering ladies; negroes, Lascars, Portuguese, Frenchmen; grimy firemen, and (shadows in the throng) hungry-looking day-laborers..." Or so Doré and Jerrold described it nineteen years prior to the day of Eórsebet's arrival. She moves, barefoot, between baskets and crates, wagons and hogshead casks, "through bales and bundles and grass-bags, over skins and rags and antlers, ores and dye-woods: now through pungent air, and now through a tallowy atmosphere, to the quay..." (once more quoting from the published memoir of Doré and Jerrold's pilgrimage).

She crosses a narrow canal bridge, which carries her from the docks, away from the anchored fleets and (to steal from the narrative of Doré and Jerrold one last time, I do promise) into "...shabby, slatternly places, by low and poor houses, amid shiftless riverside loungers...on to the eastern dock between Wapping and down Shadwell. Streets of poverty-marked tenements, gaudy public-houses and beer-shops, door-steps packed with lolling, heavy-eyed, half-naked children; low-browed and bare-armed women greasing the walls with their backs, and gossiping the while such gossip as scorches the ears; bullies of every kind walking as masters of the pavement – all sprinkled with drunkenness..."

There is almost in her a regret that the city has not made more of a challenge from the day, her one and only shore leave of this year. There are so many here who can be taken with the smallest bit of effort, the least premeditated and most lackadaisical of seductions, and how few among them would ever be missed? She could easily feast, slaughtering a dozen without any especial effort. She could forget her predator's instinctual cautions and play the glutton; the hollow created by her plunder would be no more than that made when lifting a single grain of sand from off a dune. Concealing herself within the stinking gloom of a side lane, she watches and breathes in all the heady, disorienting odors and tastes and sounds of these Citizens of the Crown. Eórsebet's senses are assailed, as though she's come upon a single gigantic organism stranded by the river's tidal retreat, stranded and rotting, but still very much alive; something too concerned with petty squabbles and daydreams and debauchery to even notice how near at hand it is to perishing.

But she'll take only one. István made of her many sorts of demons, but all are creatures of habit. And habit dictates that only one in London shall die this day by her hand. Habit reminds her that taking *more* than one might have dire consequences. A mere scrap of the frightened Székely girl she once was asks if the consequences would truly be so unfortunate, discovery and her subsequent undoing. *What sort of life is this?* it asks. Sometimes, Eórsebet listens to this voice. Sometimes, she allows it to speak at length, but only sometimes, as it inevitably fills her with melancholy and anger and memories she's no longer sure are even her own. Today, she bids it be silent, if ever it wishes to be heard again. She shows it the outskirts of hellish regions of the mind, to which she might so easily banish that voice, were it her fancy to do so. Eórsebet replies (speaking aloud, though not above a whisper) that this is the sort of life for which she has been *shaped*. And there are too many lighthouses and sea caves remaining that she has not yet harrowed, too many ships she has not foundered, countless beating hearts not yet stilled by drowning, entire oceans left unexplored. But, also, there is the unending hunger, István's hunger and her truest master, pulling her along like a cod hooked on an angler's taut line.

"I am not finished," she says, and her English is better now than when she came ashore at Dover the year before, or at Brighton, the year before that. She repeats the words, delivering them with more finality, "I am not finished." Hearing this, both the meaning and the tone, that small ghost in her withdraws and will not be heard again for very many months.

In short order, Eórsebet Soffia espies a dingy young Irishman with eyes the color of the sky on a clear November day and hair like soot. He will do. He will be more than sufficient, and as the young man is somewhat worldly, and possessed of a famishment all his own, it is a simple enough matter to lure him into the side lane and to her. She knows ten times ten thousand songs, and each one is more beautiful than the last. She sings, in a voice pitched so that none but he will hear the melody, and he thinks this must be an angel's voice. And so, as he draws near what he sees is angelic beauty, not the ruin of her, not the demon. The concealing glamour is another facet of her father's gift, though she may choose whether or not to don the mask. But it is easier to seduce a man to a warm embrace and to lost brown eyes and lips that do not stink of estuary muck. Later, in the aftermost instant left to him, when she has been bedded and fucked and he is, for the moment, spent, she will cast aside the charade. He may see the truth of her at the end, and she has always thought this her *own* singular gift. Clarity at the brink of oblivion, largesse before the void. It is no manner of kindness, however, for what unimpeachable gift in this world may *be* kind? It is one honest breath, before her sharp yellow teeth and the saltwater flood that flows out of her from every pore and orifice.

Whoever finds the broken, oddly shriveled body may wonder at the mattress and sheets drenched and reeking, at the gaping hole in the Irishman's throat. That unlucky innkeeper may cross him- or herself, may mutter a prayer before calling upon a constabulary beadle or policeman. More likely, the corpse will be disposed of in a less sensational and less public fashion. Regardless, she has never been hunted and has begun to doubt she ever shall be.

By sunset, she has slipped back into the muddy river, regretting only that another year must past before she can again step foot on dry land and take her prey from amongst the breathing multitudes. But this one rides the tides, hardly more than a shade, and her mistress is the sea, as her father was a devil. Her belly full, she finds a wreck and coils herself in between the limpets and mussels, the oysters and thick growths of sponges. She will sleep for a few hours, or a day, or, more rarely, a fortnight. She will dream of the sun and high mountain villages, of meadows dotted with goats and sheep. Of rain. And then she will awaken and slip away, unnoticed, except by the crabs and eels that wreath her like a winding shroud. The white, wheeling gulls may glance down to perceive her silhouette moving swiftly past just beneath the waves, and knowing what they see, sail higher.

The Dissevered Heart

"She is a slut who eats the flesh and drinks the blood of her granny," the cat whispers. Only, there *is* no cat, and I cannot help but think how very odd this is, as I have always had cats around me. People say, "I'm a dog person," or they say, "I'm a cat person," and I've always been a cat person. But not in *this* dream. In this dream, there is no cat, and, yet, it *is* a cat who says, quite clearly and with an unmistakably feline accent, "She is a slut who eats the flesh and drinks the blood..."

I lack the language to properly describe this paradox, the disapproving, chiding cat who isn't there. I'm a painter, not a poet, nor a novelist, and words never come easily to me. Images flood my mind – unbidden, often even unwanted – but fashioning effective sentences and paragraphs of them, that's another matter entirely. I constantly marvel at those who think in narratives, especially *linear* narratives. It is an unnatural undertaking, I would hazard, laying out narratives like stepping stones, one foot in front of the other, when the human mind seems to churn, and our dreams, no matter how filled with revelation, appear to me no more ordered than a scattering of autumn leaves. And yes, in the dream it is autumn, late autumn, and where the ceiling should be there's only pastel blue sky hung above a forest of dry, rattling leaves. I raise the goblet to my lips again, and if the cat *were* there in the cottage with me, I would reply, "It's only an unremarkable claret." I would show the cat the bottle, the cork pulled from the bottle. Maybe, I would even offer the cat an opportunity to lap a taste from my glass, so there would be no doubt left in its sneering cat's mind.

"Have a bite," I would say to the cat who isn't there, and then submit a raw pink morsel, speared on the tines of the tarnished silver fork provided for me by my host. "See for yourself."

Somewhere, somewhen, what I think must be hours before my meal in the cottage, I leave the highway, which stretches north to south (or south to north, depending on one's inclinations). It forms a stark gray-black stripe stretching towards the horizon; I find offensive both its severity and its contrived violation of that irregularity inherent in all Nature. On either side, the highway is in league with autumn, and so the trees have gone all the colors of fire, or of stone, soil, clay, sand, freshly mined ore. I choose an exit, and the trees pull up their roots and move aside. None stand in my way – not a single birch, maple, oak, or sycamore – and the forest swings open like a gate, granting me provisional access to all her secrets. The radio is on, and so the air is full of music and voices, clanging and clamoring for my attention.

"You're following my directions?" she asks me, after the cell phone rings, and after I answer it. I drive with one hand, winding along the narrow road between those all-too-welcoming trees. "If you're following my directions, I can't imagine how you could possibly get lost."

"I didn't say I was lost," I reply, trying not to sound annoyed, though I am.

"You said you don't know where you are. Isn't that the same thing?"

"It would be easy to get lost out here," I say, thinking these words, in this particular order, do not quite constitute an admission of guilt.

"Not if you're following my directions," she tells me.

I want to say, *These roads all look the same.* And, *These trees all look the same.* And, *The exit signs back there on that cruel slash of highway, those also all pretty much looked the same to me.* But I say none of these things. You've never been a patient woman. Nor have I. I am gripped by a sudden, almost morbid fear that you'll hang up on me, if I say the wrong thing, if I make you angry. Your voice is a tether, grounding me in a wakeful place and time. Without it, I have only the winding road flanked by watchful trees pressing in on me. Below their heavy boughs are shadows crouched like hungry wolves.

But you don't hang up, not just yet. That will happen soon enough. You tell me, "His name was Peter Stumpp. He was a German farmer. He was put to death on the 28th day of October, 1589. In Bedbur, I believe." You describe in great detail the means of execution, how the man was tied to a wagon wheel and his skin burned repeatedly with a hot poker, how he was partly flayed alive. "The executioners took the dull side of an ax to his arms and legs," you add, "so that he would not be able to return from the dead. Then he was decapitated, and his body was burnt to ashes."

"Seems sort of silly, don't you think, breaking his arms and legs to keep him in the grave, if they were going to burn the body anyway."

She's silent for a bit, and I hear a sound in the background, behind the place her voice should be. A noise like a hard rain falling against window glass or meat frying in a skillet. "Men are spiteful," she continues, finally. "They wanted to *hurt* him, for what he'd done, for what they believed he'd done. They *needed* to hurt him, I suspect."

I take a hairpin curve a little too fast, and the wheels squeal against the tarmac. The forest is growing darker as I go deeper, which, of course, is exactly what she warned me would happen. I cradle the phone between my chin and shoulder and put both hands on the steering wheel. I'm starting to think this road is an inconstant sort of road, that it changes, wriggling like an enormous serpent. It wriggles more the less attention one pays it.

"But why execute his daughter?" I protest. "He raped the poor girl."

"They judged it a wicked union, the werewolf and his daughter. And men are spiteful, as I've said already. Then as now, men are spiteful, and superstitious, and desperately need to consider themselves capable of meting out justice to put right anything they deem wicked. Better still to erase it from the world."

"When you say 'men,' you mean 'men and women'?" I ask her, and she laughs. In the dream, her laugh has a color, and the color is almost yellow.

"Naturally, yes. Of course. I mean all humanity. Women have never been exempt from acting on their fears and need for vengeance. Women are spiteful, as are men. Children are spiteful, as are adults. Innocence is a lie we tell ourselves. And all that shit about the 'fairer sex,' that's just another lie."

The trees bend so low over the road now, weighted down by the blue autumn sky, that I hear branches and twigs scraping across the roof of the car. It's an ugly sound, one I do not wish to hear, and I start looking for a place to pull over. There's hardly any shoulder at all to this road, just weedy ditches that begin where the asphalt ends.

"Still," I say, "he killed so many people. Killed them *and* ate them, making him not only a murderer, but a cannibal. You have to draw the line somewhere. You can't have people thinking meat is meat."

There's an unexpected bitterness in her response, her yellow voice shifting into orange. "They killed Peter Stumpp and cut open his belly with the same axes used to break his arms and legs. And then a miracle occurred. All his victims, all those whom he'd slain for their meat and blood and just to watch them die, *all* of them sprang from out his innards, restored to life by the reparation of his well-deserved death and the Glory of the Lord. Amen."

"You're in a mood today."

"I'm in a mood everyday. Do you see the mailbox yet?"

And I do, as though her question has brought it into being. A dirt road on my left and a mailbox nailed to a post. I can tell it was painted some shade of green, a long time ago, but now much of the paint has flaked away and the metal has mostly gone to rust.

"Then you're not lost. That's your turnoff. Don't be late. Don't stray too far."

She hangs up before I have a chance to say anything more. For a moment, it feels exactly as though I'm falling, as if deprived now of that all but tangible auditory connection back to her, the world has dropped away beneath me. Then I hear the wheels crunching gravel and dry leaves, and I stop the car. The trunks of the trees are so near I wonder if I'll be able to open the door and squeeze through. Perhaps I'll get stuck, half in, half out, sandwiched forever between metal and wood.

I reach for the door handle, and there she is, standing near the foot of the bed. I wonder for a moment if the mailbox was just a trick, if she always meant for me to lose my way in these woods. Were there a cat about, I would ask its opinion, but there is not (as I have previously noted) a cat there in the cottage that has no roof but the crushing November sky.

"I once read a version of the story," she says, and I marvel that anyone can speak with teeth like that, "where the girl was a wolf herself. She murdered and ate her *own* grandmother, who didn't know that her beloved grandchild was a werewolf."

I tell her I've never heard that one, and she smiles, those mottled lips folding back to reveal still more teeth, and every one of them jaundiced as antique ivory. I make some lame attempt at a joke, something excruciatingly predictable – a wolf in sheep's clothing, foxes guarding henhouses. I can't recall precisely what I say, and it hardly matters now.

I've walked far enough along the dirt road, which has narrowed so that it's hardly more than a deer path, that, when I look back, I can't see the car. Ahead of me, the limbs have formed a canopy, branches knitting together to shut out that oppressive sky with this oppressive spread of dead, rustling leaves. The farther I walk, the darker grows the wood, and soon enough I'm aware that I'm no longer alone (though I'm fairly certain, in hindsight, that I never truly was). There is movement up ahead, in the perpetual dusk cast by the overhanging trees, and I begin, more fully, to comprehend the way this game is played.

Or, if thou follow me, do not believe
But I shall do thee mischief...

64

The wolf raises its shaggy head and stares at me with eyes like the scalding pokers used by the righteous men who tortured Peter Stumpp. It has her smile, this wolf, and I suppose that should put me at ease, but it doesn't. It licks its rough muzzle and sits back on its haunches to kindly wait for me to catch up.

But I shall do thee mischief in the wood.

No, it's not a wolf. It's not a wolf with her smile. Rather, it's *her* wearing the smile of a wolf. She kneels in dirt and moss, green briars and shed leaves gone brown and crisp as charred skin. She is naked as on the day she was born. Her mouth and hands are smeared with blood already drying to a sticky mess.

"What road have you taken?" she asks. "Is this the Road of Pins, or is it the Road of Needles. The Road of Little Stones or the Road of Little Thorns?"

"In the end, will it matter?" I reply, and she assures me that it will make all the difference in the world. The fate of my soul may well hang in any answer I dare utter.

"She is a slut who eats," purrs the paradoxical cat, and I lay my fork down next to my powder-blue and white Wedgwood china plate.

"She is a whore who swallows," growls the wolf who is not a wolf, squatting there on the trail before me. "Which will it be, old woman? Pleasure or duty?"

"And if I choose not to make a choice?"

"You'll taste no less sweet," the wolf replies, its crimson tongue lolling from those sooty lips and stained teeth, dripping sputum to the forest floor so there can be no question in my mind as to its hunger, its intent. "I've never yet allowed a contrary, indecisive tease to ruin my dinner. I have no plans to start this day."

Whatever undefined quality of the firmament grants our merciful illusion of past, present, future, our fixed perception of time as flowing, riverwise, from *was* to *will be,* that quality is unknown (or in short supply) in the country of dreams. So there is no surprise whatsoever that I am no longer standing on the dirt road or sitting in a cottage without a cat. So it is that I have not yet even departed the apartment I share with her. The car is still parked by the curb, and she stands at the window, the draperies pushed aside, cautiously watching the autumn sky, which smothers the city as efficiently and with the same undisguised malice that it smothers the paved and white-striped desolation of the highway and the wood.

"Lots of people with good directions get lost, regardless," she says, and she could be addressing me, or that carnivorous sky outside the window.

"A map is never a guarantee. There are damn few lies as treacherous as the false promises made by maps."

She has not bothered to dress, and I know the secret, brazen pleasure she takes in standing naked at the window for anyone to look upon.

"But they're your directions," I say.

"I'm an inveterate liar. You know that. You've always known that, haven't you?"

I realize that the window is open. Maybe she's only just opened it, and I simply didn't notice. Maybe I looked away for a moment or three. Or, possibly, I was standing on a deer trail talking to a hungry wolf. Or I was sitting in a cottage without the company of a cat. Do not trouble my dreaming mind with the arbitrary tyranny of parsimony. The window is open, and a chilly breeze stirs at the curtains. They billow and flap on her left and her right. It seems strange that I've never before noticed the bushy tail sprouting from the base of her spine, drooping down to hide the crack of her ass, reaching almost to her calves. It is a wolf's tail, lush with fur the color of dirty snow.

"Have you always had a tail?" I ask, and she laughs.

"I've always been a liar," she answers.

She reaches for her lighter and cigarettes there on the window ledge. She fishes out a cigarette and lights it, but doesn't offer one to me. She breathes smoke and tells me about the Wolf of Magdeburg and infants stolen from their cradles during a January so brutal that the Elbe canals froze solid. In Magdeburg, in the shadow of the Harz Mountains, they called that month *Wolfsmonat*.

"When was that?"

"1819," she says. "A man named Breber tracked a wolf from the snow-covered city streets across the countryside to its lair, a lodge abandoned for the winter. Turned out, the wolf was Breber's wife. The summer before, she was hunting with her husband and was foolish enough to drink from a fairy stream. When Breber found her, he killed her. What else was he supposed to do, right? But first, before he took his sword to the woman, she told him this one thing. She said, 'The night has teeth. The night has claws, and I have found them.'"

"I should be going," I say, retrieving my keys from a bowl on the coffee table. "It's a long drive."

"You really mean to go? You mean to go *that* far?"

"Did Breber know the werewolf was his wife? When he killed her, I mean."

"You think that's of any consequence? Maybe you should wait until another day to drive all the way out there. I've not even told you about Courtaud and the wolves of Paris, or the wolves of Périgord. That was February of 1766."

"And Courtaud and the wolves of Paris?"

"Much farther back. The winter of 1450, just before the end of the Hundred Years' War."

"Why is it always wintertime in these awful stories of yours?"

"Wolves get hungry," she says and takes another drag off her cigarette. "It's hard to find food in the winter, and then a pack comes upon so much easy prey, all huddled together in one place. You can hardly blame the wolves. If you're going, you should get on the road."

"It's not *yet* winter," I tell her, and she shrugs and nods her head.

"It's your call," she says, "your choice." And her tail sweeps once or twice from side to side. I have no idea what that signifies. I've never bothered learning the language of tails, and there must be so many dialects. I take a step towards the door, then stop again. In the light from the windows, the easy morning light of a November day, she is the most beautiful woman I have ever seen, the most beautiful woman I've ever loved. The sun is butter on her pale skin. Her brown hair is tied back in a long ponytail. I almost tell her how much I love her, almost.

But I shall do thee mischief in the wood.

"She's a slut. You know that, right?" And the question catches me off guard. I don't argue.

"She's a slut, and she's making a fool of you. I know that's not going to make any difference, as to whether you go or stay, what road you choose," she says. "But I'll be damned and back again if I'll have you thinking she's anything *but* a whore who can't be bothered to find a street corner."

Whatever sting you've packed into the words, I know it's nothing I haven't earned.

"The genuinely sick part is, I'll still be here, waiting, when she's done with you. After she's had her fill, I'll take whatever's left over. I'll count myself lucky to pick through the gnawed bones sucked clean of their marrow. Sort of makes me a fucking masochist, doesn't it?"

"I should be going," I say, and yes, you should, she agrees.

"Her eyes are like the moon," I say, there in the cottage without a roof, the cottage only sheltered by the sky. "They are. I'm not exaggerating. Her eyes are like a full moon rising over the sea."

The cat can't look askance, or disagree, as it isn't even there. I glance down at that neglected morsel impaled on my fork. It resembles nothing so much now as a lump of raw pork. It gleams wetly in the fading daylight. I am careful not to look directly at the full banquet spread out before me, the carcass arranged with fresh fruit and boiled root vegetables and served to me on a sterling silver tray.

But I am less careful about gazing into the wolf's golden eyes, and then *past* the wolf, to the place where the path through the woods becomes *two* paths, diverging, bisected, and expecting me to accept the distinction and embrace only One or the Other. The wolf is standing on its hind legs, indifferently violating whatever laws of vertebrate anatomy and biophysics foist quadrupedalism upon all wolfkind. It stands there before me and begins picking burs from the coarse fur that covers its six small, perfectly formed human breasts. Those nipples are sharp as thumbtacks and ooze a milky excrescence. I don't dare glance down to see what this beast sports between its long hind legs.

"Want my advice?" the wolf asks, continuing to groom.

I don't say yes, but I don't say no, either.

"That's more or less exactly what I thought you wouldn't say," the wolf mutters contemptuously, without bothering to look at me. I turn around and begin walking back towards the car, and the wolf laughs a yellow laugh, knowing my retreat is imaginary, no more than wishful thinking, and knowing full well I'd already chosen a path before I even took my car keys from the bowl on the coffee table.

I find myself standing in a room with tiled walls, blood-spattered walls of once-white ceramic tile. There is an elaborate set of knives, and scalpels, a bone saw and cleavers, and a bolt gun arranged on a stainless steel table. There are chains sporting meat hooks hanging down from the twinkling, star-dabbed darkness overhead. There are drains set into the concrete floor. Everything smells of blood and death and casual butcheries.

I find myself driving slowly along a narrow road that winds through autumn woods.

I stand at our front door, indecisive and decided, watching the sunlight washing idly across the naked body of a woman I have loved.

And the cat who does not live in the cottage in the forest says, "She is a slut who eats the flesh and drinks the blood." I wonder if Peter Stumpp might have heard this same missing (yet very vocal) cat. I wonder if it ever spoke to the wife of a man named Breber, after she sipped from a fairy stream.

Exuvium

She says, "It doesn't matter why, not really. It only matters *that*," and then seems to trail off, leaving me to wonder if the sentence is complete. Whether it has been delivered whole and intact, or if I'm waiting for some unspoken conclusion. She stands in the field behind the house that once belonged to her mother, beneath the apple trees her grandfather planted, and points up at a limb only a foot or so above her head. At first I don't see it, whatever she wants me to see; when I say so, she frowns and bites the tip of her tongue. She communicates so much with that act, displaying the pink nub of flesh caught and held tight between her upper and lower incisors. The gesture speaks volumes of impatience, but also restraint, forbearance. She stretches, growing a few inches taller, her bare feet on tiptoe now, and I see what it is she means for me to see. A large chrysalis, larger than my thumb, yellow green and smooth as latex, shining faintly in the morning sun.

"It's a monarch butterfly," she says, "or it will be, soon." She begins explaining how the chrysalis is secured to the branch by a silken pad and a bundle of hooked cremasters. "Sort of like velcro," she tells me. I wonder if she knew these things before the dreams began, or if she's only learned them afterwards, but this isn't a question I ask aloud.

"When it emerges from the cocoon, after ecdysis, the pupa will have transformed into the *imago*." There is an especial emphasis placed on the three syllables of that last, unfamiliar word, and then she rocks back down onto the heels of her feet, but her eyes are still fixed on the chrysalis dangling above us.

There's a low mist blanketing everything, the tall grass and the neglected orchard and the dry-stone walls. In another half hour the mist will have burned away. The July morning is serenaded by catbirds and the mechanical drone of various unseen insects. An iridescent dragonfly buzzes past her head, but she doesn't seem to notice it. I look away from her, out across the field to the place where the woods begin, and spot a doe grazing in the shadows cast by oak and maple branches.

Two women standing in a field, bathed by the morning, and the air smells like dew and the green apples clustered above us. In the weeks to come, they'll ripen and grow red.

It may be that day was a week ago, and it may be a scene I have concocted from my imagination, to give a suitable preface to an inexplicable present. I suspect *she* would tell me that it doesn't matter. The memories, whether false or genuine, serve the same purpose. It may be I have confused cause and effect, and I am recalling a day that hasn't yet occurred, which is the most hopeful of those three choices. I am not a hopeful person by nature. And by nature, I am not a person who may easily dispense with chronology, or the illusion of chronology, though it appears to have deserted me now.

"Not a dream," she says. "At least, not what I would ever call a dream." She's sitting on the hardwood floor at the foot of the bed. I'm sitting in a chair near the window, which looks out over the field which we may or may not have already visited so that I could see the chrysalis of a monarch butterfly. I'm as naked as she is, or, rather, I am as unclothed. I am too guarded ever to be as naked as she.

"You don't have to tell me, not if you'd rather not," and I'm thinking that *I'd* rather she didn't, and I'm thinking how selfish of me that must be. I'm not looking at her. There's an old photo album lying open on my lap, page after page of antique Polaroids of black-and-white people and places I don't recognize. She's said the album belonged to her mother and that most of the people are her aunts and uncles, her mother's sisters and brothers. Most of the places are somewhere in Ohio.

"I felt safe," she says. "That's what I most remember. I can't ever recall having felt half so safe."

"Why wouldn't you feel safe?" I ask, and she laughs. It's not a mean or mocking laugh, but it is a laugh that leaves no doubt that I should have known better than to task her with such a foolish question.

Beneath the apple tree she says, "I cannot imagine how peaceful it must be in there, sleeping through such profound changes, unaware of the constant threats outside."

"What sort of threats?"

"It will die," she replies. "If anything dislodges the cocoon and it falls to the ground, if anything happens to interrupt the metamorphosis, the pupa will die. It will never have been anything but a caterpillar. It will never have flown."

She glances up at me from her place at the foot of the bed. I don't take my eyes off the pages of the photo album, but I can feel her gaze, so I know she's looking at me. I have always been able to feel her gaze. This is nothing I attribute to any sensitivity on my part, but to the intensity of her green eyes. Sometimes, I think they will bruise me, should they happen to linger too long. The day has faded almost to twilight, and the bedroom is filling up with shadows.

"I felt such perfect peace," she says again. "I've never felt such peace, no matter how many times I might have wished for it."

There's a photograph of two men standing beside an old car. It wasn't old when the picture was taken, of course. It was new and shiny. Both the men are smiling, and I wonder what ever became of the car.

"Are you listening to me?" she asks, and I reply that yes, of course I'm listening.

She silently watches me for a moment, as if trying to decide whether or not I'm lying. And then she says, so quietly I can hardly hear her, "It's all I want anymore. To have that sort of peace. To pull the blankets tight about me and close my eyes and know that *if* I ever wake up I won't have to be me, because I'll have become something else. The something else would not recall me."

Before I can think better of it I reply, "That sounds like self-pity."

"So what if it does?" And I was almost certain she'd be angry, but there's no trace of anger in her voice. "It's humane to pity someone else, but weak to feel pity for oneself? I've never understood that sentiment. It smacks of hypocrisy to me."

I turn a page, and here are eight photographs taken at a zoo. Here's a bear. Here's a giraffe. Here's an elephant.

"I wasn't calling you a hypocrite," she says.

"I know."

"It's just, you hear all this shit about how we have to learn to love ourselves, right? How am I supposed to love someone I'm told I can't feel sympathy for?"

There's a long silence then, because I honestly don't have an answer to her question.

I'm awake, sweating and breathless, and lie staring up at the dim ceiling over our bed, gradually realizing that I *am* awake. It ought to come as a relief, but it doesn't. That the dream was only a dream, I mean, the nightmare nothing *more* than a nightmare. All those trees, and where there should have been ripening apples, there were, instead, countless hundreds of yellow-green cocoons, also ripening. The air was hot, simmering and still, and filled with the shrill screams of cicadas. But now I'm awake, and I can hear you snoring softly beside me. I turn my head towards the bedroom window, catching sight of a waxing crescent moon pinned in an indigo sky.

The next page in the photo album is blank, and the page facing it has five Polaroids from a child's birthday party, frozen moments from fifty or fifty-five years ago. A cake with ten candles, a girl in a cowboy hat, paper plates, party hats, presents wrapped in black-and-white paper and adorned with black-and-white ribbons and bows.

"No," you tell me when I ask if you know whose birthday that was. "I can't remember. My mother, she told me once, but now I've forgotten."

"Do you ever wonder what a caterpillar dreams, while in its chrysalis?" I ask her, and she frowns.

"That's a stupid question," she says. "Caterpillars don't dream anything at all. Don't be condescending."

I shrug and turn another page in the photo album, leaving the birthday party behind. I turn a page. I look out a window at the moon. I stand with my lover in a neglected orchard. All the days and nights of my life are bleeding together, and I only suspect that I should be alarmed. I'm still arrogant enough to believe I know what the mind does when forced to confront the inscrutable, and that arrogance insulates me and keeps me safe from fear.

I came home early from work one day and found her sitting on the bathroom floor, next to the tub. She'd wrapped herself entirely in damp towels and washcloths. I stood in the doorway, hesitant to infringe upon whatever peculiar sort of meditation or retreat she'd undertaken. I stood there a very long time before I was even sure that she was breathing. The bathroom smelled like rotting fruit. Peaches, though. Not apples.

This particular page of the album is devoted to school photos, and all the faces look the same, except that there are boy faces and girl faces. Such distinctions were so much clearer back then. On the surface, at least.

From her place on the floor at the foot of the bed, she once again relates the dream (which she insists was not exactly a dream). I sit and listen as though this is the first time, when it must actually be the tenth or twelfth time I've heard it. But I currently have nothing better to do. Which isn't the same as saying there aren't things I'd *rather* be doing. I sit naked in my chair, and you sit naked on the floor. If I look away from the photo album – if I look at you, instead – I see your breasts and their unexpectedly dark areolae. I see your nipples, the curve of your hips, the dark bristle of your sex, your long hair the same reddish brown as chestnuts. I see your lips, and I think how badly I want to kiss you. Maybe I have never wanted, or needed, to kiss you as badly as I do right now.

"There was a deep hole in the ground, but it wasn't like a grave. I knew going into that hole meant coming out again, even if it wouldn't be precisely me that came out. It would be another me. So it was more like a womb than a grave. I was sitting at the bottom, breathing in the musty, sweet scent of freshly broken earth, looking up at the sky. The day was very bright. I couldn't see any clouds. Something tickled me, down here, between my legs." And, in case I don't understand, she spreads her thighs wide apart and place the tip of an index finger just above her vagina. "Here," she says, and I nod, as I always do. "I stood up. I stood up in the hole, but it was so deep that I couldn't have reached the edges to pull myself out. Anyway, I glanced down, because the tickling hadn't stopped. There was a chrysalis…" and she pauses. I suppose she's either searching for some word that's escaped her or the memory of the dream is so vivid that it leaves her speechless for a few seconds. It happens every time, and I've learned to sit still and wait for this intermission to pass.

"There was a chrysalis," she says again, "*here*, right here, attached to my clit. The cremasters were attached to my clit, and I'd never seen such an enormous monarch chrysalis. It almost looked like I had a green penis." She laughs here, but I only smile. I force my eyes to return to the photo album.

"Did it still tickle?" I ask her. "After you saw what it was?"

"Yes, it still tickled. It was almost painful, actually, that sensation. I started to reach down and pull it loose. Seeing it hanging there, I felt…I don't know…violated. This was something that had been done to me, when I wasn't paying attention. This was a parasite. And then I thought no, this is no different than finding a chrysalis on the branch of an apple tree, and if I pull it off, the pupa will die."

I think about getting out of bed and going to the window, but I don't. I lie here, the darkness measured out in discrete units by the cadence of her sleeping breath, my heartbeats, the noise of crickets in the grass outside. This is the same night she asked me to look at websites of people encased from head to toe in saran wrap and duct tape, plaster bandages and bizarre nylon full-body stockings. She said, "It's sexual for most of them. Just a fetish, you know. But that's not the way these pictures make me feel."

"How do they make you feel, then?"

She laughed nervously, and turned her head away from me and the computer screen. "They make me feel hopeful," she said.

"Are you asking me for something?"

"No," she replied. "I'm not asking for anything."

"It feels as though you're asking my permission."

That nervous laugh again, this time tinged with what's meant to be contempt, I think. "I wouldn't need your permission," she replied. "I'm a grown woman, aren't I?"

I looked back at the computer monitor, at a woman mummified in swaths of silver-grey duct tape. There were slits at her mouth and her nostrils so that she could breathe, but, otherwise, no hint of flesh. Just the vague shape of her. Bondage has never been my thing, but I might have found it sexy, had she been better photographed. Instead, I found myself thinking about how much it would hurt, pulling all that tape away, and wondering what would happen if she had to take a piss.

"*This* is what you want?" I asked, pointing at the screen.

"No," she said. "This is *not* what I want. It's more like a metaphor. You know, I thought you'd get that. I didn't expect to have to spell it out." And she was getting angry, and so I got up and went to the kitchen for a beer.

And lying in our bed, watching that cold sliver of moon watching *me* – that moon like an eye barely open – I wish I'd reacted differently. Wishes aren't horses, not tonight. Not tomorrow. Not yesterday. *Wishes* is only a prettier word for *regrets*. I regret not having reacted differently. Maybe I could have mended the gash between us, or begun to mend the gash in her. I did the opposite; I pushed her farther away and so increased her alienation. Lying here, one thought (selfish, I suspect) plays over and over again – *I am not sufficient to wrap you and keep you safe, and my embrace will never give you that perfect sense of peace you're seeking.* The women in those photographs online were being restrained, imprisoned, *bound*. They desired to be bound. Too late, I realize that she's doing something else entirely, trying, however belatedly, to set herself free, and I'm unable to articulate what's so wrong with me that I cannot help.

Beneath the apple tree, she's explaining how caterpillars fashion their cocoons so that they are weak in places, along certain precise lines, to make it easier for the butterfly or moth to escape later on. She tells me that some chew their way out, while others secrete fluids that break down the silk casing. She talks about the hormones that dictate pupation. "When they leave the chrysalis, it's called *eclose*," she says, conveying the word with the same reverence for the divine that another woman might reserve for the Virgin Mary or Radha Krishna or the goddess Diana.

"So you didn't pull it off, even though it tickled, even though it hurt?" I ask, on another day, turning another page of her mother's photo album.

"No," she says from her place on the floor. "I didn't. I couldn't have. I touched it, gently, and could feel life inside. I knelt in the dirt at the bottom of the hole, and I knew that when the monarch butterfly emerged, then I'd be able to climb back out. I could hear you, calling me from someplace far away. And I could hear the birds."

"I was looking for you?"

"You were calling my name."

Here's a photograph taken decades ago, and the woman in it is standing alone in a field, looking up at the sky. She's shading her eyes with her left hand.

"I must have been looking for you, if I was calling your name."

"I suppose," she says. "You might have noticed I was missing and gone to try and find me."

I close the photo album and sit staring out the window at the twilit field and the gnarled old apple trees. It isn't hard to imagine the world beyond the windowsill as nothing more than another snapshot, bled to black and white and myriad hues of chalk and slate and ash and all the colors of an oyster's cast-off shell. It isn't hard to imagine it pressed flat and faded and worn around the edges.

There's another dream, one she's only shared with me three or four times, and so I know it's somehow more precious, or that it embarrasses her (and having these two choices means that, in this instance, I *know* nothing at all). Whenever she's described it to me, she's been very careful not to meet my gaze. She talks, and her eyes wander restlessly or stay locked on a single arbitrary point in whichever room we happen to be sitting.

"You don't have to tell me, not if it bothers you."

"Yes, I do," she replies.

"I don't begrudge you your secrets."

"I don't want it to be a secret."

I roll over in the bed, because I'd rather stare at your back, at your shoulders and the nape of your neck, than know the moon is watching me. Watching us. I ought to get up and cross the room and pull down the blinds so we have a little privacy, but I don't. One does not easily find the will to put out the moon, the way one might snuff out a candle or flip a light switch.

"We're together, but I don't know where. Not here, not in our house," she says without looking at me. "There's hardly any furniture, where we are. There's a chair where you sit, and another chair where I sit. And there's a table near me. We aren't sitting very near one another, though sometimes you seem closer and other times farther away from me. You have your clothes on, and I'm naked. On the table is a large bowl and a great pile of newspaper torn into strips. Hundreds or thousands of strips of newspaper heaped on the table. The bowl's a very deep red, like pomegranate seeds. Almost exactly that same shade of red. I'm not sure what's in the bowl. At first it seems like a paste, the sort you'd use for *papier-mâché,* but then, later, it's black and very sticky. While you watch, I dip the strips of newspaper into the bowl and lay them on my skin – my arms, my legs, my breasts and belly. I place each one exactly so, and smooth them down very carefully, making sure that no air is trapped underneath. You sit and watch. You watch very, very intently, and I'm scared and wishing you would stop me before it's too late, but you never say anything. You just sit there, watching what I'm doing to myself."

"I'm sorry," I said, the first time you told me this, and you said, "Don't apologize. It wasn't your dream."

I move closer, and the bedsprings creak, but not loudly enough to wake you. I'm trying hard not to think about the orchard and what hangs ripening in those trees, there among the apples no one will ever pick and eat. I try not to think about the gawking, inquisitorial moon. I close my eyes and bury my face in your brown hair, and there's only the clean scent of soap and shampoo, not rotting fruit. If I prayed, I would pray *this* moment is the present. I would pray what I found on the bathroom floor was only you, swaddled in wet towels and breathing so shallowly that at first I thought you were dead. I would pray that in a dream of yours I interrupted you, and the interruption was enough to forestall that terrible transmutation. But I don't pray, and wishes aren't horses. I wonder if you'll remember me.

Drawing from Life

"**I** think you, Sir, are a selfish man," she says, and then she waits, as if expecting me to defend myself, when she should know better by now. I can hear the way she's watching me.

"You might well have left behind a few coins," she says. "A morsel of food, five pebbles, maybe a spent candle nub, a handful of silver coins wrapped in silk and tucked into the stump of a fallen tree."

I listen, and the words drop from her mouth and spiral lazily down to the floor to lie there like autumn leaves. They pile up thick in a shaft of bright afternoon sunlight slipping in through the studio's tall windows, and I imagine all manner of beetles and earthworms and stinging red centipedes rustling busily about below the detritus of those fallen, accumulated words. I'm lying half-dressed on the army-surplus cot where I sleep (*when I sleep*), and I open my eyes, half expecting to see the floor blanketed from wall to wall and an inch deep with leaves and words in all the shades of a copperhead's scales.

"I've never seen a copperhead," she says. "Truth be told, I've never even heard of them before." She's sitting on a stool at the far side of the room, nude and silhouetted against the bare brick walls. It's the same stool where she sits whenever I sketch her, and today she's sitting up very straight, poised to strike, watching me and smiling. It's a wicked smile, but then so little of her is not wicked. I begin to tell her about copperheads, trying to recall if these are my thoughts or only lines she may have written down for me to say in this moment and in this place.

"They're snakes," I tell her. "Where I grew up, down South, you had to watch out for them whenever you went walking in the woods. They were hard to spot, coiled up in the leaves." She asks if they're poisonous snakes, and I tell her yes, copperheads are pit vipers, like rattlesnakes, but that she doesn't need to worry, because I'm pretty sure they don't live this far north. "The winters are too cold," I say, hoping that I'm making it up as I go along, that I've succeeded in deviating from the script, because I know how angry that makes her. But nothing else is said about copperheads, one way or the other, and I close my eyes again. I can hear her, sighing like wind through high branches, the way the wind blew on the night I met her.

"I don't feel like drawing today," I say, and I allow myself to feel brave for having said it aloud.

"But the light's perfect," she replies. "And I'm already here. It would be a waste. It would be selfish, not to work today."

I open my eyes and roll over onto my back. I stare at the antique ceiling tiles, all rust and flaking mint-green paint. The ceiling is such a terribly long way up, a nasty fall just waiting to happen, but I do my best not to dwell on that. I try, instead, to concentrate on the intricate patterns of those tiles wrought from molten iron and set into place a century before I was born. They remind me of the squares on a game board, though clearly for a game that no one has yet bothered to invent. Unless she has invented it, and we've been playing all along. It would never have crossed her mind to share the rules with me.

"I'm sorry," I say. "You're right. I know you're right. But I'm not in the mood to draw. Not today. Maybe next week, but not today." I keep my eyes on the iron tiles, trying to imagine what the game pieces might look like, and how they could be prevented from dropping to the floor to lie among all the cast-off words.

"You *say* you're sorry, but I know you aren't."

"There's no fooling you," I reply and turn my head so my left cheek is resting against the dirty sheets. She's still watching me from her customary place on the stool, as though I'm going to change my mind and get up, find a bit of charcoal and a sketch pad that isn't already filled with unfinished portraits of her. I pretend (for my benefit, no one else's) that it's the bravest thing I've ever done, watching her watching me, her brown eyes, her skin like spilled milk, her close-cropped hair that manages to be brown and grey at the same time. It occurs to me how her nipples resemble chestnuts, and I silently congratulate myself on the pun. She is thin, rawboned, as though she never eats, or never keeps anything down. She might be twenty-five, or thirty, or she might be older than all the forests of the world.

"Well, if you will not draw me," she says, "then maybe I'll tell you a story. All men are vain. It's nothing you don't have coming."

It occurs to me, as it always does, that if I'd never fucked her, I wouldn't have to listen to any this. If I hadn't fucked her, I could tell her to go away and never, ever come back. She would be banished. It's a very simple sort of magic, after all, unless you learn too late that it *is* magic. As it happens, I did fuck her, and so I lie still on my cot, smelling sweat and dust and turpentine, and she talks and I listen. Call it a curse or call it penance; I can't see the difference anymore. Her voice has lost its autumn tinge, and is become hard-packed snow piled beneath heavy clouds, and is become frostbite, and is become the longest, darkest winter night in a mountainous Scandinavian forest. I should know this one by heart, a litany I might recite in my sleep, and so it should hold no dread for me whatsoever. I should close my eyes, so at least I would not have to *see* her.

She only has a single story, but knows a hundred thousand variations upon it. This way, I cannot even seek the empty solace of monotony. No matter how hard I might try not to give her my attention, I inevitably do, so obsessed have I become with finding the way in which each successive version of the tale distinguishes itself from all the rest. She talks, shedding her leaves again, and I lie here on my cot and listen. Some part of me is actually grateful, that she's not yet done with my soul or my mind or what have you, that there must still remain something within me worth destroying. In this way, I think she is a surgeon, or akin to the pupae of certain wasps that hatch in paralyzed caterpillars and then very slowly devour their hosts from the inside out. She's making of me a husk, but is taking exquisite care to save the vital organs for last. She may be a glutton, but she's a careful glutton.

"Men do not know the harm they do," she says. "They do not care to pause and consider. Men come into the wood and they take, because they have needs. They do not look beyond those needs or consider the needs of those who have made the wood their home. Men are blind vanity, and they can no more feel the sap flowing through the trees than the blood flowing in their own veins."

I was nowhere near a wood the night I met her.

"There was once a collier, tending his kiln. He was alone and lonely, high in the mountains, a few nights past midwinter eve. And such a hard, bitter winter it was that year, and all the wolves went about hungry and with their ribs showing through their mangy pelts. The collier had built his kiln in a glen that was guarded by a Skogsrå, and while the collier tended to his billets and made sure he'd done a good job packing damp clods of earth over his kiln, the Skogsrå watched him closely from the birch that was her home. In her time, she'd seen many men that were no different from him. He came and took and left behind nothing but ashes."

I was walking home from a bar on Empire Street, the blustery summer night I met her, and she was standing alone beneath a street light at the Kennedy Plaza bus depot. We talked, waiting together for our buses. I was more than a little drunk. I'd been out with friends, and she asked me what I did for a living, and I told her that I was an artist. That I painted portraits.

"But, you should understand, it's not exactly a living," I added. I didn't notice how she stood always with her back to me. And I don't remember now whether or not my bus ever arrived, or if other people waited there with us. It seemed we stood beneath the street light and talked for a very long time, long enough that I was sobering up, and I know she went home with me. Either we rode the bus back to my studio on Federal Hill, or we walked all that way. The route is of no consequence; it only matters that I asked her into my bed.

"Understand," she continues, "I don't mean to say that the collier was an evil man. Few men are evil. Few men have within them that sort of vaulting ambition. He merely saw the wood as men have always seen the wood, as a larder handed down to them by one or another god. But the gods of the Skogsrå were far older and had charged her to keep safe the same trees this man felled for ash and pine tar. She waited until the bright moon slipped behind a passing cloud, and she went to him. He'd never seen such a beautiful maiden, and certainly not walking alone in the snowy wood, so far from any village. He asked if she were not afraid of the wolves, and when she said no, that she'd nothing to fear from wolves, he asked about bears. She assured him she was not afraid of bears, and he thought he must have found a wonderful, brave woman, indeed, if neither wolves nor bears frightened her."

I won't say we made love. There was no love that night. But I fucked her, and she fucked me. She let me undress her and then stood before me in the commingled streetlight and moonlight shining in through those tall windows. I thought I'd never seen anything so beautiful, and, confronted with the sight of her, I began to weep. She looked confused. Her brown eyes became twin pools of consternation, and she asked me if she'd done something wrong, and was I alright, and was there anything she could do to help. I laughed and wiped at my eyes, and I said, "I'm drunk, that's all." It wasn't all, not even close, but she seemed to accept the explanation, as I plainly *was* drunk. Drunk and embarrassed and feeling like an ass. She kissed me and I thought I tasted snow and spruce needles, a taste like some unfamiliar, pitchy German liqueur. We fucked on the floor, because my old army cot isn't big enough for two. It's hardly big enough for one.

"Didn't he know?" I ask her, because sometimes it's not so bad if I break up her story with a question or three (even though I know all the answers perfectly well). "He must have known about the Skogsrå, right? It must have seemed strange, happening upon this woman in that wilderness."

"Men sometimes think with their pricks," she says, and that's nothing I can argue with. "She sat with him while he tended his kiln, and in the morning he took her back to his village and soon they were wed. She made him very happy, and she gave him two fine, handsome children, a son and a daughter. And he stopped going into the forest, and his kilns were lost in the snow and forgotten. He could think of nothing but his love for her, even though the men and women in the village were wary of this outsider he'd brought into their midst, and even though she refused to go to church or allow their children to be baptized. Some said she was a witch and others that the collier had married no woman at all, but was a good man who'd been seduced by a troll or some other forest spirit."

"Filthy gossips," I say very softly, but loudly enough that she'll hear. She glares at me, still smiling, and her brown eyes are peat-stained bogs. I've tried to paint those eyes, repeatedly. It's not possible.

"People talk," she says, "then, as now."

That windy night last summer, before I knew enough to leave offerings in tree stumps or to recite the Rosary backwards or to turn all my socks wrong-side out – before I was wise in the ways of talismans and vigilant superstition – I only knew she was beautiful, and my life knew far too little beauty to refuse her. Horny single men who settle for jacking off to internet pornography cannot be expected to say no when opportunity knocks. In that way, I'm no different from her lonely collier, I suppose. Though, I do cut myself some slack, not having been raised to believe that sirens haunt bus stops. Her poor Swede (sometimes he's Norwegian, or Danish, or Finnish, or Prussian) was surely taught of the everyday yet demonic, otherworldly dangers which lurk behind birches and lampposts, hoping to catch some pathetic bastard off his guard. She might as well have caught me with my pants already down. I was damned by lust and ignorance, as fateful a mix as any. Disrobed, she climbed on top and slipped my dick inside her. She was wet as the sea or a spring thaw, receptive as the grave. Outside, the wind howled off Narragansett Bay, blown out before an oncoming summer storm, and all of Providence seemed to cringe around me. The wind howled, and soon enough I howled with it.

"So, what happened?" I ask, managing to sound as if I genuinely have no fucking idea.

"What happened," she says, "is that one night she was indiscreet. Perhaps she no longer cared and had grown bored of this man. Perhaps she just screwed up. But, either way, he saw her from behind and knew at once that he had been deceived. His wife surely was no mortal woman, but a Skogsrå, or Skogsnufvar, and he now knew that he had proof of it – the proof of his own eyes. In that instant, she ceased to be his love, and became, instead, a monster."

"Could she not be both, his love *and* a monster?"

"No," she says. "It was not like that."

"But he was *not* an evil man," I say, and she quietly watches me.

"Sorry," I tell her. "That was rude of me, wasn't it. I won't interrupt again."

"You should have drawn me," she says. "It was wasteful not to work on such a fine afternoon as this."

"Yes," I agree. "I should have. I'm a lazy bastard, and I should have drawn you." She nods once, blinks those peaty eyes, and then continues with her story.

"The collier, he was horrified, as you can well imagine. But far greater than his horror was his anger. He seized his troll wife by the hair and dragged her naked and screaming from their house, the two small children trailing after them. This wronged man took her *back* into the wood where he'd found her, to a frozen lake not far from his abandoned kiln, and he left her there, her and their two children."

"The children were blameless," I say, and she reminds me of my promise that I'd stop interrupting her.

"Still, they were, in his eyes, abominations, the spawn of an unholy union. They should die with their mother, he reasoned. He left them no fire against the cold and the wolves – and he knew well enough how the Skogsrå feared wolves. As night fell and he trudged away through the deep snow, she cried out to him for mercy, for truly she had come to love her human husband in their years together. She pleaded that he at least spare their son and daughter, but all her pleas went unheeded by all save the starving wolves. *They* heard and began to slink out of the trees, slavering golden-eyed shadows, and crept across the ice towards the unfortunate Skogsrå and her children."

A year ago, I lay on the hardwood floor beneath this pretty woman from Kennedy Plaza as she ground herself against me, and I thought, *This is how a granite cobble on a beach must feel, dragged to and fro by the tide, polished smooth and round by so many centuries in the sand.* Outside, the fierce wind buffeted the building, rattling the windowpanes in their frames, and I heard thunder booming far away and imagined the unseen lightning that must have preceded it. Her sweat dripped onto my bare chest, onto my face, except it *wasn't* sweat. It was fine, clear trickles of sticky sap, and where it touched my skin it would leave blisters that would not fully heal for weeks.

"Are you blind," she laughed. "Do you not *see* me?"

And I did see her, in the dressing mirror leaned against one wall. I looked, and I saw her from behind.

"The pack came across the ice, made bold by their hunger and by the scent of their prey's terror. The woman continued to call out to her husband, even as the daughter was snatched away and torn apart by the wolves, the daughter and then the son. And it was then, grieving and afraid and with nothing left to tie her to the world of men, that the Skogsrå raised her head and cried out the name of her sister. Hearing this, the wolves stopped worrying at the mangled corpses of her children and turned to watch the Skogsrå begging the sky for deliverance, their muzzles caked with blood and their eyes glittering like coins in the darkness.

"'Save me, please, for the wolves have come!' she screamed. And her sister, a wind rider, heard the scream, and suddenly, from out the north, there blew such a violent, chilling gust that the ravening animals were knocked off their feet and sent sliding and tumbling, whining and yelping back towards the trees at the edge of the frozen lake. Then the sister flew down and took the Skogsrå in her arms and carried her across the sky until she was whole and well again, and she no longer cried at the loss of her children, abandoned by their father and devoured by wolves."

"I don't like this story," I say, and she tells me again that I shouldn't have decided not to sketch. And I think, as I always do, how I should not have looked into that mirror and seen my lover from behind. It must not have been so very different from what the collier glimpsed, the vision that drove him to madness and murder.

"I forgive you your laziness," she says, "but there's *still* a price to be paid for giving in to sloth. And it is wicked to leave a story unfinished."

"You would know," I whisper.

"Yes," she says. "Now shut up and listen."

In the dressing mirror, I saw her back. It was pale and grey-white as the bark of a birch tree, the bark peeling back here and there in papery strips. There was moss growing upon the angles of her shoulder blades, and dull green sprays of lichen spread out across her buttocks. Her long tail, not so unlike that of a cow, swept slowly from side to side. The tuft of fur at the end of it was the same shades of brown and grey as her hair. But the worst was the hollow place where her spine should be, and *seeing* that hole in her – peering directly into that emptiness that I understood might well run on forever like a universe bereft of stars – it may be I lost my mind. Or, conversely, it may be that I became sane for the first time in all my life.

"You *do* see," she said and laughed as rain began to tap at the studio windows; I said nothing whatsoever. There was nothing to be said. There still isn't.

"When the Skogsrå was strong again, she parted company with her dear sister. She searched for the man, her husband and the father of her slain son and daughter. He was still in the house that they had shared, though now he wore charms against her kind, an amulet of cold steel and also a bulb of garlic about his throat. But her vengeance was possessed of a great patience, and she waited, and waited, and waited. Many years passed, many winters filled with starving wolves, and one day he finally removed the amulet and stopped wearing the garlic, too. His memories of her had begun to fade, the whole affair seeming little more than an awful nightmare from which he'd slowly roused. He'd been absolved of any sinful acts by a priest, and that same holy man had assured the collier that he was free of the Skogsrå's curse and was protected now by the benevolence of their god. To continue to wear heathen amulets, the priest said, was an insult in the eyes of that god. So the troll woman returned to her husband, who'd taken a new wife by then. The Skogsrå came to them both as they slept, but took care to wake only the collier. She crouched at the foot of the bed that had once been her own and spoke in the secret, timeless language of the wood, which no mortal man may hear and live. The next morning, when the collier's new wife awoke, she found lying next to her the bones of her husband, and heaps of birch leaves, and shiny black beetles looking out from the eye sockets of his skull."

"You ought to write that down," I say, glancing away from her to the tall studio windows. The afternoon sun of a summer day does nothing to drive away the chill that follows her, but I won't give her the satisfaction of seeing me shiver.

"And you should draw," she says, and I get up and find a stick of charcoal and a pad with a few blank pages.

The Eighth Veil

"They say nobody ever brings anything small into a bar. They talk a lot, don't they? They sure do." Don't call where I first tapped into that skit of bushwa, not right offhand, but it wasn't gild from the lips of a living, wheezing, blue and fucking holding human being. That much is settled and certified, so I'm supposing it was something outta one of the cinoche that deckhead Piltdown was always running whenever he was arrow enough to keep those jaundiced eyes of his peeled. Not my apogee, I admit, those four square in the winter of seven and six, laid up with that jackhole Piltdown.

But I digress. I back peddle. I burden now with then. So, yeah, they say nobody ever brings anything small into a bar. That's what I'm thinking, couched on a stool between Nettle (on my left) and Quick (on my right), my eyes on my drink, cause I'm very not into the follies and smudge that grace the stage in a place like the Ruby MacaDoo. Sickest of the chrome and meat pageants, so they say, middle slice of the ninth circle, this blind pig at the wicked shit end of Boston. Me, I wouldn't know, except that's what *they* say. And they talk a lot don't they? Yes, they do.

"Suzy didn't tell us you were such a squeam," Nettle says and hails another beer. "So, you know, me and the Quick, we had no inkling. Otherwise, hell, we could'a had this chat someplace clean." And Nettle, he laughs, all gravel and sparks, then yells at the bartender again. Meantime, Quick, well, she's too busy doing elsur on the floorshow to give a squirt what anyone's saying. Those OLED minces the Yak paid for after she caught a face-load from some Korean's muzzleneck, they shine silver in the smoke and gloom. She used to be a beauty, did Quick.

"We all got our predilections," I say, "and we all got our not-so-muches. Me, I just don't care for slaughter."

"Straight-up, tight-interfacing," says Quick, so I guess I was wrong and she *can* scope and listen in at the same time. "Old-fashioned mallee root and titties for this harp lesbyterian, ain't that the way of it, Carrigan?"

"If you must," I tell her, and she never looks away from the stage.

"Missy Quick, she sees all," says Nettle. "They think she don't, but she's hubble, this one here." Then his beer shows up, something muddy and German with a flying bear on the label, and he sucks at it a few times before saying anything more.

On stage, the screaming finally stops. No, that's not right. There's only a lull before the screaming begins anew. I sip my gin and tonic and do endeavor to think happy thoughts.

"We got the hammer on this one, and the Yak, he says you need to twig that from the get-go. Ain't no spare latitude and longitude on this job, Carrigan. Ain't no slag wax, and or we'd have used one of our own damn vaps. The Yak likes to keep it cozy and inhouse, but you know that."

"Yeah," I tell him. "I know that, Nettle. You wanna cut the jackanory and stop treating me like virgin treasure never did a bleed?"

Nettle, that ugly motherfucker, he takes another deep suck on his bottle and stares at me like, you know, that's plenteous enough violence to pop my skull. The gin in my glass tastes like toilet freshener and iodine, and I'm starting to regret the conjecture it was such a whole lot of smarts, showing up sober at the Ruby MacaDoo.

"All function," says Nettle. "Work and no play, this lady." He sets down the half empty bottle of Fliegen-Bär or what the fuck ever it is he's swilling at, and then he makes a grand production of shaking his head in disapproval. "Carrigan, you'd profit taking a page from the book of Missy Quick here, and go lightly. I spare you'll live longer."

"She's not so much as hearing you, Net," Quick says. "You're wasting air on the likes of her."

"Sure, fine," I say, speaking to neither one of these preening gatekeepers. "In one ear, out the other. So, spell it before I get bored and have to go back to Alonzo and tell him you pooched the hit, and he's out his commission."

"Scary, scary," says Quick, and she lights another butt. Nettle laughs and sips his beer.

"All right, sheba," he sighs, imbuing this moment with almost as much melodrama as that headshake of a few moments prior. "We aim, right enough, but just having some fun, yeah? No cause to get pissy on me. Everybody's friendly here, ain't that gospel, Quick?"

"*Va te faire foutre,* Nettie," she mutters around her cigarette. And me, well, I'm so goddamn puked of both these two and also the casual horrors proffered by the players of the Ruby MacaDoo's carnage cabaret, I really *am* thinking hard of strolling. Let the Yak sort it out, let Alonzo howl on me for skipping work. Either way, gotta best this sad shit. But that's when Nettle grabs hold my left arm just above the elbow, like he's gone cassandra and knows exactly what's rattling between my ears without me having to put it into words.

"You watch one round," he growls, good as a starving pit. "Just one, that's all, outta respect for the Quick, so she don't get her crackers in a jam, yeah? Then, we give you the envelope and you go on about your merry. Deal?"

And screw me raw, but I told the fucker yes, seeking the path of least impedance. That and a coward's resolve come calling. I said yeah, sure, I'll pacify you two twists, why the hell not. Why the hell. Quick, she cackled like a dragon, all smoke and scar tissue, and Nettle, he just grinned and let go my limb. Only mercy, if you see it so, there wasn't long before the next act came out, so I didn't have to sit and stew. Not too much time for the dread to build and make matters worse. The orchestra starts in with its usual thunderous prelude of kettledrums and snatch keys and tin-tin-tin, and the followspots washing red across the stage go the starkest shade of plain. The sun ain't even half that white. Pure titanium, that light, and for a moment I see the brightly more before my eyes.

Quick laughs again, and Nettle yells for another beer and a shot of Cutty Sark.

"This one coming up, Carrigan, it's choice," he says. "The grue's own grue, you might as well say. Primo."

And soon enough, I'll wish I'd taken that stroll. Fuck Alonzo and the hit, the money and the due grief I'd catch for scotching a job. I'll have nights enough past counting without sleep, and nights I'll *wish* I hadn't slept a wink. Yeah, I did a tour in Kenya and another after the Turks' glow pipped Skopje and Kumanovo. I've been down in it, danced the fray, and seen what nukes and bio do to cities and people. But it ain't pork pie when I say none of that bushwa prepped me for that one act at the Ruby MacaDoo. Nettle wasn't slinging hyperbole. It was something special.

The girl was pretty, maybe twenty-one, maybe a year more at the most. But what difference, yeah? The rodeo clowns had hosed down the plexi after the last stunt, so there wasn't any smear or brains or shit to spoil the view. In the restless spots, her skin was pale as dumplings, and she had long black hair pulled back away from her face. They'd shaved her smooth everywhere wasn't her head, and the only thing she was wearing was a nylon collar on a lead, but her handlers removed that, too, once she was slotted and safe inside the ring. First, though, one of the handlers produced a brass dermojet from her tool belt. This fetched forth the mad applause, right on cue, and fuck if I don't believe Quick came at the sight of the thing. Then the kettledrums rolled again, and the naked girl took a shot to the throat off that jet. Where I was sitting, maybe eight feet back from her, looked like they nailed her jugular, catching all that deoxygenated blood on its way back to her heart. The Barker in his crow's nest (there's always a Barker in a market like the Ruby MacaDoo) takes his megaphone in hand and starts in on his sermon.

"Them ancients called it alchemy," he bawls, "the transmutation of that which is common and without worth into something sublime and immortal. Us latter-day motherfuckers, so cast down or fallen from the wisdom of old, we trust *not* in Paracelsus and his marble-busted ilk. No, *we* squint up from the gutters of our sorry lives and gaze in wild wonder at the marvels of the high holy priests of mechanosynthesis and constructive ecophagy. We cast *our* pearls, the nacreous gems of our collective irritation, before the high glory swine of nanorobotics. Yes, and we *are* rewarded, but not with any so-called panacea or elixir of life everlasting – for we know all flesh *is* but flesh and will die and rot away. *Our* reward, instead, will be but a few precious, exquisite tick-tocks of transcendent abomination, a salve against the monotony of yesterday, the grind of today, and the crushing boredom of every inevitable tomorrow. Sit back, all you pricks and cunts and them falls reckless in between. Stoke your lusts, and behold with unmitigated awe and without charity what humanity can achieve when we put our shoulders to the wheel and check our delusions of restraint at the door."

Now, I've tapped the like before. I've heard the broods sing and the vultures trilling sweet fucking nothings into the receptive ears the hounds of Golgotha. You work this side of the street, sure, you wind up lots of places you might not ever wanna be, slaughter huts like the Ruby MacaDoo being only the example at hand. You get thick and you get numb, or you go away, one path or another. No place in this vocation for squeams. But there's numb and then there's this *here,* what's coming up, and *putain de bordel de merde* if I can't handle.

They've got the black-haired girl down on her knees, and the handlers are stepping back. The whole house is going hush, and Nettle, he leans over and whispers in my ear. Nettle, he sounds like a happy man.

"See, the shit in that jet, it's something the wetjocks at Monsanto baked a few years back. Still pitch tech, strictly off the funnies, right, but the Yak, he got his sources."

"Sure, sure," I mutter, watching the girl, the Barker's voice booming in my skull. "He's a resourceful bastard, the Yak, ain't he just?"

"Fuckin' level," grins Nettle. "Don't you *ever* let that slip your mind. Anyhow, Yak's got pals sky high, so he's been getting shipments of this soup for the dustyards out at Roxbury. Does wonders with chop disposal, it does. And the mechanics, well, they were fucking about, like mech fuckers do, got wise it makes short work of *la cucaracha* and rats and whatyougot. Plus, it's wholesome, since this soup don't crossover. Stays where you put it, does the job, and afterwards, all them bitty assemblers they go inert, A to Z."

"Nettle, I can do without all this generous fucking edification," I say back, and Quick giggles, though I can't tell if she's laughing at the convo or at the show. Hard to tell with a twist quiff like Quick, but if I were playing lot and there was rivets and rhinos on the line, I'd guess the latter.

Backside the plexi, the girl's handlers have both vacated the stage, and I'm thinking possible they don't posses Nettle's abiding faith those nanos are so wholesome, after all. Now it's just the sacrificial fucking lamb in there all by her lonesome, with the Barker's prattle raining down around her sharp as tacks.

"And for anyone in the cheap seats might be keeping score," he rasps through his megaphone, all buttery mock confidence, "ain't like she's some innocent. Ain't like you gotta lament some unfortunate done no worse than been in the wrong place at the wrong time. Holding out on her Don Juan, this walking the night always. Three strikes, hun, you're out like Fenway. So don't you fucking weep, nary a one. Better you rejoice there's still an ounce of justice left in the world."

"Okay," Nettle mutters, "that part's a lie. She's just some bitch come budget off the Mozarts. But always gotta win over the mob, right?"

I wanna tell him shut the fuck up. Ain't it harsh enough I'm sitting here *watching* this shit so I don't gotta run back to Alonzo as the empty-handed hangdog? But, no, no, no I put teeth to tongue and don't say peep. I can feel the smug coming off the Yak's boy like hot off a stovetop. I play stooge and don't give guff and don't look away. The black-haired woman's staring up into the spots the exact same way Mr. Jesus H. eyeballs the Lord on high in all those popeblower paintings. Maybe she's scoping for the Barker way up in his shadows. I don't know. But it's plain she's hurting. This lamb's sweating buckets. That's when I realize she's saying something, and that it's the same something repeated over and over again. Takes me a second to savvy out the words. Nothing profound. Just "Please, help, please, help, please help," looping like bum playback. I know, then and there, I'm gonna be hearing those two words for a considerable stretch of time. Oh, and there's another sound, one puts me in mind of walking in fresh snow, that same soft *crunch.* But here it's the noise transpires as skin, muscle, blood, fat, and hair are converted to corrosion, as a lifetime is reduced to red iron oxides.

Oh, also I realize Nettle's got a paw parked hard on my left shoulder, weighting me down, making sure I don't run rabbit on his sadistic ass.

"Shame is," he says, "it's overcook, this soup. Real rapid-fire diaper gravy. Blink, you'll miss it."

Nettle's always been bang on for exaggeration. Then again, I'm sure the untimely demise of the lamb could take all the live-long day, and Nettle and Quick, they'd *still* come away dissatisfied customers.

I watch the stage. I sit on my stool, and I'm all eyes. There are these great brown blotches spreading out along her milky hips and breasts now, blooming like a time-lapse geranium across her flat belly. This close – best seats in the house for guests of the Yak – there's no snarling it for anything but rust. Terrible fucking beauty in this spectacle, which only makes it worse. *Blotches,* that ain't the most veridical, stone-true word for it, not by half. Rust fanning out in more than approximate fractals, a geometry so precise it would pass any boffin's criteria for self-similarity. Less than five minutes since the injection, and she's having the devil's own just breathing, and rigor's already setting in. All about me, the ceaseless pother of these fine patrons of the Ruby MacaDoo is ceasing – or, more accurately, and lest I mock Nettle, I'll say the voice of the rabble is become pindrop only by comparison to its former ear-piercing peal. This drove, here's near as they'll likely ever know to that reverential silence what stains cathedrals and libraries. This is the first church of slaughter, and the Barker's sermon and the lamb's suffering makes them hard and wet down yonder.

"Lot's wife, bitch had it *easy,*" cries that disembodied voice from overhead. The mob hangs on his every goddamn syllable.

"Ravish," gasps Quick, those slash lips of hers leaking more cigarette smoke. "Utterly jerking ravish."

And I know it's close to run its course – the act and the congregation's reverie and the nanoswarm's replication sequence – *all* of its winding down to perished clockwork. Not much left for the soup to consume, so not much left to ogle at, and I expect the next act is already waiting in the wings. I catch myself leaning towards the dying woman, hanging like the rest on her parting gasps. Thirty seconds more and there's not enough meat left for a stingy bowl of fish chowder. What once was mutton is as still as the big deep six, which, of course, is what it is.

And now, now there's this trice that only *seems* to stretch a few forevers, the proverbial last note wringing an instant for all its got. Frozen like flies in amber, yeah, only it's the likeness of that black-haired woman cast in a thousand flaking shades of brown and brick and yellow. For that long, long trice, I'll vouch her nipples would have sliced you like a razor, and her clit might well have been a lancet's blade. But then it was done, done solid and for all, and she collapsed in upon herself, disintegrated in a sudden rufous cloud that spread out across the stage and rose again in billows when it met the plexi. All those twists and mutilation freaks packed into the Ruby MacaDoo clapped their hands, and their commingled fucking joy became a hurricane of cheers and huzzahs and the frenzied yelping of beasts hungry for more of the same.

"Well, well," says Nettle, rubbing at his chin. "Maybe Missy Carrigan got herself some *pelotas* she's been keeping hid somewhere. Maybe, Quick, we gone and misjudged this soldier."

Quick, she don't answer, not one way or another. She's too busy doing a line on the bar. Me, I tell Nettle to stow it and hand over, cause I ain't hearing no more, so give me the goddamn envelope with Yak's wish list and let me get to work. That's when my phone takes a mind to buzz, Alonzo yanking the chain, and finally, and at last, I'm able to look away from the stage.

Apsinthion (ἀψίνθιον)

Sometimes I forget, and, forgetting, I ask the sorts of questions I am meant never to forget I should not ask. In the last moments of fading darkness before sunrise or the warm afterglow of orgasm, for example, I forget. It's only human, as they say, and of course, it's only human. But this limp, spiritless excuse – though absolutely and inarguably true – interests her not in the least, so nothing is forgiven. And, to be honest, were she any sort of creature who'd fall *for* that sort of shit, I'd never have fallen *to* her. I forget, and ask that sort of question, and she turns away. Given what I've become, what she's *made* of me, there can be no greater punishment than the sight of her turning away. After all, this might be the last time, might it not? This might be the *final* time she turns away, and maybe she'll be done with me once and for all. I couldn't fault her; it would be fair enough. I ask that sort of question, and she turns away, and I think this is how prehistoric peoples felt during a solar eclipse. This is the fear one feels watching dragons devour the sun and imagining a night that will last forever.

"How did it start?"

"You know better than that," she says and sighs and immediately turns away from me.

Or.

"Do you imagine it will ever end?"

"Do you?" she replies, batting away my words, folding them back upon themselves, showing me the folly. And she sets her back to me.

I found her in a pool beside the sea. This is almost an accurate statement. As close as I can come to a simple explanation. It was winter, and I parked in one of the lots north of the lighthouse. The day was sunny, extraordinarily bright, and the cloudless sky was that vivid, nearly suffocating shade of blue that marks certain January and February days in New England. It was a Thursday afternoon, and there was, at most, a handful of other people nearby, a few birdwatchers with their binoculars and cameras aimed at eider ducks and cormorants. I've often wondered if anyone else present saw what happened, but I've never slipped up and asked her *this* particular question. Maybe it's because I'd rather not know the answer.

I locked the car, checked to be *sure* I'd locked the car (and that I hadn't locked my keys inside), then stood for a while at the liminal point where soil, green briars, and sea oats give way to bare stone. Gulls bobbed about like tiny boats upon the waves. Far out in the bay, a tanker was headed north, towards Providence. The ship was hardly more than a silhouette, stark against all that blue sky.

"Did you know I was coming?" I ask her.

"Did you know you were about to find me?" she replies.

"Maybe I *didn't* find you. Maybe that's not what happened at all. Maybe it was *you* found *me*."

And she says, "You might be right."

That day, my usual dirt path down to the rocks was muddy and slick. There'd been snow, a week or so earlier, only three or four inches but it was still melting, keeping the clayey ground soggy, making the ordinarily easy descent a little treacherous. But I went slowly and managed to pick my way down to firmer footing among the tilted beds of phyllite and slate without falling on my ass or twisting an ankle. Near the base of the muddy trail, there was a pool of meltwater trapped among the rocks and mostly frozen over. It was ringed round about with snow that had accumulated in whatever shadowy nooks and crannies the sun couldn't reach. The whole southern edge was buried in a small drift, protected by the perpetual gloom of a low overhang. The pool was no more than a few feet across, and only a foot deep at its deepest point. Here and there, lumps of yellow-gray phyllite peeked up through the crust of ice and snow. There was, at first glance, nothing remarkable about the pool, and I might have passed it by without so much as a second thought.

"But that's not what happened," she says, as though I need reminding. "You didn't pass it by."

"No, I didn't," I agree, and she smiles, revealing all those small, sharp teeth crowded into gums the color of a robin's egg. "But what if I had?" This sort of question isn't forbidden, even if it's not exactly encouraged.

"Someone else would have come along, sooner or later."

"You're sure of that?" I ask.

"Yes," she says. "I'm sure of that. Some things truly are inevitable, given enough time." She leans close and nips at my left shoulder, drawing a stingy trickle of blood, which she instantly licks away. There's hardly any pain at all, and I understand this is because she's not presently in the mood to hurt me.

"Be careful," she says and smiles again. "You're starting to taste like regret."

"And how does regret taste? I imagine it's bitter."

She shakes her head. "Then you're mistaken. It's not bitter. Regret tastes like dead roses and stale bread. Regret tastes like dust."

I was about to pick my way around the frozen pool, when something lying on the bottom, beneath the ice, caught my attention. And now I know that damnation (for want of a better, more precise word) can be exactly that uncomplicated, exactly that matter of fact. I won't say "exactly that impersonal," because she's left too many of my questions unanswered, so I can't be certain. I can have my suspicions, but they haven't been confirmed. They've not been dismissed, either.

"Regret," she adds, "tastes like the fruit of the Tree of Knowledge of Good and Evil."

That winter day, I stopped and stared into the pool at my feet, looking down through the translucent, distorting lens of the ice.

"And did you like what you saw there?" she wants to know, or at least wants me to think she does.

"It was wicked," I reply. "What I saw there was a wicked, wicked thing."

"That isn't what I asked," she says.

I recall, distinctly, the confusion I felt that day, standing there, gazing into the ice, being unable to figure out *what* I was seeing. But, yes, from the very first I had no doubt it was a wicked thing, whatever it was. That much was clear. My mouth went dry and cottony. I felt the hairs on the back of my neck prickle. I started sweating, despite the cold northwestern wind. I felt vaguely nauseous. I got an erection. And I sat down on the rocks at the edge of the pool, and I suppose it would not be inaccurate to say that I gawked.

"You could have walked away," she says. She laps at my shoulder again, and her breath smells like cardamom and low tide, blood and dying fish. "You had that choice, even once you'd noticed what was in the pool."

"I believe I only had the illusion of choice."

"Believe what you wish. That doesn't make it true."

I squatted beside the frozen pool, and pondered the identity of the wicked thing trapped there at the bottom. My initial impression was that it must be some sort of a doll. Parents are always bringing their children down onto the rocks, so maybe it was only a lost ragdoll. But then, I realized it looked nothing at all like a doll of any sort, and I was unable even to remember what had given me that impression. My next thought was that it must be a dead crab, maybe one of the big blue crabs, flipped over on its back. I could make out the serrated claws, the spines along the margins of its carapace, the four pairs of legs.

"It looked nothing at all like a crab," she says and laughs. "But you know that. You know that perfectly well, don't you?"

"Yes, I know that," I tell her, and she sits back and watches me from the foot of the bed. In the dim light from a reading lamp, her skin is very like the iridescent sheen of motor oil spilled on wet asphalt. Her heavy-lidded eyes are either all pupil or may as well be.

And I did see it wasn't a blue crab, almost as soon as I'd become convinced that it was. I bent closer to the ice, squinting, trying to get a better view. Overhead, herring gulls wheeled and cried out to one another. Back towards the parking lot, I could hear the rasping calls of crows and jays. I glanced up at the sun, shielding my eyes against the harsh glare; just a little brighter, I thought, and the winter day would collapse into a tonal inversion of itself, a color negative with all the blues shifting towards yellow, all the reds towards cyan, the greens to magenta. I felt dizzy and lowered my head, staring at the pool again until the vertigo passed.

"And then you thought it was a star," she says.

"Yes," I nod. "Then I thought it was a star. A rusty cast-iron star."

"That wasn't so very far from the truth. Hardly anyone ever gets that near the reality of it." And then she quotes the Book of the Revelation of John, *"And the third angel sounded, and there fell a great star from heaven, burning as it were a lamp, and it fell upon the third part of the rivers, and upon the fountains of waters; And the name of the star is called Wormwood: and the third part of the waters became wormwood; and many men died of the waters, because they were made bitter."*

"The *men* were made bitter?" I ask. "Or was it the *waters* that were made bitter? It's not clear. I think that's a faulty translation."

"Would you like to hear the original Aramaic?"

"I would like to sleep," I answer. "Just now, I would only like to sleep and not dream."

"Don't be a coward," she whispers.

"Why? Haven't I earned a little cowardice?"

I sat by the frozen pool and stared at what I'd mistaken for a lost doll, then a blue crab, what I now took to be a five-pointed, cast-iron star. I extended my right hand and, with bare fingertips, touched the ice, which moved slightly, so I knew the water wasn't frozen all the way down, that the ice was floating on a layer of liquid. I withdrew my hand, and the ice rose again, and the rusty five-pointed star promptly became a rusty seven-pointed star. A heptagram, a Christian symbol for God and perfection, Aleister Crowley's Star of Babalon, or only alchemical shorthand for the seven planets known to the ancients. And yes, it *was* a wicked thing, but the dread it had inspired scant minutes before had completely dissolved, leaving behind only curiosity and desire. Suddenly, I wanted this thing, whatever it might or might not be, as badly as I'd ever wanted anything in all my life. I could conceive nothing more worthy of my longing, of lust, or greed, than the star. I touched the ice again, and seven points became eight.

"Some have gone mad at the first sight of it, at the first incarnation they perceive," she tells me for, I don't know, the hundredth time. I wonder at the pride of demons, keeping in mind that *demon* is, here, a word selected merely for the sake of convenience, and for its various connotations. What she is cannot *be* named. I may as well call her anything else at all, so far as issues of accuracy are concerned. "The most degenerate of men have blinded themselves," she continues, "and whores have taken their own lives rather than endure that passion. But *you*, you *did* like what you saw and wanted more."

"You can come across awfully melodramatic," I say and am relieved when she doesn't turn her back on me for having said it.

Squatting next to the frozen pool, I beheld the octagram's seemingly inexorable transformation into an enneagram; it occurred to me, perhaps belatedly, that this was not so very different from watching the blossoming of a flower, a rose, perhaps, videotaped and played back on fast forward. But then, when it appeared I would actually be able to *predict* the object's next manifestation, the rusty nine-pointed star abruptly disintegrated, and all that remained beneath the ice was a scummy red-brown heap, a somewhat star-shaped mound of sludge. A few heartbeats later, the surface of the pool cracked open, clear across its width. The splintering ice seemed inordinately loud, momentarily reducing all the other sounds of that bright day to a hushed murmur – the birds, the breakers slamming against the rocks, the wind, the clanging buoy anchored off the point – all of it. And through some unlikely, or entirely impossible, warping of the shoreline's acoustics, that crack clearly echoed, and, stranger still, each reverberation was plainly *louder* than the one preceding it. It came back to me six or seven times, no more than eight, and then just…stopped.

I wanted badly to stand and move away from that pool, but my mind was unable to spur my body to action. I stayed where I was as the clean salt smells of the sea were gradually replaced by an acrid, unfamiliar stench. I could liken it to vinegar, or a wet dog, or old coffee grounds, or sulfur. Each of these is accurate and wholly insufficient to describe that smell. Cloying. It was that, too, and I gagged and thought that I might vomit. I pictured the eggs and bacon and toast I'd had for breakfast spattered across the ice. But the queasiness soon passed, as did the stink.

"You weren't afraid," she says.

"I was startled, sure. But no, I wasn't afraid. I was disoriented. I definitely wanted to be away from there, but I can't say I was *afraid*, no. I kept thinking, if I could just get back to the car—"

"You'd have driven away," she says glibly. "You'd have driven off and never looked back. You'd have stopped coming to the sea, except in your dreams."

"Well, that's not what happened, and I see no point in dwelling on alternate, unrealized histories. I didn't run…"

"No one who has navigated that many stations of the sigil has ever run. At least, not yet. The ones who run, they don't make it past the second or third."

"The crab," I say. "The crab and the first star."

"In your case, yes. But it's always different. The sequence is determined by the initiate, and so is never the same twice. Not in ten millennia have I seen the puzzle solved the same way by any two postulants."

"Postulants," I say, and she shrugs her bony black shoulders.

"It's as good a term as any," and I agree with her that, yes, it probably is.

"And what about the time before there *were* postulants?" I ask, knowing that this is most assuredly the sort of question I am meant never to forget I should not ask. And I haven't forgotten. But the words are out before I find the courage to stop myself.

However, she doesn't turn away from me, but raises a very long and nailless forefinger to her thin lips. The gesture was simultaneously flirtatious, playful, unmistakably threatening, and evasive. And with that many-jointed finger still raised, she sternly reminds me of what I already know, that we do not discuss what she deems the time *before* time. This taboo, in and of itself, must speak volumes. It raises questions for which I will probably never find solutions. Ten millennia, she said, so only a fraction of the span of human civilization, and a much smaller fraction of the history of *Homo sapiens,* reaching back not even as far as the end of the Paleolithic. Who was she before, or does this date fix the moment of her creation, or of her arrival among men? No, these aren't questions I'll ever have the nerve to press, so not questions I will solve.

...and there fell a great star from heaven, burning as it were a lamp...

That day by the pool, I looked up from the crack in the ice, and she was crouched naked on a nearby boulder. I'd thought I had gazed upon beautiful things in my life, and also upon terrible things. I thought I'd known genuine awe and revulsion. But then, *then* I inadvertently solved her puzzle, the puzzle of her being, and she revealed herself to me, her postulant. It could be she had no say in the matter. Or it could be otherwise. This, too, is not for me to know. The dazzling winter sun danced along her monstrous silhouette, and her waxy skin – dim and rich as polished ebony – writhed with oily rainbow iridescence. She crept slowly towards me across slabs of phyllite, over snow and ice. She came on all fours, like a respectable predator. I was only dimly aware of how the snow crunched beneath her hands and feet. She dragged that obscene appendage along behind her, the twining mass of flesh and bone, cartilage and chitin that sprouts from both her sex and the base of her spinal column. It jerked restlessly from side to side as she came, not like the swishing tail of a cat, but, instead, as if it were possessed of an autonomy all its own, as though it were some symbiote or parasite. A single gull dropped from the sky and lay broken and twitching upon the rocks. And *this* is how I became haunted, though, admittedly, that word is lacking. That word is wholly inadequate and signifies nothing but the hopelessness of rendering what has happened into any language.

"Kiss me," I say, begging favors from the void.

"I would not taste regret," she replies.

"Then I won't *feel* regret," I promise, and so she comes close, and her mouth encircles my cock, and all the universe spreads out around me, as unknown and incomprehensible as the infinity contained within a frozen pool at the edge of the sea.

Three Months, Three Scenes,
With Snow

1.

The painter notices snow in the hallway on the same day that he finishes a large canvas titled *A Flock of Crows Alighting Near the Edge of the Sea*. It's a Wednesday, and the afternoon has been almost too hot to work, but he's worked anyway. His T-shirt is stained with sweat, especially at the armpits and about the collar. The apartment, which doubles as his studio, is on the third floor of a house built in 1869, and air conditioning has never been installed. There are noisy electric fans running in the few windows that are not stuck shut, but sometimes the fans only seem to make the New England summers worse, that constant drone of electric motors, the whir of plastic blades.

The painter has spent the last half hour carefully cleaning his brushes, and his hands stink of turpentine and linseed oil. He left the brushes to dry, his best camel-hair brush filberts and riggers, and went to the kitchen for a cold bottle of beer from the refrigerator. He's on his way back when he notices the snow in the hallway, which wasn't there when he walked by this same spot only a minute or two before. There isn't much of it, maybe a third of an inch, maybe less, banked against the doorsill of the closet where he keeps his coats and hats, his sweaters and an assortment of cardboard boxes filled with old receipts and tax returns and the like. The snow has already begun to melt, and the water is collecting in a fissure between the varnished pine boards. The floor is very slightly warped, so he knows the water will flow north, in the direction of the room he uses for his studio.

Instinctively, he glances up at the high ceiling, to see if the snow might have leaked in through a hole in the roof. There's no sign of a crack anywhere in the plaster, but he's considering returning to the kitchen to get the stepladder – so he can have a closer look – when the absurdity of it all overcomes his curiosity. Even if there were a hole in the ceiling, the mercury has been inching towards the one-hundred-degree mark since sunrise. It's not a question of how the snow got in, but of where it possibly could have come from.

The painter bends down, and like doubting Thomas the Apostle, presses a finger into the snow to be certain that it's real. It doesn't vanish when he touches it and is colder than he might have expected, if he'd not half expected it simply to disappear when put to such a test.

He takes a swallow of beer and stares at the snow for a moment, then wipes at his sweaty face with a blue paisley bandana. He's certain there's a perfectly obvious explanation here somewhere; he's just too hot and distracted to think of it. Surely, it'll occur to him later on, and he'll feel stupid for not having thought of it right off. He'll laugh about finding a tiny mound of snow in the hallway on a sweltering late June afternoon. Maybe he'll call his father or a friend to tell them the story, and then they'll laugh about the snow with him. Feeling somewhat less uneasy, the painter goes to the pantry for a broom and a dust pan and a dish towel to clean up the mess before it all melts and makes a bigger mess.

2.

This is a muggy Friday night, midway through the month of July. The painter is sharing a six-pack of Narragansett Beer with the red-haired woman who's been his lover, on and off, for the past three years. They sit across from one another at the tiny kitchen table, and he sips his second beer while she talks about the creation myths of the Delaware Indians. The red-haired woman is an anthropology professor at Brown, and though the painter isn't particularly interested in Native American folklore, he sometimes enjoys hearing her tell these stories. He rarely has anything much to add, or an opinion on the subject, so usually he can just sit and listen and admire her enthusiasm, even if he doesn't share it. But tonight is different; the heat is making him irritable, impatient, and he finds himself wishing she'd come to the end of this tale. The fan in the window is whirring noisily, and there's sweat on their faces and bright beads of condensation on their beer bottles.

"So," she says, "according to the cosmogony of the Lenape, that's why crows have black feathers." She smiles at him, then wipes her face on the sleeve of her T-shirt and takes another long swallow of her beer.

"Because all gods are bastards," he says.

"More or less," she replies and smiles again. "Divine gifts usually come with a price tag, some pricier than others. Fire's a good example. The crow was able to save all the animals of the Earth from freezing to death, but only by giving up its rainbow feathers and being burned black by the heat of the gift of fire. A sacrifice was necessary to receive the boon."

"Because all gods are bastards," he says again. "This Creator Who Creates By Thinking What Will Be, whatever his name was—"

"Kijiamuh Ka'ong," she reminds him.

"Right, well, if he'd cared enough about his creation to show a little foresight, if he'd given the animals fire *before* he buried the whole world in snow, the crow's sacrifice wouldn't have been necessary. The boon wouldn't have been necessary. If Zeus hadn't hidden fire from humanity, Prometheus wouldn't have had to steal it back. And so on and so forth."

"But then we wouldn't have heroes," she says. "Which is my point. Often, heroes are the men and women who willingly suffer the wrath or whim or negligence of the gods. Or, as with Prometheus, those who have the nerve to stand up to them. Regardless, there's usually a sacrifice involved." She finishes her beer and sets the empty bottle on the table.

"You want another?" he asks and points at the bottle. She tells him yes, then scoots her chair back from the table a foot or so, until the window fan is blowing directly on her. He gets up and goes to the refrigerator. He lingers there a moment, staring in at leftovers and wilted produce and a half empty plastic carton of milk while the chilly air spills out around him.

"Speaking of snow," she says, "has it happened again?"

He shuts the refrigerator door, then opens the bottle of Narragansett and goes back to the table.

"Didn't I tell you already, when you called?"

"Yeah," she says, facing into the fan now, so that damp strands of her lank auburn hair flutter about her face. "But I meant since then. That was almost a week ago."

He sits, and slides the bottle across to her. It leaves a wet streak on the table. "No," he says. "It hasn't happened again, not since then."

"So how many times does this make?" she asks. "Five, or six?"

"Five," he replies. "Only five times."

She repeats what he's said – *only five times* – in a way that sounds almost like an echo. "I came across something the other day that reminded me very much of your snow," she says. "Frankly, I've been trying to decide whether or not to even bring it up."

The painter has another sip of his own beer, but finds it's gone luke-warm. He grimaces and stares at the amber-colored bottle, the red and white label he's begun peeling off in strips.

"Well, you've sort of brought it up already, haven't you?" he asks the anthropologist, and she shrugs. "By the way, it's not *my* snow," he adds. "It just happens to be showing up in my apartment."

She nods and turns away from the window fan, moving her chair back towards the table. She rubs the pad of her left thumb over the fresh bottle of lager, but doesn't take a drink. "It's just something I read online. I was won-dering if this sort of thing has ever happened before, to anyone else, and I stumbled upon a reference that led me to some old newspaper articles."

He frowns and pulls another strip of label from the bottle, then lets the paper slip from his fingers and fall to the floor. "I asked you not to do that, not to go looking for answers."

"I know," she says. "But I find myself lying awake at night, thinking about this goddamn thing. I won't tell you, if you don't want to hear."

"I *don't* want to hear," he says. "You already know I don't. But now you've gone and started this, so you'll tell me, or *I'll* lie awake all night, wondering what the hell you were talking about."

She begins to apologize, then thinks better of it. Instead, the anthro-pologist nods and has a couple of mouthfuls of the Narragansett while the beer's still cold.

"It's not my snow," he says again.

"You know that was only a figure of speech," she sighs. And then she tells him about a report from Lancashire, UK, an article from the February 15th, 1873 issue of the *Chorley Standard and District Advertiser*. At Bank House, in the village of Eccleston, two maiden aunts and their niece claimed to have witnessed water streaming from their ceilings. Throughout the house, furniture and carpets were soaked, and the three women were so terrified they briefly vacated their home until the phenomenon ceased. Not only had these inexplicable falls of water occurred on cloudless, sunny days, but when the ceilings of the affected rooms were examined, the plaster was found to be perfectly dry, without exception.

"That's it?" he asks, trying to sound underwhelmed, when she stops for another swallow of beer. She wipes her mouth on the back of her hand and shakes her head.

"No, it's not," she replies. "There were a couple of other articles, but…" and she trails off. She doesn't look up at him, but keeps her eyes on the tabletop.

"Did either involve snow?"

"No. There was another fall of water at a farmhouse in Wellesley, Ontario in 1880. In 1919, a rectory in Norfolk – that's Norfolk, England – well, this one was even stranger. It wasn't just water, but also showers of paraffin, petrol, sandalwood oil, and methylated spirits, spewing from the walls and the ceilings of the rectory. Thirteen showers were recorded, and fifty gallons of oil were supposedly collected in buckets and wash tubs. At one point, a quart was falling every ten minutes."

"So, I should count myself lucky," the painter says, pulling the last of the label from his beer bottle.

"We should talk about something else," says the anthropologist, glancing over her shoulder at the window and the fan. "I'm sorry I brought it up."

3.

And here's where it ends, to the degree that anything may ever be said truly to conclude, following from an assumption that the precise moment of any given beginning may be pinpointed. On a rainy night near the end of August, almost three months after the painter discovered a drift of snow in his hallway, he wakes from a dream of fire and thunder and the faces of those he has lost in his lifetime. Or perhaps he wakes *into* a dream, as the parameters of dreaming and the unconscious mind may well be as arbitrary as our definitions of beginnings and endings. He sits on the edge of his bed, listening to the rain on the shingles, which sounds to him very much like the sizzle of bacon in a hot skillet. He waits for the awful images from the dream to fade, but they cling stubbornly to whatever life he has unwittingly given them. He watches the red LED display of the digital clock radio beside the bed. He considers calling the anthropologist, even though it's after three in the morning, and even though they still haven't made up following a particularly silly argument only a few days earlier. Besides, what would he say to her? That he had a bad dream and doesn't want to go back to sleep for fear it isn't done with him? It's hard for the painter not to imagine her anger and confusion and everything she might say before hanging up on him.

When he finally realizes that he's grown tired of following that steady procession of blocky red numbers counting off the seconds until dawn, he gets up and goes to take a piss. To reach the bathroom, it's necessary to walk past the hallway closet where, eleven times since June, he's come upon small, unexplainable accumulations of snow. Distracted, possibly, by his aching bladder, he notices nothing out of the ordinary on the way to the toilet, but on the way back to his bedroom, he stops in front of the closet door. There's the faint, but unmistakable, sound of wind coming from the other side.

For a moment, the painter considers ignoring it, going back to bed, and trying to forget about it. Whatever's causing the sound will either go away or it won't. It will either recur on some other, future occasion or it won't. The novelty of this peculiar patch of hallway has long since faded, and he's tired and has be sharp for a two o'clock meeting with a gallery owner on Wickenden Street.

"Fuck you," he says aloud. "I'm going back to bed."

But he doesn't go back to bed. He stands there at the door and listens as the impossible wind which seems to have originated or been trapped some-how inside his closet quickly gathers strength, buffeting the wooden panels with enough force that the door has actually begun to rattle on its hinges.

"Fuck you," he says again, more quietly and with considerably less conviction than before. He reaches for the doorknob, expecting it to be cold, perhaps *so* cold that he'll quickly pull his hand back or risk frostbite. This is an expectation born of innumerable scary movies and horror stories, a cliché so ingrained as to resemble, in the moment, a truism. Yet he finds that the antique brass knob is no cooler than it would be on any late summer night. It quivers gently, transmitting vibrations from the shuddering door into his palm and fingers.

He turns the knob and opens the door.

Later, he will not actually *remember* opening the door, any more than he will remember the trip to the toilet or the details of the nightmare that woke him. He won't recall sitting on the edge of his bed watching the clock or the urge to call the anthropologist.

He opens the door, and there's no sudden gust of wind, no numbing gale to force him backwards as an anticipated blizzard swirls out into the hallway. He stands at the threshold and stares into what should only be a modest space – two and a half feet deep by three and a quarter feet wide –

bounded by three walls, and filled with clothing hung on coat hangers and bulging cardboard boxes stacked on the floor. This is only his hall closet, after all, and so it should be no larger or smaller than his hall closet has ever been and should hold nothing that he has not put into it. But there are no coats, no windbreakers, no Gore-Tex parka, no sweaters, no baseball caps, no coat hangers or steel rod to support them, no umbrellas or walking sticks, and not a single cardboard box.

There is what he at first takes to be a vast black sea lapping hungrily at the sill and stretching out across that hideous, implausible void beyond the door. But, only seconds later, the painter realizes his mistake, for a sea is, by definition, a *presence,* and what lies before him could only be accurately defined as an *absence.* An absence of light, of substance, of sound, of heat, almost an absence of existence. Except that there *is* the hill. There's no meaningful way to judge how far away from him the hill lies, for it seems unlikely that this anti-space is amenable to any unit of measurement. Fifty yards may as well be a hundred, or vice versa. But it's near enough that he can make out certain details without his glasses and despite his nearsightedness.

The hill is white, being almost entirely shrouded by the mantle of a deep snowfall. Indeed, snow is still settling lazily out of the nowhere and nothing that surrounds the hill. He watches as the drifts grow taller. Here and there, outcroppings of a dark stone, like shale or slate, are visible, where the snow has not yet hidden the rock from view. And at the crest of the hill stands a single tree. Or, if it is not actually a tree, there is nothing else the painter would know to call it. It is at least the rough approximation of a tree, an alikeness, and it clutches at the hill with an approximation of gnarled roots and raises an alikeness of branches to the void. The tree is not quite as pale as the snow, and no leaves or coniferous needles cling to its barren limbs. The branches sway, this way and that, perhaps disturbed by that vanished wind that only moments before battered at the closet door. Or it may be they move of their own accord. Watching them sway, the painter is reminded of the arms or tentacles of some invertebrate stranded by the tide and struggling now over the sand to regain the safety of the waves.

The painter is about the slam the door shut when he sees that the limbs of the tree are not completely barren. There are three objects perched there that bear a faint and passing resemblance to enormous, malformed crows. They shift restlessly from foot to foot, and their sharp beaks peck at the ashen bark of the tree, leaving behind small but ugly gashes that weep. The tree that is not precisely a tree bleeds oily rivulets that drip and spatter the snow about its trunk. Only later will it occur to the painter that the limbs were not swaying at all, but writhing, racked with pain from the gouging beaks of that alikeness of crows. It's a thought he will always keep to himself.

Workprint

A week has passed since Helen Farrow unlocked her post office box and discovered the large kraft envelope stuffed inside, half folded, slightly creased, even though the box was plenty large enough that it could have lain flat. Upon opening the envelope, she found it contained nothing but a color glossy 8"x10" still shot from a movie that, near as she has been able to determine over the past seven days, has never been made. The envelope bore no return address, only a smudged Pasadena, California postmark. The still was printed on sturdy, standard-weight, resin-based Kodak paper, complete with a developer's "Kodachrome Print" stamp on the back, dated January '85. There were also a few all but indecipherable lines scrawled on the back in sloppy cursive, with what appeared to be a purple Sharpie.

As for the image printed on the paper, she found it so fantastically grotesque and pornographic that her first impulse was to rip it apart and toss the pieces into the nearest trash can. Be rid of it. Forget the whole thing. But standing there in the busy, bustling post office, staring at the still, her initial revulsion very quickly melted into curiosity. After all, here was a mystery, and though it wasn't precisely the sort of mystery that was her stock and trade, it was still an unanswered question. She slid the still back into the envelope, put the envelope in the leather satchel that also held her laptop and a half-edited print-out of an incomplete manuscript, and walked back to her car.

That was Monday morning. This is Monday, again.

And Helen Farrow is sitting in a yellow naugahyde booth near the back of a tiny coffee shop on Mass Ave. The place is crowded, mostly with MIT students who come for the free WiFi. It's really a bit *too* crowded for her liking, but this is where Otto wanted to meet. He said the coffee here is good, though he knows she doesn't drink coffee, but she didn't feel like arguing. Three days back, on Friday, she sent him a scan of the still and admitted she'd been unable to make heads or tails of it, despite her experience with the history of lost and unfinished films. Of course, most of her work has been confined to misplaced cinema of the early Twentieth Century, the teens and twenties, and her interest in movies really doesn't extend much past the forties. Even if it did, she's never cared for horror or science fiction flicks, and certainly not pornography, especially nothing so outlandishly perverse as the image delivered to her a week ago in that anonymous envelope. That's more Otto's taste, but, as of his last email the night before, he'd had no luck solving the puzzle, either.

He arrives almost fifteen minutes late, disheveled as usual, and orders an Americano and two pieces of almond biscotti. Helen orders a decaf chai latté, and Otto makes a joke about not trusting anyone who can't handle caffeine.

"I already have enough trouble sleeping, thank you," she says. "And this thing hasn't exactly been helping." She slides the envelope across the table to him, and he stares at it a moment or two before picking it up.

"It doesn't bite," she says. "At least, it hasn't yet. Who knows, maybe you'll be the first."

Otto smiles and winks at her, then takes the photograph from the envelope. He sets it in front of him, stares at it for two or three minutes, and then whistles softy and shakes his head. Then he turns it over again, squinting at the writing on the back.

"Just so you know," he says, "this baby is raising eyebrows all over the web. It's a certified fucking enigma. I've already had one collector in Kyoto offer me five hundred dollars for the print."

"But you still have no clue whatsoever."

"Oh, I've got clues," he tells her. "Hell, I've got clues coming out my ass, but they just aren't leading anywhere."

The waitress brings their order, and Helen sips at her chai while Otto chews at a piece of his biscotti and takes turns reexamining the front and back of the photograph. He finally leaves it lying face down and taps it once with an index finger.

"Clearly, 'R. Bottin' is meant to refer to *Rob* Bottin," he tells her, and he pronounces the surname *Bow-teen*. Helen shrugs and admits she's never heard of anyone by that name. "Of course you haven't," Otto frowns. "You're a philistine. You've probably never seen *The Howling* or *The Thing* or *The Fog* or–"

"So, this guy's a director?" she asks, interrupting him; Otto sighs and glares at her.

"No," he says with exaggerated patience. "He does makeup special effects. Werewolves and aliens, monsters, that sort of shit. *This* sort of shit."

"Oh," says Helen, feeling annoyed, but not half so stupid as Otto probably *thinks* she feels right now. "It wasn't done with CGI, then?"

"Not in January 1985, it wasn't. Anyway, look at this," and he flips the photo over. "That's all strictly analog, Farrow. Some pretty spiffy animatronics and prosthetics work going on here. Looks like latex over transparent polyester, some silicone, urethane, foam rubber, methyl cellulose, all that old-school stuff. You really *don't* know the first thing about anyone or anything after Hitchcock, do you?"

"Otto, did you actually just use the word *spiffy?*" she asks, deflecting his question with one of her own. She turns the photograph over once again and points at the handwriting on the back. "And what about 'The Sick Rose'?" she asks him. "What's that supposed to mean?"

"Well, the only thing I've come up with is a poem by William Blake. I'm assuming that's a dead end, but I did write it down." Otto fishes a crumpled, medium-sized Post-it note from a pocket of his jeans and smoothes it out next to the photo. "'The Sick Rose,'" he reads, "from Blake's *Songs of Innocence and of Experience,* first published in 1794. You want to hear this?"

"You went to the trouble to write it down, so why not," she says and takes another sip of the chai.

"Why not," Otto nods and reads aloud from the Post-it note, "'O Rose thou art sick, the invisible worm that flies in the night in the howling storm has found out thy bed of crimson joy. And his dark secret love does thy life destroy.' Happy stuff, but I don't see that it has bearing on our problem."

"Mind if I keep that?" she asks, and Otto shrugs and gives her the note.

"Next question," he says and finishes his biscotti.

"Were there any films released in 1985 that this Rob Bottin guy was involved with?"

"Yes, there were," Otto tells her, wiping crumbs off the front of his T-shirt. "Two, actually. Joe Dante's *Explorers* in July and Ridley Scott's *Legend* that December. Some cool makeup effects, but they both tanked at the box office. In fact, you could say that Scott's film almost ended his career. You could even say it was a bomb of *legendary* stature." And Otto pantomimes a rim shot, but Helen doesn't laugh. "Anyway," he sighs, "your enigma here, it definitely has nothing whatsoever to do with either film. That much I *can* safely say."

Helen tries not to scowl, though she very much feels like scowling. This whole affair is beginning to seem like a joke at her expense, someone else's idea of funny. For all she knows, Otto arranged to have the still sent to her, and he's sitting across from her silently, secretly laughing his ass off. She drinks her chai, which is getting cold, and takes turns watching him and the ugly, impossible scene in the photograph.

"Otto, you got friends in Burbank," she says.

Otto makes a great show of looking hurt, that she would ever entertain such an idea. "So the fuck do you, Farrow. We're film buffs, for shit's sake. I did not have this picture mailed to you, so just get that notion out of your head right this second. I have better things to do with my time, lady."

"Fine. I was just kidding," she tells him, even though she wasn't. "So if this shot's not from either one of those films, maybe it's from something else Bottin worked on, something that was never completed, or maybe the date's wrong."

Otto picks another biscotti crumb off his T-shirt, flicks it away, and shrugs. "Those possibilities crossed my mind," he says. "But we can pretty much rule out the first one. I know his work, and, fact is, he's never done a movie that this image would fit into. The creature, and the general theme, sure, it's reminiscent of the designs he did for Carpenter's *The Thing*, but not only was that film made in '81 and released in '82, it had an all male cast. And there's pretty much nothing else remotely like this anywhere in the man's oeuvre until *Mimic*, but *Mimic* – not very good, by the way – didn't come along until 1997."

"So what about unfinished films, or projects that never got beyond pre-production?" she asks and puts her cup down, deciding not to finish her tea.

"Not that I'm aware of, but I have my feelers out," and he wiggles all ten of his fingers at her. "Maybe somebody will know something I don't. That's happened maybe once or twice."

"Oh, well," Helen Farrow says, truthfully more irritated at having wasted most of the morning than disappointed that Otto's come up empty-handed. She reaches for the Post-it note with the William Blake poem. "I can't sit here all day," she says. "I'm supposed to talk with my agent in a couple of hours, and I need to get to the market before then."

"Still working on that piece about von Stroheim and *Greed?*" he asks, and Helen nods.

"Yeah, but I'm having trouble tracking down this Rick Schmidlin character, the guy at Turner who oversaw the so-called recreation. He's not returning my calls or emails."

"Doesn't that prima donna shit piss you off? I mean, how hard is it to take five minutes and answer a goddamned email, right? He could at least have the decency to tell you to fuck off."

"Nothing much surprises me anymore," she tells Otto, and then she reaches for the photograph, but he stops her by picking it up again.

"Otto, didn't I just say I need to get going? It's almost noon."

"There is *one* thing this shot keeps reminding me of," he says, more or less ignoring her. "A moderately wretched, low-budget Brit film called *Xtro,* directed by Harry Bromley Davenport – no one you've ever heard of, and for good reason. *Xtro* was released 1983, the year after *The Thing.*"

"Bottin worked on it?"

"Hell no," Otto scoffs. "Bottin would have still been recuperating from working himself half to death in Alaska and British Columbia on Carpenter's film. The effects for *Xtro* were done by Robin Grantham, who's actually worked on a few decent films. Anyway, I'm not saying I think there's an actual connection between that film and your mystery still here. Just that when I look at it, that's the film that immediately comes to mind."

"And it's wretched," Helen says, eyeing the door longingly and just wanting to be out of the booth and out of the cramped coffee shop.

"Okay, maybe not *totally* wretched. It has a few good moments, here and there. But definitely moderately wretched. There was this great stupid glut of films after *Alien* came out in '79, all trying to cash in on Scott's success." Helen makes a halfhearted effort not to look impatient while Otto reels off a catalog of films she's never heard of and never intends to track down. Movies with titles like *Galaxy of Terror, The Intruder Within, Scared to Death, Inseminoid,* and *The Deadly Spawn.* "All these filmmakers churning out cut-rate extraterrestrial invasions," Otto says, "just like back in the fifties. It's fucking amazing how many of them blatantly ripped off Giger's biomechanoid design from *Alien,* especially William Malone's *Creature* – also known as *The Titan Find,* by the way – but then you could argue that the premise for *Alien* is lifted from *It! The Terror from Beyond Space,* or that *Doctor Who* episode, "The Ark in Space." For that matter, A. E. van Vogt actually initiated a lawsuit against 20th Century Fox, claiming that Dan O'Bannon's screenplay plagiarized a couple of the stories in *The Voyage of the Space Beagle.*"

"Otto," Helen says as sharply as she can without raising her voice, and she plucks the photograph from his fingers. "That's all very fascinating, but I've got to get going. Let me know if you turn up anything relevant, okay?"

Otto blinks and furrows his eyebrows, his expression reminding her of a sleepwalker who's been shaken roughly awake. He glances at his empty hand, and she half expects him to ask if she's interested in the offer from the collector in Kyoto.

"I'll call you," she says, returning the photo to its kraft envelope, and before Otto can reply, Helen Farrow gets up and squeezes between other customers and other booths and steps out onto the noisy sidewalk.

The day seems quite a bit longer than it has a right to, longer and considerably more annoying. The talk with her agent is anything but encouraging, yet another editor passing on her proposal for a book treating the risqué cinema of pre-Production Code Hollywood, which makes five now. A third attempt to contact the man who oversaw the 1999 restoration of Erich von Stroheim's famously lost epic *Greed* meets with an uncooperative personal assistant, and she discovers a leaking pipe beneath the kitchen sink. Helen hardly has time to think about the mystery shot or Otto or obscure science-fiction films until she sits down at her desk with an unappetizing cold dinner of leftover Chinese takeout. The microwave seemed to require too much effort, and so she's settled for Kung Pao chicken straight from the refrigerator. As she eats, she opens her Gmail account and finds not one, but two emails from Otto waiting for her. The subject line of the first reads simply "RE XTRO," and she clicks it first:

> Talked with dude who has a few pre-production sketches and storyboards from both XTRO and ALIEN but nothing there even remotely like your picture. Didn't expect there would be. But if you ever want to see woman give birth to a full-grown man or au pair cocooned and turned into egg-making thingy, check it out. Japanese hentai freaks must be wild about this one. Subject of aliens raping and growing inside human hosts very damn popular in the 80s, we can blame Scott and Giger for this obviously. I'll keep looking. You keep watching the skies.

She has no idea what the last lines means, but writes it off as one of Otto's allusions to some B movie or another she's never seen. The subject line of his second email is "A possible lead?" Helen spears a water chestnut on the tines of her fork, extracting it from the mess inside the grease-stained Chinese takeout box, then opens the email:

So this is interesting. According to someone I know who reviews for Video Watchdog and a couple of blogs Bottin DOES have a lost film. Sort of. After THE THING he was hired to do creature design for director named Bob Perkins, of whom I do not know jack shit. No listing at IMDb or Wikipedia. Get this. Film was called THE SICK ROSE (bingo!) and the alien baddies seem to have been of the body-snatcher assimilation variety. Please tell me you've heard of INVASION OF THE BODY SNATCHERS. But there was supposed to be a twist. Woman falls in love with one of the monsters, and there was gonna be this Beauty and the Beast angle at work. Something like that. Rumor is Bottin got as far as constructing several of the aliens, and maybe some test footage was shot, but then this Perkins dude lost his backers and the project was scrapped. My guess is your mystery photo is from the test footage. Right now I'm looking into who was supposedly cast in the film, who that woman on the bed might be, but not turning up much. Presumably she would have been the lead. Supposedly Susan Sarandon was cast in female lead, but that doesn't look like her to me. Also, I'm told director committed suicide a few weeks after production folded, and various other mishaps in conjunction with film. So you can put this one in the cursed folder as well as the lost folder. All I have for now, but I'll keep digging. How could I have not known about this puppy? Ciao.

Helen logs out of her account, figuring there's nothing waiting there she hasn't read that's so important it can't wait until later, and she's not in the mood to respond to Otto. Otto will keep. She sets the takeout box aside, reaches for her leather satchel, and removes the envelope. For several minutes, she sits and stares at it, at that smudged Burbank postmark, and her own address printed in large blocky letters underneath. She realizes for the first time that the handwriting on the envelope isn't the same as the handwriting on the backside of the print. It should have occurred to her right off, but didn't.

She slips the photograph out of its envelope, wondering how many times she's repeated this simple act over the course of the last week. Too many, surely. She sets both down on the cluttered desk beside the computer, with the still shot lying on top of the kraft paper. Helen licks her lips, tasting soy sauce and peanuts, and wishes she had something to drink. She almost gets up to go to the fridge for a soda, but then the moment passes and, instead, she sits gazing at the photograph. It truly is hideous, Helen Farrow thinks, no matter how clever or resourceful this Bottin fellow might have been at stringing together the abomination perched menacingly above the actress on the bed. She can't imagine anyone finding anything the least bit entertaining or even erotic about such a nightmarish tableaux, any more than she can fathom why it was mailed to her.

She shuts her eyes, but when she opens them again, the photograph is still there, of course.

A woman lies naked on a narrow bed. The walls are bare plaster painted almost the same shade of blue as a swimming pool. The bed sheets match the walls. A single bare light bulb mounted on the ceiling illuminates the scene. The floor is hardwood, and there's a careless pile of discarded clothing lying next to the bed. The actress is blonde, and Helen supposes she does bear a resemblance to Susan Sarandon, Sarandon as she would have looked in the mid eighties. Her eyes are shut, and it's almost impossible to tell what she's meant to be feeling in the scene, whether its pain or terror or ecstasy. The actress is almost, but not quite, expressionless. She lies flat on her back, legs spread and knees bent, her hands either fondling herself or the monster's bizarre phallus. The photo's not clear enough to be sure which. Maybe she's meant to be doing both at once.

The creature looming over the supine woman reminds Helen more of a praying mantis than anything else. Except it's not green or brown, like all the mantises she's ever seen, but jet black with bulging crimson eyes. Helen can only assume that the rugose appendage dangling from the creature's belly and buried deeply in the woman's vagina is meant to be some manner of reproductive organ and that the actress, the character the actress is playing, is copulating with this thing. If Otto was right about the "Beauty and the Beast" parallel, then she's doing so of her own free will. The creature is exuding some manner of thick bluish slime that drips from every inch of its body and covers much of the bed and spatters the actress' skin.

But the worst part of it is the form that has begun to take shape on the thing's back – a waxy-looking copy of the woman's head and torso, her breasts and shoulders. The eyes of the replica are the same shade of red as the eyes of the actress' insectile lover. The forearms of the replica are raised, fusing at the elbow with the hindmost pair of the creature's six jointed legs. There is the impression of motion, that if one were seeing the film itself and not merely a still, that the half-formed imitation of the woman on the bed would be taking shape right before Helen's eyes. The lower part of the replica's body dissolves in a seething mass of tendrils and raw coalescing flesh, and the head is not precisely bald, but what's growing from it, curling backwards in tangled strands, isn't anything she'd call hair. Helen reaches for the nearest book, a copy of *The Silent Cinema Reader,* and quickly hides the still from view.

"That's enough," Helen Farrow says. "That's *more* than enough." After she's had a long hot shower, she'll answer Otto's email and tell him that if there's really someone in Kyoto crazy enough to PayPal her five hundred bucks US for the photo, it's a deal. A fool and his money, the bills she has to pay, etcetera. She never wants to see the thing again, and whatever curiosity she might have harbored as to its origins has faded. She stands and, reaching into a pocket, finds the Post-it note with the Blake poem written on it. There's a wastepaper basket beside her desk, and she wads the neon-yellow slip of paper into a tight ball and drops it in the trash.

Tempest Witch

The sea has many voices. Many voices and many gods. Even dreaming, I know that I'm only recollecting these words, this thought, that my unconscious mind has pilfered them from a poem I've read, years and years ago, and could likely never quote while awake. Many voices. Many gods. And yet She stands on that jagged granite promontory, a stark and furious contradiction to Eliot's claim that there are many. She will have me know there is but this one. She spreads wide her white arms and fluttering, tattered raiments, which are the arms and raiments of a hurricane, and She howls. Her voice is a hurricane's roar. Her breath a hurricane's breath. The winds that whip the waves to frenzy and cause the waters to dash themselves against the shore, these are merely the consequence of Her sighs. No more engine would ever be required to drive the oceans. No more than a sigh. Though, in the night of this dream there *is* more than a sigh. Considerably more than a sigh. She stands on the rocks and howls. It is a cry sufficient to shatter all the waters of the world and set the sky to writhing. It is the song that chews away mountains, grain by crystalline grain, until they are only sand again. Until they are sand or silt, beaches or muddy strands or the slime at the very bottom of the deepest depths. She sings apart the continents, given time enough, and time enough I know She has. As the convections of inner furnaces spur the courses of those land masses – so they plow and skitter and careen about the globe, rearranging themselves over aeons – it is by Her voice that they are given shape. By Her breath does the water move, and yet, also, I know there is no dividing Her *from* the water. She *is* the sea. I understand this perfectly well, whether I am watching Her howl from the deck of a tiny ship foundering in the storm She has sung into being or watching from the safety of the rain-lashed shore. It is the needful limitations of my dreaming ape's mind that has fashioned Her the semblance of a woman. No shape would She otherwise wear, unless it were the ever-changing, and therefore indefinable, form of all the seas combined. And if I were to lay a name upon Her, this would be equally arbitrary, equally inconsequential. Even as I look on, squinting through the rain and wind, shielding my eyes with my hand, She is busy turning a trick to defy my dream's demands of Her. Where my sensibilities would grow a woman's legs, She has, instead, sprouted the coiling arms of an enormous octopus or squid. They slither over the rocks and vanish into the breakers or wrap themselves tightly about the granite crags, as if to make clear any doubt about Her grip upon the land. I feel myself sinking and am certain that I must be watching from a ship, after all. I am on some barque or whaler, and, in the throes of this tempest, the sea has dropped away beneath the hull. I am thrown to the deck, and for a moment the moaning of the timbers below me is almost as loud as the storm, or, rather, as the screaming white shape who has given birth to the storm. The ship rolls violently to starboard, slamming back down into the sea, and for the space of several seconds I'm certain that she'll capsize. I grit my teeth and squeeze my eyes shut, and in that darkness of my choosing do I imagine that Her many arms have reached out and found me. Even now, they must be twining themselves about the ship, looping, spiraling all the way up into the masts and rigging, and with a single gargantuan tug will they pull me under. In the space between one heartbeat and the next they will close together like a fist and shatter the planking, crushing the futtocks to splinters, making of stem and stern no more than driftwood. That much force would be an effort without effort for Her, and She might exert it on a whim. I can hear water crashing over the gunwales, splashing out across the weather deck. I open my eyes again, expecting only foam and spray before the darkness of the abyss is laid bare to receive me. But the ship has righted herself, *if* truly she had rolled. I cannot now trust that I can trust my sense of things, for I suspect it is all a dream, and I know the deceptive truthfulness of all dreams. The mind sees clearly in sleep, but many lies may be required to build a single certainty. I try to stand and am thrown once more to my hands and knees. Nevertheless, impossibly, I can look upon Her, still and all, even though She is no longer, strictly speaking, *before* me. The vessel pitches and heaves, drawing about on the vicious currents She has summoned, and I behold Her perched upon that mean scrap of stone. All around, the sea appears to boil from the restless activity of Her serpentine arms. They are so many in number, I can't count, and I suspect the number isn't fixed. The howling white woman is not bound by the laws of any science of living matter, and so all morphology, all physiology, is rendered indeterminate. Every cell must be in perpetual flux, an evolution governed not by natural selection, but by will alone. "Imagine that," I say, and plainly hear myself speaking the words as if there's no wind to drown my voice, no waves, no creaking wood. "Imagine that She is never anything She does not desire to be. But you must simultaneously imagine that She *has* no desire, or nothing we might ever recognize as so conscious an emotion as desire." And you tell me I'm not making sense, and here we are strolling along the Cobb. You've gotten a little ahead of me, following that demilune of boulders forming the protective harbor wall. "I half imagine," you say, "that Chinese poppy fields deserve more credit for your interpretations than does any faculty of reason. If I did not know better, I'd lay the blame on opium pipes." But you do know better, and I glance over my shoulder at the flat calm of the harbor and the sun off the sea sparkling almost bright enough to blind. In that instant, I can't say what has become of the ship that ferried me, or its crew. Was that some very old memory – frayed about the edges, worn smooth as a pebble – or is the dream intent on beguiling me with false hopes and misdirection? I strongly suspect the latter. I'll not be fobbed off by this pleasant illusion of a life I've never lived, of a love and a city by the shore and of a particular late summer day I've never known. "Can't you hear it?" I ask, and you turn and watch me, watching silently for a time. Then you ask, "Can I hear what, Jonathan? I hear the waves, and the gulls. The bells at St. Michael's were chiming the hour, but they've stopped now. You don't look well. I think we should go back." I don't tell you, but I don't feel well, either. I feel sick, and weary. I feel lost. "You don't hear the wind?" I ask, pressing my luck. You smile and reply, "Sure, there's a breeze," but you sound confused and worried. *Have I already drowned?* I wonder. *Has the barque been dragged under, and are all aboard lost? Is this brilliant afternoon nothing more than pretty pictures painted on torn canvas sails?* "Yes," I say, "I think you're right, Sebastian. I think we should go back. We should never have come out so far. It isn't safe." And woven through the roar of that hidden squall, I catch a sudden crack like canon fire. That's the bowsprit snapping away, broken as easily as a matchstick between my fingers. If I were to shut my eyes, I'd see the forestays, torn free and whipping madly in the gale. If I *were* to shut my eyes, it occurs to me then, this sunny day would dissolve, and you with it, so I do *not* shut my eyes. I do not so much as blink. "Poor souls," you say, frowning and picking at a loose thread in your waistcoat. "They perished. Had I been any god of power, I'd have sunk the sea within the earth, before it was able to swallow up that good ship and all the fraughting souls within her." Your words don't startle me, but they do give me pause. I've called you Sebastian, my love, and have no memory of having ever called you by the name Miranda. *Both* names may fit you, one quite so well as the other, just as I stand *both* on the listing deck of a sinking ship *and* upon this ancient breakwater of Portland Stone and mortar. Still not daring to close my eyes, I stare at the limestone beneath my feet, at the impressions there of ammonite shells and other Jurassic mollusks. "So, have you seen Her?" I ask, comprehending now that the layers of duplicity and pretense are at last peeling back. "From afar," you reply. "Never half so intimately as you, Jonathan. I wouldn't hazard it, for I would fain die a dry death." I stand listening and gnawing at my lower lip. I taste salt, which might be blood, or might only be the spray dried upon my mouth. "She is a pale demon," I say, "pale as marble or an alabaster effigy. About Her left arm are twined two banded serpents, and it's this same arm She has leveled at me. It is with the forefinger of that left hand that She stirs the cauldron of the depths and takes aim at my soul." You laugh, and it pricks me, that laugh. It is both mockery and cruel delight at my situation, and I marvel that your moods may change at least as swiftly as those of the sea witch and the disposition of Her realm. "You always were so clever," you say – Sebastian, Miranda, who- and whatever you may be. "How is it that this lives in your mind? What *more* do you see in the dark backward and abysm of time?" I ask you please not to taunt me, if only because I have loved you so long and so wholly. "It's not my dream," you answer. And at this I finally find the courage to shut my eyes, which is to say, I *open* my eyes, and that sun-drenched day on the Cobb breaks apart, whether it were real or only wishful thinking. I am, instead, kneeling on the deck of the nameless broken ship, as it races down the backside of a titanic wave, plunging headlong into the yawning trough beyond. The ruins of the shrouds are draped all about me, and they dance a fierce tarantella in the blow. I muster the strength to raise my head, that I might gaze out across the tortured brine towards that razor jut of granite where still She stands, directing the storm, governing its beat and tempo, much the same way that a conductor with his ivory and ebony baton might direct an orchestra. She is *so* white against that roiling, horizonless backdrop of intermingling sea and sky. She might well have been chiseled by a daemonic Michelangelo from a slab of Carrara marble – yes once already have I likened Her to a marmoreal effigy, but each time I catch sight of Her, this analogy returns anew. The sea witch strikes me as far too perfect a form to have ever been arrived at by the dumb and random processes of Nature. A visage this terrible must surely have been crafted by *conscious* hands, by an imagination most terrible, most exquisite, most sublime. Far back on the Cobb, from the sanctuary of that parallel dreamspace, you'd like to know if she's meant to be Scylla or Sycorax. I ask what difference it would make, and you admit it would make none whatsoever. She is, as I have said, the Sea. No other name is necessary or fitting. I try, again, to stand, and this time catch hold of one of the dangling stays and manage to remain more or less upright. The waters are being whipped into a maelstrom, a vast counterclockwise whorl turning at Her insistence, turning with the wind. The scudding ship, now entirely at the mercy of this vortex She has conjured, has attained a tremendous rate of speed as it traces the rotating periphery. I'm helpless *not* to watch Her. How does a man turn away from the face of his demise? How does any being ever turn away from Her? And from the Cobb, I hear your voice: "It might well be your salvation, Jonathan, if only you would avert your eyes. In so doing, possibly, this hold She has on you might be severed." And you, dear indifferent Sebastian, you're not *pleading* that I look away. You do not even sound particularly concerned. The words are casually offered up, just a suggestion, and you care not whether I heed or disregard them. "The entire crew might be saved," you add. "There is no crew," I reply, though the wind steals my words and I do not hear them. I trust you do, Sebastian. "There's no one but me, and it would be more correct to call this unfortunate barquentine a casket than a ship." You don't disagree, and I try not to hear anything more you may have to say. This will be simpler if it finishes without you. Yes, my passage down to Her will be eased if I allow myself to forget that you might ever have existed, if I can forget the rooms we shared on Bridge Street, not far from the place where the River Lim empties into the sea, and forget the taste of your lips, and the color of your eyes, which I always thought were so like the sky. You were only another dream, Sebastian. And now my heart and faith must be given over to Her. She is a jealous god and would have no other gods before Her, as they say. The ship (or casket) crests another towering wave and rushes down its farther side, descending into yet another trough. I'm pitched forward and almost lose my footing, slipping, sliding on the deck, swinging now from the broken stay like a codfish hooked and wriggling upon a troller's line. And I notice an odd thing then (though shortly will I notice far odder) – though the ship is caught in the maelstrom, pulled widdershins round and round, and though She stands there on Her rock at the very center of the whirlpool, I am always *facing* Her. Not once do I get a glimpse of Her back or see Her in either left or right profile. *Perhaps,* I suppose, *She turns with the waters, and it's no more than an illusion.* This is a dishonest supposition, because I know stranger physics are at work here than those of Newton and Euclid, Johannes Kepler and Galileo Galilei. Indeed, *nothing* we were taught at University will serve me here. And I am full in that knowledge, but still clinging to the cold comfort of self-delusion, that She is only turning in time with the maelstrom. Even after all I've seen, my mind reels at the assault against rationality required of any other explanation. I can push Sebastian away and die alone, but I cannot abandon *all* reason. Oh, and something is hauling itself from the water, crawling out onto the exposed granite behind Her. Whatever its true pedigree, the thing puts me in mind of a great lizard – albeit a lizard half as large as an ox – and I wonder if the creature is some manner of familiar, a lesser imp that She's bidden swim up from the perpetual gloom of black submarine canyons to aid in my undoing. But if She even notices the arrival of this huge saurian, She shows no evidence of having done so. Perhaps it's not a familiar, after all. Perhaps it's only been attracted by the magic, the way that spoiled meat attracts flies. I marvel that it was not snared in Her thrashing tentacles, that it has passed unhindered through them. And here, precisely *here,* as my eyes, so briefly distracted, drift from the lizard-like monstrosity, past Her innumerous arms, and back to the pallid figure of a woman standing upon that crag, *here* am I seized by an epiphany. Neither word seems too strong – neither *seized* nor *epiphany* – for the realization which grips me is of a certain that violent *and* that sudden, intuitive, and profound. I behold Her, perched upon that mean scrap of stone, Her exposed breasts, Her coal-colored hair whipped back from Her face and high noble forehead by the wind that is the consequence of Her sighs. By the hurricane which is Her voice. While I make a habit of avoiding Biblical correspondences, it seems very appropriate to say that, in that moment, the scales fell from my eyes. And, in contempt of my resolution to forget you, Sebastian, I once again hear you speaking to me from that never-was bright day on the Cobb. It will be your voice that frames this awful revelation. You'd have it no other way. "Do you remember when we were last in Swanage, the Punch and Judy show we came upon when we were walking along the beach? Do you remember those horrid glove-puppets, and the way the children all crowded about?" I do, of course, but don't say so. I'd rather not grant you that satisfaction. But I remember, and now I see that the squirming tendrils which appear to sprout from the place where the sea witch's legs ought to be and snake away into the breakers, I see, violently, suddenly, that I've gotten it the wrong way round. The bow of the ship abruptly rises, buoyed by the highest of all the waves yet, one I know she'll never be able to navigate. The ninth wave of superstitious seafarers, and of Tennyson, *gathering half the deep and full of voices.* The wave that will bear me down. I can hear the foremast toppling as a barrel rolls past and is smashed to kindling against a capstan. And at last I make out what has been right *here,* in front of me, all along, the slimy, half-submerged bulk which I mistook for nothing more than foam and bladderwrack and kelp. I perceive two bulbous eyes set atop that gelatinous mass, and, like me, they also appear to be watching the sea witch, rapt and unable to do otherwise. But the arms I thought Hers, in point of fact, belong rather to It, and they are not *entering* the water, but *emerging* onto that stingy bit of land. In my dream, there is not a witch, and there is no howling personification of all the world's oceans to conjure a hurricane. In my dream, there is only the *likeness* of a chalk-white siren, no more sentient than a child's glove-puppet, no more conscious than the grotesque, worm-shaped lure I've read can be found at the tip of tongues of certain species of turtle. These reptiles, we are told, lie in wait at the bottoms of ponds, their mouths gaping wide so that any passing fish might see the twitching lure within their hungry jaws. Everything I believed I'd apprehended about Her is a falsehood, and *this* is my thought as that final calamitous wave falls over the ship and, waking, I am not swallowed by a raging sea.

In Memory of Frank Frazetta

Fairy Tale of the Maritime

There are tales sea monsters tell their children to get them to behave. "Eat your krill, or you'll go the way of poor old Cetus, slain by some ne'er-do-well like Perseus." Or it might be, "Take care you never swim too near the surface, or you'll end up like that fool merrow Coomara, his lobster pots emptied of souls by meddlesome Jack Dougherty." The mothers of leviathans and mermaids have no shortage of cautionary tales, promising dreadful fates to unwise fingerlings who disregard their warnings. There are abyssopelagic religions, practiced in the basalt cathedrals of that midnight zone, founded upon this or that piscine or crustacean martyr who ran afoul of a vicious landlubber. "It's all devils and fishhooks, driftnets and tartar sauce up there," the hermaphroditic hagfish mutter as they worry at the bones and tattered blubber of sunken whales.

They're traitors, deserters, scoundrels all, the million-times great grandchildren of the those lobe-finned Devonian heretics who turned their backs on the ancient womb of the sea and crawled out into the sun.

There's not an honest soul among them.

Some dolphins, possessed as they are of a more scientific bent, have theorized that prolonged exposure to the direct rays of the sun lead inevitably to moral degradation. Another school of thought, championed by manatees and dugongs, blames various skeletal adaptations to terrestrial locomotion. Almost all will admit, however, that much of the evidence is anecdotal.

But the division remains between those ashore and those who've never forsaken the water, even if that division may be complicated and blurred by the perversities of the semi-aquatic (and among these, seals, sea lions, walruses, those serpents of the Family Hydrophiidae, otters, saltwater crocodiles, sea turtles, and mudskippers are usually listed as the worst offenders). The division remains and is given lip service even among sub- and eulittoral dwellers, crabs and barnacles, periwinkles and limpets. "We are of the sea, and shall ever be," as one of the catchier catchphrases puts it.

But, for the time being, let's settle on one single tragedy, and on one generally accepted as more hearsay and rumor than outright legend.

Long ago, a child was born to a woman who, during her pregnancy, was frightened when she came unexpectedly upon the carcass of a shark while strolling along the beach near her village. Several months later, the woman gave birth to a beautiful daughter, radiant and fair in all respects save one: each of her hands was possessed of only three fingers and a thumb, and the webbing between the fingers was almost as pronounced as the webbing between the toes of a gull or cormorant. Despite the protestations of the local priest – who deemed the infant a spawn of its mother's detestable congress with some oceanic demon – the village accepted the girl as one of its own.

And as she grew to be a girl and passed from girlhood to womanhood, her beauty doubled and trebled. At first glance, most men (and no few women) found her irresistible. But so too did the curse of her nativity increase three-fold. When she shed her baby teeth, they were replaced with a double row of recurved and serrated fangs that would have done any mako or hammerhead proud. The webbing between her fingers also appeared between her toes. And lastly, her sky-blue eyes deepened in hue until they were blacker than roofing pitch, and it was no longer possible to distinguish iris from pupil. Some claimed her eyes refused to cast a reflection and that each month when her menses came around it wasn't blood she bled, but brine.

Still, she wasn't banished from the village, though the aging priest did do his damnedest. She was endured, suffered, tolerated, allowed to remain among those whose flesh had not marked them as an abomination. She lived alone in a rundown cottage at the farthest edge of town, and some might have judged outright exile kinder than the way the people of the village shunned her. Once a week, they left groceries, along with whatever toiletries and sundries she might need, in a wicker basket near her doorstep. It was deemed preferable to having her wandering through the streets and markets. She found her clothing among the ragman's castoffs, and she knew better than to attend mass. So, she sought her own gods, fashioning them from the roar of the breakers, from foam and spray, from mist and the roiling clouds preceding winter squalls. She left offerings of bread and honey on the shingle, and the tolling of a buoy was to her as sacred as any church bell. By new moon and full, she burned candles on her windowsills. At neap tide, she laid wreaths of heather and lavender on the quay. Years passed, and, in her solitude, the daughter of the woman who'd been scared by a stranded shark grew ever stranger and more distant from her own kind. She was the legacy of their prejudice and fear, as surely as she was the product of whatever *in utero* calamity had shaped her countenance. She all but forgot the fellowship and comforts afforded by family and friends. She existed apart.

"I don't see where this is headed?" muttered a young cod, and several adolescent flounders were quick to agree.

"All this nonsense about a human woman," sighed an indignant haddock. "Are we actually meant to feel pity for her? How does that teach us to *avoid* her sort?"

"She *is* meant to be the villain of the tale, yes?" asked a suspicious whiting. "Otherwise, it's shaping up to be an unpardonably subversive yarn."

"These humans certainly are a right superstitious bunch," the haddock added. "It's taught me that."

At this, the enormous old conger eel who was telling the story scowled from its hole in the mud and said, "Interrupt me again, and the whole lot of you can run afoul of North Sea trawlers and hungry pelicans, and I'll not lose even a single night's sleep over the loss. Now, if I may dare continue–"

The years passed, and the woman who lived in the ramshackle cottage by the sea took to swimming in the cold waters of the harbor. The webbing of her hands and feet carried her easily out beyond the jetty. Fishermen whispered of having seen her as far out as Dogger Rock and the shipwreck near Cutters Nubble. On warm days, when the mist burned off by mid-morning, she was espied sunning herself naked upon the rocks, as if the seals had adopted her as one of their own.

The villagers stopped leaving baskets outside her shack, for, after hearing such accounts of her brazen habits, none wanted to come so near. But it hardly troubled the woman, because by this time she'd learned to seize herring and pollock and smelt with her razor teeth. She ate them raw and forgot the need for cooking fires and bubbling pots. She dined on stalks of kelp and feasted on mussels. She cracked the shells of crabs and picked out every morsel of sweet white flesh. Some of the trollers began to complain that she was having an adverse affect on their catch, and soon she was being blamed for everything from torn nets to fouled lines. One angler went so far as to swear he'd drag her up with a gaff hook and gut her himself, if ever he had the opportunity.

Shortly thereafter, the harbormaster's handsome son disappeared, and four days hence his body fetched up in a tangle of rope and seaweed. He'd been so savagely gnawed identification would have been impossible, if not for a heart-shaped mole on the back of his neck. One or two suggested sharks had done the deed, but it was generally agreed that it was the work of the strange black-eyed woman and that too long had they permitted such a fiend to dwell in their midst. A bounty was posted, gold and silver for her head, and one night past Easter Sunday, the priest led his parishioners down to the shore with flaming brands, and they burned her cottage to the ground and broke apart the stone walls. Some said loathsome driftwood idols were discovered among the ashes, untouched by the flames. The ground was sown with salt and sprigs of dried rosemary.

The woman watched the fire from half a mile out and knew she could never again return to the village. Only briefly did she mourn the loss of her home and what few meager keepsakes she'd owned. She understood that the sea was her only home now, and so that night she swam East'ard, farther than she'd ever ventured before. Out past the ledges to a last, lone spire of ragged granite known as Fiddlehead Rock. Men rarely came near to the Fiddlehead, as the currents here were unaccountably treacherous, and maelstroms sometimes opened up, even in fair weather, powerful enough to swamp a dory and drag her to the bottom. Freezing and exhausted, the strange woman hauled herself from the waves, and sat shivering as a cold and cheerless April sun rose above the nether banks.

She shivered until there was no strength left in her to shiver anymore, and then she curled into a nook and resigned herself to death. She was a mighty swimmer, yes, and few fish escaped her jaws, once she set her sights upon them. But her body was thin and deficient in the insulating layers of the blubber that would have kept her warm. Likewise, her human blood lacked antifreeze glycoproteins that keep such fish as cod hale and hearty in those frigid climes. But the sea didn't forsake her, and before sunset a trip of jar seals found her. Barking, they clambered up onto the rocks and packed in close around her, their bodies shielding her from the icy wind and a light snow that had begun to blow from the north.

"It's kind of you," she told the seals, "To come when all mine own have turned against me. There's solace knowing I'm not yet utterly disowned."

The stars came out, and the moon rose, and in her dreams, the seals murmured secrets to which few women had ever been privy–

"Seals," sighed the indignant haddock. "You hear that? There's a *reason* they say, 'Never trust a seal.'"

But the old conger eel silenced the impolite fish with a baleful glare and just a few choice words about the perils of sushi chefs.

"Where was I?" asked the eel.

"Mouthy seals," the suspicious whiting prompted.

Yes, right – the seals met her below the sea of dreams, and they told her of an immemorial evil that dwelt in a cavern six-hundred fathoms down.

"Wait," one of the adolescent flounders interrupted. "*What* sort of evil did you say it was?"

"Equatorial," said the haddock.

"No, no. Dictatorial," the whiting chimed in.

The conger eel smacked its wide lips and made mention of the fact that it had missed luncheon to tell this tale, and how a few bites of whiting would surely hit the spot. There were profuse apologies, then, and the eel continued:

A full six-hundred fathoms down, they told her, where the rocks formed the landward end of a silty submarine canyon, were grand halls carved long ago by the chisels and picks of a race of giants that had descended from the sky. Over the aeons, almost all these beings had perished, for they warred endlessly amongst themselves over every petty dispute and difference of opinion. So, they died off at one another's hands – all but one, that is, and that one had emerged hardened and cruel from all those ages of war. Some among the seals said it had gone mad, though others believed the creature's wickedness and barbarity was part and parcel of its natural disposition.

"They sail between all the stars," a bull seal barked, "in ships of iron and fire. They carry their wars with them wherever they do."

"Why are you telling me this?" the woman asked the jar seals who had saved her life as they darted and dove and swam in circles about her.

"It seeks a bride," the bull seal replied. "And it seeks a bride of man. Already has it taken brides from many of the people of the sea and none have yet pleased it. It grows ever more spiteful, and we worry that even Father Kraken and Mother Hydra have deserted us from fear of this devil's depredations."

She gazed towards the surface, watching the silvery bubbles that leaked from her nostrils as they raced away. It was more than she could comprehend – and she told the seals this – that even the Mother and the Father had cause to fear this star-spawned evil, for were they not all and everything, existing even unto the day when the seas would boil away? Did not Poseidon and Amphitrite themselves kneel before them? The seals grew anxious, then, and answered her questions with nothing more informative than a round of impatient stares.

"And you'd have me seek this beast and offer myself as its bride? Is that the price for having guarded me against the chill?"

"No," the seals replied in unison. "Our favors are freely given, without need for compensation. But it is also true that we have prayed that a daughter of man would come who might deliver us."

The woman awoke then, and it was still an hour before dawn. The seals had not deserted her, but crowded in on all sides, close and warm. She watched the twinkling stars, distant and cold and unknowable, and wondered at what awful mysteries they held and what scourges had escaped them to circumnavigate the glittering Dome of Heaven.

When the sky had gone from velvet black to violet to the grey of weathered slate, the seals said their good-byes and left her. She'd made no promises to them. But the woman's heart was heavy, knowing as she did that she *would* go below to be the wife of the beast and that she might never see any seal again, nor the gentle light of a morning sky. She lingered a while longer on the Fiddlehead, imagining herself safe and snug back in her cottage, imagining the villagers had not marched to the beach and burned it. Then she climbed resolutely to the rock's highest point, watching and listening as a noisy, cawing flock of gulls whirled about her, as though beseeching her to reconsider her decision. She thanked the birds for their concern, fared them well, warned them against crosswinds and sudden downdrafts, and dove into the choppy water.

The woman swam down and down and down, the sea about her growing ever darker and colder, until the only light came from the bioluminescence of lanternfish and squid, and there was no warmth remaining whatsoever. It seemed to the woman that she was no longer descending into the abyss, but had somehow risen far into the sky and the photophore glow was starlight. *This,* she thought, *is why the beast holds to the deep places, for these realms are so very much akin to the emptiness that lies between the worlds.* She went down farther than the bold *spermaceti* hazard, to the very haunt of the giant squid.

"How is it she held her breath that long?" the whiting wanted to know.

"And why didn't the water pressure crush her flat?" one of the adolescent flounders asked.

The old conger eel ignored them both, for clearly they were taking this all far too literally, and it could not be bothered with the questions of such obtuse and disagreeable students.

Deeper still, the woman at last came upon the den of the beast, cut into the stone untold *millennia* before her birth, perhaps before the birth of the first man.

"Was it carved out so long back there would still have been crinoids?" the whiting inquired. "And trilobites, would there still have been trilobites? And plesiosaurs, and ichthyosaurs, and ammonites, and–"

In a single gulp, the conger eel swallowed the inquisitive whiting, and, after eyeing those still remaining to be certain the lesson had been taken to heart and head and swim bladder, it resumed:

To call the den a mere cave, or even a cavern, would never have done it justice, not by half. Peering in through the gloom, the woman saw that her entire village could easily fit inside, thrice over. The ceiling was supported by magnificent columns fashioned from rock, whalebone, and coral. The floor was tiled all in starfish, iridescent abalone shells, and the skulls of drowned sailors, ingeniously fitted together to form grimly spectacular designs, spirals within spirals, a maze to capture the eye and hold it forever.

She heard the voice of the beast before she saw its face.

"Are you the best that they could send to me?" it demanded, and the sea pressing in all about the woman cringed at the sound.

"I wasn't sent," she replied. "I came willingly and of my own accord. It was my choice."

There was a long moment of silence, and then the walls of this titanic pit trembled with the laughter of the beast. It was like unto thunder and to waves driven out before an advancing hurricane, like the grinding of continental plates, one upon the other. Silt and chunks of granite were shaken loose from the walls and ceiling to rain down about the woman.

"Of course you did," the beast said. It drew nearer, and for the first time she beheld its face. It was not so large as she'd expected, though it was certainly hideous. The head was bulbous and mottled, and two eyes as big around as dinner plates stared back at her. Like her own eyes, they were as black as pitch or polished ebony. If the thing had nostrils or a mouth, they were hidden beneath the writhing mass of ropy tendrils that sprouted from its face. These appendages almost seemed possessed of a life all their own, and two or three slithered free of the rest and wrapped themselves about her arms and waist. The beast's touch was colder than the water at the bottom of the sea, and its skin wept a sticky slime that glowed faintly wherever it touched her.

"Willingly, you consent to be my bride?"

"Would it matter if I didn't?"

"Not in the least," the beast replied. "Though I admit, this acquiescence amuses me. No one has ever before *offered* herself to me. My wives have all been given, or stolen, or in one case, purchased."

"So, I'm something new, something rare."

"And precious," the beast said.

"And precious," she agreed.

It considered her for a time, and the woman didn't struggle against the tendrils that had twined themselves about her.

"You are different from other men and women," it finally said. "You have been marked by the sea, marked before your birth, I'd wager."

"It's a wager you'd win," she told the beast.

"I might name this a flaw and send you back to your people, and wait for a truly human bride. It may be that's what I *should* do."

"*My* people, as you name them, want no part of me. They have driven me out and would of a certain put me to death if I were to return to them."

At this, the tendrils holding her grew tighter, but she didn't wince at the pain.

"If your cunny is not even fit for the sport of men, what need have I of it? You do me insult, woman."

"No, my Lord," the woman said. "For you must know that all men are fools, and most of their women are soft and weak and not fit to wade in the surf, much less find their way down to your glorious sanctuary. Most women would be driven insane by your somber eminence, and they would wither to dust at your first touch. But, being half a daughter of the ocean, I'm made strong and I can abide so prodigious a husband. You may well send me back, or dispose of me as you wish, but the loss will be your own."

And the beast was charmed by such daring claims, and by her bravery, and so it took the woman for its wife. For her bride price, the star-spawn gifted the woman with gills, tucked in beneath her chin, for she could not be expected to hold a single breath indefinitely. It gave her body the ability to endure the cold and the weight of the sea and changed her skin to the phosphorescent epidermis of hadal mollusks and chaetognaths. Transformed, the beast judged her a very fit bride, indeed. She was spirited away into the farthest reaches of that grotto, to her marriage bed which was a towering forest of tube worms growing round about a wide metallic slab she guessed might have come from the sky-faring ships the seals had described. It bedded her there, and the strange woman whose mother had been scared (and scarred) by a dead shark accepted the rough affections of the beast. When it entered her, probing her most secret recesses with indescribable organs, she didn't cry out, but made as if she welcomed the intrusions.

And for many seasons she remained with the beast, far longer than any other of its mates had. She listened to its stories of battles and rivals and far away globes. She told it tales of the lives of men and the gods they worshipped, stories the beast found too absurd and fabulous to believe. It showed her a chamber where it had arrayed all the bleached skulls and spines of its brethren, those who had been slain until it alone remained on the earth.

"You will live here forever?" she asked. "Alone, content with no company but mine?"

"No," it answered. "I'll rise, one day or night not too far distant. You will rise with me, wife, and together will we sweep away all the paltry works of mankind, and those few humans I leave alive will be my slaves, and cattle for our appetites. Then others will arrive from the stars, tumbling forth from the heavens, and the entire world will be remade to suit our needs. No longer will we cower in caves at the bottom of the sea. Men will know *true* gods, and cease the worship of their childish fancies."

Hearing these words, at first the woman's heart was gladdened. Had not the people of the village called her a monster and shunned her and left her alone where none of them would ever have to look upon her and be offended? Had they not, in the end, torched her little house and sought to do murder against her? She found that she hated them, perhaps more than she'd ever paused to realize, and it pleased her to think of them all falling before the rage of the beast and then being forced to gaze in horror as she walked unharmed in the creature's shadow, an accomplice to the slaughter.

"Will you be content with conquering the domain of men?" she asked. "When you have felled them, will you leave the sea to its own devices?"

The beast snorted and shook its pulpy, malformed head. "What sort of hollow victory would that be?" it demanded. "No, no. Nothing will be done by half measures. Everything that walks or creeps, that runs or flies or swims, will know my will and bow to it, unless they would be crushed and left to oblivion."

"Even the peoples of the sea?"

"Yes, even the peoples of the sea."

"Even the seals?"

"Yes," growled the beast, growing short with her. "Even the seals will be decimated and enslaved before I am done. What possible love have you for seals?"

"None at all," she assured the beast in a tone that it could never have taken for insincere. "They are hardly more than dogs who've learned to swim, filthy, rutting curs. I was only curious."

But in truth, she'd never forgotten the kindness of the seals who'd saved her life that night at Fiddlehead Rock, and who had swum through her dreams, and, in their way, sent her down to the beast. She might have no love or pity for humanity, but she owed the seals a debt that would not go unacknowledged or unpaid.

In his hole there in the bottom of the sea, the beast taught her all the unearthly arts and sciences of faraway spheres, of its own race and the many races they had conquered and absorbed in their aeons-long march across the sky. It taught her to reshape metal and stone and every manner of living thing, to force them to her needs and desires. It showed her how all forms are only temporary, transitory states of being, arrangements borne of chance and happenstance that can be altered and made more perfect by conscious intent. And in so doing, the beast inadvertently taught the woman the key to its undoing. She surely never would have found it, otherwise.

One day (or night, for who can say which it ever is in perpetual darkness) the beast returned from hunting whales to find she'd made something new of the slab where they slept together. She held it up, and the metal glistened by the cold blue-green light radiating from her flesh. Seeing this creation, the beast was pleased. His efforts had not been wasted, for only an apt, attentive pupil could have found such precise angles and planes in the raw material of that slab. There was no need to ask the purpose of what she'd made; that much was clear.

"It is a weapon," he said.

"Yes," the woman told him. "It is."

"And a formidable weapon, I think."

"Then you indeed flatter me, my Lord, for you must have, in your life and wanderings, seen instruments of destruction beyond anything I can possibly hope to envision. What I've made here, I have to confess, is little more than an amalgam of tools with which I am already familiar. A sword, an axe, a scythe, a blacksmith's hammer. There's nothing truly novel about it. Even the hinges and these moving parts I've copied from memory."

"You do yourself grave disservice," the beast admonished, still busy marveling at her craftsmanship, which he considered hardly more (or less) than an extension of his own. "With this, you will lay to rest multitudes."

"Maybe," she said, "but it was fashioned with only one enemy in mind." And before her husband could ask what she meant, the weapon the woman had made from the metal slab unfolded and its blades swung towards the beast, cleanly dividing its short neck from its shoulders. Gouts of oily blood gushed from the wound, staining the water about her, and for a time the woman was still, only half believing the task had proved so simple. And now it was done, and the seals would be safe, as would be the people of the village.

She didn't mourn the beast, but she did feel an odd pang of regret. *It's wrong,* she thought, *that those eyes should never again look upon the stars, when the stars are their mother, sure as the sea is mine.* So she lifted the severed head and swam away from that place, knowing that she'd never return. She swam up and up and up, the sea growing increasingly brighter and less heavy about her. She'd been below so long that the light stung her eyes, and she'd become so accustomed to the crushing weight of the deep ocean, that she feared she might melt away in an instant and lose herself in those pelagic, upper regions. The warmth also caught her by surprise, as she'd been cold so long she'd forgotten what it meant to be anything but cold.

The woman swam into a strong West'ard current and let it carry her away, past the nether banks and Fiddlehead Rock and near the ledges before she finally rose to the surface. She was relieved to find that the sun was down, that night lay across the face of waters, for the woman was certain she couldn't have survived the sun, even on a cloudy day. She lifted the beast's head above the waves, directing its unseeing eyes towards the glimmering constellations, though she'd never learned from which particular star it had come. This was the best she could do, and it would have to suffice. Thick blood still leaked from the shattered base of beast's skull, blood that assumed a dimly crimson hue by starlight.

"I really *don't* understand where this is leading," began the haddock, but the conger eel fluttered its short pectoral fins in such a way that said, without the need for words, *Wait, please. We're almost done.* And recalling the fate of the unfortunate whiting, the haddock decided waiting wasn't such a bad idea, after all.

The woman floated at the surface of the sea, the beast's head still borne aloft in her webbed hands. She watched a falling star as it streaked across the southern horizon and winked out, all come and gone in the space of a single heartbeat. And then she released her grip upon the disjoined head, letting the current take it from her. She knew well enough that in a day or so it would be carried ashore somewhere near the village. It would likely be found, whatever remained after the gulls and the crabs had had their way with it. In death, the creature that would have been their doom would become nothing more than a mystery and an affirmation of the villagers' fear and contempt for those same depths that kept them fed.

The woman drifted in the acrid cloud of the beast's blood, tasting it so that she would always remember precisely what it had been and what she had done. The seals came to her then, and seeing she was no longer fit to survive on land, they led her once again away from the shallows.

"You've saved us all," the seals said, and they thanked her, each and every one.

"I have," she replied. "I've done that, but I've done many other things, as well, and none of us can presently suppose the full consequences of my actions. Many things will come to pass because of what I've done, and because of what I've done many things will never come to pass."

"Do you grieve?" asked one of the cows.

"I might," the woman said.

And seeing that dawn was not so far away, the woman bade the seals goodbye. Once again she sank down and down and down into the lightless domain that had become the cradle of her second birth and now would always be her home. She whispered prayers to Father Kraken and Mother Hydra, and to other gods, some who have names and some who will always be nameless. As the villagers had turned their backs on her, so too did she turn her back on the surface world, and never again did she rise, but kept court in the eternal night of abyssal trenches and the plateaus of seamounts, tended to by retinues of anglerfish and viperfish, brittle stars and spiny holothurians.

And then the conger eel was silent, and the nervous students suspected it had dozed off without actually finishing the story. This wouldn't be the first time such a thing had happened, and none of them could make heads nor tails of what they'd heard. If it were a cautionary tale, where exactly was the caution? If it was a morality tale, what was possibly meant to be the moral? But none among them dared wake the storyteller to ask these or any other question, lest they wind up with the whiting, being slowly digested in the gut of their instructor. It was safer by far to simply, quietly swim away and not worry themselves over the ramblings of a senile old conger eel. There would be some explanation farther along, or there would not. After all, it couldn't possibly have been more than a fable, they reasoned, for everyone knows that a human woman has never become a daughter of the sea.

— 30 —

It has too often occurred to you that there is no end to the incarnations that Hell may assume. Hell, or merely hell, or simply damnation. And that most of these incarnations are the product of your own doing, restraints, and limitations. You certainly do not need Dante Alighieri, Gustave Doré, Hieronymus Bosch, or St. fucking Paul and his Second Epistle to the Thessalonians to paint the picture for you. You know it well enough without reference to the hells of others. You sit in the black chair in front of your desk, and it stares you in the face. Hell sits on that same desk, splashed across a glossy 17-inch LED screen framed in snow-white polycarbonate. Hell is the scant few inches between your eyes and that screen, the space between any given story's climax and the fleeting moment of relief when you can finally type THE END and mean it. And know it's true. Hell is the emptiness that prevents you from reaching the release that comes with those six letters. You have precious few wards against this Hell. Prayers are worse than useless. Barring intervention, solution will only come when it comes, when it's good and ready, deadlines be damned (not unlike you).

In interviews, you have played the braggart and spoken of the effortlessness of finding endings. You've said how you generally allow them to take care of themselves. You've also said that the only *true* endings are organic, an inevitable outcome dictated by the path of the story and cannot ever be things that may be determined *a priori*. Not things which should be known beforehand and then written towards. You once said, in a moment of inspired, self-congratulatory arrogance:

No story has a beginning, and no story has an end. Beginnings and endings may be conceived to serve a purpose, to serve a momentary and transient intent, but they are, in their fundamental nature, arbitrary and exist solely as a convenient construct in the mind of man.

Oh, how you smiled when you cobbled together that stately gem. Nabokov and Faulkner should have been half so clever, you thought at the time. Still and all. These proclamations will not now save you from Perdition. Sure, you've thirty-four fine-tuned pages of text trapped there in MS Word 11.2, but without those closing paragraphs – however organic and arbitrary they may prove to be – you have only thirty-four *worthless* pages.

So, you sit and stare.

Like fabled Jesus in olive-shrouded Gethsemane, you'd sweat blood, were that an option.

For the better part of this week in January, you sit and stare at that deadly precipice which lies a third of the way down the aforementioned page thirty-four. Somewhere in you should lie the conclusion, which ought to be perfectly obvious. Which should, as you've said, follow from all the rest, no matter how arbitrary the final text may prove to be. It only has to tie everything up neat and pretty. You ask no more than that.

You sit and stare.

You read the last lines you wrote aloud, repeatedly, until they've been drained almost entirely of whatever meaning they might once have held. You recite your stalled-out, dead-end litany:

Not like the dogs and rats. Not like us.

You drink bitter black coffee and chew your ragged nails and prowl the internet, finding momentary solace in the distraction offered up by various sorts of pornography you manage to pretend are "research." You answer email. You look over your shoulder at the calendar nailed to your wall, and you note all the days marked off and how few remain. You gaze out the window at the windows of other houses and at stark, leafless trees, at shivering squirrels and sparrows. And nothing comes to you. And nothing comes. And nothing comes again.

And on the seventh curs'd day of this rapidly accreting void, you bite down hard on the proverbial bullet. Being damned (as has been made clear), there remains within you hardly any fear of falling any farther into this or that flaming or glacial or shit-filled pit. You *know* your particular Hell, and you've been consigned there by your own inability, and you will be consigned there again, and again. If time permits, you admit defeat and hide failure in a computer file labeled simply, honestly, "Shelved."

But today time does not permit. You haven't the luxury of surrender. Today requires a balm, and having reached the point of "at any cost whatsoever," you bite your lip (like that bullet) and accept the steep price of that balm.

You have a photocopied sheet of paper you found thumbtacked to a bulletin board of a coffeehouse you frequent when you can afford to do so, which isn't all that often. You keep the flier inside a first-edition copy of Richard Adams' *Shardik* (Allen Lane, 1974). There's no significance to the book you chose; the selection was made at random. Random as ever random may be. You take out the photocopy, which is folded in half, and you smooth the creased paper flat against the peeling wood laminate of your desk. You light a cigarette (because this is the sort of day made for backsliding) and squint through smoke at the words printed on the page, the cryptic phrases that required many weeks to puzzle out, having been accompanied by no codex. You have three-times before resorted to *this*, this last resort (the white flag most assuredly isn't a resort, unless you decide that homelessness is an option).

When all else fails, you take out the flier. Across the top of the page are printed two words, spelled out in all caps and some unfamiliar bold-face font: ENDINGS GUARANTEED. When all else fails, this is the parachute that might see you returned safely to terra firma, with nothing shattered but your dignity and another drab of sanity.

When all else fails, you go to see the fairies.

On your way out of the apartment you share with your girlfriend and three cats (two Siamese, one tortoise-shell mutt), you pause before a mirror. The woman who stares back at you looks sick. Not flu sick or head-cold sick, but *sick*. Her eyes are bloodshot and puffy, the bags beneath them gone dark as ripening plums. Her complexion is only a few shades shy of jaundiced. At forty, she could easily pass for the rough end of fifty, or fifty-five. You grab your wool cap, your keys, and your threadbare coat. You forget your mittens. You think about leaving a note, then think better of it. Your sudden absences are not unexpected, and you're not in the mood to write anything at all. A grocery list has more of a plot and considerably more subtext than you're willing to undertake at the moment.

You shut and lock the door, follow the stairs down to the lobby, and step out into the bright, freezing day. The sidewalks are slippery with ice, and the streets and gutters are filled with a slush of white-gray-black snow, a week old and still not completely melted away. There's also sand in the slush, and salt, and all manner of trash – broken beer bottles, plastic soda bottles, torn bits of paper, cigarette butts, what looks too much like a soiled diaper to be anything else.

The photocopied page is in your coat pocket now, and you absent-mindedly finger it as you walk to the bus stop. The thing about fairies, you think, is that they have an inordinate fondness for red tape, a sort of ritual fetish, a hard-on for ceremony, that amounts to nothing more than magical bureaucracy when all is said and done. You dutifully jump through the hoops if you want what they're selling, and you inevitably pay them an arm and a leg for the fucking pleasure. Sometimes literally, or so you've heard. So far, you've been lucky in your dealings with the local Unseelie and haven't lost any limbs, or very much of your mind. Just your dignity, which seems like a fair enough shake, since dignity is a commodity few writers can afford.

You catch the bus on Westminster. It's almost empty, and stinks of sweat and diesel fumes. The bus is too warm, overcompensating for the winter weather. You stare out at the ugly, slushy Providence streets. You pull the flier from a coat pocket and read it over again, though you've long since committed these weary stations of the cross to memory. Your fingers have worn the flier as smooth as rosary beads. You've looked for other copies, on other bulletin boards, or stapled to telephone poles, or duct-taped to the see-thru Plexiglas walls of bus stops. But this is the only one you've ever seen. It might be the only one ever sent out into the world, and you might be the only sucker who's taken the bait. But you seriously doubt it. More like you get one shot at the brass ring and one shot only. Pass it by, and the chance won't ever come again. You've imagined all sorts of fliers like this one – not *exactly* the same, but the gist would be the same. Maybe fliers promising fertility to sterile would-be parents, riches to the destitute, houses for the homeless, sex changes to transsexuals, banquets for gluttons, true love for the lovelorn.

You ride all the way through downtown, across the river, to College Hill. You get off when the bus stops on Wickenden Street. There's a narrow alleyway between a Thai restaurant and a used record shop, a shop that sells actual vinyl records instead of CDs. You walk all the way to the back and stand beside a dumpster and empty cardboard boxes that once held Singha and Chang beer. The alley stinks of rotting food and urine and dirty snow, but at least you don't have to wait very long. The goblin that lives beneath the pavement peeks its head out the fourth time you knock your wind-chapped knuckles against the dumpster. It recognizes you straightaway and smiles, showing off a mouthful of crooked brown teeth.

"Oh," it mutters and rubs its indigo eyes. "You again. The poet come lookin' for a rhyme. The word beggar." The goblin's voice sounds the way the gutter slush looks.

"I'm not a goddamn poet," you tell the goblin, glancing back towards the entrance to the alley to be sure no one's stopped to watch you talking to nothing they can see, because they don't have a ticket, because they've never found a flier of their own.

"Fine. The spinner of penny awfuls, then. The madame dyke of the story papers. What the fuck ever you wish." The goblin stops smiling and begins chewing at one of its thick pea-green toenails. It seems to have forgotten you're standing there.

"Same as before," you finally say when you've grown tired of waiting. The goblin stops gnawing at it's foot and glares up at you. "I need to find Pigwidgeon again."

"Of course you do," he snorts. "Color me surprised. Didn't think you'd come for the time a day. So, what you got to trade? Ol' Pigwidgeon, you know he don't like being disturbed, so we ain't talking trinkets and baubles. You know that, right?"

"Yeah, I know that."

"Right. So, what you got to trade me, poet? What's it you can bear to part with this lovely afternoon?" The goblin farts and goes back to chewing its toenails.

"A memory," you tell it. "The memory of my first good review in the *Washington Post* and how I celebrated the night after I read it. How's that?"

"A mite stingy," the goblin mumbles around a mouthful of big toe. "What you think I want with the wistful reminiscences of a mid-list novelist?"

"It's better than last time," you reply. "That's what I've got. That's *all* I've got for you today."

The goblin spits, then glares at you again. It's indigo eyes swim with an iridescent sheen like motor oil on a mud puddle. "Well now," it sneers, "look at who's went and got herself all pertinacious. Look at who thinks she's grown a backbone. You calling the shots now, poet? That how you got it figured?" and before you can answer, the goblin has begun to crawl back into it's place beneath the asphalt.

"No, no, no," you say too quickly, all at once close to panic and silently cursing yourself for mouthing off, for trying to circumnavigate protocol. You shiver and glance towards the entrance to the alley again. "It means a lot to me. It really does. It's not a bauble. It's one of the most precious—"

"Seems that way to you, sure," the goblin interrupts. It's crouched half under the blacktop, half out. It snickers and closes one eye. "Always the way with mortals. Your heads all full of junk seems *precious,* but what you think don't necessarily go and make it so. So, sweeten the pot, or I'm going back down to finish my nap, which you so rudely disturbed, might I bloody well add."

And you want to tell this little green shit to fuck off. You want to turn and walk away, get back on the bus, go back to your apartment and the empty place where page thirty-four dried up. But you know yourself well enough to know better, and you're too cold and tired to stand here haggling with the goblin all damn day. Easier to concede. Old habits die hard, and you've been conceding your whole life, so why get haughty and stop now?

"That review and the memory of the celebration afterwards," you say once more, then hastily add, before you can think better of it, "*and* the last hour of my life."

The goblin grins his dirty brown grin, and his ears perk up, and his oily blue-black eyes shimmer. "Now, that's a whole lot more like it, poet. Got yourself a deal. In fact, you can keep the silly old review. Got no use for it. The hour's ample fare." And so he tells you where to find the elf named Pigwidgeon, the sulking, melancholy elf who never leaves his dusty attic, but who's dusty attic is never in the same place two days in a row.

You feel something icy and sharp pass through your belly, colder times ten than the bitter January air, and for a second you think you might vomit. But it passes. The goblin has what he wants, and he gives you an address on Benevolent Street (the irony isn't lost on you) before scurrying back beneath the alleyway. You want to run away and not look back, but you don't dare. That's one of the first lessons you learned about fairies: Never, ever run away. It inevitably makes them suspicious and apt to reconsider the terms of any bargain. So, you stand staring at the empty cardboard boxes for a little longer, smelling the reek from the dumpster, then you *slowly* turn and walk away, repeating the address over and over to yourself.

As the sun slinks down towards dusk, trading late afternoon for the last dregs of the day, you follow the goblin's directions and the red-brick trail of Benefit Street. Hands stuffed into coat pockets, you walk quickly between stately rows of 18th and 19th century architecture, that procession of gambrel roofs, bay windows, and sensible Georgian masonry. You pass historical landmarks and the towering white steeple of the oldest Baptist church in America, the red clapboard saltbox where President Washington slept on more than one occasion.

You turn right onto the steep incline of Benevolent Street, and here's the address you've been given, just one block from the Brown University campus. You silently stare warily at the building for two or three minutes, because you're pretty sure it wasn't there the last time you passed this way. You're pretty sure that the houses to the east and west of it once abutted one another, with hardly ten feet in between the two. But you know the routine well enough not to question the peculiarities and impossibilities that accompany this journey. Not to look too closely. You've entered a secret country. So you let it go, full in the knowledge that the house that wasn't here a week before (though it looks at least two hundred years old) won't be here the next time you happen by this spot.

The front door isn't locked, and the house is empty. No furniture. No evidence of occupants. No rugs or draperies or pictures hanging on the walls. You climb the stairs to the second floor and then the third (never mind that when viewed from the street, there were clearly only *two* floors before the attic). At the end of a narrow hallway, you find the pull-down trapdoor set into the ceiling, and you tug at a jute rope, lowering a rickety set of steps that lead up into Pigwidgeon's moveable garret.

Even in the dead of winter, the attic is bathed in all the sharp and spicy aromas of autumn. There are tapestries covering the walls, hiding patches of the peeling wallpaper from view, and the elf sits in a tattered armchair in the center of the room. This is the garret's single piece of furniture, the entire house's single stick of furniture, so far as you can see. The chair is upholstered in satin the color of pomegranates. It looks like cats have used it as a scratching post.

You learned Pigwidgeon's story the first time you listened to the flier and grew desperate enough to go seeking after ENDINGS GUARANTEED. Here he sits, the spurned fairy knight who fell in love and wooed Queen Mab of the Winter Court and so brought down upon his head all the ire of Oberon.

"Where is my wife, thou rogue?" quoth he,
"Pigwidgeon, she is come to thee;
Restore her, or thou diest by me!"

His skin is pale as milk, and his hair is even paler, almost translucent. It almost looks spun from glass. His silver eyes are filled with starlight.

"You again," he sighs in a voice like soured honey and wilted flowers. His voice is as weary as you feel, and there's about it a blankness even more absolute than the stubborn emptiness on page thirty-four. Seeing him, hearing him, you want to turn tail and run away home.

"The hob sent you," he sighs. "The hob can't keep his mouth shut, not if some delicacy is dangled before him. One day, I'll take up needle and sinew and sew that filthy squealer's lips together."

You almost say, *I can come back some other time,* but all days are the wrong day to seek an audience with Pigwidgeon, and you've already paid too dear a price to turn back now. Instead, you say, "You know why I'm here. Ask your price, and I'll pay it. I need to find the shop. I have a deadline."

"And you take the easy way out," the fairy sneers. "You sorry, pitiful mortals, so willing to barter with your souls, rather than unriddle a bewilderment by your own faculties. You're cowards, every mother's son of you, every mother's daughter, every whore or rake's bastard child."

"Then my failings are your gain," you reply. When facing Pigwidgeon, nothing is more sure to tilt the scales in your favor than an out-and-out admission of human weakness.

"You'll regret this, one day or one night," he assures you. "And, given how short the span of your days, the regret shall come sooner rather than later."

"You're not telling me anything I don't already know."

The fairy scowls and picks at the ruined upholstery.

"Would you give me every drop of blood in your veins?" he asks without meeting your eyes. "Would you grant me every breath you would have taken from this moment on?"

"I think that would defeat the purpose," you reply. This is part of Pigwidgeon's song and dance, dog and pony, the exorbitant arrangements he suggests before naming the same price he always asks.

"Would you grant me the life of the woman you love? Would you give me both your eyes?"

And, just like always, you refuse him these things. And, just like always, he finally, inevitably, demands his reward for sending you off to the one who knows the current whereabouts of the shop that sells the services advertised on the flier from the coffeehouse.

"Fine," he says and stops picking at the frayed pomegranate upholstery. "Then it's settled. Take off your clothes, woman. Take off your clothes and come to me. Every stitch. Every scrap. Come to me naked as the day you were birthed."

You begin to undress, and Pigwidgeon smiles from his raggedy throne. The air in the garret is as warm as an October evening, and no warmer; when you stand before the hungry fairy, your arms and legs are pricked with gooseflesh. He raises his alabaster head and furrows his brow, appraising his purchase and, as always, finding it wanting.

"Such an ugly, hollow countenance," he frowns. "And yet one such as you was deemed fit vessel for a soul, while all the fair folk go without. Proof of the madness of God."

You agree with him, purposefully making the same mistake you always make, and Pigwidgeon stands and slaps you so hard you taste blood. He tells you to be silent unless told to speak, and you nod and stare at the bare floorboards, your feet, his boots. This is nothing you haven't earned, by your own shortcomings, your own devotion to the path of least resistance. You're temptation's bitch and won't ever argue otherwise.

"I've seen more comely bogarts," he whispers, leaning close. His breath smells of dying roses. "I've seen cowslug sprites with a more rightful claim to beauty. But even the foulest clay may be fashioned into an exquisite simulacrum, in the hands of a skillful artist." Then he paints you with a glamour that he might spend the next hour or two pretending you're not the aging, corporeal woman whose come to beg a good turn. You become the image of his lost queen. You are clothed in her chartreuse and malachite complexion and a gown woven from dew and spider silk (which your lover tears away). You take him inside of you. And you suffer the violence and gentle moments of Pigwidgeon's affections and deliver all your lines on cue, as scripted fifteen score years before you were born.

You have never yet learned, nor even tried to learn, why the second and third and fourth fairies move about as they do. Why each time you seek the shop, their whereabouts have changed. You suspect, though, that it may not be the fairies who move about, but, rather, the thin places between worlds that shift, those points on the city map where they may be encountered. You also know far too little about the taxonomy of fairies to know, for certain, what the third creature in the chain might be rightly called. You could make guesses, and you have, but they're not educated guesses and you set little stock by them. Were you a betting woman, you'd never play those odds. But she is always called up from water, and like Pigwidgeon and the alley goblin, her price is fixed. You come to her knowing what it's going to cost, knowing exactly what you'll lose and exactly what you'll gain. The hob takes a memory. The elf takes your body and the pretense of passion. And the third fairy, she takes a song. It's a bad joke. You can gain her indulgences for a song, when there's nothing the least bit cheap about the fee.

By the time Pigwidgeon is done with you and has restored your own face, by the time you leave his attic and the house that won't be there the next time you visit Benevolent Street, sleet is falling from the cloudy Providence sky, a sky that glows orange with reflected streetlights and the lights of parking lots and all the bright lights that burn because human beings will never cease to be afraid of the dark. You have a feeling there will be snow before dawn. The air smells like snow.

Last time you sought out the blue lady (you don't even have a name for her), the elf sent you to the old marble drinking fountain (ca. 1813) in front of the Athenaeum. The time before that, he sent you to the muddy banks of the Seekonk River behind Swan Point Cemetery. This time, he says you can find her in the women's restroom of the train depot on Gaspee Street across from the south façade of the capitol building. You catch a taxi, because you're too cold and much too tired to walk all the way from College Hill.

The restroom is all mirrors and white tiled floors, the stench of disinfectant and the lingering undertone of urine that can't be scrubbed away. But it's empty. No one sees you enter, unless it was whoever sits on the other end of the security cameras. This isn't going to take long. It never does. But there's still the fear that someone will walk in and find you talking to yourself. You do as you've been told and enter the third stall on the left and flush the toilet four times after dropping a sprig of thyme into the bowl (you only almost laugh at the undeniable absurdity of the ritual). Then you return to the long mirror above the row of sinks. Whatever else she might be, she's punctual, and you don't have to wait very long. She appears behind you, and you know better than to turn and look directly at her. Do that, and she'll vanish. Do that, and it'll be as if she were never there, and worse, she'll never come to you again. Usually, you manage this trick with a compact; tonight, she's made it easier.

"I remember you," she says. "You're the poetess."

"I'm not a poet," you reply. "I write novels," and she smiles at that.

"I remember you," she says again. Her voice is all the innumerable sounds that water makes. You could make a list of analogies as long as your arm and never reach the end. Her voice has been fashioned from all the wet places of the world. Her voice is a prosopoeia of water.

"I need to find the shop again," you tell her. "I need to find the shopkeeper."

She smiles, unhinging her jaw to reveal row upon row of translucent needle teeth that would be better suited to the mouth of some deep-sea fish. Just another wonder in the tedious string of wonders, that she can speak with teeth like that. Her eyes are as black as hot tar, and they gleam and glisten beneath the fluorescent bulbs. Her skin glistens, as well, the deep blue of glass infused with cobalt ions. Her lips are the vivid Majorelle blue of Berber burnouses. Her long wet cerulean hair hangs down about her shoulders and breasts, but doesn't conceal either sapphire nipple. There's webbing between her fingers and toes, and she's never come to you dressed in any garment more modest than her flesh. She drips, and rivulets wind down her legs to puddle at her feet.

"Then you'll sing for me," she says. "You'll sing for me a sweet, sweet song you'll never hear again but that it brings a sense of regret and loss so keen as to be almost unbearable. You'll never hear this song again without weeping. From this night forth it will always be a lament, a requiem, the most sorrowful of threnodies and nothing more, so choose carefully, poetess. And remember, it has to be a song that is dear to you. Dear to you almost as much as the woman you love. Take the time you require. I am patient. I can wait."

But you decided before you left home which song it would be this time. So you answer her immediately. And she licks her narrow lips with a tongue like India ink.

"Now," she says, "you must sing it for me, each and every word, every note. You must sing it with all your heart, understanding this will be the last time you shall take even the meanest portion of joy in the act."

You half heartedly pray to a god you haven't believed in since childhood that someone will come in and interrupt. You wish someone would. A passenger in a hurry, late for her train. The janitor. Anyone at all would do.

But then your weakness passes, and you sing for her, a Kris Kristofferson song your father taught you.

She shuts her black eyes and listens.

The eerie acoustics of the depot's restroom makes something lilting and unfamiliar of your voice. This is a song you love, and now you're letting it go forever.

"Oh," she said: "Casey, it's been so long since I've seen you.

"Here," she said: "just a kiss to make a body smile.

"See," she said: "I've put on new stockings just to please you.

"Lord," she said. "Casey, can you only stay a while?"

When you've finished, she leans forward and whispers the whereabouts of the shop into you ear (always your left ear, never the right). Her teeth click, and her breath smells like seaweed and silt and brine.

"Your voice is lovely," she says before stepping back and fading from view. "You may come sing for me any time."

You stare at your dingy self in the mirror for a while, and splash your face with water so cold it stings. You dry your face with a brown paper towel from the dispenser mounted on the wall.

The blue woman didn't give you an address. Instead, she gave you an image, the awareness of a point in space and time, a conjunction where and when the shop will be, very briefly, accessible by any who are trying to find it. Odds are very, very good that you're the only one. You know that, which somehow makes the whole business that much worse. You can't excuse your actions with a simple "Everybody else is doing it, so why shouldn't I?" You attempt to find consolation in the fantasy that there exist a thousand other copouts at least as execrable as whoring oneself out, piece by piece, to a quartet of fay. The attempt fails utterly, but you settle for the meager solace of having tried. After the train station, you walk. The sleet has changed over to enormous snowflakes that spiral lazily down from the orange Rhode Island sky, frosting the city, dusting lawns and rooftops and sidewalks. If it keeps this up, by morning the unsightly crust of the last snowfall will be buried and hidden decently away, and the snowplows will be making the rounds.

You consider catching another taxi. Two or three pass you by, but you don't flag them down. Suddenly, taking a taxi seems like another brand of cheating, that warm, effortless ride for a few dollars. Better the long walk through the night and the gathering storm, better the wind's tiny, invisible knives slicing at your unprotected face. If you can't butch up and withstand the incompleteness of page thirty-four, much less summon the acumen necessary to complete it, you can endure so minor a tribulation. Let the two-mile walk be your half-hearted hairshirt; it's hardly St. Catherine of Siena with her sackcloth and thrice daily scourgings. You put one foot in front of the other, leaving tracks in the freshly fallen snow.

Past the Biltmore and the bus mall, you ford the slate-dark Moshassuck River at Kennedy Plaza. Heading east, you cross South Water and South Main and Benefit streets to Waterman, which leads you all the way to Hope Street where you turn north. Your shoes are wet and your feet are on fire. You grit your teeth so they don't chatter and manage to block out the worst of the chill by counting your footsteps. You wonder if any among the fairies practice mortification of the flesh. But, then, why would they? With no souls to lose, why ever deny or punish themselves the way that women and men do in all their fruitless bids for forgiveness and salvation. The fairies know better. Even Pigwidgeon locked in the cloistered, mock-asceticism of his garret is a decadent, sating his darkest appetites whenever the opportunity arises.

You let Hope Street lead you all the way to the redbrick and silver dome of the observatory. If there's any significance in being treated to two domes in a single night, it's lost on you. All that matters is that the blue woman hasn't led you astray, and waiting between you and the observatory is what could easily, at first glance, be mistaken for a tall, unframed looking glass. It's not a mirror, of course. It reflects nothing at all. It's most decidedly accurate to say that its function is, in fact, the opposite of a mirror's. It wasn't constructed to reflect anything, but to permit entry.

You spare a single glance over your shoulder, at the snow piling up, the dark or glowing windows of houses, the street, the stark, bare branches of trees. Your fingers brush across the photocopied flier stuffed into your coat pocket. And then you hold your breath and step through the quicksilver doorway.

You smell nutmeg, mildew, and ammonia, each in its turn, before you step out into the shop. Then there's only a comfortable, musty smell. Just as it's entryway might be mistaken for a looking glass, the dimly lit interior of the fairy shop could be confused with a certain variety of New England antique shop. Not the upscale sort, but the sort that's all clutter and dust, random odds and ends. Odds, mostly. The walls are lined with sagging shelves and wooden red-lacquered apothecary cabinets. On your first visit, you browsed through the drawers of those cabinets. One was stuffed with old theater tickets, the next with doorknobs, a third with bridge and subway tokens, a fourth with skeleton keys, a fifth with the feathers of songbirds, the sixth with a mismatched assortment of chess pieces, and so on and on and on and on. Dried bundles of herbs, peppers, and corn droop from the low ceiling. There are rows of formalin filled jars, and the milky eyes of countless species of fish, serpents, rats, and indescribable fairy creatures gaze blindly out as you walk down the long aisle that leads to the glass display counter and the hulking cash register that seems to double as a typewriter and telegraph machine.

"Took your own sweet time *this* time, poet," the peddler of endings says from her place at the register. The crone of sticks and warts and pebbles is sitting on an aluminum stool that creaks and wobbles alarmingly whenever she moves, as if it's always poised on the verge of dumping her onto the cold concrete floor. "Thought maybe you'd lost your way, or your nerve, or both."

"It's snowing," you reply.

"Does that, most every winter," she snickers and chews at the stem of her ivory pipe. Opium smoke curls from the bowl, forming question marks in the musty atmosphere of the shop. Where her eyes ought to be, there are fat yellow spiders spinning crystalline webs. She points the seventh finger of her right hand at you, raises a bramble eyebrow, and tilts her head to one side.

"I paid them," you whisper. "I paid them, every one."

"You wouldn't be standing here if you hadn't, now would you? Seems somewhat south of likely, don't it?"

You agree and try hard not to stare too long at anything in particular.

"Put you through the wringer," the crone mutters. "Can see that much. A right wicked lot, those three. Steal the meat off your bones, then complain the marrow's not sweet enough by half. Hardly seems decent after all they done, but now I have my own small query."

"I know."

"Ain't so much, mind you. Not after those three. A formality, and hardly more."

"I'm not complaining," you say.

"Very well," she nods, and you imagine one of the yellow spiders is gazing directly at you. "I'd ask why you do this to yourself?"

"What else would I do?" you answer.

"And is it worth it?" asks the crone, blinking her arachnid eyes. "All this hurt for another puny tale?"

"It's what I do," you say, same as every time before. "I write stories. There's not much else to me. And my stories have to end somewhere, even if the endings escape me." The words tumble like lead from your chapped lips.

"Fair enough," says the crone. "Fair enough."

"I held out as long as I could," you add, though she hasn't asked for more. "This time, I made it a whole week."

"Not my place to judge," she replies, and plucks the pipe from her mouth long enough to spit at a clay bowl on the counter. She misses. "Figure you're gonna do plenty enough of that all on your own, poet."

"I'm not a poet," you say.

"Of course you're not," she grins, then presses a single brass key, and the cash register blares a cacophony of thunderclaps, church bells, and the high, cruel laughter of children. She leans over, reaching beneath the counter and rummaging about for a moment. The stool totters and sways, and she curses in several languages all in a single breath.

When she sits up again, she's holding a small white linen bag, tied at the top with a carmine ribbon.

"This is a fine one," she says. "Don't think you'll have any room for complaints. Best denouement I've dispensed in a hare's age. Won't find none better nowhere, not on earth nor heaven nor anywhere in between."

You thank her, and she spits again, misses the bowl again, and instructs you to think nothing of it.

Next time, I'll make it two weeks, you think.

"Of course you will, baby girl. Now, best be on your way. The wheel's turning." She jabs a twisted, thorny finger back the way you've come, and you turn away from the counter, slipping the linen bag into your pocket.

"Fare thee well, poet," the crone says before you step through the argent roil of the unmirror and out onto the curb outside your house. You almost slip going up the icy steps to the front door, and you have more trouble than usual with the lock. Your lover may have waited up for you, and she may not have. She's grown accustomed to your nocturnal walks and hardly ever asks where you've been.

You'll untie the crone's bag in the morning, after you've returned the flier to its place between the pages of *Shardik,* after breakfast and coffee and your first cigarette of the day. You won't think about what it's cost you or how much it'll cost next time, or the time after that. You'll have your ending, guaranteed, and a few days from now you'll loathe every word you've written. There will be no more satisfaction than you find when you take a piss, but none of that matters a whit, not so long as the check clears. You'll email a copy to your editor in Manhattan, print out a copy for yourself, and file it away.

You'll do your best not to dwell on whatever you lost the night before. What's done is done, and regret never paid the bills. You won't worry much what editors or readers will think of the ending.

It only has to tie everything up neat and pretty. You ask no more than that.

For Robyn Guilford, wherever she has gone.

The Carnival is Dead and Gone

"This ain't nothin'," Chaser tells me as we weave and push and squeeze our way through the first-floor crowd. The air stinks of tobacco smoke, hashish, pot, burning cocaine, pipe-blazing acronym chemical concoctions to spawn hallucinogenic epiphanies that are no more or less true than any other lie. The air smells like sweat, bile, vanilla, shit, frankincense, piss, sandalwood, spilled beer, vomited beer, smoldering sage, hot steel, mold, bergamot, frying meat. The air pulses with two hundred voices screaming to be heard above one another and throbs with toothache bass spilling from speakers mounted almost everywhere and with the hammer-on-iron intonations of the talker, unrolling his spiel for the marks. "If this ain't nothing," I say into Chaser's left ear, "what the hell would something be?" So she points at the floor and tells me, just wait until we're below. "Just you wait, you fucker, and you'll see exactly what I mean." And I will admit, I'm a taut cherry to this whole menagerie, this scene, to be perfectly fucking quaint, if you will. I wouldn't even have asked Chaser to get me into a shitpit like this shitpit if the Feed wasn't asking for a tale, half a thousand words to sum up the likes of Golden Merry and the other Ballyhoos dotting the Lower East Side. Those catwalk streets suspended above the floodwaters, those rotten-apple dangling habitations where the clubs have popped up last two or three years. Down here, Manhattan real estate is just shy of free, and it shows. All these cast-off and stolen shipping containers welded together into some vague semblance of architecture. All these long and windowless rooms and their sordid exhibitions. Cross the olden times sideshows with Bangkok sex clubs with abattoirs, do that, and you're getting close to shitpits the likes of Golden Merry.

"Now," Chaser screams at me in a shrill falsetto she must have cultivated for just such an eventuality as this, "We'll look about, sure. But don't mistake this for the real deal. This is the poseur pedestal, that's all. Most these chumps and bumps, you ain't gonna catch 'em dead down in the hold. Mostly, they come 'cause this is the place to be seen and score and no more or less than that."

Chaser is a font of social commentary.

A regular pop-culture virtuoso.

So, she gets us vodka and schnapps, and I take in all the "this ain't nothin'" I can glimpse between the yammering patrons. I've done a little homework, hence it's not all a revelation. The towering display of pickled punks, just for example. Jars of formalin or whatever keeps them best preserved. I've read most are shipped in from Pakistan and India and Korea, because the late war was good for the mutated fetus trade. All those free-range isotopes might as well not go to waste, might as well give us something besides cancer. Though, the jars hold not much of anything I *wouldn't* deem tumors, malignancies excised from swollen bellies, ectopic whatsits gone pale as cheese in their see-through sarcophagi. Maybe not all spawn of women, because I glimpse appendages and organs not even the most radiated DNA base sequence misfire could produce from a human genotype. And sure, I know lots are fake, what the menagerie scene refers to as *gaffs*. Oh, that's one especially charming aspect of the shitpits, the resurrection of carny argot what died off by the end of the 20th C, and they offer it up with straight faces and beaming, earnest sarcasm. Fuck'em.

One end of this shipping crate, it's the famed (to use the term underhandedly) carousel. Chaser bulldozes her way through the crowd, me yanked along all slipstream like, until we're pressed up against the low metal bars keeping the horde from swamping the creaking, clanking contraption. Now, back in the overrated Once Upon A Time of yore, I know because (as noted) I done my research, these amusements were wooden horses or wooden camels or ostriches or huge goddamn kitty cats or whatthehellever. But now ain't then, nor even close, and tastes are not so tame as once they were. This ride is not its historical predecessor, meant for squealing children out for brass rings and the pure up-and-down, roundabout joy. This is The Wheel. Read about it already, so I knew what to expect, more or less, and it's about the worst, says Chaser, we're gonna see topside. Fuck the sword swallowers, the hermaphrodite what eats live rats, the popeye, pierced and holotatted, Evelyn the Python Lover, fuck the dancers and the sex acts and contortionists with their backbending, frontbending, dislocations and enterologies. This is The Wheel of Flesh, as advertised on the gaudy canvas panoramas strung up outside the shitpit. As ugly (in the eye of the beholder, I will grant) as you're gonna peep first floor, Chaser assures me. And it's maybe not bad enough to make me have second thoughts. I already had my second thoughts at the stench of the place and the fucking noise. But, on the other hand, The Wheel does give one pause. Even one whom, like myself, has come here oh so boldly thinking himself prepared for the puppet show. I have been forewarned, visually, but the shots were grubby, nubilous as fuck all and back. But still, it's not so much. A turn on, even, and I go so far as to laugh and tell Chaser we ought have a spin. Just joking, but joking says a lot, right?

The Wheel goes round and round, tilting a little in it's revolutions, a purposeful wobble to add that extra zing. No one ever gets enough, so you gotta have the extra zing, a dash of capsaicin to eyes already scalded by lachrymatory phenacyl chloride sprays. It's all goddamn over-stimulation down on Carny Row, so let it come as no surprise, you sorry rube. Chaser, she points to the gaily appointed gallopers on their shiny poles. She points with the prosthetic right hand could pass for real if she bothered, but Chaser won't wear a cosmesis, better whirring joints and bolts and exposed wires. Lost the hand to a case of the rot two years ago, which ain't so not to be expected, you spend as much time as she spends slumming the Lower East. I know she got it off a whore, but she won't cop to that. Anyway, she points, like I wasn't already gawking at the living women and men in their leather harnesses and polyurethane stirrups and the up-and-down pole shoved up their distended assholes, urethras, vaginas. I know the specs, how the machinery keeps them safe from fatal injury. But I *also* know a few months at that job takes a toll on a body. Stay on too long, come the prolapsed bits and pieces and such like. The air is split by what only sounds like a calliope, and those men and women go round and round, bearing the various weights of their riders, seemingly with no strain at all. Bodies painted and polished, so they might *pass* for wood, contacts so those eyes look no more than inert. Bells and whistles to complete the illusion. Sometimes, two or three bound ingeniously together, saddles in improbable places, anatomies held in place with trusses and struts and invisible wires, spines supported by metallic cradles. What's more, pay the extra $250, you can have a jolly rollicking bj or hand job or fuck while the you take your spin. A few are fitted with artificial orifices or phalluses to this very end, as their actual crotches and points of entry are being employed by The Wheel's most basic needs. We watch for half an hour, maybe, but we don't ride. Oh, I do consider the centaur, and a mossy dryad, but Chaser is all ribbons and bows about dragging me below for the main attraction.

"Pace yourself, kiddo. Miles to go 'fore you blow your wad, eh? Don't want to shoot the whole lot upstairs. Like I said, ain't seen nothin' yet." She yells, and I'm mostly still having to read her lips (which I'm absolutely no good at, by the by). "Seem," she says, "you're just the sting the strong-arms got their sights on. The easy money."

"You say so," I say, it not mattering to me whether she hears or doesn't hear. Maybe better if she don't. Last thing I need is Chaser getting ticked at me, leaving me down here to fend for myself. Last thing I need is to miss my deadline because I can't keep my mouth shut and my libido on a short leash.

"Glad you like, though," she says and smiles her silver grin (rot took most her teeth, too). "Always a plus on my end the newbs don't bolt or sick up on my shoes. Then again," and here the well-measured pause to make my resolve wobble same as The Wheel. "Then again, you ain't seen nothin' yet. So we'll see what we'll see."

She tears me away, and we reenact our weave and push and squeeze feat of derring-do and eventually reach the green door that admits the bold and brave to The Sink, as the lower level of Golden Merry is generally known. The door's surrounded by glowing blue neon tubing and two bouncers, one male and one female, and both look like they could take down a grizzly bear if the need ever fucking arose. Not just nobody goes down to The Sink, as there have been incidents, but I have Chaser and she's a regular at the ballyhoos. They know her face, know her creds, know she's not gonna start any sort of ruckus down below.

We stand in front of that green door, green-blue because of the neon, and she chats up the towering caryatid juicers, those anabolic ripped son-and-daughter of bitches, and I think it's just a shame they're not identical twins. That would make for yet another fine attraction in the shitpit freak show. Anyway, the not-twins, they *unlock* the green door for Chaser, literally, and we step across that threshold onto an on-beyond-rickety spiral staircase, rusty steel winding down maybe thirty feet through clouds of smoke so dense it burns my eyes and I have to be very careful I don't miss a step and go tumbling ass over tits. Just like upstairs, a lot of it's cannabis and what have you, but there's a lot of smoke-machine action going on, as well. "You didn't tell me I'd need a goddamn respirator," I grumble, but probably not loud enough Chaser actually hears me. We come to the bottom, and there are two more bouncers, both male this time, or at least passing for male, and they pat us down roughly while making polite chit-chat with Chaser. She told me to expect this, because, like I said, there have been incidents, some involving weapons, some others involving cameras, which are strictly forbidden, same as upstairs only more so.

Then we're past the security goons, and right away I notice there's maybe only a third the crowd there was upstairs. Which is a relief. And it's not half so loud down here, so I figure there must be some pretty good soundproofing overhead (or underfoot, if you're topside). Chaser leans close and says, "First off, we get a few of the Question Mark Shows," and it turns out they're not so different from the pickled punks upstairs, excepting it's a lot harder to look at them without feeling at least a little queasy. "Probably two thirds are just silicone and whatnot," Chaser adds. Not that this bit of intel makes looking at them any easier. I will note, for one, unlike the pyramid of fetal teratisms above, this lot's mostly the purported corpses of adult malformations. There they are, all lined up in lexan tanks of yellowish fluid. The ones that have eyes gaze blindly out at we voyeurs. Chaser seems to get off on them, and we dally here longer than I'd have thought, given what I've been told lies farther along the shipping-crate hallway. "Jesus and Allah," she quietly exclaims and points at one tank in particular. A naked female thing, its mottled skin reminding me of nothing so much as a fine Gorgonzola, emphasis on *gorgon*. Her or its arms are folded across the sunken chest, the withered breasts, and I will not here attempt an accurate description of the genitalia that so fascinated Chaser. The whole hideous thing gets me thinking of fungi, of the sorts of infections you hear about coming out of the blight zones down in Brazil and Ecuador.

"We could move along," I say, "and I wouldn't mind at all."

"Oh, come, come," she replies. "You got the stomach for this shite. I fucking know you do, so don't go getting squishy on me right off the bat. You tellin' me she's given you the willies?"

"No," I lie, and I'm a lousy liar so I know she knows I'm lying, but whatever. "But I want to see the hardcore attractions, all that crazy bushwa you been going on about."

Chaser stares at me a few seconds, then glances back at the Question Mark (later on, she explained they're called that since no one bothers to label any of them and you have to guess at what you're seeing). "Fine," she says. "But Jesus and Allah, that one makes me wet," and she points again.

"You're easy," I tell Chaser, and she punches me in the arm hard enough I'm sincere as a coronary when I curse and tell her to stop being a goddamn cunt.

"And you, my dear, you're a squeam," she snickers and takes my hand and leads me through the other Clems, all those hard-ons and sweaty palms and racing pulses. No one looks at me. No one looks at anything but the exhibits, all lined up bright as Christmas. But down in The Sink, the talkers (the scene eschews the term "barker") aren't bellowing like their first-floor counterparts. Most have headset mikes, so no need to shout. And softer voices are far more effective, I find. These talkers, they have the luxury of titillation and sultry insinuation. Also, no pounding music down below, and I think that's because it would only prove distracting. And there's no tolerance, I think, for that sort of distraction in The Sink. People have come to see what people have come to see, not have their eardrums reduced to jelly by deafeningly, aggressively shitsome djs.

Not gonna dwell in loving detail on all we see while strolling through the lengthy corridor of The Sink (three of those containers, laid end to end, and dangling only a few feet above the water where Delancey Street used to be). I endeavor not to think about whatever's holding this whole place up giving way and dropping into the bay. Not too damn high on the list of ways I want to punch out, drowning in that filthy water, trapped in a tin box full of freaks and the assholes who make of them a fetish.

But I digress.

We pause, in turn, before almost every stage and podium and, yeah, to be honest, the cages, too. Lots of genetic and surgical and biomech make-overs down there, and it ain't no lie to say some are easier on the eyes than others. The mermaid is more than decent enough. Sexy enough. She's one of the sites I'd read about beforehand, and even seen a halfway not-crappy photo of, floating somewhere in the offgrid d-stream. I haven't meant to imply I'm too good or above getting off on bizarro Ballyhoo fare. But, now that I *say* that, I remember I've already set down my reactions to The Wheel (and here I am digressing again). The mermaid, whom the talker calls Djullanar the Sea-Girl, after a tale from the *Arabian Nights*, isn't so much the old cliché beauty only fishy from the waist down that most would expect. Oh, there's a tail, long and sinuous, the color of coal, more reminiscent of an eel than anything else. Anguilliform. The skin on her chest and back, throat and face, is several shades lighter, and nearer an iridescent deep, deep blue than anthracitic black. Her fingers are exquisitely long, and webbed all the way up to their clawed ends. So, not so much hands as paddles, to get anatomical, nomenclatural, and just imagine, I think, the right damn damage she could do with those talons. For talons they certainly were. Her tank is filled with water top to bottom, no breathing space left above, so the docs had made this one fully fucking aquatic. The gill flaps (operculae) are right there below her sharp chin line, and they rise and fall, pumping water across feathery crimson filaments. Her breasts are so small as to be almost unnoticeable, and she has no nipples. A line of stickleback fins extends from a spot between her shoulder blades all the way down to the end of that eel-like tail. No visible scales, and this, too, makes me think of eels. Or sharks. I'll get purple and say her eyes are orbs plucked from out a starless, moonless sky, all those decades back before when the heavens were not yet set ablaze by the omnipresent glow demanded by humanity's collective nyctophobia. Her hair trails like tangled seaweed, and I can't help but wonder if she's ever been permitted to swim free. Or if her keepers fear she'd make for the open sea and never come back to be stared at in the shitpits of NYC.

Chaser, she reaches over and grabbed my crotch, giving me a good fondle, and she laughs. "Oh, yeah. This is more *your* speed, ain't it, buckaroo." And she laughs again, insisting we move along to other abominations. Or so most would name the denizens of The Sink. "Don't shoot your wad over one little tadpole," Chaser taunts, but I keep quiet.

We stop more briefly before a double amputee, serving beer from the spigot where her cunt ought to be. How do you resist a thing like that, eh? Besides, the nitroglycerine smokiness has gone and fearsomely parched my throat and mouth. Chaser plays the good host and ponies up the cash. The amputee positions the glasses between her thighs and pulls back on the pub-style tap handle. It's some German beer, yellow as urine. She smiles and thanks us both. She's a pretty girl, and I can't help ponder the fate of her legs and the hardware packed inside her torso. That the beer is icy cold only makes me that much more curious. Almost curious enough to ask, but before I risk such a rube *faux pas*, Chaser's already shoving me along again.

We were an item once, Chaser Jay and I. But that was far ago and long away. She was still a boy back then. Or, she would protest, still forced to *masquerade* as a boy. Either way, I probably loved her, might still, but she's a transient, nomadic beast is she. She's never, ever gonna settle for anyone for good.

I think, I do, more's the fucking pity.

I'm jostled with unwelcome expedience past a number of other gloriously grotesque fantasy beings made of bone and respirating flesh. I catch glimpses. A tall man hung like a horse – literally, his hindquarters the strong and hoofed hindquarters of a bay stallion. His long tail sweeps from side to side, as if swatting at nonexistent flies. He has an extraordinarily beautiful young man (no more than eighteen surely, if that), pressed against the wall of that hay-strewn pen, long black cock shoved deeply into the boy's asshole. The horse man wears a bit and bridle, as if he might, at times, carry riders piggy back. We pass a man with a perfectly formed vagina in the center of his chest. There's an ebony-skinned woman with wide leathery wings, and she reminds me of the "mermaid," unable to ever fly, I imagine, cooped up in a cage hung a few feet off the floor. She glares at the gawkers with golden eyes, and keeps those wings folded tight. I could not help but think of the Cumaean Sibyl, caged, then shrinking, shrinking until she was kept inside a jar.

There was a man who was far more machine than human being, mounted in a tangle of wires and cables and framed on the wall. *His* eyes were silver, and he bled an endless stream of data. I caught hasty sight of a woman and man somehow fused loin-to-loin so that they were locked in an unending coitus. I could have watched that one for hours stacked upon hours, had Dame Chaser allowed it. She did not. She meant me to see something all the way at the very back of this costly Dime Museum. I realized, all at once, her fierce compulsion, her determination that I *would* see whatever I would see, was the primary (if not only) motive for dragging me from my cubby up in Harlem all the way down, down, down to filthy fucking Floodland.

I finish my beer and drop the plastic mug to my feet, where it's promptly crushed by the feet of another tourist. I say tourist, but that's for certain a projection, transference. For all I know, dude's a goddamn staple of the Ballyhoo circuit. This might be his every goddamn weekend's distraction. For all I know.

"Almost there," Chaser assured me, clutching my hand so tightly my fingers were going numb.

And then, well, then we *were* there.

Another Plexiglas tank, cage, pod, capsule, whatever. It's taller than the others we've passed (not all the exhibits reside within such cases, possibly no more than half). There's a locked doorway (also Plexi) centered in the front, a keypad for a secret code to enter. Once I espy what lies (or crouches, hunkers, squats – no, no, it lies, for true) within the moist growth filling the floor and slithering halfway up the walls of the tank, I will say I was quite happy for that locked door. If this thing had ever been human, its genotype had been so altered that almost all semblance had been forsook to the phenotype. Among its bed of dun and rubbery, sweating tendrils, it pulses slowly, faintly, but distinctly. It is the color of bile, and might have been five feet, one end to the other. It sweats, too, and it quivers. It looks as much like a great lump of innards as it does a huge malformed vagina freed of the need for the rightful corpus.

"This?" I ask. "You hauled me to a shitpit for this monstrosity?" And I seriously consider pulling free my captured hand and heading back to the mermaid, who has at least made me hard. This miscreation, I've already seen ten times too much; burn out my eyes, as spake the Bard, and kindly wipe the memory of the thing.

"No," she says, placing the word as firmly as has anyone ever said the word, and then she says it again, in case I've lost my hearing in the last half hour. "No. Gotta see the show, rube. Gotta lose your virginity sooner or later, *pendejo*."

"Fuck you, *puta*."

Neither one of us speaks much Spanish, excepting what one needs at a taco truck or to swap insults. We are each a culinary and profane aficionado of language, which makes us all but fucking illiterate. I keep waiting for my content manager to demand I do something about that, but she keeps ignoring the deficiency.

So, we watch the pulsing lump of flesh, though, beyond it's ugliness, there was very, very little to be seen. Once the initial shock faded, it teeters at the verge of boring. I actually yawn, and Chaser ribs. But then…then.

A man in a harlequin's latex bodysuit and a jangling jester's cap leads a nude woman towards the tank. Those assembled pass to afford the two unobstructed passage, and all at once, I sense the hushed awe of ritual. This, I understand, is what Chaser has brought me here to see. This is her kink, and she wants so badly to share. She wants so badly, I think, to discover it can be mine, as well. The woman is pretty in no particular way. Her hair is long and a bluish-silver grey, like clouds before snow. Her eyes, I note, are emerald green. The harlequin punches a code into the pad, and there's a retinal scan, too. All about us, the gawkers have grown silent. Chaser isn't the only one come to see this and this alone. The woman steps into the tank, and in the instant before the door is shut and locks behind her, I hear the squish of her bare feet against that spongy matrix into which the meaty blob is snuggly nestled. After the Harlequin Man shuts the door, all sounds from within the tank are mercifully fucking muted (which only makes them a little less bearable, mind you all).

"Seen enough, I wager," I say, turning away, but Chaser turns me right back to face the tank and the scene beginning to play out within.

"You gonna stand still and watch, priss. No way you pussy out on me now."

And I don't. She's already got enough to lord over my pate. I stand behind her, reluctant as reluctant goes, yeah, and put my hands on her strong shoulders. The Harlequin Man has disappeared, so maybe he sees this all the goddamned time, and it's nothing but boredom and routine to him. No need of him now. He'd only distract.

The girl looks back at us once, and I cannot name here that expression.

Not regret.

Not fear.

Akin to resignation, but far, far more complex than the faces of the resigned.

"What's coming," I whisper, "whatever it may be, she wants it?"

"Maybe," Chaser whispers back to me. "Maybe not. Some are volunteers. Some are cons, death-row sorts. Lots are malignant, so don't got much time left no ways. She takes away the pain."

"She?"

Chaser points at the tank, at the innards-vagina thing. "Yeah, man. *She.* Got too many names to name, but she's the One True *Maha Shojo*, you got that? She's Mother Hunger and the Shaper of Shadows, the World Cunt."

Then someone in the little crowd shushes us and glowers.

I shall put it down as succinctly as I may. I dream of the next half hour far too often now. I know that writing it won't dispel those nightmares, but it has been asked of me, and ain't no living on air alone. I jump when asked, I fold my fevered nights and mornings into mere paragraphs. But, I shall be succinct as I may. The emerald-eyed woman kneels before the pulsing thing, and she strokes, with utmost geniality, what must be the lump's labia majora, analogous structures if not truly homologous. In response, what might be its clit rises like an erection, a stub of meat as big about as a…I don't fucking know…a carrot, the Horse Man's cock, a policeman's baton? It's darker than the bile-colored body, a yellow that's hinting at orange. The woman's feet have sunk up to the ankles in the spongy mess on the floor. But, she strokes this obscene anatomy, and five minutes pass, ten, and the lump splits open down its dorsal midline (college biology coming in handy), right along the top. It yawns wide like a toothless mouth, ropy strands of bile-colored mucus spanning the maw. The woman pushes her hair back from her face, which seems odd, though, no, I can't say why. And then she reaches inside, her arm disappearing up to and just past the elbow. I can feel Chaser tensing, the muscles of her shoulders and back tensing, and, though I cannot see her face, I imagine she's not even blinking, would not miss even that much of whatever this is happening before us. What comes next comes quickly.

This part is merciful. Later, there is no mercy.

The woman leans forward and pushes herself head first into the pulsating lump. Immediately it closes about her, those vile lips closing about her hips. The woman doesn't struggle, and I ponder the cocktail of drugs that made her so willing, so pliant. A sort of peristalsis begins then, and the remainder of her body is swallowed. I know no better word than swallowed. And soon even her feet are lost to view.

A gasp escapes Chaser, and she has her jeans unbuttoned and her hand working down there. Others are engaged in similar acts, tending to themselves or companions; some, perhaps, to complete strangers. What do I know, noob to this Second Circle of a Ballyhoo Inferno. I feel no such titillation. But I do *feel*: a confusing alloy of anticipation, nausea, curiosity, and fear. My upper lip is damp with perspiration, and my brow, as well. It trickles down my face and burns my eyes.

"What happens?" I ask Chaser. "What happens next?"

"Shut the fuck up," she growls in her old "male" voice, and that's what I do.

Here is what happens.

The lump (which sometimes I almost think of as one of Mr. Lovecraft's shoggoths – who remembers him?; I want to call it the vagina dentata, only it is possessed of no teeth, so far as I can see) swells, almost to twice its original size. It seems to ripen, like a piece of fruit, the sickly yellow going all at once a vivid red, a vivid and bloody red. A pomegranate, I think, in that witnessing instant, Persephone's damnation, temptation, her godsforsaken lot there for all permitted entry to scry. Yes, an enormous pulsing pomegranate. The lump grows ever more rigid, that skin that earlier had seemed almost pulpy. And then, again *all at once*, as I begin to guess some version of the impending outcome, it splits itself open again. This time I can hear it quite plainly, even through the Plexi. The sound of a head of lettuce torn in half. That sound precisely. And it disgorges or vomits forth something coiled fetal, roughly the size of the woman who went into it ten minutes previously. This excrescence is shrouded in a bile-colored membrane. The lump spasms several times in quick succession, then seals itself shut again and…what words do I choose? I choose *deflate*. It deflates, returning to the sickly yellow-green thing we'd first glimpsed. The excrescence in its – I will say cocoon, for I have ever after *thought* cocoon – has begun to writhe. This is the worst so far, as I thought surely it (she) must be dead, only a gobbet of indigestible shit after a fine and willing banquet. But now I see it is not *that*, and it is not that at *all*.

"I don't want to watch anymore," I say. Or only do I think I say, because no one shushes me or looks at me or responds. Hardly matters, natch, as I don't turn my back on the biopunk's crackerjack *tableaux vivant*. I take this to mean, *I do most assuredly want to see this, any words to the contraire are only some flaccid attempt to assuage guilt and the illusion of my humanity.* Fine, we (the we of I) call it that.

The membrane tears, and in what rolls out there is still the vague outline of the woman. The writhing, coiled-up ghost of her, as if shrink-wrapped in the thinnest rubber wrapping. Still am I watching on, while the spongy organic mattress that supports the autonomous vagina thing absorbs her and makes her a part of it. Or *she* makes herself a part of it. Was there a conscious choice, eh? Was there a decision to accept the gift of the One True *Maha Shojo*, Shadow Shaper, World Cunt, Carny Sideshow Eyesore?

When three or four minutes trundle, what the woman has become is indistinguishable from the rest. "She isn't dead," Chaser whispers, shuddering with delight at the moment of her climax, devoured (in her own way) by orgasm.

"She isn't dead," I whisper back, the most breathless fucking echo. My lungs feel emptied, my belly roiling, my dick hard as planks of *Piratinera guianensis*, my bowels loose and threatful.

"No."

"What is she, then?"

Chaser turns about now, and she holds me tight, like she hasn't held me in years. This should make me happy, but it doesn't.

"Sleepin'," she says, and I realize she's crying. "Sleepin' adrift in the solitude and love and endless pleasure always denied her. Now, she'll live long as the Mother lives."

I blink, I think. I blink a few times, and swollen with skepticism, I ask, "You believe that, kitten?" I ask.

"I believe that most sincere."

There's a little more as we partake of our Exit from The Sink, a few sights seen along the way, but it is all anti-apogee after that penultimate consumption and expulsion. Chaser no longer seems interested in much of anything. We have a few tequilas at the bar topside, then find ourselves back out in the steamy New York night, July and neon and damp roadways from the rainy day. I hail a taxi, but Chaser says she wants to walk. I don't argue.

Scylla for Dummies

The lady in the aquarium tank. Upon seeing her for the first time, they inevitably ask the question of HOW. And they ask it fully expecting an answer at the ready. Or, at the least, they expect some acknowledgement of the question's validity as to what she has become. Surely, in an age of reason, science, quantum physics, images from the surface of Titan, neuroprosthetics, the mapping of genomes, data transfer at the speed of light – an age of *information* and *information overload* – surely there must be an answer to her. All things come with their HOWs in convenient tow, accessible and attached like online manuals or a helpful FAQ accompanying the purchase of this or that miraculous gadget. When their skeptic's questions go unanswered, some quickly grow suspicious of fraud or, worse still, the hoarding of valuable knowledge that *should be free.* Or which should at least be available for a cost to those fortunate few who can pony up the fee. These are the people who, more often than not, scowl and turn away. The people who feel cheated. Hoaxed. Bamboozled by some latter-day bit of humbuggery, as though Barnum were not dead and buried and the paying public safe from his deceitful shenanigans.

Still, here she lies. Here she rests perpetually behind laminated, steel-reinforced glass framed in silicone caulking and concrete, 80,000 gallons of saltwater for her private ocean. Her bed, twenty-five feet from side to side, twelve and a half feet front to back, seven feet deep. All about the colorful tiled walls of the room that holds the tank loom pumps and machines, contraptions to regulate water temperature, elaborate chugging filtration systems to increase circulation and supply adequate gas exchange at the surface, insuring the water is properly oxygenated, converting ammonia to nitrate, removing phosphate, monitoring the water's alkalinity, salt content, and the necessary levels of chloramines.

A dry recitation of these facts and figures is sometimes enough to pacify those who come demanding the HOW of her transformation. But the rest, the women and men who arrive and humbly take their places on the wooden benches arranged before the tank or who kneel at the modest altar arranged before her are all but deaf to facts and figures. They have never needed a HOW. These are the ones who consider the WHY of her, but, even so, are too grateful for her presence to press the question very far. She simply *is*, most of them conclude. She is a *gift*. She is profane, yes, and yet as holy as any splinter from a true cross or any Buddha sitting cross-legged in stony meditation. Of course, in secret, a few will devise their own and forever unspoken explanations of the HOW: swimming, she was raped by a mer-man, or a rapacious porpoise, or even a manatee; walking carelessly in a tide pool, she sliced her feet on the venomous nematocysts of coral; she drowned in an undertow, but, like Christ, was resurrected after three days; she is the illegitimate daughter of a mighty humpback whale and a maritime whore. But, even in fashioning these veiled fictions, they understand the Greater Truth, returning to sanctity and gifts cast up on the sand and shingle.

So, here we have the doubters and the supplicants.

We dismiss the former, as they will never open themselves to the Abyss, and the Abyss is the true parent of her. If one studies and learns to read the runes and mosaic spelled out in the arrangement of tiles in this semicircular chamber, they'll *find* answers, to both HOW *and* WHY. Not answers fit for the skeptics and rationalists, for merely considering the possibility of them can drive a sane mind to madness. There is knowledge there that makes a sanctuary of insanity. The tiles that speak of Mother Hydra and Father Kraken, Jörmungandr, of the Esoteric Order of Dagon, the Open Door of Night, Y'ha-nthlei, Jacova Angevine, Proteus, a rotting house at the edge of the Pacific built by a man named Dandridge, wild Thessalonian cults that still worship Scylla, and, and, and…and the tiles make an *incoherent* whole of these disparate mythologies. All are compass needles pointing to the same true north and heralding a Flood to shame Noah's Deluge and the Cretaceous epicontinental seaways, to make the cataclysmic release of Glacial Lake Missoula or the filling of the Black Sea or…be done with it and dismiss all previous floods. The tiles speak of the day when the oceans will tear themselves from their basins, and the Abyss will crush the cities of men, and all dry land will vanish forever more.

The words on walls will not – nay, *cannot* – be spoken by human tongues. Surrogate chants and supplications must suffice. The writings of Ovid, incantations from Nordic and Celtic and Inuit and Polynesian tribes cribbed from this or that anthropological text. Or bits of poem. A few lines from Tennyson's "The Coming of Arthur" seem, to some, especially apt, and so they pray them like the Rosary:

Wave after wave, each mightier than the last,
Till last, a ninth one, gathering half the deep
And full of voices, slowly rose and plunged
Roaring, and all the wave was in a flame

But now we turn our attention to the Lady herself. Now we speak of the fact and form of her, though the sum of this anatomy is beyond the descriptive capacities of *any* surviving language of man. We do our best. We make do.

She reclines in a substratum of quartz sand, granite cobbles, and slabs of charcoal-colored slate. Once, it was possible to tell where she ended and the other inhabitants of the tank began. But that time is years in the past, and the distinction has long since ceased to have any relevance. The more she becomes them, the more they become her, the nearer to that day we are all drawn, the nearer to that Ninth Wave, roaring and all in a flame. A first, casual glance might mistake her for no more than an oddly shaped reef, one that by happenstance has mimicked the outlines of the female body. But a casual glance is worthless here. Most of her skin is obscured now by bulbous and branching growths of countless genera of Alcyonaria, Anthozoa, and Zoantharia – a dead and stony cloak to shelter tiny living polyps that will secrete hard carbonate exoskeletons and so bury her that much more. Within the crannies of the coral and the nooks that are still identifiable as a woman are all the creatures to be found in any tropical reef: snails and bivalve mollusks, shoals of bright and darting fish, twisting polychaete worms, urchins and starfish and brittle stars, crabs and spider-like banded shrimp, sponges, tunicates, and less well-known cnidarians. She is scabbed with razor-sharp barnacles, and an elderly lobster watches from the flowing algal tangle of her hair. A very tiny octopus nestles in the cavern between her thighs. One breast has not yet been encrusted by the coral, and where there was a nipple and areola there is now the holdfast and stinging tentacles of a frilled anemone. Most of her face and neck can still be seen – the sharkish gill slits along her throat, the iridescent pearls that were her eyes, rows of serrate teeth and needle fangs when she chances to open her jaws.

All this, the reduction of her, is folly. It contains nothing of the Truth.

Her head is turned (permanently, now) to the left, towards the altar and towards her worshippers. Very rarely, almost never, she gazes back at them, through her own reflection in the glass. Each, in turn, feels the chill in their blood and the tingle along their spines – instinctive and prehistoric reactions, autonomic responses to a predator's attention programmed when the ancestors of humanity were shrew-sized beasts clinging to Paleocene trees.

And the last part to be considered here, the offerings. The feeding of Our Lady of the Unearthed Reef. Of the marine prophetess. Of the harbinger.

Always, she is ravenous.

There is no sating that appetite, but the faithful do their best. The most timorous bring nothing more than offerings of cod, monkfish, or mackerel wrapped in butcher's paper. Fresh, but dead. She accepts these oblations, but they aren't the delicacies she craves, the sacrifices made by the most devoted. Upon the altar, between scented candles and unspeakable soapstone effigies, there are two surgical tools cradled in carmine velvet: an electrical bone saw once used in autopsies and a pair of 209 mm rib shears. Lost in her eyes, she receives freshly amputated fingers and toes, entire hands, ears, tongues, and genitals (a medic is always present to tend to the wounds, and very few prove fatal).

The floor around the altar is crusted claret.

Once a month, on the night of the new moon, a man or woman presents himself or herself to the priestesses who guards the tank and Our Lady. He or she arrives, is bathed and consecrated, then bound by the ankles and raised, dangling head-down on a slaughterhouse hook, above the tank. Both the jugular and carotid arteries are opened simultaneously with obsidian knives, and the body bleeds out, turning the water in the aquarium red. The drained corpses are burned on pyres hidden in rocky seaside coves a few miles from the room that holds the long tank. None of these willing offerings have ever screamed or tried to back out. She sings them siren songs of exaltation and magnificent, terrible beauty, lulling them as a mother lulls her child with a lullaby. And they are her children. They are all her children, those who have accepted her and accepted what is to come.

And even the scoffers, those unfortunates, the blind askers of HOW, even they are haunted by her. She returns to them in dreams and unguarded moments. She prowls their daydreams. They know her vengeance and stay awake or swallow pills in vain and pitiable attempts at forgetting the holy-unholy face of a goddess.

Figurehead

Here is the tale of a tree nymph, if you chance to believe in that sort of thing. Which is to say, in *this* sort of thing. The sort of story that requires of the reader either the willing suspension of disbelief or a superstitious mindset untainted by reason and science. *That* sort of story. *This* sort. It's not necessary to begin with the traditional "once upon a time," though, for some, it helps. Four words to trigger, or, at the very least, four words that prime. Sheer repetition has long since conspired to render (depending upon one's predilections) of the five syllables of those words either a tired cliché, a comforting overture to coming entertainment, or a grandiose revelation of the mythic, legendary sort. It is worth noting that the Great Religions of the world eschew "once upon a time" in all their holy books, fearing fictional connotations, which is rather like a dog eschewing four paws and its bark for fear of being taken *for* a dog.

But if you are of any sort who listens – and many, it shall be noted, are too insecure in this or that dogma to listen to fairy tales, which this is to be, give or take – then may you not be displeased by the following:

Once upon a time – long, long ago – there lived in a forest a dryad, a nymph who inhabited the bole of a great oak. She'd been the oak's faithful companion and sole lover since the first sprouts pushed their way up through loam and earthworms from the bitter, astringent meat of Mother Acorn. With the tree, she grew. Her arms for sky-reaching limbs, her feet for taproots digging down five feet or more in that first year alone. And now so many years have passed since. A century or more. Easily a century. With the tree, she unfolded, rising stout and strong among a hundred – nay, a thousand – other trees. Oaks and maples, hawthorn and spruce and ash. The symbiotic dryad bathed in summer rains, drinking and pulling nutrients from the rich and ancient soil. The photosynthetic chlorophyll of the oak's broad leaves captured photons that had traveled a hundred and fifty million kilometers from the blazing furnace of Sol Invictus, crossing

90 million miles, on average, racing through space at 186,000 miles per second. Through the magic of chemistry (if you wish it to *be* magic), the photons reacted with water and carbon dioxide from the roots and leaves to form simple sugars. The tree then shat forth free oxygen and water vapor. In this way was the nymph nourished across the decades.

She had, of course, other *divine* nourishment. For one, the offerings left by satyrs and fauns and that rutting lot. For another, from time to time blessings were passed down from the gods. Her sisters inhabited other trees, and they spoke through interweaving branches. Dryads are shy creatures, rarely showing themselves except when the goddess Artemis Agrotera, Potnia Theron should happen to stroll by. The dryads kept to themselves, and the years rolled past. Summers faded. Chilling winds came, and the dryads spoke one to another of the advent of winter's chill, and, with the descending sap, sank into the deepest recesses of the trees, huddling and sleeping there until spring. Only the ladies of the evergreens stood tall above the snow and under the lead-grey skies. The rest withdrew, and they dreamt the dreams that dryads dream. I do not know those dreams, but I fancy they are filled with the business of nesting squirrels and with bright days and cooling thunder showers.

Here we could digress. Here we could also discuss the hamadryads, those several daughters of Oxylus and Hamadryas – Ptelea for elm, Morea for the mulberry, Syke for fig, fair Aigeiros for *Populus nigra*. Best, though, that we not (more than we already have), for that's another tale for another time. Many tales, in truth. Turn aside, and the story at hand may well be lost, dissolving like mist in the heat of late morning.

Aristotle is believed to have said something like, "Change in all things is sweet." But, then, Aristotle was not a dryad wedded to a tree in a forest that had so long endured the seasons and the casual depredations of Nature. Hence, let's suppose we can forgive his ignorance.

But accept this – for some, in change may lie horror and dissolution.

Not *all* change, of course. For the dryad was accustomed to, and at peace with, and, indeed, *one* with the rhythms of the seasons and the changes those rhythms wrought upon the oak and, by extension, upon herself. And if a storm felled a sister, if wind or lightning found its mark, there were always other acorns, strewn across the floor of the wood. There were always other homes, other companions waiting to be born.

But the change with which we are here concerned is not *that* sort of change.

The herald of the change in question was a young woodcarver, the apprentice to a renowned shipwright, and the young man arrived in the wood with an axe. A very, very sharp axe. He came into the forest with ill intent (a subjective call, admittedly), and that was the intent of taking away. It might be that he came believing in such things as dryads, and it might be that he did not. That part of the story has been forgotten and doesn't much matter anyway. But what is remembered is that after admiring the trunks and heights of many great trees and dismissing them all, he came to the oak in which our particular dryad lived. The woodcarver had a keen eye, and in the oak he saw all the qualities he required. And so he hefted his sharp, sharp axe and made the first blow.

And the tree screamed.

Now, this is a thing he'd never heard before, having kept always to the edges of the forest, where trees were younger and more vulnerable to the ravages of man. Where there were no dryads. He had not even imagined a tree *could* scream, and at the sound, startled, he dropped his axe and stared up into its mighty branches.

"What witchery is this?" he asked. "What curse is laid upon a tree that it might scream with a voice more disarming than that of a frightened, hurting woman?"

And at this, the dryad stepped from out her oak, or, rather, she bled out from the shallow gash left by his axe and the strong arms that wielded it. So it was, here, he first laid eyes upon her, and though the woodcarver had beheld many marvels in his life, not one could match the countenance of her, not even by a fourth part.

With the voice of a breeze rustling leaves, she asked him, "Why have you done harm to my tree, which is my home, and which is my lover, and which is my charge, and which also guards me night and day?"

For two reasons, he didn't answer straightaway. Firstly, he was overcome with the strangeness and beauty of her. Secondly, for a few moments he had no idea what to reply to such a question. The sight of the dryad had driven from his mind his purpose for coming to the copse, for needing the wood of her tree, his trade that demanded the constant sacrifice of trees.

"Tell me, Sirrah!" she demanded. "Tell me now, this very instant! What malign being do you serve, to brandish an axe against me and mine?"

"None," he managed to reply. "I come on my own."

She stared at him, momentarily at a loss for words. Perhaps in other woods, dryads knew of lumberjacks and woodcarvers, but not in this wood.

It had never once occurred to the dryad that a man (an odd sort of beast she only vaguely comprehended, even when faced with one) could be a threat, could desire what he had no right to desire, because a tree owns itself, as does a dryad, and, presumably, a man. To fell a tree, then, is to rob it of that which you have no right to take. Yet, men have always taken trees, as the need has struck them, the need or the whim. Thousands of years before the first inklings of any civilization, men felled trees. Mesolithic hunters made grassy, open country of forests, to attract the animals they preyed upon. Then came the Neolithic and the more evolved cultures of that age, and men cleared countless acreage for their crops. Even their crude stone axes were sufficient to the task. Stone-Age woodcarvers gave way to Bronze-Age woodcarvers gave way to those of the Iron Age, and each fashioned better tools with which to clear greater tracks of land. But the dryad was aware of none (or very little) of this. The dryad understood only that a mortal man had wounded *her* oak.

"I couldn't have known," he stammered. "That it was your oak. Or that it was anyone's."

"But now you are the wiser," she told him. "And now you will depart our wood, and, if you *are* wise, you'll never walk here again."

This is when he explained to her that, by trade, he was woodcarver to a shipwright – one of the best on all the Aegean – and the shipwright required the wood from not just any tree, but from a great tree, such as her own. He could leave *this* oak be, certainly (though it was perfectly suited to his needs), but that would only mean he'd have to choose another. He stared at the dryad, and she stared back at him. She hardly seemed much of a threat, this slender creature. But perhaps she possessed magic of which he was unaware, and so was far more dangerous than she looked to be.

"Go away," she said. "Go away and trouble us no more."

Staring at her, taking in all the *details* of her, he was charmed by a sorcery that was not her doing. Or which she cast unintentionally. Not only had he never set eyes on a wonder to rival her, he'd never set eyes upon a woman equal to her beauty. A strange fay beauty to be sure, but beauty all the same. And he was a young man, with all the appetites of a young man. He took in every minute aspect of her anatomy: her skin more like the mossy bark of a fallen log than the skin of a young woman (for sh*e appeared* young) and her hazy grey-green hair that was mossier still. Her small breasts, with nipples so like the buds of flowers that might, at any moment, open to reveal bright and delicate petals. Her face was long and narrow, as were her eyes, which were blacker than the blackest pitch. Her eyes were a night sky from which the capricious gods had devoured the moon and all the stars. Her lips were the color of slate, and her ears tapered to delicate points, tipped with sprigs of herbage. Her legs and feet were subtly twisted, almost as are roots before they disappear into the detritus of a forest floor. Her sex (which was, actually, the very first thing he looked at, despite the way I've ordered his observations) was hardly more than an especially symmetrical knothole, but, all the same, a knothole pleasing to his eyes in every way possible, and seeing it, he at once began to grow hard. And though not an evil man, not as genuinely evil men go, here were two things: the oak – which he needed – and the dryad – which suddenly he desired more than ever he'd desired a *human* woman. And a grim sort of scheme occurred to this not-genuinely-evil man, the fellow who had never in all his whole life *schemed*. Consider this the price men pay for looking upon such beings and creatures as inhabit the deeper regions of any wilderness.

"I'll strike a deal," he said, unable to look away from her.

"A wager? Why would I wager with so base a thing as you, a ravager of trees?"

"Because," he said, "it would save your tree. And it's a simple enough matter."

She gazed at the oak, and then she gazed longer still at the man and his deadly axe. "What is your wager?" she asked at last, but uttering silent prayers that Artemis might yet intervene and drive this man from the wood. Or slaughter him. Or, best yet, make a tree of *him*. She prayed, but if any heard her, none replied.

"Let me bed you," he whispered, shamed by the words, but speaking them anyway. "Lie with me, and I'll spare your tree, and I'll leave your forest, and never return again." You will at this point, no doubt, question whether or not I have lied, and he was a wicked man all along, but, then, you've likely never seen a dryad.

"*Bed* me?" she asked, so taken aback by his offer that she only just barely found the words and only just barely spoke them, "Lie with *me?* You, a mortal man, hardly higher than the beasts that roam the forest and fields and swim in the seas?"

"You and I," he countered, "were we not both created by the same gods? Did not Zeus have a hand in the birth of my race *and* in the birth of yours? Yes, of course. So how is it you name me the inferior?"

"You misspeak, Sirrah. I am a *deity* in this wood," and she tried not to raise her voice, as all of this was foul enough a situation without alarming other trees and her sisters. "I am in the retinue and favor of the goddess Artemis the Hunter, and you…you are gravely in error. Unlike you, I do not die, nor do I grow old, nor can I fall ill. I am immortal, a gift the gods denied you and all your kin."

"Yes, that's true," he quickly replied. "But isn't it also true that all the nymphs love singing, and dancing, and wine, and that they are amorous, wanton beings, keen to mate with men? Isn't this what I've been taught, what the priestesses and scholars say? So, isn't this the truth of it?" (Questions which, I suppose, make a lie of whether or not our woodcarver believed in dryads before meeting the Lady of the Oak.)

She could *not* deny that what he said was true of her kind. But so old was this wood, and so many ages had it been since she'd beheld men, those old habits had fallen from her like autumn leaves. Now, she had only her one lover, the oak, and had become loyal and tamed, after a fashion, and was left with no wish to lie with this mortal who had, already, taken up an axe against the tree and who had not yet even properly apologized and asked her forgiveness.

"Do I misspeak?" he asked. "Do I truly?"

"You do not," she relented. She peered into his green-brown eyes, as shallow as a puddle caught in the crux of trunk and limb, searching for deceit. "You will be true to your word? I give myself to you, and you'll not touch this oak again, nor put axe to any other tree here? You will leave our forest and never return?" And after a moment's reflection, she added, "Nor send another to act in your stead?"

"I am an honest man, a man of integrity, and I will stand by my promises. So, come now. You've little to lose, everything to gain."

It seemed that way, regardless of her loathing for his impermanent flesh and her lingering doubts as to his sincerity. What other chance did she have to drive him from the forest and save the tree? And she silently vowed, *I will give him nothing but my body. He'll have no part of my spirit. He'll never know more than the surface of me. Nothing more.* The man undressed, and together they settled into a cradle formed by the oak's enormous roots. He had his way, and she denied him nothing of her dryad's form. His callused hands cupped her breasts, finding them softer than the rough, bark-like appearance of her skin had led him to expect. He slipped inside her, into sap and mucilage, so finding the fuck a bit stickier than the taking of a

178

human woman. Her mossy hair spread about her face like a crown or halo, and she smelled of more than the oak – of bergamot, wild roses, lavender, hyssop, bay, and frankincense. He breathed her in, filling his lungs with the intoxicating scents of forests that had grown in the world eons before the creation of mankind. When they kissed, she tasted of cedar and rosemary.

She wrapped her strong legs about him, and it did occur to her how easily she might crush his back and ribcage. If any other ever came searching for the lost woodcarver, they would find the ancient roots grown around the corpse, as if he'd lain there a hundred years. This thought occurred to her, but she remembered how vengeful men are and imagined, in their fear and anger, that they might answer her murder of the woodcarver by felling and burning the entire grove. She pushed the thought away; it would be over soon enough, when he'd sated his fleeting mortal passion.

But even as he came and spilled his seed into her, the woodcarver found he'd fallen in love with this fantastical creature, and he resolved then and there to have her always, to *take* her to be his wife, and the opinions of other men be damned if they should look upon the union as profane.

"I will have you," he said. "Forever, for as long as I am alive I will have you. Never have I held anything to match the beauty and the grace of you."

"You may not have me, Sirrah, for I have pledged myself to the oak and will seek no other husband until the tree has lived out the span of all its long seasons." Then she pulled herself quickly from beneath him and dissolved back into her tree.

The woodcarver, his cock still dripping cum, swore then and there he would not be denied by her. He would *kill* the tree, ending the span of all its long seasons, and surely, he told himself, she would then have no choice but to accept his affections. So, standing naked in the forest, he took up his axe, swinging it with all his might until, at last, after many hours of sweat and toil, he sent it toppling over. He heard the oak (or its lover) scream again, as it crashed to the ground, taking the limbs and leaves of many of its companions as it went, and for a while the air seemed to rain the sundered clothing of trees. Smiling at his handiwork, the woodcarver called out to the nymph, "Now your husband is dead and gone, so come out and return with me, and be my wife."

But she did not come out. She did not even answer him.

Inside the fallen oak, she wept. Shattered, she cursed all men, and she cursed the gods for having *made* men. Hearing the dryad, her sisters wept, but so feared the selfsame fate that none of them dared strike out against the man.

"Come out," he said again. "Come out," he demanded, "and walk with me back to the town by the sea, where we will be wed."

She did *not* come out, but, in her sorrow, swore forever to be one and the same with the tree and never again to leave the sanctuary of its rings. In truth, the tree was not yet dead. Felled, yes, but the deaths of trees are protracted agonies. Slowly do they surrender life, and so that much greater was the horror that she felt.

"I will not," she cried from the oak, and the not-genuinely-evil man found himself changed and his heart hardened at her refusal.

"I'll not ask again," he declared, but no voice replied except the birds, singing their sadness from the branches of other trees, the verdant crowns of other nymphs. The woodcarver, denied, was gripped by fierce anger, and resolved that he would possess the nymph, and that always would she be his. If not by consent, by force, and if she would not leave her tree, then he would do what he'd intended at the start. He would take the oak from this shadowy, wicked wood. And so other men came, other men with other axes and with saws, and they carved the trees into many smaller parts, and then loaded their grisly handiwork into horse-drawn wagons that hauled away the ruined oak – now only timber – to their marble city by the shimmering blue waters of the sea.

You'd not thought this would be the sort of tale with a *happy* ending, did you? Surely, you didn't come here expecting the sort of whitewashing that the Victorians inflicted upon the tales of Perrault and those of Wilhelm and Jacob Grimm? If so, you'll be sorely disappointed, though it is never my *intent* to disappoint. Honest women and men know the scarcity of "happily ever afters," same as they understand the arbitrary nature of "once upon a times." But, this said, I will not belabor the ending, not draw it out any longer than necessary. I won't revel in its tragedy and malice (though, I admit, the perversity to do so resides in me, and to do otherwise is therefore a shade of self-denial).

As it happens, the woodcarver, apprentice to that master shipwright, had sought out the oak for the figurehead of a fine new galley, a trireme that would sail to war in Assyria and survive to see battle with other fleets in other wars. The shipwright had left the exact physiognomy of the figurehead to the woodcarver's discretion. And, still seething from rejection, he chose for its countenance the form of the dryad, that men would possess the treewife, and that he wouldn't be robbed of the sight of her. He chose only the strongest planks, which he glued together, clamped, and doweled. Beneath the roof of the shipwright's workshop, he took hammer and chisel in hand and set to work. He worked day and night, neither sleeping nor eating, pausing only to drink and relieve himself. Under his busy, determined hands, the face of the dryad emerged, and his memory fashioned it almost as beautiful as it had been when she stepped from the tree. He shaped her breasts, her belly, shoulders and thighs. He carved her strange sex and the wreath of her hair. About her legs, instead of feet (he couldn't have her walking away) he carved elaborate scrolls and acanthus leaves, squirrels and foxes. In her hair he placed sparrows and nightingales. He painted the figurehead as true to his memory as he was able, even down to the inkiness of her eyes. And then she was taken from the workshop and placed upon the prow of the new trireme.

"Now," sneered the woodcarver, "for all your immortal existence will you be cast out upon the rolling sea. There will be times when the galley is rowed within easy sight of shore, of green forests perched high on limestone cliffs. But you will do no more than look upon them with your new wooden eyes and only despair and long for their embrace. Many times, you will sail near to *living* trees," he bitterly told her, "but always will you be bound unto the remnants of your *dead* husband. Eventually, you'll sink and lie rotting on the slimy bottom of the sea, shelter for crabs and worms, at best your glove of Venus become no more than an eel's narrow mansion."

Though she did not speak, he knew she heard him.

The day the ship was put to sea, he watched, full in the knowledge he'd likely never glimpse the oaken figurehead again, as he rarely caught another glimpse of his art once it left port. The sails billowed in a stiff gale and the oars rose and fell, propelling her – the abomination he'd *made* of her – far, far away.

And here is the end of it, or what we shall settle for as an ending.

Within a fortnight of the ship's departure from the town by the sea, the woodcarver's anger and his satisfaction at having exacted so perfect a revenge upon the haughty dryad turned to grieving. And he turned to wine and was dismissed by his master. Within another fortnight, he swallowed a draught made from hemlock – *Conium maculatum*, as it would eventually, centuries later, be named by Carl Linnaeus – and went to his own ignominious death.

As for the dryad he had cursed, bound to the bones of her oak, she would – true to his words – never again step foot on any shore, nor know the intimate embrace of any living tree. There were nights when the sailors and galley slaves, who knew nothing of the origins of the figurehead, swore they heard the unearthly wailing of a woman drifting out across the waves. Hearing her cries, the Nereids – Nereus and Doris' fifty seafaring daughters – came and did their best to console her. But finding her inconsolable, they were left to follow in the wake of the trireme, weeping for the wood nymph as they'd once wept for Achilles' suffering at the death of Patroclus. The dolphins followed with them, and, in deep places, whales sang laments to the dryad.

One night, seized by a fearsome gale, the ship was dashed upon a rocky shore, and precisely as the woodcarver had expected, the figurehead was washed out to sea and sank to lie in silt and darkness, too lost now to even feel the warmth of the sun. And there she would lie, even after the coffin of her husband had decayed and dropped away to reveal her true form, not the mockery carved to imprison her. No longer sane, she coiled among the slithering, blind serpents that haunt the dark, having forgotten who and what she once had been. No god or goddess came to her rescue, for there were still so many dryads in the world, what mattered the loss of one.

If you *are* the sort who has listened, then I'll leave you here. You will take from this tale of treachery what you may, or whatever you may not. We each of us hear a story through the obscuring gauze of our own experience, our own beliefs and prejudices. Many do not even mourn for murdered oaks, and it's much less likely they will worry over the fate of a tree nymph who was damned by the hand of a spiteful woodcarver.

> *The seaman spread his sails to the winds he did not yet*
> *understand, and what had stood long on high mountains*
> *now tossed as keels on unknown waves…*
>
> Ovid, *Metamorphoses*

Down to Gehenna

And thus, joy suddenly faded into horror, and the most beautiful became the most hideous, as Hinnom became Gehenna.

Edgar Allan Poe, "Morella" (1835)

1.

There can be no proper naming of this place, as it has no proper boundaries and exists nowhere and nowhen. We may say that it is, and beyond that, we may say very little regarding either its special or temporal geography. This is not a matter of geographers, where they toil in the realm of cosmogony or quantum cosmology. Neither planetology nor carefully drafted maps based upon Dante's *Divina Commedia* will be of any use here. We may retain a few useful metaphors – up and down, to and from, in and out – but only for the sake of convenience. Still, there is no accounting for human folly. To wit, the tales of a "Well to Hell" drilled in the wastes of Siberia in 1989. So say the crackpots and gatekeepers of urban legend and Christianity-Made-Fact, and they say too that when geologists lowered a microphone nine miles down into the unexpected vacuity, a microphone resistant to temperatures of two-thousand degrees Fahrenheit, "to their astonishment they heard the sounds of thousands, perhaps millions, of suffering souls screaming." Further embellishment adds that "A luminous gas shot up from the drill hole. A brilliant being with bat wings then coalesced, with the words in Russian: 'I have conquered' visible against the sky." See, too, claims by a Mel Waters of Ellensburg, Washington that upon his land exists a hole of possibly infinite depth, or the physicists quantifying the singularities at the hearts of black holes. Leave all such fancies and equations behind. They will not serve you here. Nor will hope. Nor will sanity. Nor will imagination, for what good is imagination in a territory where all things are realized, sooner or later, again and again, towards infinity.

We shall say only that it is a place.

We shall say only that it is a place inhabited by regret and the self-persecution of women and men since apes foolishly stood upright and viewed the horizon and asked themselves questions better left unasked.

We shall say that it is *that* place.

We shall speak of its tenants, and perhaps these words will amount to a warning or, at least, a parable of caution. Maybe, though, it can be little more than pornography, as is Hieronymus Bosch's *The Garden of Earthly Delights* and his *The Fall of the Rebel Angels*, or, likewise prurient, the works of Gustav Doré meant to illustrate the works of John Milton. Obscenity (precisely like Beauty) is in the mind of the beholder and nowhere else. Abandon all intent, ye who enter here. Abandon all. Divest yourself of time and salvation and, above all else, the idea that the flesh is immutable. Do not suppose damnation or a cleansing antechamber to any Heavenly Kingdom. You won't find Sisyphus pushing his stony burden up any steep incline. You shall find nothing but that which humanity has decreed it owes itself.

"The mind is its own place, and in itself, can make heaven of Hell, and a hell of Heaven." And here we are in the regions of the Mind. Not the Mind after death, for then the Mind fades like a summer shower, or an echo, or ripples across the surface of a pond. This is the Living Mind which has strayed down some or another dark hallway of the "soul" and having followed hallways of incalculable length, width, and height comes at last unto The Place. No one turns and walks the million miles back, though he or she is entirely free to do so. One does not face such deserved anguish and the truth of such deserved anguish only to set one's back to it. There is, here, by choice and not decree, no looking away.

Imagine *any* landscape and that landscape will be found in this Place.

Imagine any condition at all and that condition is made manifest.

Here, possibility is inexhaustible. And all possibility is made actuality. Here. In this Place.

The Apostles might have glimpsed it, but they could, at best, tell only lies of what they saw. They hid beneath their pious beds. Old Testament prophets spun their ecclesiastical fairy tales that, at best, were echoes, and, at worst, were lies. But the Place did not and does not serve the agenda of any religion. It is, and it is without *purpose*.

Is that not worse?

2.

We shall, regardless of the truth, as a concession to the above-slighted Signor Alighieri, call what follows an *Il libro dei dannati* (with apologies to Mr. Charles Fort):

This man, who failed at three suicide attempts, sits in a very tall chair (mahogany with inlaid nacre), and there is no poison he has not swallowed. He sits before a screen replaying every moment that led him to such loathing of his existence. He pulls triggers and fashions jute nooses. He injects drain cleaner into his veins. He lives, and one begins to suspect it's not that he wishes to die, but only to suffer. Each and every attempt to end his life gives him a throbbing erection, but he will not permit himself to masturbate. So long as he exists (and none here are immortal) this will be the routine of his perdition. It will not vary, excepting in his ever more ingenious means to fail at dying.

This woman who crouches in the thickets of a Permo-Carboniferous swampland. It has taken her centuries – one would suspect – to grow the thick skin she never possessed in the World beyond this Not World. She never suffered the slings and arrows of outrageous fortune, for there was nothing outrageous about her fortune. She was plain, and, each time she gazed upon glamour, she imagined herself the most frightful sort of ugly. Here, her skin has not only grown thick enough to endure catcalls and slights that were never more than fabrications. Here bony plates have grown below her epidermis – paramedian, lateral, ventral, cervical, and appendicular osteoderms – until she as much resembles the mating of a human and an armadillo, or ankylosaur, or aetosaur, as she ever did a woman. No arrow will ever pierce her now. No cruel words will ever find her heart. She has curled into a tight, impenetrable ball and lies inside the stump of a fallen tree, and there she has lain for half a century.

Here is a woman at the edge of a sea. The archetype for any and all seas that are filled with water (taking case to distinguish this sea from hydrocarbon seas of methane and ethane, et al.). She kneels on a razor carpet of barnacles and muscles. She wraps herself in shrouds of bladderwrack. When this woman was sixteen and pregnant and considering an abortion, at the last moment she changed her mind and walked out of the clinic. One week later she miscarried, and she carried the stillborn to a rocky shore and cast it into the waves. She drew lines of cause and effect where none existed. She imagined divine retribution in the absence of any condemning deity. So, eventually, she came *here*. And she kneels and prays and her knees and calves bleed, while her sex swells until it hangs between her legs like a melon, ripening in all the colors of a bruise. The pain is beyond anything she may have (here's that word again) imagined. The tumor continues to grow, and one "day" develops a distinct groove. When she rouses herself from pain and delirium, she cautiously presses a fingertip to the groove, and the melon-like protrusion splits open. It spills onto the granite a writhing mass of yellow-brown tentacles, two dozen, twice that, twice that sum again, which drag her into the water, to the deep places where she will be forever reunited with the object of her innocent malfeasance.

This Place is rife with contradiction and oxymorons.

Here, the man who castrates himself once an hour, only to watch his penis sprout anew from the gory stump of its predecessor. Before he found these regions, he dreamt he raped a woman, and then dreamt he raped a boy. He performs his surgeries with an assortment of blades which he found in a tiled room lit by flickering fluorescent bulbs. He has placed each amputation in a jar of formalin. They line the shelves of walls that stretch away in all directions.

Here are loves, two women. Before coming Here, they loved only from afar, allowing social mores and a marriage to divide them – though they'd loved each other from childhood. Each came separately, and there is no record of how long it took for them to find one another (time Here is, at best, slippery and unreliable). Naked, they embraced, and the fusion of their bodies began at once. Watching this process, you might be reminded of wax dolls, one laid atop, one laid below, abandoned to the heat of a July afternoon. But she and she will never again be divided. There is only one now, and it huddles in a lightless corner, always embracing herself.

This is a civilization's grandest freak show. It's collective fucking guilt. One supposes every sentient species must possess an equivalent, unless mankind-womankind in unique. Which is doubtful in the extreme.

This woman's genitals long ago became the calyx of an orchid. Specifically, the calyx of *Laelia anceps*. What were her labia became pink petals (the palest pink, bleeding into white about the edges). What had been her clit underwent a more elaborate metamorphosis, reshaping into the bloom's column, which is divided into the female (stigmatic) and male (pollinia); we might, therefore, suppose her a hermaphrodite. The anatomy of the flower is, in truth, far more complex, and many scientific terms would need be employed for an accurate description, but our attentions should not be drawn to the minutiae of botany, even a botany this bizarre.

She stands in lush gardens, relying on such insects as ants and bees, but she is also capable of self-fertilization and often resorts to asexual reproduction. The gardens are strewn with her offspring. But the crime she thinks herself to have committed…we will leave that to some other cataloger of these pitiful wretches bound by their own grief and self-disgust.

In a tower of glass and steel that reaches towards clouds it may never gain, in the subbasement of that tower, is a machine that was once a woman. She is only gears and pistons, a chugging engine that was her heart, all cogs and flywheels and oil dripping to concrete floors. She exhales steam and consumes great mouthfuls of coal. Her belly is a furnace. In the days of Queen Victoria she lay herself down on the tracks before a locomotive, or so it is said, even though this is no Land of the Dead and so generally not the realm of suicides.

We will draw attention to one more, and then put this Place behind us forever, and we will do our best to forget.

He stands in an autumn forest and has long since ceased to be anything more than a hive, a honeycomb.

3.

The universe, though devoid of any unifying consciousness to call its own, is nonetheless awash in intelligences, though each is – so far as is presently known – divided one from the other. Working from a single data point, we will speak only of the human race. The human universe is, likewise, awash with irony. Indeed, so prevalent is irony that we might speculate that it, above all else, is the defining quality of *Homo sapiens*. Forget all those characteristics of the phenotype to which anthropologists have assigned such great importance. Irony is a simpler concept than morphology and genetics and social behavior. So, to wit (again), consider another Place. It would truly conform to the Christian notion of Hell, except there is no lake of fire and brimstone, and there is no suffering. There is not even proper judgment. Yet, it is a land of the dead, and there are those who would deem it a land of the dead who have lived out the course of evil lives. It is best described as a congregation of like-minded souls. They dance genteel waltzes and dine thrice daily on the most delectable of delicacies. There is no pain here and no want. There is not even boredom. If there are demons, then the demons are these residents themselves.

In life, they all wielded power over weaker men and women.

They bathed in charisma and fear.

They made absurd promises and cut anyone who dared to expect the fulfillment of those promises.

In this place, on down mattresses and silken sheets, they screw and laugh at the deaths and suffering they inflicted in their days.

They are privy to a heretical secret: Mankind fashioned all its fictional bogeymen so that fewer would take notice of the true monsters who walk among them, these murderers and despoilers, despots and queens and kings. Common men with razors. Common women with tubs of blood. Those who only followed orders. Zealots and slavers, usurpers, those who cheered in Roman coliseums and gathered for hangings, those who were inquisitors, conquistadors, ruiners of dreams and propagators of nightmares. Those who used and took and devoured and consumed, never pausing to consider the consequences.

Those. In this Other Place.

But, despite the privileges afforded to the wicked, we should note one crucial difference between those lands of self-mortification and these lands where the cruelest of the cruel are eternally rewarded. Look about the hinterlands of the latter, and, if you look long enough and hard enough and from the very corners of your eyes, you may perceive the shadowy forms of guards. We will not be so presumptuous as to give them names, neither as a group nor each as an individual. They are like unto the titans of legend, and their shoulders vanish into thunderheads and mist. But they form an impenetrable ring about the circumference of *this* Place, that these dead will not ever escape back into the Lands of the Living.

There is not even the possibility of return. Some speculate this follows from the inmates' refusal to engage in any rite of penance. It hardly matters, truth be told, if truth we dare attempt.

Here there are walls, and no one has delivered him or herself.

There all are free to leave, and yet no one ever has.

The Granting Cabinet

There is nothing remarkable about the cabinet, except that it is so very unremarkable. It is rendered remarkable by the fact of its sheer ordinariness. It stands somewhat taller than wider, perhaps seven feet by five. Front to back, it cannot possibly be more than two feet deep. It is marked by no ornate scrollwork, gilding, or mother-pearl inlay. It was carved from some blond wood, oak perhaps, and – despite the sense that it must surely be an antique – there are no obvious scratches anywhere upon its varnished surface. Therefore, you may say that it has been well cared for, or simply left untouched. Regardless, it is a tall cabinet, and to the eye perceiving it from without, it is only a cabinet and nothing else. Some might call it a *wardrobe,* and not a cabinet at all. But whatever is or whatever is not in a name, we'll not concern ourselves with that here. *Cabinet* is a sufficient enough word, this piece of furniture that, as has been said, when viewed from the outside is unremarkable, except that it is so very unremarkable (and, of course, many would miss this subtlety). Entrance to the cabinet is gained by way of two doors, which open outwards, one on the left and one on the right. Set into the right door is a keyhole, and in the keyhole is a small brass skeleton key. The skeleton key is as unremarkable as the cabinet itself, and you might stand a long time in the farthest corner of an attic, or in a bedroom, or in a musty basement, considering the cabinet and the lock and the key.

You might extend a hand, with inexplicable hesitancy or wariness, and run your fingers across the varnished wood. The blond wood unmarred by any evidence of use.

You might do that.

Or you might be the less careful or more curious sort, and you might immediately take the key's oval bow (a horizontal oval) between thumb and forefinger and turn it clockwise. The hinges are not rusted, so perhaps someone has kept them well-oiled. Or it may be, by some unfathomed agency, that these hinges require no upkeep. You might, then, turn the key, which unlocks both doors at once.

Or you might first stare a while at the cabinet, or gently run your fingers across the polished wood.

I'm doubling back upon myself, which is only a problem in so much as any given woman or man's patience may be strained by a narrator who repeats herself.

What matters is that almost no one fails, in their own time, to turn the key and open at least one of the doors. Usually the right. There is an iron handle attached to each door, and they readily swing open on those agreeable hinges. At first glance, the cabinet will appear empty. There's not even an assortment of old wire coat hangers (though there is a rod that could support coat hangers, and, for that matter, coats). The unremarkable back of the cabinet is easy enough to see – depending where the cabinet has been encountered. If the lighting is poor, the back may be difficult to see, but this, too, is unremarkable.

It is at this juncture that we must pause to divide those who encounter the cabinet into two categories, those who close the door and those who step inside. Either class could be further sorted, should we also pause to consider their reasons for closing or entering the cabinet, but the mind is inscrutable and only a very *few* of those reasons could ever be listed, a few drawn from a potential infinity. It's difficult to see the profit in an exercise which, from the outset, is understood to be in vain.

Now, set aside the people who walk away. They are of no concern here.

And set aside all who have stepped inside, excepting *you*. There is no more time to discuss all who have entered than there is to examine the reasons some enter and others do not. So, only *you* are of consequence here. You, or should we prefer a less immediate, a less personal voice, let us say *this woman* and remain more safely in the third person. Yes, let's do that. Too many find the second person awkward, anyway.

This woman, she has found the cabinet in the attic of the house that once belonged to her mother and father, but now belongs to her and her two brothers. The house is in the countryside, far from the city where the siblings live and work, the city none of them have any intention of leaving. Which is why the house is being sold. Not for greed or want of cash, but merely because it would not be practical for any of them to relocate to so rural a location. But first, before the arrival of potential buyers, first the house must be emptied of the belongings of the mother (who outlived the father by seven years). Conveniently, the mother has already emptied it of most of the belongings of the father. And the woman – *your* avatar – has agreed to deal with the attic, and in the attic she has found the cabinet, which she's never seen before. She's quite *certain* she's never before laid eyes upon it, even though she spent many days during her childhood playing this or that game of pretend in the cluttered attic.

Being who she is, having lived the life she's led, she's one of that category who doesn't hesitate before turning the skeleton key and opening the doors (yes, both; not only the right or left). The sunlight through an attic window is sufficient that she can see how empty the unremarkable cabinet is, that she can see it's empty.

(This is not the first story that has been written about a cabinet, of course. Let that be noted now, since it was not noted earlier. Hopefully, no one will already have protested that this story too readily brings to mind, say, the wardrobe of Professor Digory Kirke, the wardrobe that was a portal, and through which the four Pevensie children gained access to a magical land of snow and lampposts and helpful beavers. This cabinet is not to be mistaken for any other, from any other work of fiction, if only because, as unremarkable as it is, this account is to be considered no work of fiction. Whether you choose to believe it or not, of course.)

So, she turns the key and opens both doors, and, as she is shorter than the cabinet is tall, steps inside. This act doesn't seem the least bit odd to her – entering the cabinet. It only seems odd to her that she's never *seen* the cabinet before. She reasons that her mother bought it fairly recently.

But why, she thinks, *would Mother have bought such a fine, if admittedly unremarkable, cabinet, only to have then hidden it away up here?* Which is to say, she's begged the question.

She pulls both the doors shut, and *this* action she does find odd, though finding it odd, she does it anyway and without a moment's indecision.

Sometimes, a storyteller is forced by the circumstances of her life to pause in the telling of a tale. This tale of an unremarkable cabinet in the attic of a dead woman and the actions of her daughter is a case in point. And sometimes, in the space between stepping *away* from the story and returning *to* the story, the particulars of the story are muddled or lost. Of course, all of it being perhaps a fiction after all, the substitution of that earlier account with a newly conceived account, a newly conceived continuation, is, by definition, as *true* as the original text would have been.

So, I will continue, having been forced to pause, but the continuance, I feel it only fair to say, is a new road, as I have lost the one down which the daughter of the dead woman was originally meant to walk. If there is a library where lost and untold stories are kept (and I believe no such thing), then should you ever gain access to that library, perhaps you may stumble across the road not here taken.

Robert Frost, yes.

As I have said already, being the woman the daughter is, she turns the key, opens the cabinet doors, steps inside, and then, without hesitation, pulls them shut behind her. As I have said, before the pause and the taking of this new story road, she *does* find it odd, closing the cabinet doors, though, still, she does so anyway.

For a time, she sits very still inside the no-longer-empty cabinet, which is musty and smells like dust and cedar blocks, mothballs and stale, closed-away air. This is what she smells, even though there is no evidence of either mothballs *or* cedar blocks. She suspects she smells the ghost of them, lingering from a time when the cabinet held clothes and those clothes needed to be protected from hungry insects and their larvae. She sits very still, and is aware of few sounds except the beating of her own heart, which seems louder than it has ever seemed before, even though she isn't frightened and obviously hasn't exerted herself.

And then she thinks, *Doors lead somewhere. This is the purpose of doors. If only into an empty cabinet, doors lead somewhere. This cabinet has two doors, so perhaps it leads* two *places.* She is aware, immediately, how peculiar this thought is, that last bit, and wishes she could take it back, but is old enough to understand that thoughts can't be retracted, and even if you try not to think about having thought them, you'll probably find yourself thinking of very little else.

"This cabinet has *two* doors, so perhaps it leads two places," she says aloud, without having meant to, and, without having meant to, she makes a choice between one door and the other. It was only ever an illusion that they granted entry to the *same* place. We might consider (though this is also inaccurate) that they granted access to a sort of lobby or foyer, from which two paths diverged.

Yes, Robert Frost again.

The woman in the cabinet experiences a moment of vertigo or dizziness, not unlike what one may feel after stepping out of an elevator that has just descended, or ascended, several floors at once. As though the world below her, and around her, has been made very briefly unsteady, or as though it is she who has been made unsteady. It's a familiar enough sensation; you know what I mean. Well, probably.

After the moment of vertigo, she is aware there was no sense of falling, or of rising, though there was, just before the dizziness, a distinct *thump,* as though the cabinet were lifted and then set down on the attic floor again. She's afraid, a not entirely inexplicable fear, but it comes and goes – the being afraid – so quickly that she's hardly aware it was ever there.

I'm dreaming, she's thinking, trying to recall having climbed up the stairs and opened the attic door.

A dream is a wish your heart makes...

Walt Disney's *Cinderella* (1950), which borrowed heavily from Franz Liszt's Transcendental Etudes. Specifically, Etude No. 9 in A-flat, "Ricordanza."

But the woman in the cabinet clearly can recall climbing the stairs and entering the attic. She clearly can recall most of the day before she found the cabinet, as well as the day before, and the day before that, and so on (though, as is normal, the memories grow vaguer as they grow farther from the present moment). Then she falls back upon clichés and pinches a bit of the underside of her left forearm between her right thumb and index finger; it hurts, but, if she's dreaming, she doesn't wake up. This, though, is of little consequence, as we are treading the boards of old wives' tales.

Have I neglected to mention how dark it is inside the cabinet? If I have, well, it was, indeed, very dark inside the cabinet. The woman was swaddled all in darkness. Except...when she first entered the cabinet and closed the doors, there was a razor-thin shaft of sunlight slipping in between the two closed doors, and now that light is gone. Now, the darkness seems so absolute it almost makes her straining eyes ache, so she shuts them. She reaches out and finds that where there were two doors, now there is only one.

This cabinet has two doors, so perhaps it leads two *places.*

Having made a choice, now it has only one *door.*

The making of choices presents a peculiar (if not inevitable) paradox: in choosing, one diminishes the available pool of choices, but it is equally true that in choosing one often creates new choices that did not previously exist.

Even if, as is the case here, the choices that have been made were unconscious, or even accidental. She considers this very problem, eyes closed, sitting on the floor of the cabinet, smelling cedar and dust. *I reduced my choices by choosing, so now one door. But I may leave the door shut, or I may open it.* And with this thought comes the strange certainty that there is a third choice available to her, that she might make the choice to simply return to her dead mother's attic, and to that place where the cabinet had two doors. She can't escape the certainty that this is exactly what any sane woman would do, or at least any woman who is not who *she* is and so has not lived the life *she's* led.

We might fairly here consider the matter of freewill, but that would, regrettably, only slow the narrative.

The daughter of the dead woman opens her eyes, extends her right hand, and pushes open the cabinet door.

And it has happened once more. The narrator has had to part with the narrative for a space of weeks and comes back now uncertain, not only of her original intention, but of the revised intention, created after her first necessary setting aside of the piece. So, I find I must now make something up (and here, yes, the story becomes well and truly a fiction, more's the pity). We have a second road not taken (I can quote Robert Frost all day and night, though some find him trite and sentimental).

So the daughter of the dead woman – whom, you will again recall, is functioning as your avatar – in whose attic the unremarkable cabinet was found has climbed inside, and she has experienced a peculiar sensation, and she has made a choice, and she has opened the one door where before there were two.

A dream is a wish your heart makes
When you're fast asleep,
In dreams you lose your heartaches,
Whatever you wish for, you keep.

(A writer friend once said to me, "Lawyers are making things very hard for Modernists." Of course, they always have, right from the start. And this parenthetical might have been a footnote, but, as much as some hate digressions via parentheticals, many more hate footnotes.)

But she believes she is *not* fast asleep. She believes she is fast *awake.*

Behind her, the cabinet has vanished. She thinks, *If it were ever really there.* And so, let's eliminate another likely infinite set of choices. No matter, as she has lost all heartaches, and she will wish, always, to keep *this.* This life which the only seemingly unremarkable cabinet has granted her, even if any memory of whatever was before has already faded from her mind. And, I will say here, do not judge and condemn her for this realized dream; the Heavens and Hells that can be summoned by the human mind are endless lands, and how can any one be objectively judged better or worse, righter or wronger, than any other? (Lawyers leave relativism alone, for it often serves their purposes.) However, here the tale, twice interrupted, thrice begun, here it assumes a difficult nature. As it is *your* tale, and I do not know *your* own heart's deepest or darkest or most forbidden or most beloved fantasy. The woman whose mother has died being you, the woman who has opened the door to a granting cabinet which may never have existed, I cannot know *her (your)* mind. Though, what a neat trick *that* would be.

The best I can ever do is thumb through a few hypotheticals, a very few if we consider the scope of possibility, and leave the rest to *you,* and *you,* and *you, ad infinitum.*

She stands in a forest of cedars and almond trees. The ground is rocky and volcanic, having long ago been spewed from deep within the earth. I cannot begin to name all the wild flowers: allium, crown anemones, the Cretan iris, *Lupinus pilosus,* Barbary nut, *Trifolium uniflorum.* And certainly she does not know the names of any of these species. You do not, if this *is* you. She walks between the gnarled trunks, four clopping hooves, reaching up with two human arms unchanged by the cabinet's granting of a forgotten wish. Once, she dreamt she was a centaur, one among the Kentaurides, and the dream was forgotten as an adult. As was forgotten how much desire she'd invested in the dream or how much desire had birthed it. She drinks from the sparkling pools that lead down to the sparkling seas. It is long days and long nights, blessedly long, before she finds a mate. She was unaware she was even searching for him, until they see one another across a meadow. They embrace first, the way a man and woman would embrace. They kiss – no words are spoken, and maybe they have no spoken language – and he licks at her brown nipples, and she rubs her cheeks along his strong arms. And then he mounts her from behind, in the manner of horses, for those portions of her anatomy are not now those of a woman. He is heavy, but she is strong and bears his weight. He bites down, gently, on her withers, and she sings. She will bear him a half-foal daughter.

No? I can try again, for all the good it will do me.

She lies in the cool silken sheets of a very wealthy woman, a woman who is one of those copyright lawyers who makes a tidy mint each year by making life so very hard for Modernists. She – you – has denied herself so long, always seeking the company of men, for isn't that what good girls do? She may now believe herself fallen, and she may not. It no longer matters. She spreads her long legs, her thighs, and the lawyer stands over her a few moments. They are both entirely nude. "Mine?" the lawyer asks. "Yours," the other woman, now her lover, replies. "Always?" and "Yes," replies the cabinet traveler, "Always." The lawyer considers this and chews at a thumbnail. "And no one else's?"

"Not ever anyone else's. Only yours."

"How can I believe? How can I know you're not a liar."

The woman from the granting cabinet, from the attic, from a city in another world, thinks for a handful of seconds before she replies.

"Only by a leap of faith," she says. "Only from one day to the next. As you trust the sun will rise tomorrow."

"The sun's never made me any promises," says the lawyer. It hasn't, of course.

"Have you ever asked it?" And the lawyer has to admit she hasn't.

"Taste me," the woman whispers.

And the lawyer kneels between her legs, running her tongue along the inside of one leg, one thigh, then the other, and the other. "Kiss me deeper," she – you – implore, and so the lawyer does, a practiced tongue pushing back the clitoral hood and finding the delicate nubbin hidden within.

Have I missed the mark again?

It's a thankless task, this.

A last try, then you're on your own.

Everything above her torso has been chiseled from a block of blue-grey Carrara marble, *pietra paesina*, cut from the rugged, scrubby peaks above an Italian village not far from Florence. From the same beds as the stone from which Michelangelo carved his *David*. Once – not quite two-hundred million years ago – the form that she has taken from the callused sculptors hands, from his skill, were the slimy beds of a warm Jurassic sea. In a former time, she knew ichthyosaurs, and the buds of her nipples and each fingertip was the calcium carbonate of dead marine creatures, later heated, folded, pressed, recrystallized, and thrust upwards into the bones of mountains. Into the block from which each day a little more of her emerges. Her nights in his workshop are peaceful as peaceful may be, but each day the morning sun arrives bright between parted draperies, and bathes her on her wooden pedestal. In an hour more, he arrives, as well, and the days are filled with the rhythm of hammer (*La Mazza*) and point chisel (*La Subbia*), rasps and rifflers. When first quarried, the block in which she was contained (if as yet unconceived), was softer, hardening in the workshop, and the sculptor stops, from time to time, setting aside his mallet, to polish her smoother than the skin of any woman who has ever lived or who will ever be born to any mother. He is working far slower than usual, for he has fallen in love with the woman from the cabinet (perhaps, if she is mistaken and it did exist). But she is no Galatea, and he no Pygmalion, and there will be no kindly Aphrodite. This concerns no metamorphosis beyond that which changed limestone to marble. So, he takes more time than he needs, for he has fallen so deeply in love with the sight of her – she who is you – and doesn't wish to part with this commission, no matter how princely the sum. Likewise, she has no wish to be parted from the sculptor, even if it were to mean forever remaining a work in progress.

She opened the doors.

The doors open out into desire. The wishes of our bloody, four-chambered hearts.

And likely as not I've missed the mark three times, so here the narrator leaves you to your own narrative devices, your own wishes. You may turn the key – or not. You may step inside – or not. You may close the doors behind you – or not.

These are not choices that can be made for another.

Evensong

The ocean at once represents death and the possibility of rebirth...
Greek Heroine Cults, Jennifer Lynn Larson (1995)

On any given day, dozens of people might see what remains of the altar. Though most will not notice it, if only because they have visited the cove too often, and so it's a familiar sight. West Cove, at the southeast corner of Conanicut Island, is a popular destination for scuba divers, fishermen, kayakers and canoeists, bird watchers, and beachcombers. So the sizable chunk of weathered concrete wedged into the granite crevice to the left of the boat ramp (left if one happens to be looking out across the water and not landward) has, to most who have seen it, become unremarkable. Often, the extraordinary, the divine, the profane becomes of little interest. Though, here, there is not need to invoke the idiom that "familiarity breeds contempt."

At worse, an occasional visitor to the cove might pause to joke about the peculiar, cartoonish image traced into the concrete however many decades ago, when it was still wet, still freshly poured. To many, the image is nothing more than a momentary amusement, what might be an odd sort of cephalopod, with the claws of a lobster visible on either side of it. The octopus-like creature, many have thought, might actually be the head of a lobster, poorly rendered. And, truthfully, the Paleolithic cave paintings – the aurochs, horses, bears, rhinoceri, and etcetera – at Lascaux are more artful than this image at West Cove.

There was more of it once, and, obviously, what remains is only a fragment, an incomplete pictograph of whatever the artist was striving to convey.

Waves and high tides have battered the image for all the many years it has existed. And it is certainly worse for the wear, hence the confusion over exactly what it is meant to depict, though most agree it's only a lobster, a conclusion bolstered by the strings of lobster pots and their bobbing floats set only a few hundred yards from shore. It might be thought, by some, a humorous sort of tabernacle erected by the lobster men, in a joking (or half-joking) effort to assure better catches. This assumption, is, at best, only a third correct.

For on a night every tenth year, a night when the tide of the *seasons* is turning from autumn to winter, a ragtag assortment of supplicants gather at the cove. By then, the trees are barren (or almost so), and the wind off Narragansett Bay quickly chills a woman or man straight down to the bone. But they come, regardless, whether the moon is waxing or waning, full or new, whether there are clear skies or there are clouds, and they are not to be dissuaded by either rain or, on rare occasions, an early snow. At midnight they gather white-robed below the parking lot, there at the boat ramp. And *they* know the identity of the image traced into the concrete boulder, its identity and its significance. They know it is a thing that was ancient before the retreat of ice-age glaciers and the flooding of the canyons and valleys that became this bay. The name is never spoken aloud – not even in whispers or hushed tones – for there would be for them no greater blasphemy than to burden and define it with a cognomen.

The low waves lapping at the shore is a metronome, setting the rhythm for the hymn they offer in veneration of the thing traced there in the concrete. They do not exactly sing and do not precisely chant. This hosanna is neither one nor the other, as are so many other aspects of their worship. Unspeakable, indefinable acts, neither this nor that. They call out, and their commingled voices are snatched by the wind and blown out across the dark waters of the cove, held between the craggy low cliffs to the east and west, the borders of this narrow anchorage.

One among them has been chosen for the honor of this offering, and always it is a woman. Setting aside the issue of sexism in blood sacrifices, it should be noted that she is never a virgin. So, at least that one cliché is dodged. She must *not* be a virgin, and better she be the wanton sort, a woman so defiled she has known pleasures and agonies for which there are not even names. Unlike her companions, she is nude beneath her white woolen robe. The libations she has been given render her immune to any discomfort from the cold. Yet, they render her not insensible, but more *aware,* more attuned, that she may bear witness to the deeper fabric of the night, layers unknown or only half-suspected by her colleagues.

The strange and indefinable hymn drifts across the cove, and, seventy-feet down, her soon-to-be lover stirs from silt and wreckage, disturbing heaps of cobbles and schools of cod, as it shakes off the sediment of another decade's slumber. It has no gender, and yet is not a hermaphrodite, nor is it gonochoric. The god of the men and women in their white robes exists beyond all concepts of sex. As it rises, a host of earlier brides scuttle away to deeper waters. It stirs, and then slowly it rises and moves silently and unseen towards shore.

The priestess – she who was never half degraded enough to be offered up on any night – speaks, though the others do not fall silent to listen. They know her words by rote, as does the sacrifice. But this is tradition, and tradition is at the root of this night. Tradition must not be deviated from. The thing moving slowly towards the shore is a thing of strictest habit, and any discrepancy in the ceremony could send it back to the deep, and each of the supplicants to their own private damnations.

"You do this of your own volition?" the priestess asks.

"I do," replies the bride.

"You go down with no regrets?"

"I do."

"You will faithfully serve XXXXXXXXXX forever more, and you understand there is no possibility of return?"

"I do."

"You forsake this human form?"

"I do."

There are other questions and other replies, but no need here to record each and every one. Better to mention the jealousy and envy of those who have not proven themselves proper courtesans for this holiest of holy nights.

"You will not ever die," the priestess assures the bride. "Beyond the transformation, you will know a life everlasting, so long as the world doth endure."

The bride does not doubt even for an instant the truth of this promise, and not only because it would be sacrilege to do so. Her ungendered betrothed has visited her dreams every fifth night of the last year, and she has glimpsed not only its face, so crudely rendered in the concrete block. She has also been shown its harem, and she has seen the immense age of many of them huddled among the submerged rocks of the bay.

"You will make of yourself a gift, and your generosity will be rewarded with the mysteries forever withheld from those not chosen."

"I shall."

"There exist no words for your fortune."

"There do not, and there never shall."

"Then the moment has come round," the priestess tells the bride. The bride lowers her hood and unties the stays of her robe, allowing it to fall in a heap at her bare feet. The priestess anoints the brides forehead, the space between her breasts, and, lastly, the hairless rise of her *mons veneris* with an oily substance held inside an empty whelk. The substance is dark as pitch and stinks of frankincense, turpentine, and fish gone ripe beneath an August sun. The bride bows once to the priestess, then makes a sign with her left hand, a sign for the others to cease their hymn that is neither a song nor a chant.

Now, there is only the whisper of the wind, the gentle shush-shush of the waves, and a fainter sound, as their god moves slowly towards the shore.

"Go," the priestess says, and these are the last words she will be capable of uttering before dawn, for any trace of her mouth abruptly vanishes from the woman's face. But she expected this, having conducted the wedding once before. She is proud that her heart quickens only a tiny bit, that her will holds panic at bay. This is her small measure of blessed transformation, and it's not to go unappreciated.

The bride turns towards the cove and the bay and her advancing mate. She kneels on the rough concrete, and the metamorphosing night reveals itself to her, every minute detail the others will miss. The gift of the libation she was given at sunset. A sight beyond sight, beyond the ken of any but her and her betrothed. It is the latter who is waking up the sea, the shingle, the starry sky spread out overhead (for this night happens to be a night of the new moon, and there is no light but the light of the stars). All the nooks and crannies of the cove doth suffer a sea-change. The barnacles encrusting the rocks at the water's edge, for example, open calcareous valves and, blinking, gaze out with eyes like ink stains, like the eyes of crows. Shoals of fish beach themselves and bleat with the voices of newborn calves. The trees and underbrush grow perfectly still, despite the stiff breeze off Narragansett Bay, while the knotted wrack writhes, rubbery fronds and swollen air bladders twining into impossibly complex patterns. Night birds fall dead from the sky, and the cries of coyotes becomes all but a cacophony. The very darkness in between the stars appears to coil and uncoil, while all those distant suns dotting the heavens pulse like a toothache. The bride sees this, all of it, but the others hear only the howling coyotes, and see the owls and whippoorwills tumbling from the sky. Several among the supplicants may catch sight of the stranded, flopping fish, but they cannot hear their peculiar bleating. For they have not been chosen, and here their part in the ceremony ends, even as the role of the bride is only beginning.

And kneeling, and with her betrothed so near now, the swollen, leathery membrane that has grown between her thighs over the last few months at last ruptures, and from that wound spill organs as completely alien to her anatomy as are the eyes of crows to barnacles. These indescribable parts of the bride squirm in the thick mucus of their own afterbirth, and, with surprising strength, pull her towards the bay. There is no pain, only joy and only ecstasy, sensation that the word *orgasm* could never begin to do justice.

The others turn their backs on her. Only the priestess is permitted to behold this marriage. And even when her tongues and lips are returned, she'll be entirely incapable of describing the form, the shape, the countenance that at last rears from the water. She might make comparisons to a thousand animals and plants, but none would be even decent approximations. It bears virtually no resemblance to the thing traced into the concrete block.

The bride raises her arms in a welcoming embrace, and that which has burst from her fastens itself to her lover. There is an almost imperceptible sucking noise, and then she is gone, and for many months will she sleep in the belly of her god. Swaddled in rugal folds and bathed in a scared stew of gastric acids and proteases, she will suffer her own *private* sea change. She will be nourished by her god's every meal, having become its cherished symbiote. And then, finally, on a night when bioluminescent copepods and squids, dinoflagellates and comb jellies set the moonlit bay afire, what she has become will be expelled from this temporary Heaven to take its place among all the brides who have come before.

The men and women in their white robes linger for almost an hour, and two acolytes tend to the voiceless priestess and tie a red silk cloth around her face, for her eyes have begun to bleed. And then the supplicants wander away. Not all at once, but by ones and twos. They can rest now, knowing their part has been done, and the furious hunger has been sated, and for another ten years the world will turn unimpeded upon its axis.

The sleepers in their houses along Walcott Avenue and Newport Street and as far into Jamestown as Blueberry Lane toss and turn and mutter as a terrible shadow passes through their dreams. But in the shadow of that shadow is a beautiful woman who leads the beast away with a song none of them will remember upon waking.

The tide rises, as it always does, as it always will, and the innocuously abominable concrete block is decently covered again.

Latitude 41°21'45.89"N, Longitude 71°29'0.62"W

Walking the jetty (she is a *woman* walking a jetty), which is not so much walking as it is mountain-goat leaping from one enormous granite black or slab to the next. I can't say if this granite was mined from the quarries of faraway Cape Anne, Massachusetts. Or if it came from quarries much nearer, from Westerly, perhaps. Either way, my rubber soles leap from boulder to boulder, these chunks of magma cooled four-hundred and fifty million years ago, the Iapetus oceanic plate colliding with and then beginning to sink beneath the North American craton in that cold Late Ordovician age, and here the protracted birth pains of the Appalachians begin. Recorded in the curve of this jetty and the bones of New England, writ in porphyritic textures, this plagioclase composition below my feet of alkali feldspar, quartz, pinkish, gray, almost white, almost black. Oh, yes, once I was a geologist, left with this head full of stone and deep time and orogenies and subduction events. I've read the book of the earth. But *that* story is not *this* story. If this is a story at all, and it may well be something else.

"A man is not a thing, but a drama." That's Joseph Campbell. Look it up.

And an axiom of Hermetic philosophy: *As above, so below*, isn't that scrawled in these rough stones I jump, from one to the next to the next? Almighty slick from salt spray to the east, where there is little refuge at the Harbor of Refuge, which, factually, lies on my *left*, to the west. The right side, on *my* right, is battered, unsheltered, unrefuged. The Army Corps of Engineers, in their toils of the 1930s, favored the west, where even at the waning of this stormy autumn day the water lies dark and placid. Mats of seaweed bobbing placidly *there*, while on my *right* an angry sea slams itself to pieces, jewel spray to, grain by grain, devour the stone, make of it sand, make it amnesiac granules to forget plutonic plumes so far below.

Turn my head to the right, and there's the beacon of the Point Judith Lighthouse, calling ships home, steering them safely from sirens and jagged, submerged granite reefs that will never be quarried in the history of humanity. I pause to stare at the glassed-in housing of the lantern room; considering the clockworks for those rotating lenses, devised and installed to time the comforting yellow-white flash that divides the gloom settling all about me.

Then I am off the jetty, and there's only scrunching parking lot below my feet, running even if I can't say why, running maybe from the sea-slammed shore at my back. Even the lighthouse would never keep me safe from the ocean's fury. "Many gods, and many voices." That's Elliot, T. S. Look it up, if you don't believe me. I'm running east towards the not-quite-*entirely*-reassuring lighthouse, and I pass a modest fisherman's memorial (those gone down to the sea, only never returned), and scale a steep hill, and then my busy feet carry me down into scrubland and salt-marsh sanctuary. First and second frosts a week since come and gone to brown, to kill, make sleep, wither away all the dog roses (*Rosa canina*), the blackberry (*Rubus fruticosus*), black raspberry (*Rubus occidentalis*) and greenbrier vines (*Smilax* sp.), poison ivy (*Toxicodendron radicans*), thick and ochre-browned tufts of smooth cordgrass (*Spartina alterniflora*) and saltmeadow hay (*S. patens*), patches of sea lavender (*Limonium carolinianum*). My careless feet repeatedly tangle in the snarls of vegetation, and so I fall too many times to count. I scrape my hands, and briers rip at my cheeks. I know where I'm going, and I know I'm late, and what's a little blood to unnamable marine, riparian, estuarine, aeolian, botanical gods?

"What, indeed."

Dash. Mad, mad dash (he is a *man*, dashing). Dashing *towards* a devil, instead of *away* from one. Oh, I know her name. Her name is etched in diamond-drill characters in the secret vacuities behind my eyes. So, mad, mad, pell-mell, headlong fucking dash, shoes sinking into squelching mud freezing cold and all but crisped with ice. My feet know where I will be when the journey has ended, when I am nearer to the lighthouse rising up before me, wink, dark, wink, dark, eye of Polyphemus trusted by all good sailors entering and exiting Narragansett Bay, the lobstermen loaded down with lobsters and the titanic container ships loaded down with tons of dry goods in metal crates. The light appears to me now less a friend than before, and more the one-eyed cannibalistic son of Poseidon and Thoosa. Many beasts have eye-shine. A giant might easily be mistaken for a lighthouse, then, it follows, yes. I've no sheep bellies, and I've not so convenient a tool as a burning spear with which to blind so great a beast. So it will watch what this trembling, falling, clumsy (*woman* running in the marsh) pilgrim will do this twilight. I can hear the cars not so far away – only some two-hundred yards north – coming and going out on 108 (also named, unimaginatively, Ocean Road), and each of those, if legal, has *two* electric eyes.

In dreams, she's shown me the grave and called me to her.

In dreams. I close my eyes, then drift away, into a magic night, and that has become *this* night. And she has rendered me a fluid flesh thing, now woman, then man, then woman, and the changes will roll on and on, so I may as well be a perpetual Tiresias ("son" of a shepherd and of a nymph), smit'er, smiting copulating serpents, priestess of Hera and/or renowned whore for seven years. I've seen no snakes tonight, and I will not; a different magick is at work upon me, dragging myself to her open grave. I know it to be open, for *in dreams* she has shown me so.

"Into the magic night," I softly say.

She, he, it. I, him, her. The required hermaphrodite. But I must be a functional hermaphrodite; not enough to possess dick and ovaries, scrotum and vagina. There must be sperm and eggs, and everything must be in anatomical, reproductive order, as with earthworms, garden snails, clownfish and wrasse, banana slugs, or, like the dragon fruit (possessing both pollen-producing staminate *and* ovule-producing carpellate tissue). At this moment, picking my way through the tall grasses and briers, my body flickers from this to that, that to this, but she has told me when I stand before her, equilibrium will be achieved. I will be perfectly one thing, but possessed of the sexual prowess of both. *Perfected,* she whispers in dreams.

A dream is a wish your heart makes, yes, or only hear, perhaps, turned round about. So, then, a wish is a dream your heart makes? How does it possibly matter, what with me so near now, and some revelation more than wishes and dreams *must* be at hand. Here is this patch of hardly dry land – hardly marsh, either – between the pond nearest the Point Judith Lighthouse and the much smaller pond near the potholed, muddy dirt road leading to that so-called Harbor of Refuge, though I found none there. No refuge. So, what with me here, running through the weeds, crash, underbrush, frightening rabbits and a fox, smelling salt and the sewage, sex stink of this sodden earth.

I come upon the open grave so suddenly that I almost plunge into it, and wouldn't *that* have been a funny, funny state of affairs, a grand *faux pas* in this nightmare or dream or rough-beast slouch towards tomorrow's damning salvation. *Fall* on you, this autumn, this *fall*. I fall on you, and would that, would that, would that break our compact? Or would she, you, take me in her, your arms and sing, "Go to sleep, everything's alright." Can the itinerary change like that? How can I know when I am only iron pulled to the magnet in that grave.

A grave dug into the blue-gray clay and glacial sands, not six by six, but plenty spacious to contain her. More than sufficient, we (I) will say. I gaze upon the perfection of that living *corpus,* and, true to her word, I am made the perfect epicene.

There is no knowing when she was laid to rest here, so no knowing how *long* she has lain here, or, likewise, who lowered her into the grave, or if she did it herself. How many spectacles has she "witnessed" on this spit of land? She must have seen, for an example, May 5, 1945, on the occasion of the sinking of the allied *SS Black Point,* a collier of its way to Boston with its load of coal. Sent straight to the bottom, and all hands lost, dragged a hundred and thirty-five feet down into silt gardens of eelgrass and crabs by the Nazi sub *U-853* (German Type IXC/40, *Kriegsmarine,* who met her own fate the *very next day,* when the *SS Black Point* was swiftly avenged). She would have witnessed the destruction of the *first* lighthouse in 1811, hurricane slain, and then seen, too, the redcoat Captain Wallace order his troops to burn the farms at Point Judith. Oh, but here I am being *homo-centric,* and how do I know she has any especial interest in the tragedies of humanity. Maybe the births of skunk kits (*Mephitis mephitis*), the April breeding hordes of horseshoe crabs (*Limulus polyphemus*; that name again, I know), and the eggs of herring gulls (*Larus smithsonianus*) are of more or equal concern. Maybe she's called members of *those* disparate species unto her, as well, and countless others, so tonight she only wears a human form because I need to *see* and be *greeted* by a human form. Maybe this is an act of indulgence and consideration, a kindness, molecular recombination. Though, part of my ragged soul would be disappointed to learn she is ever subject to considerate acts of this sort.

My gods, the beauty of her.

In dreams you're mine all of the time.

There is great pain in my abrupt physical transformation, but it was an expected agony and not unwelcome. We endure that which makes us more than ever we thought we could be. Elsewise we are undeserving and not even to be pitied.

I can here try to describe the indescribable beauty of her, if only because I am subject to such a folly: a woman, no doubt of *her* sex, at least not in this moment; a body graven from the same reddish granite I walked across out on the jetty, but polished smooth as smooth will ever be; crystalline skin catching the light of the rising moon; every detail attended to, despite this smoothness, erect nipples, the nub of her clit, every strand of hair, eyelashes, teeth glimpsed, iris, pupil, sclera, labial lips, a navel, and a hundred more particulars; almost six feet tall, *almost,* but not quite, which makes her taller than me; and that is quite enough of this delineative indiscretion, I think. I have fallen to my knees in the throes of the gift of her pain, as my anatomy is rearranged to suit *her* purposes. I kneel now in the mud and freshly turned soil at the edge of her grave (if it's fair to say *grave,* and not *bed chamber*). I have no memory of having undressed, but…

A silent prayer like dreamers do.

…I am nude now, and I suppose if she can perform such physiological alchemy what ease it would be to cause the evaporation of fabric or lead me to not remember disrobing. I have no cause to question her motives, and, besides, I know from my dreams what is to come, and it could hardly be accomplished while clothed. She raises her arms, and to one who does not even begin to grasp the what of her (as I only *just* do), that sort of person would be expecting, I don't doubt, stone in motion to shatter and rain shards. She doesn't shatter, but there is the faintest imaginable smile, and the parting of those igneous thighs to welcome her hermaphroditic creation, husband-wife-son-daughter-lover-devotee. I have ached for this moment, in all the ways a woman or man may ache (and I've forgotten which sex I began as and know that knowledge is no longer of any consequence).

"Come to me," the wind off the sea whispers.

"Climb down and let me embrace your beauty," whisper tiny black beetles scuttling about her body.

"Descend and ascend," whispers the dry blades of cordgrass.

The entirety of the night is her voice. Through other creatures, she speaks a thousand languages, this ventriloquist extraordinaire.

A bit of ragweed mutters, "I am waiting."

There is no repeating the patience of her voice. She has waited for *me* down long years, decades, centuries, millennia, and who can testify to the extent of these expanding, ever inclusive temporal units. I can't. But I will not try her patience. I am the supplicant, and I obediently go down to My Lady of Stone. With these impossible organs that are neither, and yet are both, she accepts he into her. There is no friction in our coupling, even if the only wetness is my perspiration coupled with the night's condensation on the surface of her. The coalescing of beads drawn from two oceans. And the wetness of my cunt. I slip inside, and there is cold to put Arctic and Antarctic, boreal and austral climes, to shame. I dimly marvel I am not flash frozen as if by a bath of liquid nitrogen. She slips granite fingers into me, and I *am* grown wet, as I have noted already. We lie surrounded by the earth on four sides, within the boundaries of our rectilinear marriage substratum.

I can still hear the waves pounding the shore, and it occurs to me for the first time that the sea is *jealous*. But, oh, of course! It chews at the land, struggling to chew enough that it will gain her grave and swallow her entire that she might be dashed apart by its waves and foam, and those dead (or still living) fragments of her encrusted with barnacles and mussels, prowled by hungry periwinkles. But if this could have happened, it would have happened long, long ago, and so I imagine a secret, immemorial college charged with the task of exhumation and reburial as need be, as dictated by the advancing tide and the shifting of continental plates.

My lips brush hers, and that rocky tongue probes my mouth.

My palate tingles with an almost (or entirely) electric charge. But I know granite is a silicate, like glass, and both are insulative, and so poor, poor conductors. It is me, not her, my conductive flesh, approximately 40 liters of water, some 57%, through which that current flows, if any current flows. I imagine voltage so profound as to tear my constituent electrons out of their orbits, unmaking me, and I will be a fork of lightning sparking upwards into the Rhode Island night. But I *only* imagine. Her polished tongue glides along my palate, and I shudder.

And then I hear a sound entirely indescribable. She holds me so tightly, and me being so lost in desire, there is no looking back to see the originator of that sound, which roars from the direction of the ocean. *Oh, smile and pray, like dreamers do.*

This sudden tumult could be a mountain rising from the surf, only no such noise *ever* haunted my haunted dreams. Has she kept a secret? Has she only shown me half? Have I been duped by my goddess? And for no reason that is immediately clear, I recall the fleshy growth dangling above the mouth of an anglerfish (*Melanocetus johnsonii*), so named the *esca* by ichthyologists, the bioluminescence of that organ drawing prey into snapping jaws. Is that the truth of this tryst? Is she merely a *lure?*

"No, my dear love. It isn't like that at all," mutters the grubs coiled amongst the roots all around us. "Be patient. You'll understand soon enough. You'll *marvel.*"

And I plunge deeper into her, this organ that she's given me which is almost a penis, and she slips her fingers deeper into me, into that organ that is not quite a vagina.

I am dying, and I am finally being born.

I see with new eyes the arc between the one and the other, and how there is so very little difference.

What rough beast in back of me? But there is, and never will be, the freedom to look upon that fearful symmetry, that monstrous thing monstrous and free. *And,* I think, *am I not grown monstrous now? Was that not part and parcel of her gift to me?*

The sounds of a mountain summit thrust up from the seafloor makes me think many, many things as we lie in the mud and fuck. As our bodies squirm into impossible configurations, as I am all but sick and insane with ecstasy. A mountain has risen, though, I know of a certain, and now it strides towards the shore. I cannot but help, even through the awful pain and pleasure, of displacement and tsunamis that must now be racing across the Atlantic and of the earthquake I didn't feel. Science doesn't impede, much less halt, the path of a breathing, walking mountain. We have left all science behind, all those pretty theories, hypotheses, theorems, algorithms, models, nomenclatures. We are most assuredly fallen back into those *nights of first ages,* of those aeons that are gone, *leaving hardly a sign.* Perhaps not any of the world remaining now but *me* and *she* and *it.* But we can no longer exist within the fabric of any sane universe. Or within any (relativistic) concept of sanity. We cannot *exist,* but we do. A trinity, I think, neither holy nor unholy, merely as indifferent as granite.

I do see something now, for her polished skin no longer glimmers beneath the moonlight, as the moonlight has been blotted out, as the walking mountain has eclipsed the moon and even the starshine cannot reach our hole. This darkness must even have swallowed the Point Judith Lighthouse and every speck of light from the bobbing ships far out in the sound and all lights far inland. No, no. Because I have already said we are not in *that* universe anymore, and of that I am without doubt. We are *removed.* Where *to* is of no consequence, and this is the jumble of my thoughts as we make nothing that could ever be called love, because she doesn't love me, and what I feel for her may never be contained in so short a word, so *stingy* a noun.

And then the mountain enters me.

No.

First there is *another* transformation of my body, triggered either by her or by it. By whom matters not one goddamn whit. For I *am* damned by gods, am I not? And this thought almost makes me laugh. And I understand how there is no salvation *excepting* damnation. How have I never known *that* before *this* moment. But, I was saying, another transformation, no describing it, no point, but it allows some erect organ of that mountain to take me from behind, even as I am still thrusting myself into her.

This is no simple coupling. It is a *tripling*.

Three organisms (if we are, technically, organisms) are required to complete the aforementioned arc – electric, reproductive, or what you will.

I am sure I will die. I will be split apart, regardless what they have made of me. Lava flows into that new orifice, primitive melts of kimberlite, lamprophyre, lamproite, alkali basalts drawn from mantle regions, then primary and parental melts, komatiite and picrite, and the ejaculation of the mountain ends with only mafic, intermediate, felsic, ultramafic lavas broiling my newly-formed womb at 650, 750, 950° C, and yet no part of me is immolated. But, instead, made indestructible. For what is being deposited within the me of *now* cannot be trusted to any fragile uterine lining, no mere endometrium. It needs a geode incubator equal to its violence and solidity.

I lie with her, taking her, taken from behind by a being to crumple any consciousness, and I know I rest within the kiln they have created for me. The crucible within which I am melted and forged anew.

I am terrified and not the least bit afraid of anything.

I am divided and made whole.

And then she is gone, and the mountain slides back into the sea with far less fanfare than it emerged. I lie fetal in the cordgrass and shriveled vines, shivering and gazing in turn at the stars and the Cyclops eyes of the full moon and the lighthouse. The foghorn is almost as loud as my heartbeat. The counterpoint of a bell buoy. My body is as they undid and repurposed it, and I'll have to find somewhere safe to wait out the interminable passage of gestation, which, for all I know may require a geologic, rather than biologic, timescale. But for now I can only rest, and heal, and watch the sky, hear the waves, the wind. If I were not sufficient to the task set before me, it would never have *become* my task. I am to bear into this wicked age of man the seed of its final dissolution. For now it is but a cobble growing inside me, but time is already flowing around me like a river. I am in the universe of my birth again, and here time is only time.

Another Tale of Two Cities

The people are the city.
William Shakespeare, *Coriolanus* (c. 1607-08)

Her name is appropriately Phyllida, but that is to be written off as a coincidence. Unless one chooses, instead, to read meaning into what has, in the recent past, been termed "meaningful coincidence." Her name is Phyllida, and she isn't entirely certain how it began, her reconstruction, for the Builders have never made a point of telling her. Even that word she uses to refer to them – the Builders – is of her own invention, the only word she has for them, as they have never offered up any other name for themselves. But, in most other ways, they have proven cordial and communicative.

Phyllida has thought that perhaps she inhaled them one day, that they arrived via a random inhalation. She has entertained the notion that they entered her bloodstream by way of a paper cut or a scrape or a splinter beneath a fingernail. Perhaps a toilet seat or a drinking fountain. Possibly the bite of an alien insect that had somehow found its way across the vacuum of space and survived the descent to the surface of the Earth. All of these scenarios are (each in its own way) tenable. Yet the one she most often settles on is that the Builders are an elaborate psychosomatic phenomenon, devised to fill some emptiness within her that has always existed and would have always existed, if not for their emergence.

These conjectures are, of course, irrelevant. The only thing here that matters is that the Builders have come, whether by accident or whether they chose her or whether she is their author. It only matters that Phyllida has given herself over to them completely, soon full in the knowledge of their intent, and that she has yet to regret that. They have bestowed upon her a *purpose*. They have come to love her as no one ever has, not even her parents or grandparents, no other human being. Whatever they are, they love her unconditionally for the gift of herself to them.

Sometimes she has trouble recalling how it began, and other times that part is clear as clear can be. A tiny welt on the back of her left hand, but it didn't itch or cause her any other discomfort, and so she paid it very little mind. In those days, she was a worker in the Neo-Byzantine labyrinth of an office building, in a hive not so different from what the Builders are busy making of her. She was a drone in a hive, the whys and wherefores she only ever half bothered to consider. The work paid the bills, and the work asked only a modicum of attention from her; it wasn't difficult to be a drone. If the Builders have a class that are effectively drones, she believes they must find more reward in their work than she ever did in the honeycomb of that fluorescent-lit maze of cubicles. "Veal-fattening pens," she once heard them called, and, as derogatory as the phrase was, and as laced with overt cannibalistic innuendo, she couldn't actually *disagree* with the sentiment.

But it was there, in the workaday tomb of a faceless, latter-day Minos, that Phyllida first noticed the welt, and even though it didn't itch, even though she paid it only a passing glance, she did happen to scratch it. She understands it hardly matters that she scratched it by accident. The result was the same. The Builders, in that instant, were activated, and began to flood her bloodstream, and from there moved into every nook and cranny of her physiology. When the nail of her right index finger broke the skin, there was a hardly audible *pop*. To the microbial oragnisms that are the Builders, it may have sounded like the sundering of worlds, but to Phyllida it wasn't any more than that, a *pop*. She sat in her chair a while, anonymous within her anony- mous cubicle, before the screen of her computer monitor and the mundane clutter of her desk, and stared at the place where the welt had been. Now there was a miniscule pockmark in its place, but one that wasn't bleeding, or raw, and one that hadn't released any pus. Instead, there was the briefest metallic cloud, black metallic, which put her in mind of graphite. Fitting, as the pockmark was no larger than the tip of a sharp pencil (though the welt had easily been as big around as a dime). The cloud settled on her skin, and there was a mild tingling. There was also, almost immediately, a wave of diz- ziness and nausea that sent her to the restroom. She vomited, then went to the sink and splashed her face with cold water, and stared at herself in the mirror.

The Builders spoke to her for the first time then, and it was made clear that they would leave if she took exception to what was coming, which they laid out as clearly as the blueprints of any architect – for architects they are. It surprised her that she felt no fear. She felt curiosity. And an excitement that bordered on the sexual. And, most importantly, she was suddenly gripped by a sense that she was *wanted*. Likely, it was that last that sealed the bargain between her and the invaders. A loaded word, but that's how she thought of them at first, the *invaders*. She would only begin to think of them as the Builders in the days to come.

Then you should leave, they told her. *You should leave and never again return to this place, which has never had anything to offer you but drudgery and a paycheck.*

Which is what she did, leave, though she didn't go home to her apartment. She followed their explicit instructions, for she'd soon come to understand how painstakingly the Builders had laid their plans. And those plans were sound. And she knew none better, and had no wish to disrupt them. A sanctuary had been prepared for Phyllida, a corner on the third story of an abandoned warehouse. Here she and the Builders would be safe from discovery for all the generations that were to come and go and for all the time that she would be their vessel. She undressed, shivering at the cold and damp (though assured all such discomfort would soon enough pass and never inconvenience her again), then sat down on the bare, dusty concrete, her back wedged into a redbrick corner.

"Will there be pain?" she asked aloud, not yet apprehending that her voice wasn't needed to communicate with the Builders. They answered that there would be some discomfort at first, but that it would pass very quickly; the chemists among them were already busy formulating anesthetics to ensure this, compounds that would begin to be administered before much longer, and that would thereafter be available as needed.

"You've thought it all out," she said, smiling, amazed that such thinking creatures could exist. "All the angles and contingencies."

Not all, no. But as many as we were able to calculate.

And she asked, also, "Am I the first?"

No. *I* asked. Be done with the silly artifice of third person.

No, the Buiders replied. *You aren't the first, and you won't be the last.*

Somehow, this thought was as comforting, in its way, as the promise that there would be very little pain.

Then a third question: "Will this be forever?"

If you're asking if it will be a permanent metamorphosis, then the answer is yes. But if you're asking if you are being gifted with immortality, then we must admit the answer is no. No civilization lasts. All fall, sooner or later.

And I know enough of history that I could hardly argue. Indeed, the reply made me embarrased that I'd even asked.

It will be, the Builders answered, *and none among us may guess how long. We cannot even conceive of the passage of time as you do. Our best guess would be meaningless to you.*

In the moments the exchange had required (and I was beginning to wonder if my sense of time was being altered along with my body), the Builders had already laid the foundations for their new and great city. And how long would that require of them? Decades? Centuries? How many generations had been born and died, had lived and played out their miniscule lives within and upon me? Rome was not built in a day. Very few things of beauty and function, very few things worth the effort, ever are.

The Builders spoke to me constantly, and I watched with eyes that were still eyes as ancient history was related (immemorial to their race, but which might only have occurred during my last week). I came to know almost all they knew of themselves, and I marveled that such things could be. I knew their evolution, economies, wars, sciences, and half a thousand other fields of endeavor. I knew, too, how they chose the vessels, which made me all the more grateful and surprised than I had been. I grasped the nature of all the gifts that had been bequeathed to me, no matter how fleeting they might (or might not) prove to be: a peace I'd never have known, utility and service beyond the kin of man, and the constant companionship of my inhabitants (unless I desired silence).

I watched in awe. Perhaps there was fear, too, but, if so, it was eclipsed and rendered all but irrelevant. My skin shimmered in the dim light of the warehouse (was it daylight or night, morning or afternoon, dawn or dusk?). The shimmer was almost, but not quite, the same black metallic I'd seen when I'd scratched the welt on the back of my hand. There was a sort of portal where my navel had been, and I pondered how vast its diameter and circumference must be to them, and how deeply into me it led.

Already, the Builders' unspoken voices had made me aware that my body had been firmly and forevermore anchored to the concrete and bricks, and that the process employed to accomplish this restraint had necessitated an osteological alchemy. My own bones had become the pillars, columns, pilasters, buttresses, cantilever and strap footings, piers, and caissons needed to support and hold fast what I was fast becoming, from the back of my skull and legs, along the entire length of my spine (now all but indistinguishable from the wall). My legs and feet were quickly becoming lost in an unspeakably beautiful and elaborate assemblage of spans and towers and bridges tying one knee, one ankle, to its companion. Soon, there was nothing recognizable remaining of either leg, and still I felt no panic. Nor did I feel pain. The Builders were keeping that promise. I wondered what my face was becoming, and so they presented to me an image, but I cannot imagine the words that could begin to explain it. Except to say that it seemed a mask of glass and steel, partioned into a million geometric prisms. My eyes were no longer what they had been before, though the function remained essentially the same. Only now, they were the lenses through which the Builders might view distant worlds (and I'll not conjecture their measurements of distance). I no longer had any need to blink, which was fortunate, as my eyelids had been absorbed and that matter repurposed. There was a brief and violent itching below my chin, but it vanished almost as suddenly as it began, and I recalled assurance there would be balms and anesthetics as needed.

How can a city show gratitude to its architects?

We know, the Builders assured me. *Our great-great-great forefathers who chose you chose well, and we keenly feel your gratutude, as we hope you feel ours.*

I told them, *I do. I do feel that,* finding that I'd long since lost the need for words. The honeycombed chambers of my brain had been modified for (among many other things) a communication free of spoken words.

The black-metallic expanse of Me sprouted skyscrapers thin as human hairs, but reaching fantastic heights that semed to defy any earthly gravity. I was a canvas for domes no larger than the heads of pins, and highways and backroads and tunnels burrowed and snaked around this given *corpus* in such numbers a hundred years might be needed to catalog and traverse them. The immense canyon, maw, cavern of my slack jaws held a single megalopolis to shame all of Europe and America, and from it were launched flying machines the likes of which men have never conceived. Forests of molds and mosses sprouted along my arms and thighs, were harvested, replanted, and grew again. My sex was sealed and a gigantic (all things being relative here) waste disposal facility created from my anus, flowing into hollows cut into the concrete floor beneath me. I found that funny and would have laughed, if I were still capable, and I pondered the likelihood that an evolutionary biologist might have considered that an example of exaptation, preadaptation. Afterall, why reinvent the wheel?

Sometimes I puzzled – vaguely – over the sources of so many of the Builders raw materials and was informed that everything they'd ever require, down all their Ages of Me, were contained within the body I'd offered up. It was easy to synthesize steel from the iron in my blood, concrete from the calcium in my skeleton, vast reservoirs from the water contained within me. Even an almost inexhaustable supply of petrochemicals. Indeed, more of me was now composed of various plastics than of that old flesh.

Nothing is inexhaustable, I warned, remembering distant, half-forgotten crises in the world that had given birth to my former self. *I am not without my limits to serve.*

And after I "said" this, there was a silence from the Builders, a long, long silence that might have lasted many of their decades. I felt the heat of wars. I heard the mounting panic as this sprawling city they'd made of me began to starve and wither. First as scattered voices, and then as a single united cry, I heard their prayers to me – for what other god might so systematic a race ever devise? *We listened too late. Deliver us.*

How are we to save ourselves and the children of the children of our children's children? They named me MOTHER, and I surely *would* have cried at that, *had* I been capable of tears.

I could offer them no surcease, nor any solutions. I was only what I had been made – they were my creators, bioengineers of the living habitation I was, not the other way round – and never had the First Builders, nor any subsequent generation, gifted me with any contingency. But I did see now, and seeing mourn, that this race was not so very different from my own – rushing blindly forward towards self-annihilation. Only...

Some one among them, or perhaps many minds, were able to decipher that equation my refashioned consciousness could not. Their prayers become a pledge. *We will not allow you to die, MOTHER. We see the way now. We see the path to undo that evil which we have done.* But, in truth, I found little comfort in those words. How many times had this drama been enacted? How many times had the progenitors of this population of Builders chosen a man or a woman, only to destroy the gift? Why should I have any reason to suspect their "path" was anything more than wishful thinking and folly, the fumbling grasping of desperate minds facing the end of their existence?

But I was ignorant of the resourcefulness of the offspring of my anatomy. I underestimated their genius, drawing foolishly upon humanity for an analogy, anthropomorphizing something that I now know can never be anthropomorphized. I had done them all, each and every one, a disservice.

There was a brief stirring deep in the grotto they'd made of me. A brief stirring to me, but for them I suspect the sensation might have represented the toil of many years. And then my sex, which had long ago been sealed, was reopened. I would liken that event to the parting of the slit in the roof of an observatory, and I suspected that this mechanism had existed there all along. I watched on as my vagina expelled a gleaming craft no larger than an agate or cat's-eye marble. I watched on as it floated away, only inches above the concrete. I watched until it vanished in the distance, and I instinctively understood that the Builders had constructed what science-fiction writers would have termed a "generation ship," carrying untold numbers of their race, in search of...I couldn't say what. Surely not another host, that they might abandon me. Never once had the Builders lied to me, and I didn't want to believe that they'd chosen, in fear, to begin. The slit closed again, and I waited. I might have waited a very long time. *They* might have waited a hundred times longer. Wars raged on, and the seas within me, the rivers and lakes, were poisoned beyond consumption, and the vast and towering forests of moss, lichen, and algae all but vanished. I could not deny that I *was* dying, and that it was only a question of how long my death would take. It would be a painful death, for the production of the anesthetics had been given up to other priorities to ensure the survival of however many of the Builders who still called me MOTHER and home. I writhed without ever moving, and I screamed silently. I mourned, and I wished constantly for the end of the end.

But then:

On a day, or a night (it matters not which), another had arrived at the deserted warehouse that had become my *firmāmentum* and my *raqa*. The other may have been a woman or it could have been a man. Already, the Builders had made too many renovations for me to recognize the original sex. There was too much joy that I'd not been abandoned to be much concerned with such matters. Even the agony seemed distant. Perhaps another had carelessly scratched a welt on the back of his or her hand, or neck, or ankle, and before me stood the acquiescent and evolving product of that act. The craft born in my biomechanical womb had found a donor, and it knelt before me on the concrete floor. It glimmered, that black-metallic skin and blank silvery eyes like ball bearings. And then I saw what had been constructed between its legs, where once a penis or labia and clit and vagina might have been. I would liken it to a tube, or pipe, a cylinder tightly packed with wriggling, living coils of wiring and cable. Each was almost microscopic, and had they not been in that constant motion I may never have noticed them; had the Builders not long ago created telescopes where once I'd possessed simple retinas. The gleaming figure smiled for me and spoke with a mouth not yet rearranged for other needs. I listened to sexless words, even as the slit of that hangar, launchpad, or departure bay between my thighs was once again opened, and I imagined a few who'd kept the faith. The few who'd awaited the return of the expedition, believing in its eventual success, denying failure while their world succumbed to thoughtless depredations. They'd stayed behind to open me.

The other vessel spoke, and I could not help but be astonished at the sound of another voice that was still *mostly* human.

"Will you accept me?" it said, that question delivered so gently and a second question even moreso. "Will you permit me entry?"

Could it "hear" my wordless reply? I couldn't know, and the voices of the Builders had been quiet for so long they were not there to advise me.

Why have you come? I replied.

"You are the MOTHER," it said. "And I am the MOTHER, and together we will be one, and we will reconstruct what has been wrought within and upon you. I will restore you, and we will be one. I have returned to end the pain."

Then I accept you, I whispered, and I could only hope it heard my gratitude. *Enter me, and we will be one.*

The glimmering figure leaned over me, and it *did* enter me, all those countless cables that had replaced its genitalia finding eager receptors. *Had the Builders made those,* I wondered, *or was that my doing? Had I become my own Builder, a thinking city which, having crossed some threshold, had gained control of its own formation?*

The new one becoming the Second City, soon to be the Same City, fused itself to me, releasing and inserting a million cables (docking, umbilicus), and then its lips brushed against what had been my face. A *kiss,* even if I could not return it. And all the changes that had overtaken me overtook it, my lover and savior, and I felt new life flowing into me. The world made new again by another's sacrifice. The Builders worked, and I aided them, I believe, and the membranes that divided one from the other dissolved, and Two truly *did* become One, in a marriage more intimate than any merely human consumation.

In time, even our psyches were united into a single entity.

I and it became, and are, the City. We are.

And in the shadows of an adandoned building on a street, within another city, we live as we never would have otherwise lived. And the Builders serve, and we serve the Builders, and there will be all the inevitable cycles of Creation again. In time, there may come a Third, and in eons incomprehensible to our symbiotes, even a Fourth to be accepted, incorporated, and offer this City its next salvation.

In Memory of H.R. Giger

Blast the Human Flower

1.

We linger here at the ending of worlds contained upon every single instant, every cosmic instant since that explosion of an infinite point of density and of temperature at some finite period, lying 13.75 ± 0.11 billions of years away from Now. Unless we set this moment of this story Then or in an age Yet To Come, though its arrival is nonetheless entirely inevitable, as is that reliable constant of inevitable cellular, social, planetary, solar, galactic destruction. Destruction on a scale difficult – no, impossible – for minds fashioned of mutation and natural selection to grasp, just as those brains cannot grasp infinity (towards either end of a number line, infinitely vast or infinitely small, infinite expansion or contraction). Either. Or. But still we linger here upon one of those moments, or, actually, some time beyond one of those moments, and, in truth, we linger at some age not too far removed from a moment that was only almost utter destruction. Something that passed by, or that arose from within, or fell, or grew, it hardly matters how, and certainly it does not matter why. It only matters that a cataclysm was visited upon a world, and maybe the world we know, and maybe we are speaking of humans – but maybe this is an alien world, and so we are not speaking of humans at all. But, if the latter is so, for the sake of convenience, we will consider them analogous to human beings, and we will consider their fallen civilization an analog, and the biota – before and even after the cataclysm – at least roughly analogous to our own. It may have been tectonic upheaval, a rogue planet, freezing, rising seas, war (take your pick – nuclear, biological, conventional, chemical, mix and match), gamma burst from a nearby hypernova, proton star collision, geomagnetic reversal, collision with a micro-black hole, or what have you – "infinite" possibilities. All this is prologue, past, and only relevant to those who will, undoubtedly, ask. But the situation that has afterwards evolved and permits recovery and survival of an ecosphere – no matter how diminished or altered from its progenitor – the situation is Now, so long as it is understood that Now exists within the confines of this arbitrarily linear narrative. Here we have new forests, new deserts, new rivers and lakes on newly configured continents divided and bounded by novel seas. But, back to the forests, and back to our analogous humans, unless they are homologous humans, actual descendants of *Homo sapiens.* They inhabit the ruins of the former world, not having yet risen to construct their own towers and domes and highways and subterranean dwellings (assuming they last long enough to do so). Here they are, possibly not even a separate species, not quite yet, though evolution (of a sort never before visited upon the lineage) may already be at work. A quantum leap, an occurrence far surpassing punctuated equilibrium, necessity the mother of…but you know that one. In a world shattered and reorganized, depopulated and repopulated, new relationships arise. New parasites. New examples of symbiosis, too. Which is where we are heading, or the place where, finally, we have come. These women – it remains unclear the role of males in the post-Anthropocene environment, is where we allow our collective imagination to settle. Look this way and listen up, because *this* is the moment. This is the renewal. Here is the shape of things that have come. No name for this tribe, deep within equatorial forests where trees tower in place of all but forgotten skyscrapers and microwave towers. Trees of such a dimension previously unseen on this planet, with roots penetrating and shattering ancient strata and spreading out for miles. In between them, not secret places, but guarded places all the same. Guarded by our sentient maybe women and maybe men, even though guarding is unnecessary. They are the focal point of a new religion, and it is sometimes imagined that the sacred loci of new faiths require protection, whether or not that defeats the idea of omnipotent, omniscient, omnipresent beings. For the purpose of making the story more appealing and giving our tribe the benefit of the doubt let's invent herbivores (or even omnivores) that may forage upon what is guarded – fancied enemies of our fancied epiphytes, our plants of a suitable scale that they are suited to the trees from which they dangle, drooping down hundreds of feet from the titanic branches where their roots have taken hold. It may be they developed from ancestors within the Orchidaceae, or bromeliads, leptosporangiate ferns, or cacti, clubmosses, or even cycads. But…given the particulars of morphology, orchids do seem the most likely candidate (and, actually, all non-flowering groups may be safely ruled out). Regardless, in these new green cathedrals twining vines hang down, down, down to terminate in blooms to dwarf almost any order of Animalia that has persisted beyond the cataclysm. Excepting, on the off chance, enormous ocean-faring forms now filling niches once filled by whales and giant squid. So, having postulated a mechanism and, then, set the scene – partway – here is a young woman in a sanctuary formed naturally by the aforementioned titanic roots. All men and women live within these root houses now. But *this* one is special (though not unique, as each tribe has its own, just as each tribe has its secret, sacred, guarded places). But, yes, here is a woman who has been brought to this place regularly (we'll not be precise about the frequency, the specifics of the cycle). She is brought nude – though, this isn't saying much, as her people have need of very little in the way of clothing. But what sparse apparel she might wear day to day she here removes, upon each visitation. She is the only one who has been chosen from the dozens of females in her tribe, chosen at birth (perhaps part of a matrilineal progression, following mother, grandmother, great-grandmother, and so forth, but that's the scrappiest sort of speculation).

2.

Maybe here, a small bit of history. A recounting of deep time and the concomitant emergence of both flowering angiosperm plants and the sudden radiation of certain groups of insects (if we are assuming this is Earth, and even if we're *not* a very similar situation has likely occurred on many other planets throughout countless galaxies). Sixty to one hundred million years ago, the age deemed the Cretaceous Period, after thick layers of chalk (Latin, *creta*), frequently abbreviated K, from the German *Kriede* (chalk) deposited in vast and shallow epicontinental seaways that covered many continents during the final age of the terrible lizards. But it is not geology that here concerns us – at least not directly – but, rather, the aforementioned sterling example of coevolution. It might be a which-came-first, a chicken-or-the-egg sort of conundrum, but set that aside for paleobotanists and paleoentomologists to ponder. Though the first flowering plants appear in the terran fossil record around 140 million years ago, the explosive radiation of this group cannot be attested to by fossil evidence until, well, the dates given above. In particular, let's concern ourselves with the

Hymenoptera (bees, wasps, ants, and their kin), and *there's* an interesting bit of taxonomic nomenclature: Ancient Greek, *hymen,* and *pteron,* wing. Though hymenopterans first appeared maybe twenty hundred and forty-nine to two hundred and fifty mullion years ago, trusting the fossil record, they do not seem to have come into their own until the angiosperms did likewise – or vice versa. And this all comes down to pollination. Pollin*ators.* Bees and wasps and sawflies who inadvertently carried precious pollen from bloom to bloom. Here, at long last, the flowers had an ally. But a two-way street. The honey-stomach of bees, for instance, ingesting pollen and then regurgitating honey, honey to feed the larvae of the hive. Flowers benefit. Bees benefit. And what should happen if pollinators became extinct (lets include, by the way, the Order Lepidoptera – butterflies – though their contribution to the process didn't become important until tens of millions of years later)? Or what should happen if the angiosperms die out? Symbiosis breaks down. Ends. And, by the way, what may seem like a digression to the reader – especially the impatient reader – is no such thing at all.

3.

Our third and final act.

Call it *climax* if you will, as that word will shortly become a double entendre.

The virgin girl comes once a month to the root house in her village, and, once a month, the priestesses of this nascent mystery cult (for it has begun much as other mystery cults began; Christianity, for example, which was once precisely that). In sanctuary of that living wooden structure, she lies on the loam and offers herself to the ministrations of these priestesses, and this is the way of things, the rhythm of her life, until her twenty-second year. On this day on each month (we are, of course, assuming the familiar lunar, menstrual, and ovulation cycles of "modern" humans), and she submits. That may be the wrong word, for she understands she is honored in her role and would never forsake it and betray her people. If we use the word submit, we must also say the submission is willing. Not only *willing,* but accompanied by a great pride. She will soon become the Mother, consort to the Great MotherFather who resides within that sacred loci spoken of earlier. She is the link who keeps her god and her tribe alive.

Not a sacrifice. Not a simple offering. A *bride.*

It might be the reader begins to comprehend, and it might not be. So, we enter explicit language. Holy language. An unflinching discourse on hallowed rights.

She lies in the loam, and she spreads her legs. Her clitoris is swollen, but not painfully so. There are ointments, prepared by the priestesses, who keep it engorged, and there are plenty enough men and women to slake the appetite that her constant arousal creates. It is the highest compliment, verging on apotheosis, that the Mother To Come will accept someone as a lover. There is no concern of pregnancy, as the genetics of her matrilineal line has made her infertile, excepting a single lover. On rare occasions, there have been murders and mutilations among those who would have her, though she is the one who chooses.

She lies in the loam and spreads her legs.

The priestesses have raised her from an infant, and between them there is complete intimacy (though she must never bed one of *them;* there *are* taboos).

One among the priestesses holds a small brush fashioned of wood and the hair of an animal very like a tapir. She dips it into a stone bowl, the bottom of which contains a very minute amount of yellow-orange pollen. There is no need to lift the clitoral hood, given the perpetual erection of the woman's pseudo-penis. The priestess lightly dabs the pollen from the brush upon the head of the clit, and the other priestesses chant, and the supplicant shudders and whispers a chant all her own. One which may be uttered by no other upon pain of death.

This is the Way for those twenty-two years.

And then…

The Day of Consummation arrives, always on the New Moon, darkest sky and highest tides. Not that the tribe is anywhere near the sea, and the stars are rarely glimpsed between the all-encompassing canopy of the trees.

The young woman is led by the solemn procession of seven of the priestesses to the place where seven women with seven spears (each studded with seven razor teeth from the jaws of a cartilaginous "fish" not unlike a shark) guard the seven entrances to the sacrosanct clearing. The guards part. The priestesses may not follow the Mother To Be inside the ring's circumference. She must walk these last steps alone, and alone she must welcome the long-awaited embrace of the Great MotherFather.

The drooping vines writhe, which would be unexpected of a plant to those unaccustomed to the Plantae of which- and whatever world upon which we are eavesdropping. The drooping vines unfurl, lowering themselves before the bride. Writhing, oozing an amalgam of xylem and phloem sap, a rich soup of minerals, hormones, and carbohydrates. Multiple buds the size of the Mother To Be's hands burst open, a violent blooming accompanied by an indescribable (but most assuredly unpleasant) sound. Calyxes comprised of rubbery, thick sepals, within that the corollæ – a ring of more delicate uniformly carmine petals – and these spreading to expose the anatomy of the MotherFather's sturdy gynoecium (Greek *gynaikos oikia:* the woman's house). And extending from this innermost whorl, a strong stamen ending in sticky, pollen covered pistils and anthers rich with microsporangia. The naked Mother To Be (she is naked, as she has always been when entering the root-house temple of the priestess) turns her back on the writhing vines and the erupting flowers. She kneels in dead leaves and dark, rich soil. She is becoming the Queen, in the language of the apiologists of our present culture. In the mutualistically beneficial interaction of these two species, she will feed and permit reproduction of the epiphyte, and she will deliver new life unto her waiting tribe.

This has been the Way for millennia, or for ages containing many millennia, but certainly well beyond the memory of her race.

The probing vines enshroud her, and if we were to ascribe emotions to a plant, we would say they enshroud her lovingly. Truth is, this is a behavior left over from the time when the recipient was not so willing, when the pollinator had to be restrained. The vines soon find the entry points they are seeking – ass, vagina, and the button of her carefully prepared clit.

This is love.

And nature takes its course, as they are wont to say.

When she returns transformed to her people, the Mother (no longer To Be) speaks to no one. She'll never speak again, or utter any other sound, not even in her own eventual childbirth, when she delivers the daughter of the Great MotherFather. The bloom between her legs, sprouting from and hiding, filling, rooted in her sex, is the same carmine as those of the Great MotherFather. At prescribed times, the priestesses will collect her pollen and deliver it to undisclosed locations throughout the forest, but also keeping back a portion for the next generation. The Mother will squat in the waxy cuticle (only half concealing her form) she has fashioned to support herself. Her ass will drip the richest, sweetest, most nutritious sap imaginable, a balm against all illnesses and infections and famines. She will flower annually. And when, in the fullness of time, her daughter visits the Great MotherFather, she will wither and die. She will be returned to the earth from whence all things come.

And in this way life continues and two integral parts of the forest persist beyond cataclysm.

Having lingered at ending, we linger too at beginning, for the two are inseparable. Death begets life, life begets death. A global extinction event following the collision of an asteroid six miles in diameter only presses reset. The aeons slow tangling of one galaxy with another spawns a new galaxy, home to billions of new planets. If only hundreds of those give rise to life, the negation of hundreds of other ecosystems is negated. Here there is no Good or Evil, and here there is no Justice and Injustice. Here there is Survival. Here there is Decline and Renewal.

Here.

Right here.

Camuffare

I cannot say how she came to be what she is, any more than she is able to solve that puzzle. I assumed, at the start, that she must surely be some creature that has existed since antiquity or before. Perhaps a woman hidden or "cursed" by a goddess, one meaning of to be cruel to be kind, a woman such as Phyllis whom Athena pitied and so made an almond tree. I also considered that she might never have been a human thing at all, but a being who'd only borrowed the shape of a woman for reasons even it had long since forgotten.

"Does it matter, Elaine?" she asks. If she has a name, I've never learned it. I've never even dared to ask. "Does it matter how it began?"

"You don't remember?"

She stares at me for a very long time, then. She's standing with my bedroom wall behind her, and her skin perfectly mimics the blue and white floral wallpaper, down to the most minute detail. Except for her ankles, which match the cream baseboards, and her feet, all the same shades as the polished hardwood floor. She would be invisible, if I didn't know she was there.

"I can remember being a child," she whispers, or very nearly whispers. It's the only answer I've ever gotten from her. "I remember being like you. Like any woman."

Which is why I have abandoned those initial assumptions regarding her origins. I assume that she is telling me the truth.

"I remember my skin, almost pale as milk, against the green of summer grass. I remember my mother's laughter and the sweaty smell of my father. I don't think it was so very long ago. But why does it matter now?"

"It doesn't. It doesn't matter at all. I've always asked too many questions."

This will pacify her. She'll soon forget – or behave as if she has forgotten – the inconvenient question she wishes I'd never ask again. But the question for which I suspect she wishes she had a better answer. What she has just told me, what passes for an explanation, it causes me to conjure images of a child on a summer's day. I see her in a swing, pushed higher and higher, her feet almost, almost touching the sky before gravity drags her back to earth.

"You haven't grown tired of me?" she asks. I laugh, before I think how laughter could be taken the wrong way. Quickly, I say, "No, no. I could never – *will* never – grow tired of you." I've assured her of this times now beyond remembering, but I'll repeat it as many times as need be. I can't know the cause of so deep an insecurity, any more than I can know the cause of her condition. I accept both, as facets of my unequivocal love for her. "I can't even comprehend of growing tired of you."

"Others have," she says.

"I'm not others."

"Maybe. Maybe you're not."

I don't hold this doubt against her. Unlike the remarkable *fact* of her, it's too easy to imagine these *others* becoming too disturbed or frustrated at her secrets, or merely tiring of the novelty of their lover being so consummate a chameleon. Possibly, they grew angry, even, never being permitted even a glimpse of her true face. Then again, I am assuming there is some truer face to glimpse, truer than the thousands upon thousands she has shown me and will *yet* show me.

"Tell me about the first day."

"The day I found you?" I ask, though I know this is what she means.

"The day you *noticed* me," she replies.

"Of course. The day I noticed you."

"Tell me, then, about that day."

It's the only story she ever asks for, though sometimes I do read to her. She has never *asked* me to read to her, but sometimes I do. Either she enjoys listening to me read or she kindly humors me.

"It was cold. It was a Monday in early April, and I was walking by the sea, and I remember it was almost too cold. Even with my heavy coat and gloves. I was picking my way along the rocks above Beavertail Lighthouse, watching the gulls and cormorants and eider ducks. The breakers shattered themselves against the cliffs in diamond sprays, and the water behind the spray was the same color as Coca-Cola bottles, back before everything was bottled in plastic."

"I remember when that was," she says. Maybe it's meant as a clue, but I can only guess that might, or might not, be the case.

"Mostly, when I'm at Beavertail, I keep my eyes on the sea and the birds. They calm me when the words won't come, when I've spent too many days at the keyboard and written nothing I can use. Oh, I'm careful to watch where I put my feet, the rocks are so uneven. It would be easy to twist an ankle or fall. It would be easy to break a bone, or tumble into the bay, if I ignored the rocks altogether. But, I mean, I'm not there to see them. They don't interest me. They don't soothe me.

"But that day, I was staring south, towards the point and the lighthouse and the bell buoy not far from the shingle. I sat down and was daydreaming – woolgathering, as my grandmother used to say. I was woolgathering, and I found myself staring at the slate and phyllite and calcite veins and thinking how very old they must be, and about the terrible forces that have folded and warped them, and…"

"You saw me."

"And I saw you," I agree. "I was woolgathering, staring at the rocks, and I saw you move. Did you mean for me to see you?"

"I don't think so," she says.

"Well, it's of no consequence. Whether you intended me to see you or not, I *did* see you. The rocks moved, and I saw you."

"The rocks didn't move, Elaine. I moved."

I stare at the wallpaper that *isn't* wallpaper, the ghost-white orchids against that field of Jordy blue. She's standing as still as something that has never breathed, nor ever been alive, which, of course, is part and parcel of the gift – or the curse – depending upon one's point of view. I could lose her if I looked away. Even after all this time, I lose her now and then. Lose sight of her, I mean. I think about before I met her, when that wall was painted the yellow of Van Gogh's sunflowers.

"Yes. *You* moved."

"I still don't know if I wanted you to see me. I've wanted people to see me before, men and women, but I'm still not certain if I wanted you to see me."

"Either way, I did."

"Either way," she echoes.

Once I suggested she try wearing clothing, which I thought *might* camouflage her ability to camouflage herself. I have suggested she wear makeup or even tint her skin with dye or paint. And always she has met these suggestions with the sort of silence that says *No, you foolish woman. You don't understand any of this, do you.*

Because I'm afraid of losing sight of her, and were I to do that, she might slip away. There would be no finding a person who can hide in plain sight.

"So, the rocks moved, and I saw you lying there, stretched out in a narrow crevice. Wedged into the crevice, I ought to say. Only, I could only just barely discern that the crevice existed, because your body – which had taken on all the hundreds of shades of those strata – filled it in."

"Were you afraid?"

By now it ought to be obvious that when she asks me to "tell me the story of the day you found me," she is actually initiating a dialogue we've repeated dozens and dozens of times, and in words so similar they might as well be identical. As she has made herself identical to the wallpaper.

"I remember how I held out a hand to you," she says. "My right hand. I held out my right hand to you."

"You see something like that, you'd think it would terrify you."

"But you weren't afraid."

"No, but I thought I might be losing my mind. I did do that. And I thought my eyes may be playing tricks on me."

"You weren't, and they weren't."

That day on the rocks, I'd watched her stand, her lower body shifting, and so the stony patterns rearranging on her legs and hips and belly, while her chest and torso, breast and shoulders and face, became the sea and the sky. I watched the constant roil and crash of the breakers play out across her flesh. And I thought, as I have said, of such mythical circumstances as Phyllis and Athena. I looked upon a thing that could not exist and yet clearly *did* exist.

She said – me hearing her voice for the first time – "Don't be afraid, Elaine." That she knew my name didn't even give me pause. "I've never hurt anyone," she said.

"How–" I began, but she interrupted me.

"Why does it matter *how?* Come closer. I want you to touch me. I want to know what it feels like, your hands on my skin."

Even her eyes, her mouth, every strand of her hair blended flawlessly with her surroundings, and I thought, *When I try to touch her, my hands will pass right through.*

"But they didn't," she says, and then she laughs. And I do love her laugh. It is one of the innumerable things about her I cannot help but love as I've never before loved anyone. Not even half as much.

"I thought, *I could turn around and walk away. I could pretend none of this ever happened,*" I reply.

And she asks me, as if I don't know, "But you didn't, did you?"

"Obviously I didn't. I climbed over the rocks, over the sharp barnacles exposed by low tide, and I lay my hands on your shoulders."

I lay my hands on her, and, to my surprise, she was soft as any woman might be. She laid her hands over mine, and her hands might as well have been transparent.

"You asked, 'Are you invisible.' I thought it was one of the silliest questions I'd ever heard. Though I'd heard it before."

"Yeah, I asked that, and you told me no, you weren't. You also told me you were not transparent."

She slipped her arms about me, her shifting, restless skin assuming every shade of my blue jeans and sweater. She leaned in close and kissed me, tasting of brine and shale. But I knew she wasn't of the sea. If I'd come across her in a wood, she'd have tasted of the trees and moldering leaves. If I'd happened across her at the edge of a pond, she'd have tasted of silt, stagnant water, and lily pads.

"Do you want me," you asked.

"I do, I said. I didn't even consider saying that I didn't want you. It was as if—"

"—I was the first thing in your life you'd ever desired."

"Something like that."

"Exactly like that."

"Exactly," I admit, and the wall paper seems to moves an inch or so to the left.

"So you brought me home, Elaine."

"So I did, yes."

She moves towards the bed then, and she climbs into the bed with me. The air seems to ripple, so I can *tell* that she's moving. There would be no other way to know, as that body mimics anything behind it and anything it touches or anything that touches it. She runs her unseeable hand across my legs, up past my knees, between my thighs. She comes to the brown thatch of hair *between* my thighs, and she slips two fingers into me. It's not hard. There is nothing about her that fails to make me wet.

She lowers her head and laps at my clitoris and labia with a tongue that I'll never see. She has become the blue of the sheets that almost, but not quite, match the blue of the walls. Her back and buttocks imitate my legs and feet faultlessly. The late afternoon sun falls across her back, which means it falls across the semblance of me. I lie back and stare at the ceiling. At the fan going round and round, stirring the air that's a little too warm for comfort, and in a minute or two more I'm slick with sweat. If she sweats, I've learned long since, it has the same mysterious properties as the rest of her.

She raises her head, sitting up, straddling me, and – I admit – first I do not see her. Only the ceiling fan going round and round where, in fact, I ought to be looking upon the body of my lover. She leans over me again and kisses my mouth, tasting like sex. She whispers into my left ear, "You know what I want."

I do, of course. It's in the drawer beside the bed, and she lays on her side – become the sheets, the wallpaper again, the window frame, the blue sky and pink-orange clouds beyond the window. I can feel her eyes on me, so I know she's watching my every movement as I slip into the leather harness and secure the silicone dildo in place. When I'm back in bed, and she slides beneath me, I might as well be fucking the mattress, were I to trust only what my eyes can reveal. Except. Except that there's the place where the black dildo enters her, thrusting in and out, the shaft of it seeming to appear and disappear.

She comes first, as she almost always does.

And when we're done, I lie beside her, and in the last moments before sleep, I think how precious she is to me – how precious she is, period – and how she's lost to all the world, excepting those few to whom she chooses to reveal herself. At the edge of sleep, I envy her that.

I dream of a day beside the sea, and of stones that move.

For Emma Hack

Here Is No Why

1.

In a sooty chamber perched a full seven miles above the crumbling carbon-black crags of Tire Nam Beo, a hobgoblin named Odsbodlikins opens the grate on a potbelly stove and frowns. There's the last of the peat, smoldering away to smoke and embers, with hardly a single thing left to burn in the cramped commorancy excepting his own shoes. The wolf jaws of winter howl at all eight windows, slipping through half a hundred cracks, and Jimmy Squarefoot grunts and aims his ashplant at the changeling girl crouched between his chair and old Odsbodlikins' milking stool.

"I wager *she'd* burn just fine," Jimmy Squarefoot grunts.

"Ain't nobody gonna be conflagratin' this little one," the hobgoblin snarled at his friend, who, of course, was actually no one's friend at all. The Squarefoots' role in bringing the Revolution to the Elphame is hardly a secret. They were all braggarts and were, even now, proud of their part in the consortium that introduced the steam engines and smoke stacks and textile mills to the lands below the Hollow Hills. The elves and sprites, who'd retreated to higher realms than Odsbodlikins and his ilk could afford, made an especial point in singling out the Squarefoots for their collaboration with the Outlanders, the *Despoilers,* as undying Mab had so named the consortium on her deathbed.

The Queen is dead. Better off that way.

"Now, you know I was only jokin'," snorts Jimmy, and Odsbodlikins stares at the hog-headed bogle with his left eye, while his right ponders the dwindling peat.

"I know nothin' of the sort, you two-tusked son-of-a-whore. Know your ways well enough, I do. You lay a paw on the girl and I'll watch you fall skull-first all the way down to the Dry Seas." But no sooner have the words departed the hobgoblin's mouth than he thinks better of it and quickly adds, "Ah, don't mind me, Jimmy. It's the gout. Gets me in a foul mood, you know that."

No one low as a bogle benefits from riling the Squarefoots.

"I'll see if I can't get you an extra few briquettes," Jimmy snorts. "What are friends for, after all, eh?"

"Mighty thoughtful of you, Jimmy Squarefoot," says Odsbodlikins, even though the bogle has gone back to eyeing the human girl. Well, not a girl. A young woman now, as the Outlanders reckon age, as they *do* age. True enough, also, she *wasn't* a she when a handful of pixies led the child across the Dusk Water and through the cave at Blair's Cove. She was sure enough a *he,* back then, but a steady diet of ragwort, hazel, and honey can have unpredictable and curious consequences. Leastways, it can on *this* side of the Hills. Odsbodlikins wouldn't know about the way of things on the other side, as he's not half so intrepid as pixies and has never dared venture that way. All he need know of men has long since scorched and sullied the Fair Lands, and he imagines that the Outsiders must live only a doorstep from Hell.

"Be a price, though, you be wanting a favor as grand as extra peats."

The pig thing glares at the girl a moment. Once, her unkempt hair was blonde, but now it's as black as so many other things have turned. Her eyes are still jewels, though, sapphires shining from the smudged mask of her face. What can be seen of her skin, through all the grime, is smooth as larval silk and all the gentle greens of summer (when Elphame had still known proper summer, and known it everlasting). She's wearing the rag of a frock that Odsbodlikins bought for her at the Goblin Market. A beautiful thing, in a world where beauty has been swallowed by the consequences of waste and greed.

"I done said you'll not have her," Odsbodlikins dares to growl. "I did, didn't I?"

"Aye, you did. But listen to that wind out there. Listen to it wantin' in to freeze your bones to hoar frost and rime. She worth that much to you, old man? Besides, this is only a *borrowing* favor, not a *permanent* arrangement, you understand?"

He knows – as do all the fay – the worth of a Sqaurefoot's promise, the hob named Odsbodlikins wants to say. Instead, he shrugs and sighs and sets both butterscotch eyes on what was left in the belly of his stove.

"I gets her back, and not butchered nor no other way shattered, and I gets her back before last snowfall."

"Gotta be a wee flexible on those points, Odsbodlikins ol' man. But you get her back, and that's of a certain."

"Of a certain, then," Odsbodlikins mutters, and he sighs again and nods. This is the Where and When that sees the failure of resolve, the failure of stipulations. The cold is almost bad as iron upon his wrinkled hide.

The girl is watching him closely, and were he to glance her way, he'd see the fear in her eyes. But he doesn't glance her way, because that's precisely what the hobgoblin has no wish to see and no strength remaining to bear.

"What you happen to pay for her, if I may ask?"

Odsbodlikins almost doesn't answer, knowing as he does where this is headed. But he *only* almost doesn't answer. In for a penny, in for a pound, as the Outlanders say.

"Cost me a fat handful of acorns," he replies, then summons the courage to add, "And you knows well enough, Jimmy, the worth of acorns in this economy."

"Oh, sure I do," snorts Jimmy Sqaurefoot, before he produces a change purse from a pocket of his threadbare waistcoat and counts out a fat handful and a few more than that.

"Collateral," he tells Odsbodlikins. "In the event of an accident, which, you are assured by the honor of the Consortium of the Revolution will not occur. Regardless, yours to keep, above and beyond the impending delivery of the briquettes."

"You didn't come for tea," Odsbodlikins whispers.

"Now, now, ol' man. You do, indeed, brew a fine cuppa, even if it's a might heavy on the nettle. No false pretenses on my part, but you have a need, and I am ever keen to seize a business opportunity."

"Half the tree is nipped to the bone," Odsbodlikins says.

"Half the tree ain't got so fine a treasure with which to barter warmth."

"Aye, I am as fortunate as any goblin ever were," Odsbodlikins all but sneers, hardly minding if the Squarefoot sees his impudence now. But if Jimmy is offended, he keeps it to himself. Likely, he only counts it another necessary fraction of the payoff.

"That you be," he says. "That, most of a certain."

"May I ask the name of your client?"

"No, no," he snorts. "Confidentiality and all. You ought know that."

"I ought."

Then, Odsbodlikins watches the smoldering peat until his girl and the bogle entrepreneur have gone, and there's only the wolfish wind to keep him company.

2.

When the changeling girl was a boy, she had a name, though she's forgotten it. There are times she makes a sort of game out of trying to recall "his" name, but it's a futile game that she can never hope to win – as the forgetting is part of the enchantment – so she usually grows bored rather quickly, and so the game never goes on for very long. That said, there are times when playing the game, merely for its own sake, is a dim source of comfort, and this is one of those times. After she'd dressed and found her coat (sewn from a dingy patchwork of muskrat, hedgehog quills, and gopher), the bogle hurried her out of Odsbodlikins' hovel of an aerie and into a tiny puttering gyro he'd left hovering a few feet above the catwalk connecting numerous aeries more or less identical to her master's. The catwalk and the aeries were built into an oak that had once been a living thing, rising two hundred feet into the sky above the faerie island of Tire Nam Beo. But that was before the Revolution, and now the tree is dead and rotting and would long ago have toppled over had it not been braced with an elaborate (if frightfully rusty) network of titanium-molybdenum girders of the Warren and Monzani design, relieving any single I-beam, tie, or strut of both bending or torsional strain.

"Ah, child, soon you will see that you're well enough shed of that mangy bastard," Jimmy Squarefoot assures her, then grunts and snorffles especially loudly as the gyro lists violently to larboard so that he has to wrestle with the control stick and throttle. When the copter is on an even keel again, Jimmy adds, "He's a right blighter, keepin' a prize the likes of you cooped up in a tenement amongst these cadaverous skerries."

The girl only nods, no more than having half heard the bogle's words, so busy is she with her game of trying to recall the name of the boy she once was before the pixies led her – or him – through the narrow limestone passageway at Blair's Cove.

"Not much one for casual palaver, are you?" asks Jimmy, and she answers with the slightest of shrugs.

"Well, probably that's a propitious state of affairs, when all's been said and done. The Lady Glaistig, she much prefers her play pretties not of the chatty variety."

The girl – the young woman – doesn't ask about Lady Glaistig, as the gyro whirs over the last slate promontories of the once-island and out over the featureless black expanse of the Northern Dead Sea. The sea was boiled away in the early cataclysmic days of the exchange, before the Unseelie Court fully appreciated the perils (as well as the benefits) of human technology. The girl knows nothing of this, of course, as it occurred decades before she was stolen away to what can no longer truthfully be called the Fair Lands. The plains are dotted with the weathered skeletons of leviathans that perished in that catastrophe, recognizable for what they are even from so great a height.

My name was not Bramwell, nor was it Galen, though both are fine enough names, the girl thinks to herself. *Though both are fine names, neither could have been mine. Nor was my name Geoffrey or Dominic. If one of those were, I'd remember, wouldn't I?*

As it leaves Tire Nam Beo, Mag Mor, Tirfo Thuinn, and the other dry shores of the other skerries behind, the gyro begins to descend, seeking lower, less tumultuous altitudes. They're nearing the mainland now, and the plains are no longer featureless. There are innumerable quarries, for example, where human slaves and less fortunate bogles and hobgoblins – indentured to the King and Queen and other nobles of the Court – toil endlessly to extract coal, bronze and silver ore, and fat nuggets of gold. A few miles farther, and the first smoke stacks rise against the leaden sky, belching voluminous clouds of sulfur dioxide, carbon monoxide, peroxyacyl nitrates, et al. into the poisoned air. The girl stops playing her game, having just decided that her name had definitely *not* been Oscar, as the first gaslights of the Court come into view. This might be London or it might be the greatest swarm of fireflies that ever has existed, only it isn't. It's the outlying territories of the privileged, the fay who stay warm even in the coldest depths of winter. A place the girl has never witnessed, that Odsbodlikins always swore he would ever and always protect her from. "Am I to be a handmaid," she asks Jimmy Squarefoot, speaking loudly to be heard over the drone of the rotor blades.

"Unlikely," he snorts, smiling, revealing a couple inches more of his sharp, yellowed tushes.

"Then will I be put to work in the kitchens, possibly as a scullery maid," she asks.

"Doubtful."

"A between maid, then, or…"

"You shall be an odalisque in the Lady's harem," the bogle says, interrupting the girl in a brisk manner to which she's not accustomed, as Odsbodlikins always said that just because one is of low station that's no cause to abandon manners. "Not quite a courtesan, mind you, and certainly not a concubine. Only a common odalisque. But still, child, that's quite the honor."

She almost tells the bogle that she's a virgin, Odsbodlikins having never taken such liberties.

"Oh, all the better," laughs Jimmy Squarefoot, because, of course, no mortal can hide her thoughts from a bogle. "The Lady will be delighted at the opportunity to deflower one so fair as you."

"I wish you wouldn't do that, read my thoughts. It's awfully rude."

"Then you shouldn't think," he tells her, taking the gyro still lower as a landing pad atop one of the towers at the edge of the Great Dome of the Crystal City of the Unseelie Court comes into view.

"And however would I do *that?*"

"Have you ever tried? Or even thought of trying?"

"Well…no…"

"Then, please, child, let us please not ask of one another foolish questions we have not even considered."

"As you wish, Sir," she sighs, knowing well enough she's not been *loaned* to the bogle and his assortment of potentates. Odsbodlikins has taught her that a Squarefoot has yet to crawl from his mother's nethers that is not a grifter of one sort or another.

"Don't be so hangdog, child. You've no comprehension, I'd wager and win, of the pleasures that await you in the palace of Lady Glaistig and her seraglio."

"What's a seraglio?" the girl asks.

Jimmy Squarefoot smiles again as the gyrocopter touches down – a devious, vicious, self-satisfied sort of smile – and then he snorts, "You'll see soon enough, changeling brat. Be patient."

The whir of the rotors subsides to an increasingly lazy whup, whup, whup, and she says, "I've never been especially patient, I fear," a quality of which the hobgoblin has always been surprisingly tolerant. More so than her parents or schoolmasters, in those days when she was a he.

"Most a certain, this will change, changeling," sneers Jimmy

Squarefoot. He flips switches and toggles and taps dials on the gyro's control panel as its sputtering engine powers down. "The Lady has her limits, as soon you shall learn."

"Of course," she tells him. "I've always been a most excellent pupil."

"Then you may survive," he says and climbs out of the rickety flying contraption. She waits a few moments, then follows his example. She spares only a single glance back over her shoulder towards the wastes before following the bogle across the landing pad to one of the lifts that would carry them down and into the antechambers of the Dome of the Daoine Sidhe, the sanctuary protecting one of the last vestiges of what Faerie had once been before the consortium had ushered in the days and nights of the Revolution.

3.

The girl, the changeling girl, who was, long ago, a boy, follows the bogle through a series of airlocks and revolving doors. These keep the filth and noxious fumes outside from entering the Great Dome, the Crystal City, which was fashioned after the Great Exposition of 1851 and constructed after Joseph Paxton's design (though its overall dimensions expanded very many times over), engineered by Sir William Cubitt. And, of course, the cast-iron framework of the original Hyde Park (later removed to Penge Common) framework was replaced by an exotic and somewhat magical alloy that would pose no threat to the inhabitants of the Hollow Hills. The vast walls and ceilings are cast plate glass, supplied by the Chance Brothers glassworks of Smethwick. And though the original earthly Crystal Palace had been lit entirely by sunlight shining in through the transparent walls, artificial illumination is required for the Crystal City, what with no one having glimpsed the sun in Faerie for quite some time now. Though Queen Mab had suggested retinues of pixies and bioluminescent fungi for this purpose, in the end, thousands of gas fixtures were installed. These proved far more practical. But, we are drifting into historical digression stacked upon architectural digression and losing track of our tale of the changeling girl in the process.

In her patchwork coat, ragged frock, barefoot and with hair so tangled only an enchantment would ever hope to untangle it, the girl follows Jimmy Squarefoot down so many corridors she quickly loses count. There seems to be an endless number of turns, stairways, and switchbacks. There are vibrant paintings framed in gilded frames and dizzying balconies hundreds of feet above the lowermost levels. Squadrons of the Royal Redcap Guards repeatedly stop and gruffly question the bogle, though one would think, surely, that any Squarefoot of the Consortium would be *beyond* questioning and back again. But this is not her concern, and to say that she's overwhelmed or dazzled by her surroundings would be the grossest sort of understatement.

"We will see Queen Uonaidh and High King Finvarra?" she asks the bogle, when he's done with the redcaps.

This earns her an exceptionally derisive snort from the snout of Jimmy Squarefoot. "Certainly we will not, you foolish child. You may be a fine prize, but not even half so fine as *that*."

"The Lady Glaistig," the child whispers.

"Prezactly," the bogle answers. "You are for her, delivered at her solicitation, to be bequeathed unto her and no other." Then he turns and stares intently at the girl, as if truly seeing her for the first time. "I'd think you should be cleaned up first, but she didn't specify you ought be altered in any way. So, perhaps she wishes to view you as this tatterdemalion, appearing no more than a squalid guttersnipe. It's a fit testament to the foolishness of Odsbodlikins that he kept his most and only precious possession in such a tawdry state."

"He was kind to me."

"Or so he wished you to *think,* my dear. Likelier than not, keeping you in this state, he hoped you might go forever-enough overlooked by the Court."

"He often gave me bread and clover jam and rarely had anything for himself but crusts and porridge."

But, so far as Jimmy Squarefoot is concerned, the subject is closed, and he's already leading her through more marble hallways. Finally, they arrive at an immense lancet doorway of carved oak, inlaid with elaborate mother-of-pearl, ruby, and emerald embellishments. Five especially intimidating redcaps stand guard, and the Squarefoot speaks with them for some considerable time, mumbling in the secret language of the Crystal City (unknown to the girl, of course), before the guards produce a key and unlock the doors to the Lady Glaistig's apartments. The doors creak on unexpectedly rusty, complaining hinges, but swing wide, the both of them in perfect concert to reveal the sprawling gardens within, streams and fountains, willow and rowan groves and wildlife long since perished in the world beyond the protective walls of the Crystal City. Here and there, the girl catches brief glimpses of the rainbow iridescent wings of dragonflies and pixies. The changeling girl has never imagined – much less smelled – anything a tenth so sweet, and she breathes it in deeply, again and again, her head growing drunk with the fragrance of the place.

"Well, don't just *stand* there, you dolt," grumbles the bogle. "It won't do to keep the Lady waiting. It won't do at all."

His voice seems to reach her from a faraway place, but she obeys his dim command, and he leads her past fountains carved of amethyst and diamond. The air is filled with the songs of birds, crickets, frogs, katydids, and strange fairy creatures for which she'd never learned the names.

This, she thinks drunkenly, *is Heaven. All my life has been Purgatory, and this is Heaven, at last.*

The bogle opens his tusked jaws to say something or another, in response to the girl's blissful thoughts, for the Squarefoots despise all bliss. But before he can speak a tall fay woman, taller than the changeling by at least a head, appears before them. The girl is quite certain she wasn't there only one moment before. She wears a gown of Kelly green, woven from – well, no fabric the changeling has ever seen. It flows restlessly around the Glaistig's thin body, around flesh so pale it could be fashioned of the palest alabaster. But the girl feels no breeze whatsoever, and so she knows the gown either moves of its own accord (for all she knows, it's a living thing) or by some witchery of the fairy lady's. Her eyes are entirely black as coal dust and they glisten wetly. Her hair is the color of sunflowers. She smiles, revealing sharp teeth.

"My Lady," says Jimmy Squarefoot. He bows, and the changeling girl promptly does likewise.

"Oh," says the Glaistig. Her voice is somehow both angelic in its elegance and demonic in its loathsomeness. And so the child is washed with both love and revulsion for the creature standing above her. "She is truly a rare delight, indeed. She exceeds all my expectations."

"It pleases me no end to have pleased you, my Lady," says Jimmy Squarefoot, still bowing. His voice fairly drips with an obsequious, unctuous sort of groveling that the girl would not have guessed a member of the Consortium of the Revolution would be capable. It pleases her to see him so reduced, so cowed, and this instantly leaves her disposed to admire the Glaistig.

"You have served well, pig," says the Glaistig. "Your efforts will be compensated in kind. But now you will leave me."

"Yes, my Lady," he replies, standing upright again. He spares one last glance at the changeling, and then he's gone, plodding away through the garden paths towards those high wooden doors and the guard.

"To think," says the Lady, "you were squirreled away in some goblin's hovel. Hidden from me, all this time. It's all but inconceivable."

The girl's head is still bowed, but she whispers, "Mister Odsbodlikins was always kind to me. He never once–" before the Glaistig interrupts her.

"Speak when spoken to, human child, if you value your tongue." There's no particular anger in her voice, only a matter-of-fact command. "Your Odsbodlikins will be dealt with for concealing a changeling from the Court."

"Please, Ma'am, don't hurt him."

"You will be silent, and you will *never* again dare to instruct me in any way."

And this time, the girl has the presence of mind to do no more than nod.

"Very well, then," says the Glaistig, and she moves in such a way that the girl gets her first glimpse of the fairy's lower legs and feet, the gown briefly revealing those goatish shins and ankles and hooves. "Very well, indeed. You will do quite entirely nicely. But only after we peel away those dishrags you're wearing and scrape off the strata of ordure and muck. Still, I can see the exquisite beauty behind the obscuring curtain of feculence that neglectful hob has never bothered to wash away."

The girl nods again, knowing nothing else to do.

This is when the Glaistig leans near, her breath a blend of carrion and wine and the sweetest flowers, and she kisses the girl lightly on the cheek.

"Such an inestimable gift," she purls, and now the wind that moves the Glaistig's gown lifts the changeling girl's hair, carefully unsnarling it. "You will be a gem. My other pets will be ecstatic, and you, my gift, will share in their ecstasy. Does this delight you?"

"I..." the girl begins uncertainly.

"You may answer me. No need for fear, as I have asked a question, yes."

"I cannot yet truthfully say, my Lady. I've known little of ecstasy since arriving in your realm."

"That will soon be remedied," the Glaistig murmurs, and then she places another sort of kiss on the nape of the changeling's neck, razor teeth piercing skin, and then the fairy's tongue laps at the blood oozing from the wound. There is only an instant of pain before the girl is swallowed by salty waves of euphoria and the gentle warmth of a summer's day. The Glaistig slips her arms around the girl, drawing the changeling into an embrace as kindly as it is wicked. The earthly girl – never again to be a boy and soon never again to be anything that recalls its humanity – drowns and is borne up into the bluest skies. There's not so much as a twinge when her own feet become hooves, to match her Lady's; it's only an inevitable metamorphosis and was always a part of her future. Likewise, she doesn't feel the least agony when the whorls of a ram's horns sprout from each side of her skull, continuing the Glaistig's refinements. As the girl's transfigurations hasten, the Lady bestows upon her a name, her *true* name, to be guarded as fiercely as she might once have guarded the soul that no longer resides within her.

The changeling will forever dwell in the Crystal City, safe within the Great Dome, and she'll never again be forced to set her new black eyes upon the wreck and ruin the Consortium has made of Elphame. Always will she dwell in these gardens, and always will she be the lover of the Lady Glaistig of the Unseelie Court. She will take her place, the place that was ever before empty and waiting for her to fill that void. Only in dreams will she have the faintest memories of old Odsbodlikins and his chilly hovel. And those dreams she will count as nightmares.

I'm home, the girl thinks as her Lady drinks. *Finally, I am home.*

Hauplatte/Gegenplatte

The cage that holds the girl – if she *is* a girl; best we hereafter resort to bracketing quotation marks to indicate uncertainty – was not built for the purpose of containing a girl, or any other sentient being. The woman who keeps the "girl" within the cage purchased it cheaply, though she has never yet said where. It might once have belonged to some menagerie or another. Perhaps it held a tiger or a hyena. The "girl" has rarely thought upon the provenance of her jail. It hardly seems to matter. It only matters that she cannot squeeze between the close-set iron bars, that the cage's ceiling and floor are also steel, the whole hideous affair welded together and indivisible by what she is not, or what she always has been. The cage is inescapable. She may only reach her arms out into the unconfined spaces beyond it and no more. There are times she pretends that's a sort of freedom, but she *knows* that she's lying to herself. The floor of the cage is covered with a mixture of hay and sawdust, and there is a pail where she shits and pisses. The hay is regularly changed, and the pail is regularly emptied and returned clean. But she is somehow always asleep when the cage is mucked out, and the cleanings never wake her, which is a mystery in and of itself. Her meals are slipped into the cage through a narrow slot in one corner, and, again, she's never awake when the plate is presented or removed.

There is in the darkness where she is kept no way of telling time. It has been ages, or so it seems, since she knew night from day, since she felt the touch of either sun or moon upon her skin. Only when the woman visits is there any light at all. Sometimes, the woman comes bearing a guttering torch – a rag soaked in pitch and wrapped about a wooden shaft. Or she comes bearing a beeswax candle, or an oil lantern filled, possibly, with whale oil. Sometimes, she wields a strange contraption, a silver cylinder that shines steady and white, never flickering and seemingly containing no fuel. The "girl" prefers the darkness to the latter. For reasons she has never been able to explain to herself, it makes her anxious. It frightens her and gives her strange nightmares.

The "girl" in the cage hears footfalls, so she knows the woman is approaching. Her footsteps are never heavy. They are so light that the woman might almost be floating across the stone floor. She might be capable of descending stairs without her shoes ever once touching any of the steps. There is a wooden stool set near one side of the cage, carefully placed beyond the "girl's" reach. Today, or tonight, the woman is carrying the oil lantern, and the "girl" is grateful, whispering a prayer to her secret gods that it isn't the silver cylinder.

"How are you feeling?" the woman asks. The woman never calls the "girl" by name. She may never have been given a name. Or it may only be that she's forgotten it, though she cannot imagine anyone ever forgetting her own name. It might have been stolen from her by the woman's sorceries. The "girl" is quite certain that the woman is a *very* powerful sorceress. The woman leans close, examining the "girl" for a moment, and then she takes her place on the stool, after setting the lantern on the floor near her feet (but also always out of reach of the "girl").

"I asked you how you're feeling. It's impolite not to reply," says the woman, and when the "girl" still doesn't answer, she adds, "Ah, well. Be that way. It makes little matter to me, one way or the other. But you know that. You're *looking* well this evening."

So, the "girl" thinks, *it's evening outside.* Though, of course, evening might well mean late afternoon, twilight, or night. She cannot know which the woman means, and she certainly won't ask. To do that seems the sort of concession she never makes.

"Your eyes are bright," says the woman. "That's always a good sign." At this point, the woman produces a looking glass from the folds of her skirt. The circular mirror is held within a tortoiseshell frame and has a tortoiseshell handle. "See for yourself."

The woman passes the looking glass through the bars. She does so quickly, lest the "girl" has any chance of grabbing hold of the extended hand or wrist. The "girl" doesn't accept the proffered looking glass from her, and it falls to the soft bed of hay, where it lies mirror-side up.

"Well, have it your way. Be like that. I thought it would be a kindness."

"You do not know the meaning of the word," the "girl" replies. Her voice is not what one might expect from a "girl." It's rasping, raw, and speech seems to come to her with difficulty. "Not kindness, nor mercy."

The woman smiles, cherishing what must be to her a small victory.

"Now, that's better. A shame to waste a visit in silence, or with nothing more than a one-sided conversation."

"What do I have to say to you?"

"I don't know, dragon. What have you to say to me?"

The woman calls her captive *dragon* precisely as often as she calls her *girl*.

"Only that I have no desire to say anything to you."

"Then why have you spoken?"

Instead of answering another question so soon after answering the last, the "girl" picks the mirror up from the place where it fell in the hay and sawdust. She holds it gripped as tightly as she can, for fear of dropping it. Her short ebony claws make it difficult to hold much of anything.

"Curiosity, that's also a very good sign, you know."

What the "girl" sees in the mirror isn't different from what she saw the last time. Often, what she sees has changed, though never by very much. The sorceress works her magics slowly and with exquisite care. This has been explained to the "girl" many times. The face that looks back from the looking glass has startlingly bright amber eyes, eyes with fiery yellow-orange irises ringed in crimson. Her pupils are blacker than the pupils of any other girl she can recall ever having seen. They are blacker and deeper. She has imagined tumbling into the wells of her own pupils and falling for an eternity. Where some other girl might have eyebrows, she has minute specks of bone, deep bluish and arranged more or less as eyebrows would be arranged, if she had eyebrows. She might once have, or she might never have. At this point, she couldn't ever say. The "girl" smiles, and her teeth are exactly as she remembers them: stained like antique ivory, all of them razor sharp, her upper and lower canines far larger than those of any usual sort of girl. Her jaw is ever so slightly elongated, and her tongue is an even deeper shade of blue than the specks above her eyes. Her nose is so flat it is almost no nose at all, and her nostrils are wide. She flares them, and then lays the mirror down again.

"Apologies," the woman says. "I've been distracted. I'm afraid I've neglected you. I ought to have warned you nothing's changed since last we spoke."

The "girl" would have to admit that the sorceress is very beautiful. She has thick, shiny black hair that hangs down well past her shoulders. Her skin is almost pale as milk, but in no way is it a *sickly* pale. Her lips are full, her cheekbones high and well defined. She has eyes the color of an autumn sky. Or at least what the girl remembers of an autumn sky, though she'd admit those memories could be flawed. However, the woman walks with a slight limp, favoring her right leg.

The "girl" resents the woman for her beauty (though she has never told her that), and she derives a guiltless satisfaction at the one imperfection.

"You're in no pain today, I hope," the woman says.

"No more than usual. My back itches."

"That'll pass, dear. You know it always does."

That's true. The "girl" would have to admit that what the woman has said is, indeed, the truth. The pain and the itch of healing never lasts for very long, and she's learned to live with the more minor discomforts that accompany her transformation.

"How much longer?" she asks the woman. "How much longer will it be until you're finished?"

The woman stares at her a long moment, as though the question requires the deepest sort of contemplation. Finally, she replies. "You should be more patient, dragon. It can't be rushed, what's being accomplished here. It will require as long as it requires. Are not dragons very patient creatures?"

"I've forgotten," the "girl" admits.

"You seem to have forgotten an awful lot of things. Can you even tell me how long you've been with me?" The "girl" tell her she can't, which is what she always replies every time the woman asks her that question, which is almost every time they speak.

"That worries me, your failing memory. Then again, there remain many unknown factors in this process. To my knowledge, it's nothing that has ever before attempted. What else can't you recall?"

"My name," the "girl" says.

"Yes, well," the woman says, and she taps at her chin a moment. "I regret to say I've also forgotten that."

"But I had one?"

"Presumably. I expect you told me what it was when I found you on the streets, sleeping in doorways, eating from other people's rubbish, turning tricks from the gutter."

The "girl" stares at her a moment. She blinks her amber eyes and looks away from her captor. This is another recollection that has slipped away from the "girl." The woman never wavers from it, though, so it *might* be telling the truth. Having nothing to believe instead, the "girl" in the cage cautiously accepts it as fact.

"You would be more grateful," the woman says, "if you'd not lost that memory." Too many times, it seems as though the woman can read her mind. "Or maybe you wouldn't. Maybe you're simply beyond gratitude. Maybe all dragons are."

The "girl" *does* remember being a dragon. This may be the most terrible source of torture she has endured since the woman brought her to this place. She clearly recalls her wings and soaring high above snow-capped mountains. And the deep cavern where she slept upon a cache of gems and coins and the bones of her meals. And the inferno that she could exhale at will. And she recalls how once she was a beast so immense, in body and spirit, it could never be contained in the body of a human girl. This, she thinks, is why her skin constantly feels so tight about her, so stretched and ready to tear open if she should move too quickly. By her magic, the sorceress has folded her into such a diminutive vessel. It is hard for the "girl" to imagine a blacker, more wicked magic.

"One day," she whispers in her hoarse voice, "I'll burn your bones to ash. I'll burn them to ash, and the wind will scatter them across the land."

"Will you now? See that's precisely what I mean. This utter absence of gratitude. Not once in all our time together have you thanked me for mending what you have suffered, for working so hard to make you whole."

"Because I was once a dragon, before *you* did this to me?" the "girl" growls.

"Why can I not divest you of that absurd idea. Can you not even begin to comprehend how powerful a witch or warlock would have to be to manage such a transmogrification. Hell, just *trapping* a dragon–"

"And yet that's is exactly what you did, sorceress."

"Again, a fantasy I am unable to rid you of. I am no sorceress, *girl*, I'm only a scientist. Admittedly a very unconventional sort of scientist."

So, the game begins anew. The game that is almost always part and parcel of the woman's visits. In her cage, the "girl" remains very silent and gazes towards a cold wall of granite blocks and mortar washed in the warm light from the lantern.

"If we could get beyond that delusion, it might be that you and I could make a bit of genuine progress. You have not ever been a dragon. Well, not entirely. Not yet. Of all the memories you've managed to repress, I have a great deal of difficulty accepting that's among them."

The "girl" flares her nostrils again. The air might smell, briefly and faintly, of brimstone, but she cannot be sure. She doesn't want to say anything more, not another word. She wants to remain perfectly silent until the woman grows bored and leaves her alone again. The game, the labyrinth of contradictions that has begun, is far worse than any darkness or solitude.

Go, she thinks. *Don't say another word. Go, and never come back again. Let me die down here in peace.* But if the sorceress can read her thoughts, she chooses to ignore this one.

"When I found you – cold and starving, filthy, debased – you were so eager to please me. You agreed to the experiments more readily than I ever would have imagined. Oh, I suspect you had no idea I'd eventually have to keep you down here, locked up. But you must understand that you've become something dangerous. Girl, don't you remember what you said to me? You said, 'Let me become something too strong, too mighty, to ever be hurt again.' You did say that, after our very first night together."

"I never loved you," the "girl" says.

The woman laughs softly, mostly to herself. "I never said there was any *love* about it. But the fucking was all I was after, and I knew it was all you had to offer me. Did you love the men who paid for your cunt?"

"Nothing was ever so hateful as are you," the "girl" says, despite herself.

"Not even a dragon?"

"I *was* a dragon, and I'll be a dragon again."

"Dear, there's no such thing as dragons. There never have been, and until we are finished here – assuming I succeed – there never will be."

"My heart will rejoice to watch you burn."

"Do you think me a suicide? Do you think I'd build my own doom, then set it free to be my undoing?"

"I cannot know the mind of a monster."

"But you are convinced you *are* a monster. That's what you claim, yes?"

The lantern light of the wall sways and dances as if of its own volition. The "girl" supposes it's possible that the woman's whale-oil lantern is an enchanted lantern that has been designed in such a way as to complement its mistress in all her tireless efforts to ridicule and bewilder. A lantern she has made her coconspirator, a coruscating henchman. Somehow, the face of her tormentor is less terrible than the light reflected off the stone, so the "girl" turns once again towards the sorceress. She sits up, and the barbs that sprout at the space between her shoulder blades and run the length of her spine click and rattle noisily against one another. Her tail coils itself about her left leg and gently squeezes her thigh and knee and calf, as though it is a being possessed of a sympathetic intelligence of its own and wishes to comfort her with this cold serpentine embrace. Eve's snake, wanting nothing more than to reassure.

She grits her sharp teeth, and she says to the woman, "I am no monster. Dragons are not monsters. Women and men, though..."

The woman frowns and stares a moment at the floor. Then she sighs.

"There is *no such thing* as a dragon, child." There is enough compassion in her voice to soften the emphasis. "*No such thing,* not unless I *make* it so."

"I was not *born* a human babe," the girl snarls.

The woman lifts her head and sits up straighter on her stool, shoulders back now, mustering the air of authority that she can project, when it suits her, as easily as the lantern shines. She runs the fingers of her right hand across her forehead and through her black hair. She sighs again and fixes the "girl" with her exasperated frown.

"You are such a beautiful creature. I wish I could convince you of that one truth, if I could convince you of nothing else. You agonize over whether you began as this or that, over whether I am affecting a restoration or a novel metamorphosis, and I cannot for the life of me see why. It matters only that I am making of you, dear, so marvelous a beast. Can you not see that?"

For a response, the "girl" taps the center of the looking glass with the talon at the end of her left index finger. The lightest touch is enough to reduce it to little more than glittering dust, leaving behind only the tortoiseshell frame.

"I see your liar's flesh gone to charcoal," the "girl" tells the woman. "I see the cinders I have made of you spiraling into a starless night sky. *That* is what I see, witch."

Suddenly, the woman's frown becomes the tenderest of smiles.

"Dear, watching you in so much pain, hearing the despair in your voice, I swear before God that I would return you to the streets where I found you, if only that were possible. But what would they make of you? If you were very fortunate, it would be a carnival sideshow. More likely, it would be a stoning, a hanging, or you would be condemned as a demon and burnt at the stake."

"There's no such thing as demons," the "girl" says.

"Oh, but there are dragons?" the woman asks, and she raises an eyebrow.

When the "girl" answers, her voice is both weariness and spite. "The mind of man dimly recollects the days when dragons ruled the land and air and sea, but only dimly, and he calls them 'demons.' Your amnesia created them, as surely as it fashioned the gaudy angels and gargoyles of your cathedrals, all these beings but faint echoes of the glory that we were."

"It might be the process is proving too much for your psyche," the woman says to herself. "It might be you've gone, or are quickly going, insane. Or you might have been that way when I discovered you."

The "girl" would stand then, were there room enough in the cage. She would stand and slam herself against those bars in the hope they might shatter as easily as the mirror. She would spend her fury bending the metal in imitation of the way the woman has bent her. Instead, her tail untwines itself from about her leg and seizes one of the bars. The woman calmly scoots her stool back a few inches. This is too familiar a ritual for her to be startled at the "girl's" anger.

"What was I in the beginning?" she asks, heedless of what she's said about the patience of dragon's. The woman's smile has undone her resolve, and reawakened the awful uncertainty that is never very far below the surface. "Which *am* I, bitch? A girl becoming a dragon, in a world where there never have been dragons, or a dragon – in a world where dragons are not myths – who somehow became snared in the form of a human and is now being returned to my *true* symmetry? You *tell* me this now or you fuck off and never show me your smirking face again."

The woman is frowning again, and she shakes her head. She wears a mask that she would have pass for sorrow.

"This way or that, you cannot see it matters not in the least. In the end you will be a dragon, and whether they have ever existed or whether they've never had reality beyond the dreams and nightmares of humanity, we will, together, have rendered them corporeal. Nothing more matters. You wallow in that which is of absolutely no consequence whatsoever. If this is science or if this is magic, the end result is the same. And when your transformation is complete, dear, you *will* thank me. I will have freed you, either way."

And the "girl" asks, "Did I have a mother and a father, before you stole me away? Did I have sisters and brothers? If so, there are not words for your evil."

"I thought you were always a dragon."

The "girl's" tail wraps itself so tightly about the iron bar that it *is* very nearly bent. The tendons of those scaly coils go taunt, and if it were not iron in the embrace, if it were the woman's arm or neck...

"Was I *wyrm, draca, lohikäärme*? Did I sail the skies? Am I daughter to the race of the *Lindwurms,* numbering the years of my life in centuries or millennia?"

"You appeared, only a short while ago, convinced that you began as nothing more than a girl? Which is it to be?"

"The meat and bone you feed me, have you made me into a cannibal?"

"So long as you are kept nourished, what difference does it make? Besides, it's never anyone who'll be missed. Trust me, I take great care to see to that."

There is nothing new here. There is nothing that either of them hasn't spoken during their previous meetings. And the "girl" can only wonder how many times the scene will be replayed. Her tail releases the bar, and it curls around her leg again. She lowers her head, draws her legs up against her breasts, and hugs her knees. She will not look at the woman anymore, not this time. She can accomplish that if she can accomplish nothing more. Soon, the darkness will come back, and it'll hide and soothe her.

"By the way, the wings are proving more difficult than I expected," the woman says. "It may be months before I can proceed. But dragons are patient things, as you say, even if young girls aren't."

The "girl's" breath is hot against her skin, hot enough to scald the woman, hot enough to blister. But she'll never get that close, not while the "girl" is conscious.

"Try to rest," the woman says, then stands and lifts the lantern from the floor. "Try not to fret so. It does you no good. It saps your strength, and you're going to need that, your strength. As you're aware, I'm doing my best to minimize the trauma of grafts and implants, but there are limits. Take it easy on yourself, dear. The end will arrive one day, and you *will* be magnificent. All the cosmos will gaze upon you in fear and amazement. If there are gods, even *they* will shudder at what I have woven."

There is no end to your hubris, thinks the "girl," forcing herself not to cast the thought into words the woman could hear, knowing it would somehow please her. *In your eyes, you have become a god, as is the lot – the fate – of so many of your fallen race.*

Then there's the tattoo of the woman's shoes against the floor and the stairs, and blackness closes about the "girl," and she is left blessedly alone until her keeper's next unwelcome call rolls around.

Sanderlings

1.

I can't recall the last time I was surprised by any of the unpleasant things that wash up on the beach. Familiarity breeds complacency, I suppose. Of course, here, when I speak of *unpleasant things that wash up*, I do not mean the glistening bell of a decaying jellyfish or the carcass of a cormorant, its skull crushed and neck twisted by a bad dive. I don't mean *any* of the natural flotsam carried in and out by the advancing and withdrawing tides, nothing that one may fairly expect to find stranded on a New England beach. Admittedly, my sense of fairness may be irrelevant in this day and age, and in this context, but what I *do* mean here is the refuse that makes it impossible to ever forget the nearness of humanity, no matter how remote or lonely any given stretch of shore might seem. I mean the discarded rubbers, the empty plastic water and soda bottles, the flip-flops and other odds and ends of clothing. I mean the deadly tangles of nylon fishing line, intertwined with seaweed and rope and shattered lobster pots. I mean the disposable diapers, styrofoam cups, drinking straws, golf balls, extruded PVC can rings from six-packs of beer and Coca-Cola, the fishing lures, and fluttering polyethylene grocery bags from Cumberland Farms and Stop & Shop. I mean the occasional dead pet, or syringe, or toothbrush. These are the sorts of things I mean when I say *unpleasant*. It's much, much worse in the summer; I assume that's because of the tourists.

But these things I've listed, no matter how ugly or hurtful they might be, have all become ordinary, made commonplace by the regularity with which I encounter them on my walks. Three years ago, after Mary and I moved to Green Hill from Providence, I used to carry a garbage bag with me whenever I left the cottage and followed our street to the place where it dead ends in low dunes festooned with dog roses, poison ivy, and towering sea oats. Back then, it still upset me, the sight of all that trash, and there still seemed to be some point in trying to pick up as much of it as I could. But after only a few months, I began to grasp the futility, and also the naïveté, of my one-woman campaign to clean up the beaches. Maybe it was the hundredth shriveled prophylactic or the fiftieth pair of soiled Pampers, I don't know. But there was a tipping point, and when it arrived, I just sort of stopped noticing what I didn't want to see.

I didn't sit down to write a polemic against polluted beaches and oceans. I'm not entirely sure what I *did* sit down to write, but it wasn't that. Possibly, I've begun in the wrong place, though that particular afternoon feels like the beginning, the morning I was surprised by something unpleasant and incongruent, left behind by the morning tide, waiting to be swept away again by the evening tide. Only, I showed up in between.

What I found that day, at first glance I thought it was only a scatter of ruby-colored beach glass or an unusual accumulation of cobbles weathered from the granite reefs just offshore, one or the other polished smooth by however many decades or centuries it had been left at the mercy of the waves. But then I looked closer. I stopped and sat down in the sand and picked up a piece of the stuff about the size of my thumb. No, it wasn't glass or stone. I rolled it over in my palm a few times and then held it up to the sun, pinched between my thumb and forefinger. It was translucent, but not transparent, and noticeably greasy to the touch (though that greasiness was nothing that rubbed off on my skin). I tried hard to recall the smattering of geology I had in college and the sorts of minerals that are associated with beds of granite. I remembered feldspar and quartz, but that was about all. This didn't look like either, and, besides, it was far too light, I thought, to be any sort of rock or crystal. It hardly had any weight at all, and I thought of soap, and also that it might be some kind of wax or a variety of plastic I'd never come across before.

I sat and stared at it, then stared southward out across the sound towards Block Island, a low, hazy rind of land just visible on the horizon. Three or four herring gulls bobbed lazily about in the surf, not far from shore, and there was a boat heading east, towards Narragansett Bay. That afternoon, it was a week or so past Halloween, but the weather was warm for November in Rhode Island. There was hardly any wind at all. I looked back down at the sand and counted the crimson lumps spread out around me. There were two dozen of them, at least. Suddenly, I was seized with an almost overwhelming sense that this stuff, whatever it might be, was somehow unclean, perhaps even dangerous. I dropped the piece I was holding and got quickly to my feet, wiping my hands on my jeans. But then, immediately, I felt embarrassed, as if I'd allowed myself to be scared by a garter snake or by my own reflection. I stood there for a while, waiting for my heart to stop racing, listening to the noisy, cawing gulls. Then I turned and headed back towards the cottage. That night, I mentioned what I'd found to Mary, who suggested it might have been ambergris.

"It comes from the intestines of sperm whales," she said. "There's a whole chapter about it in *Moby-Dick*. It's used to make perfume."

"I don't think it was ambergris," I replied, and she shrugged.

"Just a thought. You should go back tomorrow and see if you can find it again. Ambergris is worth a lot of money."

"I don't think that's what it was," I told her a second time. Later, before bed, I looked at photographs of ambergris online and read the Wikipedia article. None of the pictures looked very much like what I'd seen on the beach.

Mary has started crying again, and I should get up and go see if there's anything I can do for her.

2.

I did go back the next morning, after Mary had left for work and once the tide was out. But there was no sign of the odd waxy lumps any where. I was hardly surprised. The stuff was light enough to float and would have been washed away in the night. I'd not expected to find any of it remaining. Truthfully, I'd not actually *wanted* to find it again. I sat down on the sand and watched the wheeling gulls and five or six sanderlings pecking about for whatever it is that sanderlings eat. The weather was not as warm as the day before. It was windy, and there were purplish clouds moving in from the southwest, from Connecticut and Long Island Sound. Low waves broke and sloshed against the tumble of exposed boulders, and I considered going to see what unfortunates might have been stranded in the tidal pools. But I didn't.

I've never cared much for the beach, not the way that Mary does. But then, I grew up in Kentucky, in a suburb outside Louisville. I was already in my twenties before I ever saw the ocean. First hand, I mean. Sure, I'd *seen* it, in books and on television, in the movies. Still, it was alien to me, all that sky and the incessant, rhythmic noise of the water eating away at the continent. The sheer, dizzying *openness* of it, and that sense that I'm standing at the edge of a precipice, the sense that I could *fall,* if I'm not careful. They call the deep sea *abyssal* for a reason, and sometimes, I'll admit, I've often found it mildly disconcerting that our house sits less than two blocks from the shallow frontiers of that abyss. It probably doesn't help that I never learned to swim.

Anyway, yeah, I went back to the beach. I sat and watched the birds, the gulls and cormorants and sanderlings. I was shivering slightly despite my sweater and woolen coat, and I turned the coat's collar up, trying to keep the wind off my face and ears, my chapped lips.

Mary had awoken me an hour or so before dawn, and I got the sense that she'd been lying there awake for some time. Maybe she had never gone to sleep. I'd been having a nightmare, and though I can't recall much about it, I'm pretty sure it wasn't anything I ever want to dream again. She said I'd been talking in my sleep, which I do sometimes. I know it bothers her, though usually not enough to wake me, so I asked if there were something wrong. I started to reach for the lamp on the table beside the bed, but she stopped me.

"Nothing's wrong. I was just lying here, thinking, maybe what you found has something to do with the oil spill. Maybe that's where it came from."

"The oil spill?" I muttered, disoriented and groggy, glancing at the clock. "I was *asleep.* Jesus, you scared me. I thought the house was on fire, or we had a burglar or something."

"You're exaggerating."

"Not by much, I'm not."

"You always exaggerate. You know you do. I was thinking about the oil spill, that maybe what you found isn't ambergris, but–"

"Didn't I *say* it wasn't ambergris?"

"It was just a thought," she said, sounding defensive, and Mary rolled over then, turning her back to me. "Go to sleep, Clara. We'll talk about it tomorrow. I'm sorry I woke you. I shouldn't have."

"But you *did,* and now I'm awake."

"Please, just go back to sleep," Mary said again, her voice beginning to grow impatient and annoyed. "I said I was sorry, didn't I?"

"It didn't *look* like anything that would come from an oil spill," I told her, but she didn't respond. So, I lay there in the darkness, angry and angry at myself for *being* angry. I lay there, looking up at the bedroom ceiling and wondering if she could be right. I'd never bothered to learn very much about the oil spill. It happened back in January 1996, a decade or so before we left Providence and came to Green Hill. This morning, after breakfast, I googled it.

On Friday, January 19th, a tugboat named *Scandia* was towing an unmanned 340-foot barge, the *North Cape.* The barge was loaded with four million gallons of No. 2 heating oil (very similar to diesel, it turns out; it's sometimes called "red diesel," because a red dye is added during processing). At 2 p.m. that afternoon, the afternoon of the 19th, the *Scandia* sent a distress signal, that an engine fire had broken out aboard the tug and the six-man crew was abandoning ship off Point Judith. An hour later, all the crew had been hauled safely from the stormy sea, and the burning tug and the *North Cape* began drifting inexorably towards the shore.

Both ran aground five hours later at Moonstone Beach, about a mile up the coast from Green Hill. The sea was rough that day (winds at fifty knots, waves at twelve to fourteen feet), a punishing crucible scraping the boats to and fro against the rocky bottom, and by 8:30 p.m. oil was leaking from a gash in the hull of the barge. More than eighty thousand gallons spilled out into Block Island Sound, fouling the sea as well as Trustom and Card ponds. Biologists estimated that the spill killed one and a half million surf clams, nine million lobsters, and 4.2 million fish, along with scores of sea birds and fuck knows what else. From what I've read, almost *everything* died, everything the oil touched. Eventually, the company that owned the barge was forced to pay ten million in damages. The shoreline has recovered, for the most part. The birds and the lobsters and the clams are back. But there are still reminders. Look between the granite boulders, and in places you can find a slippery black scum of hydrocarbons half an inch thick. Who knows what toxins and carcinogens are still leaching from that shit.

But I didn't find anything online associated with that spill, or any other, matching the ruddy bits of material I'd come across. Still, I supposed it wasn't impossible that the wreck of the *North Cape* had produced some weird solid distillate, something that had accreted over the years, maybe an alloy formed from the red diesel and strands of kelp, from the alginate *in* the kelp, something like that. Okay, that sounds ridiculous, never mind. At any rate, I was sitting there on the sand, thinking about the *North Cape* and murdered shellfish, when the sky opened up and a hard rain began to pelt the beach. By the time I got back to the house, I was drenched.

3.

I'm making a terrible mess of this. Trying to reduce what has happened to mere words, picking and choosing from among my memories, imposing all the convenient, necessary fictions implicit in any narrative upon what has happened. I *could* say that I am only writing down these events to the best of my recollection. But I'm quite certain even that would be a lie. I am fashioning something far more subjective here. I am echoing the echoes of my thoughts, at best. And at worst, it's *all* a lie, to hide from myself some truth I'd rather not see.

Mary is curled naked in our bed, curled fetal and lost in fever and delirium, and I am sitting here, writing this down, writing it out, and trying very hard not to hear her. But also I am *listening,* because it's the least that I can do, surely, and because there's some perverse splinter of my soul that desires to share in the secrets she has glimpsed.

"*This* is what the stars hide from us," she mumbles and then begins to laugh. Only, it's not *her* laugh. I haven't heard *her* laugh in days. And it's no *sane* woman's laugh. Maybe, it's the laugh of no woman at all. It is an awful sound, which is to say, a sound that is filled with awe and which should elicit awe, I believe. I sense this, but wholly in a distant, abstract way. Where she has gone (or has been taken) I cannot follow, and I understand that, just as I'm aware of the limitations and futility inherent in this attempt to write it all down, to write it all *out.*

Now she's stopped laughing, and is whispering again, mumbling confidences, casting grim insinuations. It would have been a mercy, I think, if the visions and the fever had left her mute. A mercy to me and to her and, possibly, a mercy to all the world. Her mouth is bleeding – not blood, no, but secrets the stars hide from us. And they must have their reasons.

"Red of the writhing earth," Mary whispers, "and red of the heaving ocean, and, in between, a crimson gash of surf." There is no urgency in her voice, only the aforementioned awfulness.

There's a small glass vial on the dining-room table, lying on its side, next to my laptop. It once held 0.15 ounces of dried, ground sage. It once resided in our kitchen pantry. Now it holds five of the peculiar lumps from the beach. No, I didn't rediscover them, and I didn't put them in the bottle. Mary did. She saves spice jars, not me. The lumps inside the jar have faded to a much duller shade of red than when I found them, as though they have been diminished in some way, partially drained of whatever pigment grants them color. They are also markedly less translucent. They have become almost milky, all five of them.

She bled them, or that ruby tint forced its way in.

Mary says, "Snow that was white upon the peaks of mountains…avalanches of snow, glaring red, gushing…"

And I know I should not be putting down what she says. I *know* it, instinctively, even if I am unable to articulate *how* I know it. Even if I cannot qualify and quantify the path to this knowledge. If I could, I would not have called it instinct. I know it is wrong to transcribe her ravings, the same way that a fish "knows" that it's better off in the water than flopping about gasping for air on the shore. I know it, that's all. But this recognition seems insufficient to stop me.

"Cities were flung in the sea," she sighs. "The sea rushed back upon the ruins. The sky boils with significance. There are tempests of indications. There is a beam of light in the sky…"

But I can't write it *all* down. There's just too much, and some of it I cannot bear to acknowledge, much less repeat.

And if I were not drunk, it could be this would form a coherent account. But if I were not drunk, I'm fairly certain I would already have put "Mary" out of her misery, and then followed her myself. What has happened here, it's nothing I can now face sober. I tried. It didn't work. This probably isn't working, either, though we're both still alive. Well, I *assume* that Mary is still a living woman. She sweats, and when I check for her pulse (pressing two fingers to her throat and/or wrist) I find a pulse. Her heart still beats, and she still breathes. And she talks. But I cannot shake the impression that *she's* gone, and what has been left behind, what lies there in our bed, hurting, screaming, muttering these star secrets I should not write down…I cannot shake the conviction that the thing in our bed is little more than a husk, only pantomiming life, and what *animates* this husk, what has taken root in her body, is barely distinguishable from the puppeteer who expertly tugs a marionette's stings.

I'm not so drunk and not so frightened that I don't know how this must sound.

I couldn't paint, and, instead of trying, I drove into Charlestown, because there were a few things we needed from the market. I thought I would get home before Mary. I *meant* to, but I didn't. This wouldn't have happened, would not *be* happening, if I'd not left the house, or if she'd not returned early from work and Providence, or if I'd not been so goddamned distracted that the brushes and palette and canvas and my mind had refused to cooperate with one another. If not *A,* and not *B,* then certainly not *C,* either. For days I have been trying to reduce it to such a simple equation, that I might at least find some comfort in guilt. No absolution, but at least blame.

However, there's a lingering suspicion that nothing here has occurred that was not *meant* to occur. And that's not like me, reading teleology into accidents. Seeing purpose or intent when reason would dictate there's happenstance and only happenstance. It's as alien to me as the sea.

4.

Whenever Mary stops muttering and falls asleep – or perhaps I should say, when she falls *silent* and closes her eyes – the bedroom walls are washed with a coruscating red glow. The glow is...what's that word? The glow is *rutilant,* but unsteadily rutilant. Red as blood or rubies or the skin of a pomegranate. It makes me think of an indoor swimming pool, of the bright pool lights shining from beneath the chlorinated water and dancing along the blue-green cinderblock walls of a natatorium. But I should be clear that I cannot tell whether or not Mary is the source of the red light. It writhes across the wall (and ceiling), but she does not appear to project it. Also, when I stand between her and the wall, I cast no shadow on the latter, and I have begun to wonder if the light is being emitted by the room itself, which has become, somehow, luminescent.

Of course, I should also note that I cast no shadow across the bed.

I half believe the light is guarding her, even if I cannot begin to imagine why. Maybe not *guarding* her, but keeping watch, all the same. Mary lies there on sweat-soaked sheets, her hands balled into tight fists as though sleep has taken her someplace where fighting is to be expected. She breathes like someone asleep, whether or not she is truly sleeping. Despite those fists and the sweat, her face becomes calm, and I can *pretend* that her dreams are not unpleasant and have brought some measure of relief, if there *are* dreams playing themselves out behind her twitching eyelids.

I sit in my chair, which I brought in from the kitchen, and I watch the red light crawling across the walls, and I watch her face, and I wait. What else *can* I do? Call an ambulance? Or perhaps a priest would be more appropriate, all things considered. No. I don't think the light would allow me to do either. I think if I *were* to go to the phone and lift the receiver with the intention of calling anyone at all, I would hear nothing on the line. Maybe static, white noise, but there wouldn't be a dial tone. I think if I tried to use a cell phone, the results would be more or less the same. The internet connection is fine, but I haven't tried to use it to contact anybody. I have these thoughts, and surely, surely they mean that I must be paranoid, that I've been afflicted with some psychosis. I stare at the red lights on the walls and try to believe that they are only a hallucination, but I haven't yet been able to persuade myself. I watch Mary, and I smell her sweat, and the vomit and urine drying on the floor and on the bedclothes, and these are completely tangible experiences, these sights and sounds. Only wishful thinking suggests anything to the contrary.

It's 4:35 a.m., so it's been nearly eight hours since I noticed that Mary had gotten quiet again. She's hardly stirred in all that time. I only have the light for company. I haven't spoken to anyone since day before yesterday, the last time that I dared to leave Mary alone. I've spoken to no one since the boy on the beach. And it just this moment occurred to me that I never said anything about him. But that only seems strange if I imagine anyone will ever be permitted to read this, and I don't. The light will never permit anyone else to read this. My laptop will crash, and the file will be erased or corrupted, unrecoverable. The motherboard will be fried, and everything on the hard drive will be lost. Something like that.

4:38 a.m., and I wish I could convince myself that Mary's in a coma, and this time she's not going to wake up. She'll remain mercifully unconscious until she dies. That would be much preferable to all the other possibilities that I've entertained. That would be infinitely fucking preferable.

The boy was alone on the beach, not very far from where I first came across the lumps of reddish…well, whatever it is, whatever *they* are. I left Mary by herself yesterday morning, because I had to get out of the house, if only for half an hour or so. I couldn't have been away for much longer than that. Likely, I won't be allowed to leave the house again. I'm surprised it let me leave that once. But, I've digressed. The boy…

He might have been twelve, maybe thirteen. He wasn't wearing a coat. That's the very first thing I noticed when I saw him standing there, well back from the water. It was only an hour or so after sunrise, and the morning was bright and clear, not a cloud to be seen anywhere. The sort of morning Mary has always loved the most. The sky was filled with noisy, wheeling gulls, and I could easily make out the low silhouette of Block

Island, nine miles to the south. But it *was* cold, bitterly so, and there was a stiff wind blowing from the northwest. And the boy was standing there staring out to sea in nothing but jeans and a T-shirt. As I came closer, I could see he was also barefoot, and I wondered who the hell lets their child run about on the beach half-dressed on a frosty morning in November. When I was only a few feet from him, he turned and looked back over his right shoulder at me. He wasn't smiling, but there was nothing disagreeable about his expression, either. Nor would I call it blank. He wasn't expressionless. For a moment, I thought maybe he didn't actually *see* me, though he was staring directly *at* me. His hair was blond, so blond as to be almost white, and his tan made me think of the summer people. Just when I was growing sure that he really *couldn't* see me, he nodded once, curtly, and then looked back out at the sound.

"Aren't you freezing?" I asked him, and the boy only shrugged his thin shoulders.

"Not really," he said. "I haven't noticed."

I glared at his back for a moment or two, at the wind ruffling his pale hair and cotton T-shirt. He wasn't wearing gloves, either, and his hands hung limp at his sides. His cheeks, his ears, his nose, and the tips of his fingers had all gone an angry pink from the cold, whether he felt it or not. I forced myself to stop staring at him, and stared across the sand at the waves, instead. The wind was slicing spray off the crests of the whitecaps as they roared towards the beach.

"It's a beautiful day," the boy said, and I realized he wasn't shivering. His teeth weren't chattering. I've read that happens in the latter stages of hypothermia. "I think I might have even seen a whale, just before you walked up."

"There are whales in the sound?" I asked.

He looked over his shoulder at me again, frowning slightly this time, his forehead creased, a sort of incredulity in his eyes (which were a slaty grey, more grey than blue). "Don't you live here?" he asked.

"Yeah, I live here. I just didn't know there were whales, not this close to shore."

The boy shook his head, a gesture that seemed to convey pity as much as disbelief, and he went back to watching the sea. "Well, there are whales," he said. "Finbacks, humpbacks, right whales. I think it might have been a finback, if I saw a whale. They're the second largest living species, after blue whales. But I bet you didn't know that, either."

"No, I didn't know that."

"It's true. They're very big whales. Bigger than most of the dinosaurs were."

"I'm afraid I don't know much about dinosaurs, either. I've never been much of a naturalist."

And all of this was only serving to compound the sense that I'd somehow stepped outside of what I'd always assumed to be reality. The boy and our conversation on the beach were simultaneously bizarre and mundane. I would almost call it "surreal," if only because surrealism is a subject with which I'm more familiar. I know a great deal more about surrealism than I do about whales or dinosaurs, or ambergris, or whatever has happened to Mary. In his manifesto, Breton claimed that surrealism was founded upon a belief in "the superior reality of certain forms of previously neglected associations." He said, "It tends to ruin once and for all other psychic mechanisms and to substitute itself for them in solving all the principal problems of life." Which makes it sound a great deal like a virus, like William Burroughs' parasitic word organism. Is that what I found lying on the sand, what Mary put in an empty spice jar and brought into our home, a virus from outer space? Maybe it wasn't washed up at all. Maybe it fell.

And these were my thoughts, more or less, an approximation of my thoughts the same way what I'm writing here is an approximation of my dialogue with the blond-haired, barefoot boy. I thought something very like, *Maybe it wasn't washed up at all. Maybe it fell.*

And he said, as though prompted, "Up from one place, in a whirlwind, and down in another."

He did not so much as look at me when he said it. His eyes remained fixed on the sea, the landward fringe of that greater abyss, restless and shimmering beneath the morning sun. Maybe he was trying to spot another whale, bigger than most dinosaurs. Maybe he was waiting for some sort of reaction from me. I didn't ask him, and I didn't bother with goodbyes. I left him there and walked as quickly as I could back to the house. I locked the doors, and checked to be sure the windows were locked, and I haven't gone out since.

I'm going to have to stop writing now. I think Mary is waking up.

For Ramsey Campbell

Interstate Love Song
(Murder Ballad No. 8)

"The way of the transgressor is hard."
Cormac McCarthy

1.

The Impala's wheels singing on the black hot asphalt sound like frying steaks, USDA choice-cut T-bones, sirloin sizzling against August
blacktop in Nevada or Utah or Nebraska, Alabama or Georgia, or where
the fuck ever this one day, this one hour, this one motherfucking minute
is going down. Here at the end, the end of one of us, months are a crimson
thumb smudge across the bathroom mirror in all the interchangeable motel
bathrooms that have come and gone and come again. You're smoking and
looking for music in the shoebox filled with cassettes, and the clatter of
protective plastic shells around spools of magnetically coated tape is like an
insect chorus, a cicada symphony. You ask what I want to hear, and I tell
you it doesn't matter, please light one of those for me. But you insist, and
you keep right on insisting, "What d'you wanna hear?" And I say, well not
fucking Nirvana again, and no more Johnny Cash, please, and you toss
something from the box out the open passenger window. In the side-view
mirror, I see a tiny shrapnel explosion when the cassette hits the road. Cars
will come behind us, cars and trucks, and roll over the shards and turn it
all to dust. "No more Nirvana," you say, and you laugh your boyish girl's
laugh, and Jesus and Joseph and Mother Mary, I'm not going to be able to
live in a world without that laugh. Look at me, I say. Open your eyes, please
open your eyes and look at me, please. You can't fall asleep on me. Because
it won't be falling asleep, will it? It won't be falling asleep at all. We are now

beyond the kindness of euphemisms, and maybe we always were. So, don't fall asleep. Don't flutter the eyelashes you've always hated because they're so long and pretty, don't let them dance that Totentanz tarantella we've delighted at so many goddamn times, don't let the sun go down on me. You shove a tape into the deck. You always do that with such force, as if there's a vendetta grudge between you and that machine. You punch it in and twist the volume knob like you mean to yank it off and yeah, that's good, I say. That's golden, Henry Rollins snarling at the sun's one great demon eye. You light a Camel for me and place it between my lips, and the steering wheel feels like a weapon in my hands, and the smoke feels like Heaven in my lungs. Wake up, though. Don't shut your eyes. Remember the day that we, and remember the morning, and remember *that* time in – shit, was it El Paso? Or was it Port Arthur? It doesn't matter, so long as you keep your eyes open and look at me. It's hours until sunrise, and have you not always sworn a blue streak that you would not die in the darkness? That's all we've got here. In for a penny, in for a pound, but blackness, wall to wall, sea to shining sea, that's all we've got in this fluorescent hell, so don't you please fall asleep on me. Hot wind roars in through the Impala's windows, the stink of melting tar, roaring like an invisible mountain lion, and you point west and say take that next exit. We need beer, and we're almost out of cigarettes, and I want a pack of Starburst Fruit Chews, the tropical flavors, so the assholes better have those out here in the world's barren shit-kicker asshole. You'll just like always save all the pina colada ones for me. Then there's a thud from the trunk, and you laugh that laugh of yours all over again, only now with true passion. "And we need a bottle of water," I say. "No good to us and a waste of time and energy, and just a waste all the way round, if she ups and dies of heat stroke back there," and you shrug. Hey, keep your eyes open, love. Please, goddamn it. You can do that for me, I know you can. And I break open one of the ampules of ammonia and cruelly wave it beneath your nostrils so that both eyes pop open wide, opening up cornflower blue, and I think of startled birds bursting from their hiding places in tall grass. Tall grass, there's so much of tall grass here at the end, isn't there? I kiss your forehead, and I can't help thinking I could fry an egg on your skin, fry an egg on blacktop, fry an egg on the hood of the Impala parked in the Dog Day sun outside a convenience store. You ask me to light a candle, your voice gone all jagged and broken apart like a cassette tape dropped on I-10 at 75 mph. I press my fingers and palm to the sloppy red mess of your belly, and I do not dare take my hand away long enough to light a candle, and I'm so sorry, I'm so, so sorry. I cannot even do that much for you. Just please don't close your eyes. Please don't you fall asleep on me.

2.

All these things you said to me, if not on this day, then surely on some other, and if not during this long Delta night, then surely on another. The blonde with one brown eye and one hazel-green eye, she wasn't the first, but you said to me she'll be the most memorable yet. She'll be one we talk about in years to come when all the rest have faded into a blur of delight and casual slaughter. We found her at a truck stop near Shreveport, and she'd been hitching down I-49 towards Baton Rouge and New Orleans. Sister, where you bound on such a hot, hot, sweltersome night? you asked. And because she was dressed in red, a Crimson Tide T-shirt and a red Budweiser baseball cap, you said, "Whither so early, Little Red Cap?" And she laughed, and you two shared a joint while I ate a skimpy dinner of Slim Jims, corn chips, and Mountain Dew. Eighteen-wheeled dinosaurs growled in and growled out and purred at the pumps. We laughed over a machine that sold multi-colored prophylactics and another that sold tampons. And would she like a ride? Would she? 'Cause we're a sight lot better than you're likely gonna find elsewhere, if you're looking for decent company and conversation, that is, and the weed, there's more where that came from. How old? Eighteen, she said, and you and I both knew she was adding years, but all the better. She tossed her knapsack in the back seat, and the extra pair of shoes she wore around her neck, laces laced together. She smelled of the road, of many summer days without a bath, and the world smelled of dinosaur trucks and diesel and dust and Spanish moss; and I love you so much, you whispered as I climbed behind the wheel. I love you so much I do not have words to say how much I love you. We set sail southwards, washed in the alien chartreuse glow of the Impala's dash, and she and thee talked while I drove, listening. That was enough for me, listening in, eavesdropping while my head filled up with a wakeful, stinging swarm of bees, with wasps and yellow jackets, courtesy those handy shrink-wrapped packets of dextroamphetamine and amphetamine, Black Beauties, and in the glove compartment there's Biphetamine-T and 40mg capsules of methaqualone, because when *we* drove all damn day and all damned night, we came prepared, didn't we, love? She's traveled all the way from Chicago, the red-capped backseat girl, and you and I have never been to Chicago and have no desire to go. She talks about the road as it unrolls beneath us, before me, hauling us towards dawn's early light. She tells you about some old pervert who picked her up outside Texarkana. She fucked him for twenty bucks and the lift to Shreveport. "Could'a done worse," you tell her, and she doesn't disagree. I watch you both in the rearview mirror. I watch you both, in anticipation, and the uppers and the prospect of what will come, the mischief we will do her in the wood, has me more awake than awake, has me ready to cum then and there. "You're twins," she said. It wasn't a question, only a statement of the obvious, as they say. "We're twins," you reply. "But she's my big sister. Born three minutes apart on the anniversary of the murder of Elizabeth Short," and she has no goddamn idea what you're talking about, but, not wanting to appear ignorant, she doesn't let on. When she asks where we're from, "Los Angeles," you lie. You have a generous pocketful of answers at the ready for that oft asked question. "South Norton Avenue, midway between Coliseum Street and West 39th," you say, which has as little meaning to the heterochromatic blonde as does Glasgow smile and Leimert Park. I drive, and you spin our revolving personal mythology. She will be one for the books, you whispered back at the truck stop. Can't you smell it on her? Can't I smell what on her? Can't you smell happenstance and inevitability and fate? Can't you smell victim? You say those things, and always I nod, because, like backseat girl, I don't want to appear ignorant in your view. This one I love, this one I love, eating cartilage, shark-eyes, shark-heart, and black mulberry trees mean I will not survive you, when the truth is I won't survive *without* you. Backseat girl, she talks about how she's gonna find work in New Orleans as a waitress, when you and I know she's cut out for nothing much but stripping and whoring the Quarter, and if this were a hundred years ago she'd be headed for fabled, vanished Storyville. "I had a boyfriend," she says. "I had a boyfriend, but he was in a band, and they all moved off to Seattle, but, dude, I didn't want to fucking *go* to fucking Seattle, you know?" And you say to her to her how it's like the California Gold Rush or something, all these musician sheep lemming assholes and would-be wannabe musician posers traipsing their way to the fabled Northwest in hopes of riding a wave that's already broken apart and isn't even sea foam anymore. That ship has *sailed,* you say. It's sailed and sunk somewhere in the deep blue Pacific. But that's not gonna stop anyone with stars in their eyes, because the lure of El Dorado is always a bitch, whichever El Dorado is at hand. "Do you miss him?" I ask, and that's the first thing I've said in over half an hour, more than happy just to listen in and count off the reflective mile markers with the help of anger and discord jangling from the tape deck. "Don't know," she says. And she says, "Maybe sometimes. Maybe." The road's a lonely place, you tell her, sounding sympathetic when I know so much better. I know your mind is full to the brim with red, red thoughts, the itch of your straight-razor lusts, the prospect of the coming butchery. Night cruising at 80 mph, we rush past the turnoff for Natchitoches, and there's a sign that says "Lost Bayou," and our passenger asks have *we* ever been to New Orleans. Sure, you lie. Sure. We'll show you round. We have friends who live in an old house on Burgundy, and they say the house is haunted by a Civil War ghost, and they'll probably let you crash there until you're on your feet. Sister, you make us sound like goddamn guardian angels, the best break she's ever had. I drive on, and the car reeks of pot and sweat, cigarette smoke and the old beer cans heaped in the back floorboard. "I've always wished I had a twin," she says. "I used to make up stories that I was adopted, and somewhere out there I had a twin brother. One day, I'd pretend, we'd find one another. Be reunited, you know." It's a pretty dream from the head of such a pretty, pretty red-capped girl in the backseat, ferried by you and I in our human masks to hide hungry wolfish faces. *I could turn you inside out,* I think at the girl. And we will. It's been a week since an indulgence, a week of aimless July motoring, letting peckish swell to starvation, taking no other pleasures but junk food and blue-plate specials, you and I fucking and sleeping in one another's arms while the merciless Dixie sun burned 101°F at motel-room rooftops, kerosene air gathered in rooms darkened and barely cooled by drawn curtains and wheezing AC. Strike a match, and the whole place woulda gone up. Cartoons on television, and watching MTV, and old movies in shades of black and white and grey. Burgers wrapped in meat-stained paper and devoured with salty fries. Patience, love, patience, you whispered in those shadows, and so we thrummed along back roads and highways waiting for just the right confection. And. My. Momma. Said. Pick the Very. Best One. And You. Are. It.

3.

Between the tall rustling cornsilk rows, ripening husks, bluebottle drone as the sun slides down from the greasy blue sky to set the horizon all ablaze, and you straddle Thin Man and hold his cheekbones so that he has no choice but to gaze into your face. He can't close his eyes, as he no longer has eyelids, and he screams every time I shake another handful of Red Devil lye across his bare thighs and genitals. Soft flesh is melting like hot wax, here beneath the fading Iowa day. I draw a deep breath, smelling chemical burns, tilled red-brown Bible Belt soil, and corn, and above all else, corn. The corn smells alive in ways I cannot imagine being alive, and when we are done with Thin Man, I think I would like to lie down here, right here, in the dirt between the tall rows, and gaze up at the June night, at the wheeling twin dippers and bear twins and the solitary scorpion and Cassiopeia, what I know of summer stars. "You don't have to do this," the man blubbers, and you tell him no, we don't, but yes, we do. We very much actually do. And he screams, and his scream is the lonesome cry of a small animal dying alone so near to twilight. He could be a rabbit in a fox's jaws, just as easily as a thin man in our company. We found him standing alongside a pickup broken down miles and miles north of Ottumwa, and maybe we ought to have driven him farther than we did, but impatience wins sometimes, and so you made up that story about our Uncle Joe who has a garage just a little ways farther up the road. What did he have to fear from two pale girls in a rust-bucket Impala, and so I drove, and Thin Man – whose name I still unto this hour do not know – talked about how liberals and niggers and bleeding hearts and the EPA are ruining the country. Might he have become suspicious of our lies if you'd not switched out the plates at the state line? Might he have paused in his unelicited screed long enough to think twice and think better? You scoop up fertile soil and dribble it into his open mouth, and he gags and sputters and chokes and wheezes, and still he manages to beg throughout. He's pissed himself and shat himself, so there are also those odors. Not too far away are train tracks, and not too far away there is a once-red barn, listing like a drunkard, and silver grain silos, and a whistle blows, and it blows, calling the swallows home. You sing to Thin Man, *Heed the curves, and watch the tunnels. Never falter, never fail.* Remember that? Don't close your eyes, and do not dare sleep, for this is not that warm night we lay together near Thin Man's shucked corpse and screwed in the eyes of approving Maggot Corn King deities thankful for our oblation. Your lips on my breasts, suckling, your fingers deep inside me, plowing, sowing, and by tomorrow we'll be far away, and this will be a pleasant dream for the scrapbooks of our tattered souls. More lye across Thin Man's crotch, and he bucks beneath you like an unbroken horse or a lover or an epileptic or a man being taken apart, piece by piece, in a cornfield north of Ottumwa. When we were children, we sat in the kudzu and live-oak shade near the tracks, waiting, waiting, placing pennies and nickels on the iron rails. You, spitting on the rails to cool them enough you would not blister your ear when you pressed it to the metal. I hear the train, you announced and smiled. Not much farther now, I hear it coming, and soon the slag ballast will dance and the crossties buck like a man dying in a cornfield. Soon now, the parade of clattering doomsday boxcars, the steel wheels that can sever limbs and flatten coins. Boxcars the color of rust – Southern Serves the South and CSX and a stray Wisconsin Central as good as a bird blown a thousand miles off course by hurricane winds. Black cylindrical tankers filled with corn syrup and crude oil, phenol, chlorine gas, acetone, vinyl chloride, and we spun tales of poisonous, flaming, steaming derailments. Those rattling, one-cent copper-smearing trains, we dreamed they might carry us off in the merciful arms of hobo sojourns to anywhere far, far away from home. *Keep your hand upon the throttle, and your eye upon the rail.* And Thin Man screams, dragging me back to the now of then. You've put dirt in his eyes, and you'd imagine he'd be thankful for that, wouldn't you? Or maybe he was gazing past you towards imaginary pearly gates where delivering angels with flaming swords might sweep down to lay low his tormentors and cast us forever and anon into the lake of fire. More Red Devil and another scream. He's beginning to bore me, you say, but I'm so busy admiring my handiwork I hardly hear you, and I'm also remembering the drive to the cornfield. I'm remembering what Thin Man was saying about fairy child-molesting atheist sodomites in all branches of the Federal government and armed forces, and an international ZOG conspiracy of Jews running the USA into the ground, and who the *fuck* starts in about shit like that with total, helpful strangers? Still, you were more than willing to play along and so told him yes, yes, yes, how we were faithful, god-fearing Southern Baptists, and how our daddy was a deacon and our momma a Sunday school teacher. That should'a been laying it on too thick, anyone would've thought, but Thin Man grinned bad teeth and nodded and blew great clouds of menthol smoke out the window like a locomotive chimney. Open your eyes. I'm not gonna tell you again. Here's another rain of lye across tender meat, and here's the corpse we left to rot in a cornfield, and I won't be left alone, do you hear me? Here are cordials to keep you nailed into your skin and to this festering, unsuspecting

world. What am I, what am I, what *am* I? he wails, delirious, as long corn-
stalk shadows crosshatch the field, and in reply do you say, A sinner in the
hands of angry gods, and we'd laugh about that one for days. But maybe
he did believe you, sister, for he fell to praying, and I half believe he was
praying not to Father, Son, and Holy Ghost, but to you and me. You tell
him, By your own words, mister, we see thou art an evil man, and we, too,
are surely out and about and up to no good, as you'll have guessed, and
we are no better than thee, and so there is balance. I don't know why, but
you tack on something about the horned, moon-crowned Popess squatting between Boaz and Jachin on the porch of Solomon. They are pretty
words, whether I follow their logic or not. Near, nearer, the train whistle
blows again, and in that moment you plunge your knife so deeply into
Thin Man's neck that it goes straight through his trachea and spine and
out the other side. The cherry fountain splashes you. You give the Bowie a
little twist to the left, just for shits and giggles. Appropriately, he lies now
still as death. You pull out the knife and kiss the jetting hole you've made,
painting sticky your lips and chin. Your throat. You're laughing, and the
train shrieks, and now I want to cover my ears, because just every once and
a while I do lose my footing on the winding serpent highway, and when I
do the fear wraps wet-sheet cold about me. This, here, now, is one of those
infrequent, unfortunate episodes. I toss the plastic bottle of lye aside and
drag you off Thin Man's still, still corpse. Don't, I say. Don't you dare
laugh no more, I don't think it's all that funny, and also don't you dare
shut your eyes, and don't you dare go to sleep on me.

> *Till we reach that blissful shore*
> *Where the angels wait to join us*
> *In that train*
> *Forevermore.*

I seize you, love, and you are raving in my embrace: *What the fuck are
you doing? Take your goddamn filthy hands off me cunt, gash, bitch, traitor.*
But oh, oh, oh I hold on, and I hold on tight for dear forsaken life, 'cause
the land's tilting teeter-totter under us as if on the Last Day of All, the day
of Kingdom Come, and just don't make me face the righteous fury of the
Lion of Judah alone. In the corn, we rolled and wallowed like dust-bathing
mares, while you growled, and foam flecked your bloody lips, and you
spat and slashed at the gloaming with your dripping blade. A voyeuristic

retinue of grasshoppers and field mice, crickets and a lone bullsnake took in our flailing, certainly comedic antics while I held you prisoner in my arms, holding you hostage against my shameful fear and self doubt. Finally, inevitably, your laughter died, and I only held you while you sobbed and Iowa sod turned to streaks of mud upon your mirthless face.

4.

I drive west, then east again, then turn south onto I-55, Missouri, the County of Cape Girardeau. Meandering like the cottonmouth, silt-choked Mississippi, out across fertile floodplain fields all night-blanketed, semisweet darkness to hide river-gifted loam. You're asleep in the backseat, your breath soft as velvet, soft as autumn rain. You never sleep more than an hour at a time, not ever, and so I never wake you. Not ever. Not even when you cry out from the secret nightmare countries behind your eyelids. We are moving along between the monotonous, barbarous topography and the overcast sky, overcast at sunset the sky looked dead, and now, well past midnight, there is still no sign of moon nor stars to guide me, and I have only the road signs and the tattered atlas lying open beside me as I weave and wend through the Indian ghosts of Ozark Bluff Dwellers, stalkers of shambling mastodon and mammoth phantoms along these crude asphalt corridors. I light cigarette after cigarette and wash Black Beauties down with peach Nehi. I do not often know loneliness, but I know it now, and I wish I were with you in your hard, hard dreams. The radio's tuned to a gospel station out of Memphis, but the volume is down low, low, low so you'll not be awakened by the Five Blind Boys of Alabama or the Dixie Hummingbirds. In your sleep, you're muttering, and I try not to eavesdrop. But voices carry, as they say, and I hear enough to get the gist. You sleep a walking sleep, and in dreams, you've drifted back to Wichita, to that tow-headed boy with fish and starfish, an octopus and sea shells tattooed all up and down his arms, across his broad chest and shoulders. "Because I've never seen the ocean," he said. "But that's where I'm headed now. I'm going all the way to Florida. To Panama City or Pensacola." "We've never seen the sea, either," you tell him. "Can we go with you? We've really nowhere else to go, and you really have no notion how delightful it will be when they take us up and throw us with the lobsters out to sea." The boy laughed. No, not a boy, not in truth, but a young man older than us, a scruffy beard growing unevenly on his suntanned cheeks. "Can we? Can we, please?" Hey, you're the two with the car, not me, he replied, so I suppose you're free to go anywhere you desire. And that is the gods' honest truth of it all, ain't it? We are free to drive anywhere we please, so long as we do not attempt to part this material plane of simply three dimensions. Alone in the night, in the now and not the then, I have to be careful. It would be too easy to slip into my own dreams, amphetamine insomnia helping hands or no, and I have so often imagined our Odyssey ending with the Impala wrapped around a telephone pole or lying wheels-up turtlewise and steaming in a ditch or head-on folded back upon ourselves after making love to an oncoming semi. I shake my head and open my eyes wider. There's a rest stop not too far up head, and I tell myself that I'll pull over there. I'll pull over to doze for a while in sodium-arc pools, until the sun rises bright and violent to burn away the clouds, until it's too hot to sleep. The boy's name was Philip – one L. The young man who was no longer a boy and who had been decorated with the cryptic nautical language of an ocean he'd never seen, and, as it came to pass, never would. But you'd keep all his teeth in a Mason jar, just in case we ever got around to the Gulf of Mexico or an Atlantic shoreline. You kept his teeth, promising him a burial in saltwater. Philip told us about visiting a museum at the university in Lawrence, where he saw the petrified skeletons of giant sea monsters that once had swum the vanished inland depths. He was only a child, ten or eleven, but he memorized names that, to my ears, sounded magical, forbidden, perilous Latin incantations to call down fish from the clear blue sky or summon bones burrowing upwards from yellow-gray chalky rocks. You sat with your arms draped shameless about his neck while he recited and elaborated – *Tylosaurus proriger, Dolichorhynchops bonneri, Platecarpus tympaniticus, Elasmosaurus platyurus, Selmasaurus kiernanae,* birds with teeth and giant turtles, flying reptiles and the fangs of ancient sharks undulled by eighty-five million years, give or take. Show off, you said and laughed. That's what you are, a show off. And you said, Why aren't you in college, bright boy? And Philip with one L said his parents couldn't afford tuition, and his grades had not been good enough for a scholarship, and he wasn't gonna join the army, because he had a cousin went off to Desert Storm, right, and did his duty in Iraq, and now he's afraid to leave the house and sick all the time and constantly checks his shoes for scorpions and landmines. The military denies all responsibility. Maybe, said Philip with one L, I can get a job on a fishing boat, or a shrimping boat, and spend all my days on the water and all my nights drinking rum with mermaids. We could almost have fallen in love with him. Almost. You even whispered to me about driving him to Florida that he might lay eyes upon the Gulf of Mexico before he died. But I am a jealous bitch, and I said no, fuck that sentimental horse-shit, and he died the next day in a landfill not far from Emporia. I did that one, cut his throat from ear to ear while he was busy screwing you. He looked up at me, his stark blue irises drowning in surprise and confusion, and then he came one last time, coaxed to orgasm, pumping blood from severed carotid and jugular and, too, pumping out an oyster stream of jizz. It seemed all but immaculate, the red and the silver gray, and you rode him even after there was no more of him left to ride but a cooling cadaver. You cried over Philip, and that was the first and only one you ever shed tears for, and Jesus I am sorry but I wanted to slap you. I wanted to do something worse than slap you for your mourning. I wanted to leave a scar. Instead, I gouged out his lifeless eyes with my thumbs and spat in his face. You wiped your nose on your shirt sleeve, pulled up your under-wear and jeans, and went back to the car for the needle-nose pair of pliers in the glove compartment. It did not have to be that way, you said, you pouted, and I growled at you to shut up, and whatever it is you're doing in his mouth, hurry because this place gives me the creeps. Those slumping, smoldering hills of refuse, Gehenna for rats and maggots and crows, coyotes, stray dogs and strayer cats. We *could* have taken him to the sea, you said. We *could* have done that much, and then you fell silent, sulking, taciturn, and not ever again waking have you spoken of him. Besides the teeth, you peeled off a patch of skin, big as the palm of your hand and inked with the image of a crab, because we were born in the sign of Cancer. The rest of him we concealed under heaps of garbage. *Here you go, rats, here's something fresh. Here's a banquet, and we shall not even demand tribute in return. We will be benevolent rat gods, will we two, bringing plenty and then taking our leave, and you will spin prophecies of our return. Amen. Amen. Hossannah.* Our work done, I followed you back to the Impala, stepping superstitiously in your footsteps, and that is what I am doing when – now – I snap awake to the dull, gritty noise of the tires bumping off the shoulder and spraying dry showers of breakdown-lane gravel, and me half awake and cursing myself for nodding off; fuck me, fuck me, I'm such an idiot, how I should have stopped way the hell back in Bonne Terre or Fredericktown. I cut the wheel left, and, just like that, all is right again.

Doomsday set aside for now. In the backseat, you don't even stir. I turn up the radio for companionship. If I had toothpicks, I might prop open my eyes. My hands are red, love. Oh god, my hands are so red, and we have not ever looked upon the sea.

5.

Boredom, you have said again and again, is the one demon might do you in, and the greatest of all our foes, the *one* demon, Mystery Babylon, the Great Harlot, who at the Valley of Josaphat, on the hill of Megiddo, wraps chains about our porcelain slender necks and drags us down to dust and comeuppance if we dare to turn our backs upon the motherfucker and give it free fucking reign. I might allow how this is the mantra that set us to traveling on the road we are on and has dictated our every action since that departure, your morbid fear of boredom. The consequence of this mantra has almost torn you in half, so that I bend low over my love, only my bare hands to keep your insides from spilling outside. Don't you shut your eyes. You don't get out half that easy. Simple boredom is as good as the flapping wings of butterflies to stir the birth throes of hurricanes. Tiresome recitations of childhood traumas and psychoses be damned. As are we; as are we.

6.

We found her, or she was the one found us, another state, another county, the outskirts of another slumbering city. Another truck-stop diner. Because we were determined to become connoisseurs of everything that is fried and smothered in lumpy brown gravy, and you were sipping a flat Coke dissolute with melting ice. You were talking – I don't know why – about the night back home when the Piggly Wiggly caught fire, so we climbed onto the roof and watched it go up. The air smelled like burning groceries. We contemplated cans of Del Monte string beans and pears and cans of Grapico reaching the boiling point and going off like grenades, and the smoke rose up and blotted out the moon, which that night was full. You're talking about the fire, and suddenly she's there, the coal-haired girl named Haddie in her too-large Lollapalooza T-shirt and black jeans and work boots. Her eyes are chipped jade and honey, that variegated hazel, and she smiles so disarming a smile and asks if, perhaps, we're heading east towards Birmingham, because she's trying to get to Birmingham, but – insert here a woeful tale of her douchebag boyfriend – and now she's stranded high and dry, not enough money for bus fare, and if we're headed that way, could she please, and would we please? You scoot over and pat the turquoise sparkle vinyl upholstery, inviting her to take a Naugahyde seat, said the spider to the fly. "Thank you," she says. "Thank you very much," and she sits and you share your link sausage and waffles with her, because she says she hasn't any money for food, either. We're heading for Atlanta, you tell her, and we'll be going right straight through Birmingham, so sure, no problem, the more the goddamn merrier. We are lifesavers, she says. Never been called that before. You chat her up, sweet as cherry pie with whipped cream squirted from a can, and, me, I stare out the plate-glass partition at the gas pumps and the stark white lighting to hide the place where a Mississippi night should be. "Austin," she says, when you ask from whence she's come. "Austin, Texas," she volunteers. "I was born and raised there." Well, you can hear it, plain as tits on a sow, in her easy, drawling voice. I take in a mouthful of lukewarm Cheerwine, swallow, repeat, and do not let my attention drift from the window and an idling eighteen-wheeler parked out there with its cab all painted up like a Santería altar whore, gaudy and ominous and seductive. Smiling Madonna and cherubic child, merry skeletons dancing joyful round about a sorrowful, solemn Pietà, roses and carnations, crucifixions, half-pagan orichá and weeping bloody Catholic Jesus. Of a sudden, then, I feel a sick coldness spreading deep in my bowels, ice water heavy in my guts, and I want to tell this talkative Lone-Star transient that no, sorry, but you spoke too soon and, sorry, but we *can't* give her a ride, after all, not to Birmingham or anywhere else, that she'll have to bum one from another mark, which won't be hard, because the night is filled with travelers. I want to say just that. But I don't. Instead, I keep my mouth shut tight and watch as a man in dirty orange coveralls climbs into the cab of the truck, him and his goddamn enormous shaggy dog. That dog, it might almost pass for a midget grizzly. In the meanwhile, Ms. Austin is sitting there feeding you choice slivers of her life's story, and you devour it, because I've never yet seen you not hungry for a sobby tale. This one, she's got all the hallmarks of a banquet, doesn't she? Easy pickings, if I only trust experience and ignore this inexplicable wash of instinct. Then you, love, give me a gentle, unseen kick beneath the table, hardly more than an emphatic nudge, your right foot insistently tapping, tap, tap, at my left ankle in a private Morse. I fake an unconcerned smile and turn my face away from the window and that strange truck, though I can still hear its impatient engines. "A painter," says Ms. Austin. "See, I want to be a painter. I've got an aunt in Birmingham, and she knows my mom's a total cunt, and she doesn't mind if I stay with her while I try to get my shit together. It was supposed to be me and him both, but now it's just gonna be me. See, I shut my eyes, and I see murals, and that's what I want to paint one day. *Wallscapes*." And she talks about murals in Mexico City and Belfast and East Berlin. "I need to piss," I say, and you flash me a questioning glance that Ms. Austin does not appear to catch. I slide out of the turquoise booth and walk past other people eating other meals, past shelves grounded with motor oil, candy bars, and pornography. I'm lucky and there's no one else in the restroom, no one to hear me vomit. *What the fuck is this? Hunh? What the fuck is wrong with me now?* When the retching is done, I sit on the dirty tile floor and drown in sweat and listen to my heart throwing a tantrum in my chest. Get up and get back out there. And you, don't you even think of shutting your eyes again. The sun won't rise for another two hours, another two hours at least, and we made a promise one to the other. Or have you forgotten in the gauzy veils of hurt and Santísima Muerte come to whisper in your ear? Always have you said you were hers, a demimondaine to the Bony Lady, *la Huesuda*. So, faithless, I have to suffer your devotions as well? I also shoulder your debt? The restroom stinks of cleaning fluid, shit and urine, my puke, deodorant cakes and antibacterial soap, filth and excessive cleanliness rubbing shoulders. I don't recall getting to my feet. I don't recall a number of things, truth be told, but then we're paying the check, and then we're out in the muggy Lee County night. You tow Ms. Austin behind you. She rides your wake, slipstreaming, and she seems to find every goddamn thing funny. You climb into the backseat with her, and the two of you giggle and titter over private jokes to which I have apparently not been invited. What all did I miss while I was on my knees, praying to my Toilet Gods? I put in a Patsy Cline tape, *punch* it into the deck as you would, and crank it up loud so I don't have to listen to the two of you, not knowing what you (not her, just *you*) have planned, feeling like an outsider in your company, and I cannot ever recall that having happened. Before long, the lights of Tupelo are growing small and dim in the rearview, a diminishing sun as the Impala glides southeast along US 78. My foot feels heavy as a millstone on the gas pedal. So, I have "A Poor

Man's Roses" and "Back in Baby's Arms" and "Sweet Dreams" and a fresh pack of Camel's and you and Ms. Austin spooning at my back. And still that ice water in my bowels. She's talking about barbeque, and you laugh, and what the fuck is funny about barbeque. "Dreamland," she says, "just like what those UFO nuts call Area 51 in Nevada, where that dead Roswell alien and shit's supposed to be hidden." Me, I smoke and chew on bitter cherry-favored Tums tablets, grinding calcium carbonate and corn starch and talc between my teeth. "Those like you," says Ms. Austin, "who've lost their way," and I have no goddamn idea what she's going on about. We cross a bridge, and if it's a river below us, I do not see any indication that it's been given a name. But we're entering Itawamba County, says a sign, and that sounds like some mythological world serpent or someplace from a William Faulkner novel. Only about twenty miles now to the state line, and I'm thinking how I desire to be shed of the bitch, how I want her out of the car before Tuscaloosa, wondering how I can signal you without making Ms. Austin Texas Chatterbox suspicious. We pass a dozen exits to lonely country roads where we could take our time, do the job right, and at least I'd have something to show for my sour stomach. I'm thinking about the couple in Arkansas, how we made him watch while we took our own sweet time with her, and you telling him it wasn't so different from skinning catfish, not really. A sharp knife and a pair of pliers, that's all you really need, and he screamed and screamed and screamed. Hell, the pussy bastard sonofabitch screamed more than she did. In the end, I put a bullet in his brain just to shut him the fuck up, please. And we'd taken so long with her, hours and hours, well, there wasn't time remaining to do him justice, anyway. After that we've made a point of avoiding couples. After that, it became a matter of policy. Also, I remember that girl we stuck in the trunk for a hundred miles, and how she was half dead of heat prostration by the time we got around to ring around the rosies, pockets full of posies time. And you sulked for days. Now, here, I watch you in the rearview, and if you notice that I am, you're purposefully ignoring me. I have to take a piss, I say, and she giggles. Fuck you, Catfish. Fuck you, because on this road you're traveling, is there hope for tomorrow? On this Glory Road you're traveling, to that land of perfect peace and endless fucking day, that's my twin sister you've got back there with you, my one and true and perfect love, and this train is bound for Glory, ain't nobody ride it, *Catfish*, but the righteous and the holy, and if this train don't turn around, well, I'm Alabama bound. You and me and she, only, we ain't going that far together. Here's why God and all his angels and the demons down under the sea made detours, *Catfish*. The headlights paint twin high-beam encouragement, luring me on down Appalachian Corridor X, and back there behind me you grumble something about how I'm never gonna find a place to piss here, not unless it's in the bushes. I'm about to cut the wheel again, because there's an unlit side road like the pitchy throat of evening wanting to swallow us whole, and right now, I'm all for that, but….Catfish, née Austin Girl, says that's enough, turn right around and get back on the goddamn highway. And whatever I'm supposed to say, however I'm about to tell her to go fuck herself, I don't. She's got a gun, you say. Jesus, Bobbie, she's got a gun, and you laugh a nervous, disbelieving laugh. You laugh a stunned laugh. She's got a goddamn gun. *What the fuck,* I whisper, and again she instructs me to retrace my steps back to 78. Her voice is cold now as the Artic currents in my belly. I look in the rearview, and I can't *see* a gun. I want to believe this is some goddamn idiot prank you and she have cooked up, pulling the wool for whatever reason known only to thee. What do you want? I ask, and she says we'll get to that, in the sweet by and by, so don't I go fretting my precious little head over what she wants, okay? Sure, sure. And five minutes later we're back on the highway, and you're starting to sound less surprised, surprise turning to fear, because this is not how the game is played. This is *not* the story. We don't have shit, I tell her. We ain't got any money, and we don't have shit, so if you think – and she interrupts, Well, you got this car, don't you? And that's more than me, so how about you just shut up and drive, Little Bird. That's what she calls me, *Little Bird*. So, someone's rewriting the fairy tale all around us; I know that now, and I realize that's the ice in the middle of me. How many warnings did we fail to heed? The Santería semi, that one for sure, as good as any caution sign planted at the side of any path. Once upon a time, pay attention, you and you who have assumed that no one's out there hunting wolves, or that all the lost girls and boys and men and women on the bum are defenseless lambs to the slaughter. Wrong. Wrong. Wrong, and it's too late now. But I push those thoughts down, and I try to focus on nothing but your face in the mirror, even though the sight of you scares the hell out of me. It's been a long time since I've seen you like that, and I thought I never would again. You want the car? I ask Catfish. Is that it? Because if you want the car, fuck it, it's yours. Just let me pull the fuck over, and I'll hand you the goddamn keys. But no, she says. No, I think you should keep right on driving for a while. As for pulling over, I'll say when. I'll say when, on that you can be sure.

7.

Maybe, you say, it wouldn't be such a bad idea to go home now, and I nod, and I wipe the blood off your lips, the strawberry life leaking from you freely as ropy cheesecloth, muslin ectoplasm from the mouth, ears, nostrils of a 1912 spiritualist. I wipe it away, but I hold it, too, clasping it against the loss of you. So long as I can catch all the rain in my cupped hands, neither of us shall drown. You just watch me, okay? Keep your eyes on my eyes, and I'll pull you through. It looks a lot worse than it is, I lie. I know it hurts, but you'll be fine. All the blood makes it look terrible, I know, but you'll be fine. Don't you close your goddamn eyes. Oh, sister, don't you die. Don't speak. I cannot stand the rheumy sound of the blood in your throat, so please do not speak. But you say, *You can hear the bells, Bobbie, can't you? Fuck, but they are so red, and they are so loud, how could you not? Take me and cut me out in little stars....*

8.

So fast, my love, so swift and sure thy hands, and when Catfish leaned forward to press the muzzle of her 9mm to my head and tell me to shut up and drive, you drew your vorpel steel, and the razor folded open like a silver flower and snicker-snacked across coal-haired Haddie's throat. She opened up as if she'd come with a zipper. Later, we opened her wide and sunk her body in a marshy maze of swamp and creek beds and snapping-turtle weeds. Scum-green water, and her guts pulled out and replaced with stones. You wanted to know were there alligators this far north, handy-dandy helpful gator pals to make nothing more of her than alligator shit, and me, I said, hey this is goddamn Mississippi, there could be crocodiles and pythons for all I know. Afterwards, we bathed in the muddy slough, because cutting a bitch's throat is dirty goddamn business, and then we fucked in the high grass, then had to pluck off leeches from our legs and arms and that one ambitious pioneer clinging fiercely to your left nipple. *What about the car? The car's a bloody goddam mess.* And yeah, I agreed, what about the car? We took what we needed from the Impala, loaded our scavenged belongings into a couple of backpacks, knapsacks, a pillowcase, and then we shifted the car into neutral and pushed it into those nameless waters at the end of a nameless dirt road, and we hiked back to 78. You did so love that car, our sixteenth birthday present, but it is what it is and can't be helped, and no way we could have washed away the indelible stain left behind by treacherous Catfish's undoing. That was the first and only time we ever killed in self defense, and it made you so angry, because her death, you said, spoiled the purity of the game. What have we got, Bobbie, except *that* purity? And now it's tainted, sullied by one silly little thief – or what the hell ever she might have been. We have us, I reply. We will always have us, so stop your worrying. My words were, at best, cold comfort, I could tell, and that hurt more than just a little bit, but I kept it to myself, the pain, the hollow in the pit of my soul that had not been there only the half second before you started in on purity and being soiled by the thwarted shenanigans of Catfish. Are you alright? you asked me, as we marched up the off-ramp. I smiled and shook my head. Really, I'm thinking, let's not have that shoe's on the other foot thing ever again, love. Let's see if we can be more careful about who we let in the car that we no longer have. There was a moon three nights past full, like a judgmental god's eye to watch us on our way. We didn't hitch. We just fucking walked until dawn, and then stole a new car from a driveway outside of Tremont. You pulled the tag and stuck on our old Nebraska plates, amongst that which we'd salvaged from the blooded Impala. The new ride, a swank fucking brand-new '96 Saturn the color of Granny Smith apples, it had all-electric windows, but a CD player when all we had was our box of tapes, so fuck that; we'd have to rely on the radio. We hooked onto WVUA 90.7 FM outta Tuscaloosa, and the DJ played Soundgarden and Beck and lulled us forward on the two lane black-racer asphalt rails of that river, traveling dawnwise back to the earliest beginnings of the world, you said, watching the morning mist burning away, and you said, *When vegetation rioted on the earth, and the big trees were kings.* Read that somewhere? Yeah, you said, and shortly thereafter we took Exit 14, stopping just south of Hamilton, Alabama, because there was a Huddle House, and by then we were both starving all over again. There was also a Texaco station, and good thing, too, as the Saturn was sitting on empty, running on fumes. So, in the cramped white-tile fluorescent drenched restroom, we washed off the swamp water we'd employed to wash away the dead girl's blood. I used wads of paper towels to clean your face as best I could, after the way the raw-boned waitress with her calla-lily tattoo stared at you. I thought there for a moment maybe it was gonna be her turn to pay the ferryman, but you let it slide. There's another woman's scabs crusted in your hair, stubborn clots, and the powdery soap from the powdery soap dispenser on the wall above the sink isn't helping all that much. I need a drink, you say. I need a drink like you would not believe. Yeah, fine, I replied, remembering the half-full, half-empty bottle of Jack in the pillowcase, so just let me get this spot here at your hairline. You go back to talking about the *river,* as if I understand – often I never truly understood you, and for that did I love thee even more. The road which is the river, the river which is the road, mortality, infinity, the grinding maw of history; *An empty stream, a great goddamn silence, an impenetrable forever forest. That's what I'm saying,* you said. *In my eyes, in disposed, in disgrace.* And I said it's gonna be a scorcher today, and at least the Saturn has AC, not like the late beloved lamented Impala, and you spit out what the fuck ever. I fill the tank, and I mention how it's a shame Ms. Austin Catfish didn't have a few dollars on her. We're damn near busted flat. Yeah, well, we'll fix that soon, you say. We'll fix that soon enough, my sweet. You're sitting on the hood, examining the gun she'd have used to lay us low. Make sure the safety is on, I say. And what I think in the split second before the pistol shot is *Please be careful with that thing, the shit our luck's been,* but I didn't say it *aloud.* An unspoken thought, then bang. No. Then BANG. You look nothing in blue blazes but surprised. You turn your face towards me, and the 9mm slips from your fingers and clatters to the oil- and anti-freeze-soaked tarmac. I see the black girl behind the register looking our way, and Jesus motherfucking-fucking-fuck-fuck-fucking-motherfucker-oh fuck me this *cannot* be goddamn happening, no way can *this* be happening, not after everything we've done and been through and how there's so much left to do and how I love you so. Suddenly, the air is nothing if not gasoline and sunlight. I can hardly clear my head, and I'm waiting for certain spontaneous combustion and the grand *whump* when the tanks blow, and they'll see the mushroom cloud for miles and miles around. My head fills with fire that isn't even there, but, still, flashblind, I somehow wrestle you into the backseat. Your eyes are muddy with shock, muddy with perfect incredulity. I press your left hand against the wet hole in that soft spot below your sternum, and you gasp in pain and squeeze my wrist so hard it hurts. *No, okay, you gotta let go now, I gotta get us the fuck outta here before the cops show up. Let go, but keep pressure on it, right? But we have to get out of here now.* Because, I do not add, that gunshot was louder than thunder, that gunshot cleaved the morning apart like the wrath of Gog and Magog striding free across the Armageddon land, Ezekiel 38:2, or wild archangel voices and the trumpet of Thessalonians 4:16. There's a scattered handful of seconds, and then I'm back on the highway again, not thinking, just driving south and east. I try not to hear your moans, 'cause how's that gonna help either of us, but I do catch the words when you whisper, *Are you alright, Bobbie? You flew away like a little bird,* and isn't that what Catfish called me? *So how about you just shut up and drive, Little Bird.* And in my head I do see a looped serpent made of fire devouring its own tail, and I know we cheated fate only for a few hours, only to meet up with it again a little farther down the road. I just drive. I don't even think to switch on the AC or roll down the window or even notice how the car's becoming as good as a kiln on four wheels. I just fucking *drive.* And, like agate beads strung along a rosary, I recite the prayer given me at the End of Days, the end of one of us: Don't you fucking shut your eyes. Please, don't you shut your eyes, because you do not want to go there, and I do not want to be alone forever and forever without the half of me that's you. In my hands, the steering wheel is busy swallowing its own tail, devouring round and round, and we, you and I, are only passengers.

For Neko Case

One man's pornography is another man's theology.
Clive Barker

The preceding stories, excepting "Sanderlings" and "Interstate Love Song (Murder Ballad No. 8)" first appeared in *Sirenia Digest,* Issues Nos. 44-77, July 2009–April 2012. The author would like to thank all the people who have made, and continue to make, the digest possible, beginning with the subscribers, and including Vince Locke, Kathryn Pollnac, and Gordon Duke. You guys keep on keepin' the wolves at bay. The author would like to thank all the people who have made, and continue to make, the digest possible, beginning with the subscribers, and including Vince Locke, Kathryn Pollnac, and Gordon Duke. Thanks also, grateful to all my Patreon backers. Together, you guys keep on keeping the wolves at bay. Also, a special thank you to Gail Cross for her painstaking work on the page proofs.

"Sanderlings" was first published as a chapbook by Subterranean Press (2010), and "Interstate Love Song (Murder Ballad No. 8)" first appeared in *Sirenia Digest* No. 100 (May 2014).

"Drawing from Life" and "Scylla for Dummies" originally appeared as "Untitled 34" and "Untitled 35," respectively.

This collection takes its title from Elvis Costello's song of the same name, which can be found on *The Juliet Letters* (1993).

About the Author

*T*he *New York Times* recently called Caitlín R. Kiernan "one of our essential writers of dark fiction" and S. T. Joshi has declared "…hers is now the voice of weird fiction." Her novels include *Silk, Threshold, Low Red Moon, Daughter of Hounds, The Red Tree* (nominated for the Shirley Jackson and World Fantasy awards), and *The Drowning Girl: A Memoir* (winner of the James Tiptree, Jr. and Bram Stoker awards, nominated for the Nebula, World Fantasy, British Fantasy, Mythopoeic, Locus, and Shirley Jackson awards). To date, her short fiction has been collected in thirteen volumes, including *Tales of Pain and Wonder, From Weird and Distant Shores, Alabaster, A is for Alien, The Ammonite Violin & Others, Confessions of a Five-Chambered Heart, Two Worlds and In Between: The Best of Caitlín R. Kiernan (Volume One), Beneath an Oil-Dark Sea: The Best of Caitlín R. Kiernan (Volume Two),* and the World Fantasy Award winning *The Ape's Wife and Other Stories.* She has also won a World Fantasy Award for Best Short Fiction for "The Prayer of Ninety Cats." During the 1990s, she wrote *The Dreaming* for DC Comics' Vertigo imprint and has recently completed the three-volume *Alabaster* for Dark Horse Comics. The first third, *Alabaster: Wolves,* received the Bram Stoker Award. She lives in Providence, Rhode Island with her partner, Kathryn Pollnac.

About the Font

This book was set in Garamond, a typeface named after the French punch-cutter Claude Garamond (c. 1480–1561). Garamond has been chosen here for its ability to convey a sense of fluidity and consistency. It has been chosen by the author because this typeface is among the most legible and readable old-style serif print typefaces. In terms of ink usage, Garamond is also considered to be one of the most eco-friendly major fonts.